COINCIDENCE OR...

In the bright Okanagan sunshine Lila stepped off the beach promenade curb mulling over all the things that remained to be done before the opening of the new clothing store—pick up garment covers for purchases, ensure the credit card hookups were working, ensure that there were tables and chairs set up on the sidewalk outside and that there was a ribbon for cutting.

Above the chatter of sunbathers by the shore, the nearby roar of a car engine caught her attention. This wasn't a drag strip—the speed limit was a sedate thirty kilometers an hour along Beach Avenue.

A dark SUV squealed away from the curb three cars down. It shot across Beach Avenue's centerline directly toward her.

Leap forward? Leap back? Someone on the sidewalk screamed. She tried forward and the SUV seemed to swerve to keep her in its sights until suddenly she was picked up and thrown to the curb. She landed on her hands and knees as the car roared past and was gone like a bat out of hell to disappear around the curve of the shore line.

Lila rolled to sitting. Her knees bled. So did her palms. One of her shoes sat in the middle of the street and her heart pounded in her chest. There were people crowding around her asking her questions, asking was she all right? Okay? Injured? Hurt?

It was all too much. Someone cut through the crowd and cast a shadow over the sun. The figure knelt in front of her and caught her hands, gently using a tissue to wipe the blood off, and then cleaning her knees of gravel.

When she looked up it was to peer into perfect turquoise-blue eyes, the kind you could swim in. Nathan Moon knelt before her like some kind of knight.

That was when the shaking cut in.

BOOKS BY THE AUTHOR

Romance
Ashes and Light
Shades of Moonlight
Judas Kiss
Second Spring
A Different Nightmusic
Shadow Play
Unlocking Her Heart
Unlocking Her History
Unlocking Her Grace
Unlocking Her Dreams
Unlocking Her Chances
Unlocking Her Doubts

Fantasy
***The Cartographer Universe* series:**
The Warden of Power
Impossible
The Cartographer's Daughter
Afterburn
Aftershock
Aftermath
Afterimage

Terra Incognita
Terra Infirma
Terra Nueva

Also by the Author
Mutable Things
Emberstone
Ice Dragon
Crystal Courtesan

UNLOCKING HER DOUBTS

Karen L. Abrahamson

For lovers lost and won.

UNLOCKING HER DOUBTS

Prologue

After the short flight from Vancouver, the *Schwarzenacht* corporate jet settled onto the tarmac of Kelowna International Airport—not that the thing in Johan Fehr's head would in any way consider this backwater single-runway airport international. It was international in the same way that a drug runner's dirt runway was international—a suitable surface for takeoff and landing for specific cargo that needed to be shipped. In the drug lord's world, it was drugs. For Kelowna he hadn't quite been able to parse what the shipment was—unless it was sun-wizened people trying to escape this hole-in-the-wall town. For, compared to Berlin and the cities of Europe, that was certainly all the "city" of Kelowna could be called. Even Vancouver, the third largest city in Canada, was just a wet-behind-the-ears upstart in the global city department.

The harsh noonday sun lit the sunburned hills of parched grass and drooping poplar and long-needled pine. Dust hung in the air in the shimmer of heat off the tarmac and shivered the air between him and the distant houses set amid the trees. Dry. Inhospitable and yet everywhere there were vivid green lawns, gardens, and orchards—the product of irrigation. In some ways it reminded him of ancient times. The Tigris and Euphrates had caused just such a microclimate of fresh green along those storied riverbanks. In the springtime of his youth he had dwelt there, taking his toll of the humans foolhardy enough to venture out between the daytime and the night. That was when he had stirred. That was when he had hunted. That had been when he had fed—until civilization came upon him and he found other, less strenuous ways to hunt, first in ancient walled villages and then in the dark alleys of modern metropolises.

The Learjet swayed to a stop and the engine cut off. The steward unstrapped from his seat near the front—the cabin staff knew to leave their betters alone unless called. The mahogany paneling glowed in the light through the window. The scent of recycled air still held the memory of the steak the body, Johan Fehr, had eaten as his in-flight meal and the red wine he'd drunk with it. Unfortunately, regardless of the reasonable food and the light doze he had managed on the flight, the body was still tired. A full sleep had eluded him for the past few days because the heart of this body had pounded, the blood rushed through the veins, all out of the excitement that came with the decision that Johan Fehr himself would take action. He had wasted too much time waiting for others to complete the job that must be done. This time it would be completed.

He would recover the bracelet and his power would return, for surely if he salvaged the power remaining in the two unopened doors, it would give him the strength to reclaim that which had been lost at the opening of the five other doors. He would feed in the old ways once more. The power of two doors was not inconsiderable. This close to the woman who wore it, he could feel her heart beating in sympathetic rhythm to his own.

He closed his eyes, taking the moment to revel in the intimacy. It was the sensation he had always relished before he killed.

The steward checked on the pilots and then cracked the door to the tarmac. Dry air rushed in carrying with it the scent of sage and airplane fuel. The Johan body inhaled.

"Ready to deplane when you are, sir. The pilot reports that the limousine is waiting."

The steward's footsteps retreated to his cubby at the front, leaving his master to do what he wanted.

With a sigh he opened his eyes and scanned the file he'd been reading, his finger trailing down the photographs of the six women. After a thousand years of no news of the bracelet, so much had happened in the barely three months since the bracelet had been found. All his attempts to retrieve his treasure had been blocked at every turn. His bodies stopped, some actually killed— him forced to abandon them and return, depleted, to Johan Fehr, until the only way he could approach the women was to fly like some common human, trapped in this body.

All caused by these women. His jaw clenched.

Each was lovely in her own way. Lovely enough he would enjoy their death, but truly it seemed he had saved the best for last— for this would be the last. In this powerful body he would surely prevail. He ran his fingertips over the photo again, imagining the silver singing on her wrist, imagining the sweetness of the fear he could evoke in her through his little jokes. Her fear would feed him and make him strong again. Auburn haired and with hazel-flecked eyes, she was the only one left amidst the bevy of beauties who had not already worn the bracelet. There was one way to be sure, for just the sound of her voice would tell him.

He picked up his cell phone from the table beside him and dialed the number his investigator had listed in the file. Not that he needed the file. He'd stolen the number already from the mind of a policeman.

The telephone purred at the other end. The best for last, and he closed his eyes at the pleasure the thoughts of her death evoked. The body's fingers worked, the large knuckles cracking. It had been a long time since the Johan body had taken direct action.

It had been even longer since he was directly involved in killing.

Chapter 1

Six-thirty in the morning and Lila Weber sipped a cup of maple-flavored milk tea as she stood on the wide front porch of the large red-and-white heritage house that had belonged to her grandparents. This late in September, along the porch edge bright copper pots held fading displays of red and white petunia and purple heliotrope that scented the air like baby powder. Across the street, beyond the white gate and hedge of the house's yard, lay the uneasy waters of Okanagan Lake, still dark from the night. It was the last of the dog days of summer, and the days were shorter, the dawn later, the nights—thankfully—cooler. But it also meant fall was here and the long gray days of winter would follow all too soon.

The rush and hum of the highway traffic at the base of the mountain behind the strip of flat land that held the sleepy town of Peachland had increased with the onset of September's workdays as people returned to their jobs from holidays. The sound was no longer just white noise. A breeze from the south picked up moisture, the scent of sage and pine, and an unusual coolness as it ran up the long narrow lake. She shivered.

She still wore her clothes from her morning yoga—navy leggings and a lavender sports bra—both still damp from her workout. Her thick auburn curls were a damp, tangled ponytail on the top of her head, so the breeze cooled her neck.

Cold, actually. Soon the wind would come from the north all the time and it would be too cold to stand outside to cool off and drink her tea. The thought saddened her. Something about this time of year always brought thoughts of endings. Maybe it was the fact that the summer people, who usually staked out their piece of beach even this early in the day, had mostly departed with Labor Day. The number of morning joggers had decreased to a trickle on the promenade along the water. Maybe it was because all the important things of her life had mostly happened at this time of year—the death of her parents and grandparents, other things that had been less painful but no less important.

Her fingers strayed to the silver links of the bracelet around her wrist.

Or maybe it was the bracelet. God knew the troublesome thing caused strange reactions within its wearer. The darn thing had been nothing *but* trouble ever since she brought it into the house. She'd like nothing more than to get it off. After causing innumerable problems for her friends, who had, one-by-one, put the bracelet on, the time had come for her to face the music and wear the infernal thing. She had no time for this kind of thing— not with a business to run.

She sipped her tea, savoring the smooth tannins and the slight sweetness of sugar. Soothing. That was what she'd been going for. Something to soothe the bad dreams that had been disturbing her the past three weeks. So far it wasn't working.

And this month was supposed to be one of beginnings—the opening of the new clothing store that she and Victoria Angelucci had partnered on. It would bring Milanese custom fashion to the Okanagan, the first of its kind, and would build on the jewelry store, *This and That,* that had already made Peachland a destination.

The first rays of sun over the bald gray mountains across the lake shattered golden in the lake's small waves and caught on the silver of the bracelet.

No, she was not going to dwell on endings, though wearing the bracelet meant she wore a target on her back. It was her turn, that was the only reason she'd put the darn thing on. That, and someone had to keep it from the reach of the creature that was seeking it. The trouble was, she'd put the bracelet on three weeks ago after it fell off of Victoria Angelucci's wrist, and too many nights of dark dreams had followed.

A sound from the house brought her around and a sleepy blonde figure in violet satin pajamas and robe padded into the *This and That* jewelry shop that occupied the front of the house. The front door opened with a little ding-a-ling from the silver bell above the door, releasing the scent of incense as Victoria Angelucci stepped out onto the porch.

She was a beautiful woman of lush hair and lusher curves à la movie stars of the Brigitte Bardot era, but sleep still muddied her features. This was her last morning as a guest of Lila's. After a month and a half staying in Lila's guest bedroom, she had leased a condo just down the street and above the clothing shop that she and Lila were opening. It meant that Lila would get her house, her sanctuary, back to herself. After the events of the summer, she couldn't say she wasn't looking forward to it.

Victoria slumped onto the turquoise-and-mandarin-cushioned wicker loveseat that was part of a grouping of wicker furniture on the covered porch. She put her slippered feet on the cushioned ottoman, closed her eyes, and held out a phone.

"This—this thing would not stop ringing. It is for you," she said in her Milanese accent.

Frowning, Lila accepted the phone. A call this early in the morning did not bode well. In fact, the phone call on top of the queasy feeling she'd had in the pit of her stomach since she finally got up this morning had her hesitating to answer.

"Man or woman?" she asked, but Victoria had laid her head back to catch the first warm rays of sun and simply waved the question away.

Bracing herself, Lila brought the phone to her ear. "Hello?"

There was silence a moment, but the sound of breathing came over the phone.

"Hello? This is Lila Weber."

The line went dead.

She looked at the phone before clicking it off, a tingle of dread pooling in her stomach as she sank onto the fan-backed, peacock chair that others called her throne. The phone felt unfamiliar and unwelcome in her hand. She set it on the ottoman and scrubbed her hand on her thigh.

"Who was it?" Victoria turned one bleary eye toward her. They had both been up late the night before with discussions about the store's grand opening and dealing with issues about Victoria's visa.

Lila shook her head, the chill she'd been feeling coalescing into cold even though the sun was finally warming the air. "I don't know. Whoever it was, they hung up as soon as I said who I was. It's odd. I had a similar call yesterday."

"He. It was a man that asked for you."

If anything, the day went colder. Lila rubbed her arms and wished for a sweater.

"I don't suppose that bodes well either, does it?"

Victoria sat up and pulled her dainty muled feet onto the floor again. "Do you think this has something to do with that thing again?"

She nodded at the bracelet, shuddering delicately.

"Do you? But why would the creature call me? It's done things much more insidiously up until now—it doesn't phone to announce itself."

"Would it not call if it knew it could upset you?"

Lila didn't know how to answer. The creature, who was somehow connected to a German named Johan Fehr, had dogged them all summer since the bracelet came into their possession. The bracelet, however, seemed to have a mind of its own, refusing to come off the wearer's wrist until the woman had found her soul mate—a man associated with one of the ornate doors that formed the links of the bracelet. So far five of her friends had found love and happiness and she was happy for them, but love—well, love wasn't what she was looking for anymore. She'd long ago given up on love for herself. If anything, she was married to her store.

She held out the bracelet to catch the sun's rays and the link shaped like an arched door with ornately-filigreed, scrolled-iron hinges momentarily blinding her.

With this store and the grand opening of the new one and trying to research the story behind the bracelet, she was busy enough.

Love was definitely the last thing she had time for.

§

For the umpteenth time, Nathan Moon hung up the phone and wondered what in God's green earth he was doing. He sat in his room in the Kelowna Marquis hotel, supposedly enjoying the blue and white view of the lake and the marina that sat at the base of Kelowna's most prestigious hotel. Instead, here he was in the glass-walled room, agonizing over whether to actually talk on a phone call.

With a groan he tossed his phone on the white leather couch and stood to pace the length of the white plush carpet to the base of the baby grand piano one more time. Money might get him the best room in the house, but apparently it didn't get him the balls to talk to a woman he hadn't seen in about fifteen years. Stupid. Idiot. Disgusting. Sissy.

"What are you, Moon? A momma's boy? A weak-willed, lily-livered coward?" he said choosing dialogue straight out of one of the 1940s movies that he'd cut his teeth watching in Hollywood.

He strode across the room to the bar and poured himself a glass of orange juice from the carafe that room service had delivered this morning. He considered adding a shot of vodka but wasn't that just the kind of thing his father had done that had led to his parents' divorce? Damn it. A drink would help to work up the courage, but the sun was barely up over the mountains let alone over the yardarm. Surely to goodness Lila Weber wasn't that daunting and the two of them *had* been rather good friends, but this time—this time he'd like things to end differently.

And if you want that to happen, then maybe you have to start somewhere? Like a screenwriter starting a script, the hardest thing was the empty page. In this case it was all the empty years between them.

Orange juice in hand, he crossed back to his phone and slumped on the couch. The view truly was stunning—blue lake and green mountains, a single stately sailboat running up the lake before the morning wind. In front of the hotel, the huge, shaggy cottonwood shaded a waterside walkway. The kind of view people would pay top dollar for, even more so for top billing in a penthouse suite like this. He was a man with enough confidence in himself he'd told the big studios to piss off and had gone independent. Surely any woman would be impressed by this address.

Except maybe Lila Weber. That was one of the things that had always impressed him about her—the trappings of Hollywood power really hadn't seemed to mean anything.

He stabbed redial on his phone.

The line hummed in his ear and then began to ring at the other end. What the hell he was going to say after all this time he wasn't sure, but he'd think of something. He and Lila had always been good at conversation while they stood around on the set between takes. He remembered the girl-woman dressed as a goddess, with Grecian toga flowing around her slim figure, the cording of the toga tied up high under her breasts, her auburn curls tumbling about her shoulders with a fine netting of jewels across her forehead and makeup that glittered on her high cheekbones. Her eyes had been huge and liquid. Her lips the color of wine so that every time he'd been with her he'd wanted to kiss her.

He hadn't, of course. He'd been living with Celia back then and he was loyal to her even if he'd already had the feeling that she wasn't the one. Besides, Lila Weber had only been seventeen, seven years his junior and jailbait at the time.

The phone clicked as someone picked up and he held his breath.

"This and That, Kylee speaking." A bright, but harried female voice at the end of the phone.

Not what he was expecting. He almost hung up again.

"I'm sorry. I was looking for someone. A woman named Lila Weber. I'm an old friend from her Hollywood days and a mutual friend gave me this number." Mutual in a pig's eye. He'd spent weeks digging around for her number, had been close as damn to hiring a private investigator to find her.

"Who's calling, please?"

So the voice on the phone did know something.

"My name's Nathan Moon. I worked with Lila on a movie a long time back. Maybe you saw it—*The Battle for Olympus*?" That usually impressed the locals.

He settled back on the couch. This was going to work. Lila'd come on the phone and he'd arrange a date to take her to dinner. Sort of sweep her off her feet.

The pause on the phone lengthened, but then the chipper voice returned. "I'm sorry, Mr. Moon, I know Lila Weber and I'm also aware that she really would like to forget her short period of fame and be left in peace. Thank you for your call. Goodbye."

The connection went dead, leaving him eyeing the phone.

"What the hell was that?" he said, dropping the offending handset in disgust.

Heck, *where* the hell was that? He knew Peachland was a backwater town in a backwater eddy of British Columbia, Canada, but the way the woman had answered the phone, it sounded like she was in a store of some kind. Was Lila reduced to a store clerk now?

The thought was almost impossible to believe, but maybe he could make like the hero in *Pretty Woman* and ride in and sweep her off her feet—rescue her, as the case may be. Poor kid. Things obviously hadn't gone well for her. Fifteen years—a lot could change. She could be married with six kids by now. Hell, the voice on the phone could be her daughter! But he just couldn't picture Lila Weber like that. No, Lila Weber had been too much like the goddess she played in the movie—too far above most mortal men. He was probably a fool thinking he could woo her even now, but hey, didn't most of his movies feature determined men who overcame the odds?

He pulled up the search engine on his phone and stabbed in *This and That* and *Peachland*. The system sought and then brought up the option for *This and That: Jewelry and Unsung Treasures.* That had a Lila Weber ring. He brought up the website.

A background image of a lake—probably this one—overlaid with a misty image of the inside of a store with dark wainscoting and gleaming glass cases. Then writing faded into existence as the misty image faded further.

This and That provides custom-made jewelry of precious and semiprecious stones from around the world. The proud home of Regulus Designs, come and see the latest stunning pieces destined to grace the runways of Europe.

This and That Jewelry and Unsung Treasures: Open Monday to Friday 9:30 a.m. to 5 p.m. Open Saturday 10 a.m. to 6 p.m. Phone to arrange a private viewing outside these hours or contact the store to arrange a jewelry party at your home.

Links at the top connected to a gallery, a page on arranging a private party, and a page on *Regulus Designs*, as well as an "About" page. He clicked on About and a clearer image of the store appeared and began rotating to give a full view of the interior— much like real estate used for a three-sixty degree tour. On top of the image more writing appeared.

Opened in 2010 at its current location at 1520 Beach Avenue, Peachland, This and That is the lovechild of three friends who love beautiful things and who are determined to share that beauty with the world.

Hardly a Hollywood headshot and credit sheet. He tossed the phone on the couch again, then scooped it up and headed for the door. He was not going to sit here like some jilted ex-lover. Even if things didn't work out with Lila the way his far-too-vivid imagination had envisioned, he still would like to see her again—even just as a friend.

Down the elevator and through the lobby to the heat that was a lot like Los Angeles on the very best days—no pollution and very little humidity, but with a breeze off the lake that kept things downright pleasant. In the parking lot he climbed in the dark gray rental Mercedes. Hot. He keyed on the car and opened the sunroof to let out the heat and catch the breeze. Then he tapped the voice recognition GPS and turned on the a/c.

"*This and That: Jewelry and Unsung Treasures*. Beach Avenue, Peachland."

The GPS computed and provided a map of the turns he needed. If only it would be as easy to secure a route to Lila.

Chapter 2

Returning to the store from a run to the printer's in West Kelowna, Lila parked her Ford Escape in the carport at the rear of the house and hauled the box of cards and pamphlets from the back. The final announcement cards for the grand opening of the clothing store had finally arrived—late, of course. In addition, Chloe and Kylee had been planning informational brochures about the proper care of individual jewels or crystals that they could provide to each customer. Chloe was a crystal healer and believed that a jewel's owner should understand how to maintain the positive vibrations of their stones. So far their test run of brochures had been eaten up by store patrons, so they'd finally committed to the not inexpensive full printing.

She lugged the box around the car and across the flagstone back patio that was unusually silent since Reggie—Reggie Lewis of *Regulus Designs*—had taken a day off from her design studio to be with her daughter at a horse show. Her sweetie, Cesare, was off in Milan, supposedly dealing the final death blow to the lawsuit that had haunted Reggie. The turquoise and yellow wicker patio furniture beckoned for her to just sit and take in the sun, but she had no time. In fact, it felt like years since she had. She might live in one of British Columbia's summer playgrounds, but she rarely played herself. As a businesswoman, who had time?

Balancing the box on her hip, she opened the back door to the kitchen and stepped inside into coolness. The kitchen was her favorite room of her house. It was her grandmother's old summer kitchen, with a bank of windows that spanned the entire back of the room, including the door. Broad marble counters spread under most of the windows except at one end of the room where there was a comfortable, old-fashioned nook with more turquoise and yellow and tangerine cushions. The room's walls were white, but the cupboards were sunny yellow. Stainless steel appliances were an update along with the copper fan hood above the gas range that sat in its own alcove.

Lila set the box on the table and eased her back, then went to the fridge. She was just pouring herself a lemonade when Kylee appeared from the darkened hallway, Chloe on her heels. Both women looked concerned. Kylee was the latest addition to *This and That*. The petite blonde had been Lila's high school best friend and had turned to Lila when her latest love had gone wrong. She'd since partnered with Chloe's vintner brother, Brett. As usual, today she wore a brightly colored floral dress, her bright hair in a cute cut that just skimmed her chin.

Chloe was everything that Kylee was not, average height with hip-length brown hair that she tamed in a braid, her uniform was a caftan tunic with matching leggings. Today they were a pale lavender that brought out the hints of violet in her eyes. Chloe was a long-time friend with a passionate belief in psychic talents.

Lila looked from one to the other and sipped her drink. "What?"

She looked down at herself. Was something wrong with her outfit? She wore a sleeveless navy shift that skimmed her body and navy-and-white spectator flats. "I haven't peed myself. And I'm not wearing my breakfast. What gives?" Another sip of the thirst quenching lemonade as Kylee and Chloe looked at each other.

Kylee crossed the room to catch her hand.

That someone had died was the first thing that crossed Lila's mind.

She set down her glass and felt suddenly afraid. "What's happened? Who's hurt?"

Kylee shook her head. "It's nothing like that. But Victoria mentioned those two weird calls you've had." She swallowed. "Another call came while you were out. I don't know if it means anything but—well, I gave him the kiss-off."

"Tell her what he said," Chloe urged.

"He said he was looking for Lila Weber, and all I could think of was the bracelet you're wearing." She nodded at the silver links gracing Lila's wrist. "He said he worked with you on a movie a long time back and he mentioned *Battle for Olympus*. Knowing the problems you've had with fans in the past, I told him that was part of a life that you'd put behind you and that you'd prefer to be left in peace."

Lila nodded. That was the instructions that all her friends had. All of Peachland, too, at least all of the old-timers, and they guarded her privacy from the fan boys and fan girls who still showed up occasionally. Unfortunately that single film had gone on to be a cult classic that had made the careers of most anyone associated with the project, but all it had done for her was make her very certain that the Hollywood lifestyle was not for her.

"It sounds like you did exactly right." She took another swallow of the lemonade and felt the heat from outside dissipate.

Kylee shrugged. "Maybe. Maybe not, too. You see, this one wasn't exactly like all the usual fan-boy calls. This one introduced himself and he said he worked on the movie with you. He said his name was Nathan Moon."

Lila almost dropped the glass. No way. No how. It couldn't be. That blast from the past just couldn't be here—unless...

She turned to lean on the counter and peer out the window into the backyard. Nathan Moon. Nathan—handsome-beyond-belief—Moon. The man she had thought she might love but never done anything about it because she'd been seventeen and stupid enough to already have been swept off her feet by a Hollywood producer who'd turned out to actually mean it when he said he was going to make her a star. She and Nathan had spent three months sitting in lawn furniture getting to know each other while the piece was shot in the desert outside of L.A.—standing in for Greek highlands. Nathan Moon, who she'd dearly wanted to run away with, but who treated her like a little sister. Nathan Moon, who she had finally, after fifteen years, put out of her mind.

"Why would he want to find me?" she asked no one in particular.

"Maybe he realized he missed you," Kylee offered.

Lila shook her head. "Why would he want to find me now? After all these years? That makes no sense."

She turned back to them, her hand covering the bracelet. "Don't you think it's a bit strange he calls me now? After all the trouble my friends have had when they wore the bracelet? A blast from the past just means danger, doesn't it?"

"Could be," Kylee said.

"What I want to know is just who is Nathan Moon?" Chloe said. She drummed her fingers on the counter and arched one eyebrow. "Long as I've known you, I've never heard of Nathan

Moon and I've certainly never seen you go wonky like this—especially not at the mention of a man. So just who was this guy to you?"

That was the thing with Chloe: far too astute, and once she got an idea in her head she was like the proverbial terrier that wouldn't let go.

Sighing, Lila leaned back on the counter and took another sip of lemonade seeking her steady, clinical self. "Nothing more than a friend, really. He was an assistant director on the movie I did. We spent a lot of time talking, that was all. Okay?" She went to push past to the door but Chloe had her by the arm.

"Nuh-uh. Not going to happen, sister. The look on your face says there was something more—a lot more—about this guy."

With a roll of her eyes, Lila turned back to her. "Damn it, Chloe, why don't you learn to leave things alone? There was nothing else. He was nice to me, the one nice thing in a situation I would rather forget ever happened. Making *Battle for Olympus* was not my shining hour, okay? And now I think I need more than this lemonade. I'm going for a walk to stretch my legs and get myself an iced coffee. Anyone want anything from the café?"

When both women just shook their heads, she abandoned her lemonade and headed for the front of the heritage house with a growl. "Damn women and their stupid suspicions."

As if there was something between her and Nathan Moon. It had been so long she could barely remember what he looked like—except his almost turquoise-blue eyes.

And then there had been that grin of his.

Would you just stop! You are a business woman. You have better things to do with your time.

She shoved out the front door of *This and That* after switching the little open sign back on because Kylee and Chloe must have switched it off before they came to talk to her. Then she half ran down the porch steps. Darn friends, anyway, thinking they could grill her like that. Not that she hadn't done some grilling herself over this very romantic and very dangerous summer.

Away from the shade of the porch, the heat fell on her head and shoulders like a hammer. Her dress might be lightweight cotton, but navy blue wasn't exactly the most cool color she could be wearing. She crossed the street for the promenade, thinking to distract herself with the last antics of the toddlers and pets that played in the water. That was half the fun of living so close to the lake. Water was like a magnet for all the best things in her life. Chloe, Brett, and Kylee were all part of her summer memories from long ago.

She headed north along the water, letting the sound of the waves and the remaining summer people and the faint scent of suntan lotion ease away her frustration. It was only a block and a half until she came even with the bakery café that leaked delicious aromas of fresh bread and cookies and the pungent promise of fresh coffee. She could have made equally good coffee at home, but that would have required her to continue to face down her inquisitors.

The café sat in the corner of a newer development with expensive condos up above, one of which Victoria was subletting fully furnished until all her residency documents came through. The building also housed the clothing shop that Victoria and Lila were opening and there was already a buzz about the event. As she stood there, a couple of summer people paused to read the announcement in the fledgling store's front window. It was designed by Kylee and showed a few of the pieces that would be available along with the grand opening date. They'd also named the shop *The Next Thing: Victoria's,* playing off against the association with *This and That.*

Everything was in place for the opening. Victoria's seamstresses were busy finishing off the last few pieces, the music was arranged, as was the food. The Peachland mayor, Haifa Samuels, had been invited, as had city council and the local media, including *This and That's* longtime client Marcia Oldstrum, publisher of the Kelowna Herald.

Lila stepped off the curb mulling over all the things that remained to be done before the opening—pick up garment covers for purchases, ensure the credit card hookups were working, ensure that there were tables and chairs set up on the sidewalk outside and that there was a ribbon for cutting.

The nearby roar of a car engine caught her attention. This wasn't a drag strip—the speed limit was a sedate thirty kilometers an hour along Beach Avenue.

A dark SUV squealed away from the curb three cars down. It shot across Beach Avenue's centerline directly toward her.

Leap forward? Leap back? Someone on the sidewalk screamed. She tried forward and the SUV seemed to swerve to keep her in its sights until suddenly she was picked up and thrown to the curb. She landed on her hands and knees as the car roared past and was gone like a bat out of hell to disappear around the curve of the shore line.

Lila rolled to sitting. Her knees bled. So did her palms. One of her shoes sat in the middle of the street and her heart beat a quick tattoo. People crowded around her asking her questions: Was she all right? Okay? Injured? Hurt?

It was all too much. She blinked, trying to make sense of it all, and considered the blood seeping from her grated palms, the bracelet gleaming around her wrist. Darn thing still hadn't come off. Someone cut through the crowd and cast a shadow over the sun. The figure knelt in front of her and caught her hands, gently using a tissue to wipe the blood off, and then cleaning her knees of gravel.

When she looked up it was to peer into perfect turquoise-blue eyes, the kind you could swim in. Nathan Moon knelt before her like some kind of knight.

That was when the shaking cut in.

§

Holy hell, that had been close. The dark blue SUV hadn't even slowed. If he hadn't been hurrying to catch up to the woman he thought was Lila, he never could have caught up to her in time to help her. The roar of the engine had seemed to freeze her just long enough that there was no way she was going to get out of the way in time. He'd barely had time to grab her and throw her and himself out of the way. Where he'd got the reaction time for that, he couldn't say. He was no hero.

"Lila, your hands and knees are scraped but otherwise you look okay." At least physically. By her thousand-yard stare, she might have hit her head; or she was in shock, at least. "Is there somewhere else you're hurting?"

She licked her lips and then her gaze shifted, slowly coming into focus on his face. "My pride?"

A glimmer of a smile appeared on her lips and suddenly she was Lila again—just as he remembered.

"Could you give me a hand up?" Her voice was stronger, as she got her legs under her.

"I've called the police," said a spandex-clad, male jogger. "I got most of the license plate—I think."

The barista from the coffee shop appeared with a white metal first aid case and Nathan wanted to sweep Lila off her feet to the nearest chair, but had to content himself with his arm around her waist. She felt slim and fine as a reed in his grasp, though she was limping. Her scent of baby's breath and roses caught in his nose.

On the sidewalk patio in front of the café, he settled her in one of the wrought iron chairs in the shade of the awning and sat down across the table from her, the breeze ruffling his hair. Someone brought them both water and she sipped, holding the glass with shaky hands. She watched him over the rim as he set to cleaning her knees for her.

"So is this one of those meet-cute situations?" Her brows rose in speculation.

"Could be, if you want it to be. I guess it depends on what happens, doesn't it?" And just like that, it was like they were fifteen years younger and the world was their oyster—a young star in the making and a top director-to-be. Except it didn't happen like that, because Lila walked away and now she didn't respond—just seemed to be contemplating what he had said.

"So how have you been? It's been a long time," he said to break the awkward silence and distract her from the sting as he used antiseptic wipes on her injured knees.

She shrugged and held out her palms for his ministrations. "And how has Hollywood been treating you? Wait—don't tell me—I've managed to see all your pictures, I think. I really enjoyed *The Sultan Shuffle*. It was my favorite."

"You saw *Sultan?* Heck you and about fifteen other people. It was my first indie film and never got picked up by the theatres."

"I saw it at an indie film festival here in Kelowna, so someone must have liked it enough to bring it in."

He grinned and spread salve on her scrapes. "One of the other fifteen people. But thanks. Your opinion means something. It wasn't quite what I had set out to make, but it was close." Before expediency demanded that he compromise a little to succeed commercially. Like that had worked.

"So what brings you to the Okanagan? A shoot?"

"You" was the answer he wanted to give, but he was saved or prevented from revealing himself by the arrival of the ambulance. Under the force of blue-and-white clad paramedics, he was shoved aside while they checked Lila over. Over her protests they concluded that she should come with them to the hospital to make sure everything was okay.

"But I don't have time for this! I was just going to get a coffee and head back to my office."

The paramedic, a burly, middle-aged blond, eased her onto a stretcher and strapped her down. Panic filled her eyes and she reached for Nathan.

He was more than glad to take her hand.

"I hate to ask. Would you go down the street to my store, *This and That?* Tell them what happened and they can come and pick me up at the hospital. Okay?"

The paramedic was levering her up into the ambulance.

"You really don't need to do this. It's just scrapes and bruises, I'm sure," she said to the paramedic.

He slid the stretcher the rest of the way into the vehicle and then grinned at Nathan. "Some people just don't know how to take care of themselves."

He could believe that about Lila. She always pushed herself to give everything she had.

"Which hospital?" he asked. In L.A. they were too many to count.

"Kelowna General, where else? Check Emergency. They probably won't keep her, but better safe than sorry."

The blond paramedic joined Lila in the back and slammed the doors behind him. The driver set out for the hospital. Nathan watched them turn onto the highway and then turned back to Beach Avenue.

The red-and-white house waited. He'd talk to her boss. Sighing, because this wasn't exactly how he saw himself reentering Lila Weber's life, he headed down the sidewalk.

The red-and-white house was the kind of place that a location scout would take note of. Its broad covered front porch spanned the entire breadth of the place, and the copper hanging baskets overflowing with fading red, white, and purple flowers gave it a heritage feel and a gentility equated with the old south. And yet the two-story structure had a sense of *gravitas*—of being a serious part of the town's history, even if it was just a house. This house belonged, not just to whoever owned it, but to the town. And while Peachland looked like it was gradually being rebuilt to fit the current preference for concrete condos and townhomes, this house held onto the grace of the past and had a presence that wasn't going anywhere anytime soon.

Odd, that he got all that from the place, but there were some places that just spoke of—home. A beloved home.

He let himself in through the little white picket gate and climbed the porch stairs two at a time. The place looked just as well groomed up close. Comfortable wicker loveseat and chairs decked out in bright summer colors. Squeegee clean windows and discreet little "open" sign by the door.

He shoved inside and caught a face full of incense as a bell tinkled above him. Then he was inside and found himself facing two women, one of whom was serving a customer. The other— brunette with a long rope of braid—eased herself from around the dark wood and glass cash counter where an incense burner before a small brass Buddha released a thin coil of potent smoke toward the ceiling's crown moldings.

"Welcome to *This and That*." she said. "May I help you?"

He felt totally out of his element because the place felt so—well—other. Feminine. New-Agey. Misty, as if it existed in both this and another dimension—an effect it achieved through gray-lavender paint and dark wainscoting that he'd have to remember for future movie sets.

"Um. Yeah. My name's Nathan Moon. I'm looking for the owner. I was just down the way at the coffee shop and there was an accident."

The women in the shop seemed to take a collective breath, both the customer and the small blonde clerk turning to him.

"Lila," said the brunette with eyes that had turned the most amazing violet.

Nathan nodded. "Yeah. She was almost hit by a car and she seems only scraped up but the paramedics thought she should go into the hospital for a check-up anyway. She asked me to come let her boss know what happened. I gather she was on her coffee break."

The brunette and the blonde looked at each other as if he was missing something.

The brunette held out her hand and he shook it. A small tingle ran up his arm.

The woman's concerned face eased into a smile. "Pleased to meet you, Nathan Moon. I'm Chloe Main. This is Kylee Jensen and this is Franny Graystone, one of our favorite customers."

Chloe almost looked like she was gloating.

"So you own the store?"

Chloe Main shrugged. "Sort of. In partnership with Lila." She arched a brow at him. "So Lila's okay?"

Nathan inhaled and sighed. Of course Lila'd own the store. She wasn't the kind to be satisfied being a clerk. "From what I could tell. I checked her out right after it happened."

"I'll just bet you did." The sotto voice comment came from the small blonde.

When he glanced at her, she met his gaze innocently.

He turned back to Chloe. "Lila said she was going to need a ride back from the hospital."

"Uh-huh. Did she now." Chloe checked her watch. "Gee, that could be a problem. I've got some healing sessions booked and Kylee has to watch the store. I guess we could call Reggie..." She glanced at the little blonde, who nodded.

"If it would help, I'd be happy to pick Lila up," he offered.

"Really? That's a very kind offer, Nathan. If you wouldn't mind. But just so you know, Lila can be kind of bitchy when she's surprised by something, and you picking her up will definitely be a surprise to her."

Forewarned was forearmed. He nodded. "Okay. That's good to know. I'll head into town then. See you in a while."

Chloe preceded him out to the porch. "Thanks so much for helping us out. You know, I think Lila's mentioned you. You're a friend from way back, aren't you? Someone she knew well, but not well enough?"

What could he say? A small flush of heat ran up his neck as he shrugged.

The darn woman smiled as if she knew better, so he hurriedly left her on the porch and headed out to the Mercedes. Funny thing was, he was almost sure he heard her chuckle.

§

Chloe reentered the shop feeling a sense of satisfaction.

"You are a very bad woman," Kylee said from the cash counter as she rang in Franny Graystone's latest purchase.

"Funny, I always thought of Chloe as an agent for good," Franny said as she punched in her credit card code.

Chloe drew herself up to her full five-foot-seven. "I *am* an agent for good, but it's about time Lila Weber got as good as she gives. She's always nudging someone along into romance. Now it's her turn. Didn't you hear who that was?"

"I heard. Nathan Moon," Kylee said.

"And who's Nathan Moon, aside from a man good enough looking to leave me fanning myself?" Franny asked, demonstrating, her bright blue eyes flashing under her stylishly cropped gray hair.

"Someone from Lila's hidden past," Chloe said with a dramatic flourish of her arms. "Someone who got away before Lila ever got to express what she felt for him—or that's what I'm thinking. 'Course it was a long time ago and chemistry can change, but him showing up right now? Well, what do you think?" she asked Kylee.

"Could be a coincidence."

"Or good timing. Just when Lila Weber needs to find her soul mate, Nathan Moon comes calling. I'd say that's a pretty good omen, wouldn't you, Franny?"

Franny nodded and took her leave. Chloe watched her down the porch and turned back to Kylee. "Perfect timing, given Lila's wearing the bracelet. And there's something else. I was worried, when he walked in, that he might be Fehr's latest victim, but he's clean. More than that, when I touched his hand, I got 'True'." Chloe often got a single word description of a person the first time she met them. "How's that for an auspicious beginning?"

"Lila's still going to be *pissed* at you." Kylee shook her head with admiration.

"Let her be. She didn't make things easy for me when Jas came a-courting. Now's payback time."

She was still chuckling an hour later when she went for lunch.

Chapter 3

Kelowna General Emergency was about the last place Lila wanted to spend her morning. So she'd scraped her hands and knees. So somewhere along the line she'd torn her dress and bruised herself all up her left thigh and hip and shoulder. She wasn't *hurt*. At least not bad enough to warrant the nurses and doctors who bustled around and had her taken down for x-rays. She'd been forced to wait in a clam-pink alcove with hospital green curtains, inhaling air that was an awful medley of antiseptic that couldn't quite hide the scents of vomit, urine, and feces.

She was worried, though. It had taken a long time for her hands to quit shaking and her heart to slow. She kept playing the scene in front of the café over and over in her mind. The car had pulled out as soon as she entered the crosswalk. It had gunned its engine as it did. Had it really aimed directly at her? It felt like it had, but that was all in the moment. She hadn't really been paying attention. The driver was probably just some kid with a beefed-up car who hadn't been paying attention either.

Except, maybe he hadn't been a kid. It could have been something far more sinister.

She looked down at the bracelet and slid it around her wrist, examining the doors. One was a small arched wooden door surrounded by vines. Another looked like it was girded in iron like doors from North Africa. Still another had a small gargoyle head door knocker and next to it was one with square lintels. One door was made in two pieces like a Dutch door and then there was the one that she thought of as hers—a curved door with the lovely ornate elvish hinges. The last door was also arched, but had hinges shaped like leaves and a small padlocked chain around its waist as if to make sure that it stayed closed.

The clasp of the bracelet was a small, ornate, silver key that slipped through an equally ornate lock. The trouble was, the darn bracelet clasp didn't come undone until it apparently decided to on its own, so Lila was stuck with it. Could the thing that had been trying to get the bracelet all summer have aimed that car at her?

But that was too crazy. The creature trying to recover the bracelet had been far more devious in the past. It wouldn't try to run her down—would it? But if the car had hit her and she'd died, the bracelet would have come off, wouldn't it? The creature could have got what it wanted. She shivered on the hospital bed until the nurse brought her a heated blanket. It couldn't be true. It just couldn't.

It took until one o'clock before they were satisfied that indeed the worst wound was to her dignity. Of course, that dignity took a serious second hit when, still nursing her worries and wearing only one shoe, she came limping out to the emergency waiting room.

"Lila."

Damn it, what the heck was Nathan Moon doing here? He leapt to his feet, a smart phone in his hands. He looked good, though. Better, even, than he had all those years ago and certainly better than he had in Peachland when his presence had radiated fear and concern. Now his blond, chin-length hair was shoved neatly behind his ears and his magnetic turquoise eyes worked their magic so she almost couldn't look away.

She forced herself to. "Where're Chloe and Kylee?"

She sought desperately around the waiting area, because surely to goodness they had to be here. She needed to talk to them and the others about whether her suspicions could possibly be true.

"Chloe said they couldn't get away so I offered to pick you up."

She was going to kill Chloe Main. And maybe Kylee, too. Those two together were too much like bad news and she knew exactly what this was all about. Payback. She gritted her teeth and looked back at Nathan. Well, the least she could be was gracious. The man had saved her hide.

She sighed. "Then I guess I should thank you. A top Hollywood director and he still has time to be a chauffeur."

"Just call me a Renaissance man."

He offered her a white plastic grocery bag. When she opened it, it held her missing shoe.

She pulled it out and started to laugh when he went down on one knee to help her put it on. "Don't you think this is a bit much?"

"Hey, you're the one who wanted 'meet cute.' This is about as cute as it can get." He stood and half bowed. "M'lady."

He looked good, with his square jaw and well-defined mouth. With his longish hair, his faint shadow of beard gave him a bit of a dangerous look. He still had the broad shoulders she remembered and rugged build that looked natural instead of bought in a gym like all the other Hollywood men. But still...

"Saccharine," she said with a dismissive shake of her head. "So where are we parked?"

She led off, determined to get there on her own, but the car was parked farther away than she'd expected and when Nathan's hand found her elbow and offered support, she wasn't in any condition to fend him off. She let him guide her into the multilevel parking lot and to a big, dark grey Mercedes sedan.

"Hollywood must be paying you very well," she said with a low whistle.

Nathan frowned. "It is kind of opulent, isn't it?"

"How many people do you think can afford one?" She turned to look a challenge at him and he grimaced like a guilty kid. "Let me guess: you've got two back home."

A charming Nathan wince that she remembered. "Well... maybe not two... but one convertible..."

And maybe she was pushing him just a little bit much.

"So does it drive as nice as it looks?"

He perked up like an excited kid, just part of the Nathan Moon who had charmed her so long ago. "Come on and I'll show you."

He held the door and she settled into brown leather as soft as butter. When he was seated beside her, the engine started with a roar, then settled into a purr as he backed them out of the parking spot. Coming out of the parking garage, he opened the sunroof and drove the car out into a blue Okanagan afternoon.

The smell of warm lake water and well-watered gardens met her as they cruised through the quiet, leafy streets that led back to the highway and south to Peachland. She felt his glances as she looked out the window and held her hair in a ponytail against the wind.

"Would you like me to close the top?" he asked and nodded at her hair.

"Would I still get the sun in my face if you did?"

He shook his head.

"Then I think this is good. I can get rid of the hospital smell."

She caught his gaze on the ripped shoulder of her dress and self-consciously pulled the hole closed.

"You know, aside from the scrapes and bruises, you're looking very good," he said, grinning at her as he steered them over the bridge to West Kelowna. "The jewelry business is treating you well?"

"Well enough. Why? You surprised I became a working girl?"

"It's not a goddess, is it?"

She turned to him, irritated. "Did you ever think that maybe I prefer to be a real person, not something out of fiction?"

"Whoa!" He held up a hand as if to fend her off. "I didn't mean anything. I was just thinking things have changed since you left the set."

Left? More like ran. She hadn't even stuck around for the wrap-up party. The thought of another evening of being pawed by Simon Grafton, the producer who had discovered her and who had become her lover, had sent her scurrying for the airport home to her mother and father. After the movie came out, there'd been a lot of offers but she'd turned them all down, fired her agent, and gone to university. Nathan—well, Nathan had been her one regret. The man she couldn't seem to forget even after all these years even though they had never even kissed.

"It was kind of abrupt, wasn't it? But it was a long time ago." My God, she was reverting to the obsequious speech pattern she'd copied when she'd lived in L.A.

"You think years mean everything?"

"Years mean change." She poked at her cheek. "A few more wrinkles. A few more lines. A lot more smarts." She tapped her head.

He matched her grin and she saw that he wasn't exactly the young man she'd known way back then, either. He had genuine smile lines around his eyes and mouth—enough to make her think maybe she could just relax.

"How come you're so nice to me when I'm being a bitch?"

He laughed and shook his head, as he skillfully guided the car through traffic. "Would you believe that Chloe warned me?"

"She did, did she?" She crossed her arm over her chest. "Remind me to give that friend of mine a talking to."

But she settled back into her seat and realized that talking to him had cleared the shadow of fear away. She allowed herself to consider Nathan Moon. He looked good in the car, the way he controlled it so casually with his long-fingered hands. He really was the best-looking man.

But she wasn't interested in him, just like she hadn't been interested fifteen years before. Okay, maybe she'd been interested back then, but he hadn't been available and neither had she. Fifteen years later, she just plain knew better.

"So you still haven't said what brought you to Kelowna. It's a little off the beaten path for someone who lives and works in L.A."

He glanced at her as he turned the car off the highway into Peachland. "Who says I live in L.A. anymore?"

"You don't?" Interesting. If she believed him.

"Well... I keep a condo there. Most of the time I've sort of been wandering from project to project. A way to see the world, you might say." He flashed her a bright smile that wouldn't look out of place on a movie star. "And that brought me here."

"And I'll ask again: why?" The man was seriously avoiding the question.

"I've never been here before. It was some place new. But really? I was somewhere in the middle of nowhere, central USA, and I got thinking of my past and my future and remembering old times and that brought up you. So I got it into my head that I'd look you up. See how many kids you had and what lucky guy you married and all that."

He didn't look at her as he guided the car into the curb in front of *This and That*. "There. Home safe and sound."

He was out of the car and gallantly around to her door while she still pondered what he'd said. If she just answered that she wasn't married, it would sound like she was putting him on notice. That was not going to happen. The fact that he'd thought of her—well, people thought of old acquaintances all the time. They didn't often do something about it, however. But that was Nathan. Always doing the unexpected.

He helped her out and the touch of his hand—more callused than she would have expected—sent a tingle up her arm that she still remembered from so many years before. The bracelet felt warm on her wrist—which had to be the product of exposure to sunshine. She'd been holding onto her hair, after all.

"Thank you. Would you like to come in? The least I can do after you rescued me is offer you a coffee. Or maybe you'd like to have dinner and talk about old times?"

Damnation—had she just said that? She never just spoke without thinking it through.

He grinned. "That sounds like a great idea, but let's see how you feel later. You might not want to go out this evening. So let's get you settled inside now."

And with that he slung an arm around her shoulder, his hand on the small of her back, just like he had on the set years ago. Older brother to younger sister, and yet somehow this felt different. Maybe his hand felt a little warmer. Maybe she was just more aware of his masculinity and his musk and cedar scent.

She could relax right into him—but she wouldn't. That would be entirely too familiar because what did she know about Nathan Moon now?

Acclaimed director who quit making blockbusters to pursue his art. He'd been in the tabloids a time or two for his involvement with women and speculation that one of the top ten eligible bachelors of Hollywood would soon tie the knot.

He never had, as far as she knew.

Beyond that, nothing. But that was enough for her to know that he wasn't the man for her. She'd been in Hollywood and seen what it expected of people—the casual sex traded to get what you wanted, the relationships discarded like someone's trash. No one ever seemed to think about how relationships were precious gifts and took work just like the rest of life. Nope, she might have been infatuated by Nathan as a girl, but as a woman she understood all that he stood for. She wasn't up for that at all—no matter what a scheming Chloe Main might think.

But she could still be cordial.

He opened the door to the jewelry store for her and a guilty-faced Chloe and Kylee both leapt up from where they'd been rearranging a display in one of the glass cabinets.

"Lila!" They rushed over to her. "Are you all right?"

"I'm fine. Just fine—thanks to Nathan here." She turned around in realization. "It was you that shoved me out of the way, wasn't it?"

"From what we're hearing—Beth-Anne from the café popped down to see how you were—Nathan here practically picked you up and threw you. He just barely got out of the way himself."

"So you're telling me this guy is a hero?" She turned back to Nathan. "There'll be no living with you, now, will there?"

He shoved his hands in his pockets with an "aw-shucks" look. "You prefer humble. I can do humble."

She rolled her eyes. "This guy is just a frustrated actor. Watch out for him. You!" She wagged a finger under Chloe's nose. "You and I are going to have a little talk later, and you—" she turned to Kylee, "—you are on notice."

Then she strode toward the beaded curtain that led to the rest of the house. She turned back to Nathan.

"Are you coming? The kitchen's this way."

§

Lila Weber was all business as she stood there by the beaded curtain at the back of the misty-colored shop. The light from the windows that gave onto the porch placed a perfect soft glow on her face and hair that his lighting grips would scramble to recreate. The two other women—Chloe and Kylee—were looking from Lila to him, and just why did he feel that he'd walked into the middle of something he didn't quite understand? There was certainly an undercurrent in the room and though there was humor, there was also a tension. He'd felt it coming off Lila in waves at the hospital. The fact he felt it again now said it was more than just the incident.

It was the kind of subtle undercurrent that a director could despair of ever getting out of his actors and onto film.

Finally he shrugged and followed Lila through the curtain. It fell shut behind him with a gentle clack-clack-clack of the beads. Down a long hall that held faded, mostly black-and-white photos of people he didn't know living their lives together along a curve of beach that had to be the lake out front.

He paused before one of a much younger Lila—perhaps not much older than she'd been in Hollywood—with an older couple who both had their arms protectively around her. There was a strain around Lila's eyes even though she was smiling.

"That was just after I got home from L.A.," she said coming up beside him. "I came up to my grandparents to try to get my head on straight again."

"It looks like they loved you very much," he said looking down at her. She might be tall for a woman, almost five foot eleven, but he was a good four inches taller.

She nodded thoughtfully. "They were the best. I used to come up here every summer and lots of weekends, 'cause Mom and Dad were always away with their business. I still miss Grandpa and Grandma at times. This was their house."

And by the way she motioned to the place, it always would be. Her place now, obviously, but always the place that had made her who she was, as well. He laid his palm on the wood wainscoting in the hall with new appreciation. She wasn't just a partner in the jewelry store—it was her baby, in her house, with her friends. A new kind of family to replace what she'd lost?

He followed her into the kitchen with a pang of sadness. Maybe it meant she had everything she needed.

"Nice room," he said, looking around. With its bright colors and airiness, it was the kind of room you could see in a television commercial for some kind of breakfast cereal, but it was also the kind of room he could see for a family drama. All the deep issues would be aired at its counters, the solutions found around the intimate nook.

Lila moved around the room like she belonged there.

"Espresso? Latte? I've gotten pretty good at them because my star boarder, Victoria, is Italian."

He asked for espresso and wandered the room, touching the small mandarin-colored fish salt and pepper shakers, admiring the kitschy turquoise wall clock and the view of the patio out the broad bank of back windows before slipping into the cushioned nook. The place spoke of comfort and family and an underlying humor.

"You look like you belong here," he said as she shifted around the room, a small espresso maker burbling on the gas range. A pot of milk steaming.

"I do. This is home. It's where I belong. I've loved coming here ever since I was a kid. I can't imagine not living here."

She glanced at him as if putting him on notice, then turned back to the espresso and poured a small cup for him and a latte for herself before joining him at the table.

"You'll have to forgive Chloe and Kylee. They have this notion that you and I are meant to be something other than friends and acquaintances from way back when." She looked at him as if expecting him to agree that such a notion was foolishness.

"Oh. Well. Who wouldn't think that when some strange man out of your past comes calling?" he waggled his eyebrows at her.

"You're not helping." She shook her head. "You see, it's something about this darn bracelet." She tapped the silver links that he'd admired on her arm. "They've started to believe that it has the power to help the wearer find their soul mate. You calling out of the blue got them speculating that you might be mine."

"Now that *is* interesting." He sampled the espresso and nodded. "Good. Now tell me more about this soul mate thing?" It was the kind of far-fetched idea you'd see in the movies.

She boxed his shoulder. "How about not and you tell me about what's been happening with you? I read the tabloids. I see you're still in them. I think the last thing on the cover was Michelle Langston devastated because you broke up with her."

Sitting in that sunny kitchen across from Lila evoked such a strong sense of *déjà vu* that for a moment Nathan almost felt dizzy. It was so much like all those sunny afternoons on location, sitting under a tent awning with the desert blue sky and then with the blue ocean of Catalina standing in for the Grecian coast. She was without a doubt one of the most beautiful women he had ever met and the most charming thing about it was that she didn't act like she knew it. She just—was.

He sighed. "Michelle was just a little too high maintenance. Insecure enough that I had to reassure her all the time. Eventually it wore me out. People have to take some responsibility to make themselves feel good. It has to come from inside—not from someone else."

"Wow. That's pretty deep for Hollywood." Their eyes met for a moment and she jerked away as if burned. "The problem is that Hollywood expects you to be the other way—feeding off of everyone's adoration."

A shiver ran through her and suddenly he understood. "That was the reason you left, wasn't it?"

A soft smile came to her lips. Then it hardened. "A little. In all honesty I can understand how it happens. I just didn't want it for me."

"So you left and didn't even say goodbye."

She took a long sip of her latte. "Would it have mattered? I needed to leave and you needed to stay. I'm sorry if I hurt your feelings, though. I didn't want to, but I knew if I hung around long enough for goodbyes, I might not get out of there at all."

A haunted look swam into her eyes and then was gone again. Something about her time in L.A. still was raw after all these years.

He frowned, but didn't push. "So you made it back here. Just how does a Greek goddess come to run a jewelry store?"

And like that she laughed, the same husky laugh he'd always remembered. They were back on safe ground, but it left him wondering just what had happened. She'd been an item with Simon Grafton. That, he and everyone knew. It was Simon's *modus operandi* that he always bedded his female stars. Of course there'd always been a lot of rumors about him, too, because a lot of those stars seemed to flame out and burn after their relationship with Simon was over.

Lila was talking about how she'd met Chloe while she was in college and the long-haired woman had introduced Lila to crystals and semiprecious stones. The two of them had made jewelry to wear themselves, but the pieces caught on. They'd met Reggie Lewis, the third partner, at a local artisan market and the three of them had got to talking after Reggie reworked an old piece that Lila had bought at a flea market. By then Lila's grandparents had died and had left her the house. She still had residuals coming in from her time in Hollywood. So she and Chloe had headed off on a trip to Morocco, Israel, and India, three places that they knew they could find jewelry and stones. They bought amethyst and other stones in Morocco, visited a kibbutz in Israel where they bought fine jewelry, and found a factory in India where they bought more jewelry and selected stones. They got connected to a gem supplier and bought more, and came home with enough inventory to open a store.

"So we decided to use the front parlor of the house. And the rest is history. Sales were really slow at first, but word of mouth spread quickly and we tried to have displays at summer markets and that got people thinking about us. At the same time, Peachland was starting to become a destination, so that helped, too. And voilà! A successful store." She held her hands up beside her.

"I'd say it's amazing, but then I shouldn't be surprised because you were always an amazing woman."

Her thick lashes veiled her eyes. "Thank you. That's kind. But it wasn't just me—there were three very hard-working women involved. Most of all, I think we have to thank Reggie, because it was her inspired creations that really started to get us noticed. Poor kid—she's had a time of it this summer."

"What happened?"

She shook her head. "Does it really matter? You don't know her and I'm boring you with these small town matters. You must be bored silly after L.A."

On some level she was right. The place was extremely small. A sleepy summertime town just waking up to all the new development he'd seen on the hillsides and what he could see in town. Change was coming. Maybe it was because he was sitting across from Lila, but it didn't feel like the small, dying towns he'd visited in the center of America.

"Surprisingly, no. This place feels different. There's a vibrancy here." He caught her hand and turned it over, exposing the angry red pepper of scabs across the heel of her palm. "It really is so good to see you, but I think I've kept you here too long. You must want to rest after all you went through this morning." He reached over and gently tugged the ripped shoulder of her dress closed. Such pale smooth skin, but he didn't touch.

At his intimate gesture, Lila froze, then bolted up out of her seat. "You're right, of course. And I've totally taken up too much of your day. Listen, I know I spoke of dinner, but if you'd rather not, that's okay."

From smooth, confident Lila, she suddenly looked uncertain and a little shocky. He stood and caught her arms, too aware of her satin-smooth skin and the muscle underneath.

"I'm not backing out of dinner unless you're not up to it. If that's the case, we'll find another time. But for now, let's just say I'll pick you up at seven."

She turned her lovely hazel gaze on him, but there was something about it that was questioning. As if she didn't believe him. Almost as if she didn't trust him.

"So seven?" he repeated.

Finally her gaze fell and she nodded. "All right. For old time's sake."

"But you'll call me if you're not feeling up to it?"

She nodded.

"Good, then. I'm staying at the Grand Marquis." He leaned in and placed a small, brotherly kiss on her cheek, and then released her to head back down the hall and out the front.

Kylee was showing a customer earrings, while Chloe was just seeing another customer out as he crossed the room for the door. She held it open for him.

"How'd it go?"

"As well as can be expected, I guess." He cocked an eyebrow at her. "She's pretty darn certain we're not soul mates, though."

Color flooded up over Chloe's features as he grinned at her and headed out to his car.

He reached the white picket gate.

"When she's wearing the bracelet, she's most likely wrong," she called.

He half-turned to her and she winked.

Interesting.

Chapter 4

At a quarter to seven, Lila stood in her bedroom eyeing the contents of her closet. Her room was a place of comfort to her, just like the kitchen was, but instead of a room of turquoise and mandarin accents, here the room had a white Shaker-style dresser, full-length mirror, and headboard in a room of pale Nantucket blue. Gauzy white curtains flowed floor to ceiling in the dormer windows to either side of the bed that held a quilt of white with blue flowers. A white porcelain vase on the dresser held a spray of white freesia. Beside the vase lay a mirrored tray with antique silver-backed hairbrush and comb—once a treasured possession of her grandmother's. It was a tranquil room that filled one end of the second floor of the house and overlooked the water, but at the moment, with the stack of discarded clothes on the bed, it looked anything but tranquil. Instead it looked like a whirlwind had hit it.

All because of Nathan Moon.

With a sigh, she stepped back from the closet. She wore a pale pink bra and panties, which was certainly *not* enough to go to dinner in, but as for what to wear, she had not the faintest idea.

"Damn you, Nathan! Look what you've done! I was a perfectly calm, collected businesswoman until you blew into town." She ran her hands through her hair in frustration and picked up a square-necked brown dress off of the bed. It would fit her well—it always had—but did she want to look like a businesswoman for this dinner?

The answer should be "yes," but something inside her said "no." Nathan Moon had come a long way to see her. He'd even risked his life. The least she could do was put her aches and pains aside and put a little effort into her appearance, whether she wanted to or not.

So—not brown. She discarded the dress again. Black would be entirely too formal and her navy dress that would have been fine with some fancier jewelry had gotten ruined today. Not trousers and not a skirt and blouse.

That left a suit—too much about business and not enough about old friends—and a cream-colored, sleeveless cotton dress that went with a cream silk shantung jacket. Far too dressy, but what choice did she have? Sighing, she slipped the dress over her head and zipped the back. Perhaps she'd put on a few pounds since the last time she wore it, because it felt like the dress was a second skin the way it hugged her body.

It looked good, she knew, but too much like she was trying too hard. But maybe if she dressed it down...

She pulled flat-heeled gladiator sandals of gold from the closet and a simple cream sweater with a gold fleck in the knit. With her hair down and loose, it would almost do. She added trim gold earrings and a gold watch and studied herself. Maybe...

A knock came at the bedroom door.

"Come on in to my disaster." She slumped beside the bed as the door opened.

"*Madre di Dio!* Lila, what has happened?" Victoria came into the room looking soft and breezy in a white, loose-fitting linen blouse over black leggings that showed off her shapely legs. Her hair was a casual tumble from a fall on the top of her head. She looked at Lila and horror bloomed in her eyes. "All these beautiful clothes in a jumble—and you—you look like a school teacher for your lovely man!"

"He's not my lovely man and you haven't even met him."

Victoria shook her head and marched from the door to Lila. "Chloe, she told me. No! You cannot wear this! The people will laugh and say who is this mouse, Lila Weber?" She tugged the sweater off of Lila's shoulders and tossed it on the bed and studied Lila critically.

"The dress is good, yes? Good lines. But not these, surely!" She bent and unlaced the gladiator sandals. "You must have better footwear, yes?" She stepped into the closet and inspected the contents, coming back with a set of strappy heels.

"These! These will show off your legs."

Lila waved her off. "And break an ankle, most likely. I haven't worn them in years."

"No." Victoria stomped her foot. "I am the designer. I will not have the partner in my store going out with a handsome man looking like she does not know how to dress. I know you, Lila. Why do you sabotage yourself tonight? And those—" She motioned at the earrings. "Those are too safe. You must have others—something Regulus, I think." She went to the dresser and the large jewelry box that stood beside the vase of flowers, to begin pawing through its drawers.

"Aha!" She turned triumphantly back with a long, silver chain from which hung a large, silver, clasped amber pendant. She carried them back to Lila, who felt a tad chagrined and a tad overwhelmed by Victoria's forcefulness.

"This isn't a date, Victoria. It's merely two old friends going for dinner."

"So you say, but he is a good-looking man, no? You do not want to look like the charity case with him, do you?" She arched a shapely brow.

"Charity case?"

"As if a handsome man has taken pity on the poor ugly duckling. You are a beautiful woman, Lila. A beautiful woman should always outshine the man she is with." She settled the long chain over Lila's head. "No, this is too long, but the pendant is right."

She went back to the jewelry box, Lila trailing after her to stop the destruction of the order she kept the jewelry in.

"What about this?" She reached past Victoria and pulled out a smooth, braided silver band that would sit like a collar around her throat.

Victoria switched the pendant to the new necklace and fastened it around Lila's neck. "There. Much better, do you not think?"

It actually was—like the torque fashions that were in style and yet something different and beautiful that set the copper highlights of her hair gleaming. "Okay, I guess."

"Okay! You are *bella*—beautiful, as you should be. But you need different earrings, too. Something large and dangly that a man could catch in his teeth, I think." She grinned wickedly and started opening drawers again.

"Hold it." Lila held up her hand. "I think I know what you're after." She pulled out another drawer in the jewelry case and produced a small box. Opening it, she pulled out a set of earrings that she'd loved when she purchased but rarely worn. They were fashioned like candelabra with a cascade of small amber beads so that they caught the light like golden chandeliers.

She held them up to her ears, finally getting into the fun of Victoria's mood. Let Nathan be wowed. She knew where she stood: there was nothing between them except a little friendly history. The earrings didn't seem as large and gaudy as she'd feared. Instead they peeked through her long copper curls as if meant to be.

"Put them on. Put them on," Victoria urged.

She did.

"*Perfetto!*" Victoria stepped up beside her. "Do you not see the glory? You will blow him away."

Lila had to smile as she turned this way and that in front of the mirror. "I just might."

She went to grab her sweater again, but Victoria slapped her hand. "A shawl. One of your pashminas."

Dutifully, Lila went to her closet and pulled out the drawer that held her collection. Victoria, who had followed, reached over her shoulder and pulled out a black one.

"This. To match the shoes, and you are complete."

Lila swung it around her shoulders and studied herself in the mirror. "He is so going to get the wrong idea."

"And that is the right idea, is it not? He is handsome. He is your friend. Would it be so bad if it went beyond friendship?"

Lila shook her head, feeling suddenly deflated. "Maybe. Maybe no. I don't know. You see, I had a huge crush on Nathan way back when, but he was involved with someone and so was I. I never told him how I felt. I just left and then fifteen years later, out of the blue, he shows up. All I know is that he's Hollywood and the people in that town chew other people up and spit them out in little pieces. I don't want anything to do with that."

Victoria busied herself tugging Lila's dress this way and that as if to get the best fall out of the cloth. "I suppose that is reasonable. But you do not know what this one is like. He may not be Hollywood, as you say."

"He grew up there. He's lived there all his life."

"But sometimes things are not as they appear. Even in the Arabian Nights, it is that way. A prince maybe a pauper and a pauper a prince. A genie may be trapped in a bottle. A princess may be a swan. This man, this Nathan, may be something beyond Hollywood. You do not know until you look."

"So you're telling me I need to keep an open mind?"

"That is exactly right. And given my Daniel is working tonight, I will live vicariously through you while I sit in my room and try to find the secret to this beautiful thing." She caught Lila's hand and brought her wrist with the bracelet up into the light. "It is such a beauty, too. Mysterious. Like you."

Victoria patted her hand and released Lila. The brass clock on the bedside table chimed seven times, and as if on cue, a knock came at the front door of *This and That*.

In Nathan's world it was show time. She took a deep breath, but for some reason felt butterflies just like she had whenever she walked in front of the camera.

§

Downstairs, Victoria tried to make her hang back to make an entrance, but Lila refused. She left Victoria in the kitchen, reading, and went to the door herself, purse in hand.

Nathan stood on the porch, resplendent in a smoke-gray suit, white shirt, and black tie with amber-colored stripes. His blond hair was combed back in wings around his face and though he'd clearly just shaved, he still had the shadow of a beard that gave him a hungry look. His turquoise eyes widened when she opened the door.

"Wow. Look at you! And here I thought you left the goddess in Hollywood." He looked down at himself. "Good thing I wore this. I was thinking of a jacket and jeans…"

"If it's any consolation, I was significantly less dressed up until Victoria got a hold of me. She wouldn't let me out of the house until I let her turn me into this."

"And I'm the lucky guy who gets to enjoy it." He offered his arm, which she was relieved to accept given the stupid heels she was wearing. Together they went down the porch steps to his car and he held the door for her.

"So where are we going?" she asked, trying to get into the fun of the evening.

"I asked around and now you'll just have to wait and see."

"A secret, then."

"A surprise." He grinned and had the nicest crinkles around his eyes. For a moment she allowed herself to feel the attraction, but then she let it go. It was a vestige of her extinct youth, wasn't it? Something left behind in her evolution into the woman she was today.

He turned the car around and drove out of Peachland as dusk settled over the lake. The mountains across the water were tinged golden with the last sunlight, but the lake had been leached of color. Now that September was here, the days had shortened significantly and she was glad of her pashmina even though Nathan had the car's roof closed.

"I used to pick peaches at a friend's orchard just down there," she said as they drove past a precipitous turn off the highway. "It was hard to get to, but the peaches were worth it. Most of them were the size of small grapefruit. The couple that owned the place are still holding on, but for how long, I don't know. These days I find myself saying goodbye to things I loved about Peachland more and more."

She shook her head and glanced at him. "I guess you wouldn't understand that. Things are always changing in Los Angeles."

But surprisingly he nodded. "I think I understand. I grew up in L.A. but we used to go out to Carmel and Malibu all the time. Neither are the same as they used to be. The old family diners and hangouts are gone, replaced by high-end restaurants that cater to high-end tourists. If the prices had been as high when I was a kid, my family couldn't have afforded to go there."

Perhaps it wasn't quite the same as her sense of loss, and just why was she feeling that way tonight anyway? Even if this was going nowhere, here she was in a fabulous car with a handsome man going to dinner somewhere. She was not going to be a downer this evening. Victoria would approve of that decision.

She caught Nathan glancing at her legs and was both pleased and a little uncomfortable. *Get over it, woman. This is Nathan Moon, and haven't you thought about him a time or two over the years and wondered what might have happened?*

"So what do you think of the Okanagan?" she asked as a safe conversation while he wheeled them through West Kelowna and down toward the floating bridge. He turned right off of the bridge into a quiet area of elegant old houses that backed onto a small canal that had been created to allow boaters to dock at their yards.

He thought a moment. "Different, I guess. In a good way, of course. Desert, but not Death Valley. Wine country, but not Napa or Sonoma. Mountains, but not the Sierra Nevada. And then there's you, different from all those Hollywood women."

She frowned. "Just what does that mean? That we're all just a pale imitation when California has got the 'real thing'?"

"Hold on, before you get upset. I mean maybe this place is special because it's different. Not any of those places—it's the Canadian Okanagan."

He guided the car into the curb and turned off the engine. "Just like you're different from every other woman I've ever known. Sure, I have met other women who had similar traits to you, but you're the only one that has all the traits that are you."

Her heart did a little tha-thunk, but she was so not going to fall for this man. "Now that *is* the Nathan Moon charm. Too bad I know what you're doing."

She didn't wait for him to help her, but swung open the door and slid her legs out to stand before he could get to her. When she stood in her heels, she could just about look him eye-to-eye. "So just where are you taking me, because this looks just like a suburban street."

"It's a surprise. I asked around at the hotel and they told me about a supper club called Moveable Feast that specializes in doing pop-up dinner parties around the city. There's one just down the block tonight. It's a set menu, but the food is supposedly a cavalcade of the best of British Columbia."

He caught her elbow and tucked it into his side, but a movement down the block caught her eye. She glanced back, but there was nothing there—just shadows under a maple tree in the front yard of a stucco house with an arched portico over the red front door.

"Lila? Is something wrong?"

She found him looking at her, his hand warm on her arm, her wrist tingling under the bracelet. She tugged her arm free to walk beside him. "I love this part of Kelowna. So far the heritage designation has saved the neighborhood. But now you tell me there's a restaurant here." She started down the block not sure where she was going, just knowing that she needed to step away from Nathan's presence; but he caught up.

"Here," he said and turned her up a sidewalk toward a two-story stucco house with round windows flanking a blue-painted door. Heliotrope filled huge barrels flanking the entrance and purple wisteria hung in clusters around the door. Lights filled the interior and the sound of music came through the door along with the scent of strawberries, peaches, and fish cooked on a grill. She felt a pang of hunger and allowed Nathan to usher her inside.

It was clearly a home, with unique, vivid artwork and what looked like antique African masks high on the walls. A living room of brown leather couches and red Persian carpets opened onto a large yard, with a flagstone patio decorated with small white lights in trees and with occupied tables scattered amid the flower beds, glistening with white tablecloths and crystal goblets. Along one side of the flagstone patio, a bar had been set up, and on the other side a tuxedoed man at a piano played soft music. Another door at the rear of the house clearly gave onto the kitchen. A black-clad waiter met them and led them to a table in a bower of roses, their sweet scent perfuming the air.

"This is amazing," she said as she settled into her chair. And more amazing was the fact that Victoria had seemed to know and made sure she was dressed appropriately. She and Nathan might stand out in Peachland in their finery, but here they fit right in. She'd have to thank Victoria later.

Nathan ordered a bottle of local wine and then sat back to look at her. "You realize every man in the place is looking at you?"

"Why? Have I got toilet paper stuck to my shoe or something?"

He shook his head. "They recognize you, I think. Or they've dreamed about someone like you. The goddess. Most of these guys might not remember the movie, or admit having seen it, but their body remembers you. Simon Grafton wasn't wrong when he cast you as the goddess. In fact, the success of the movie seemed to hinge on the fact that he got it exactly right."

"O-kay, you can stop now as I am suitably embarrassed." The heat flushed up through her face and she felt uncomfortable. She took a deep breath. "So—what are you working on these days?"

The wine arrived and she waited as the sommelier poured Nathan a sample so he could taste the rich red wine. When he nodded his approval, the sommelier poured the wine and left them. Nathan took another sip.

"It's very good. Surprisingly so, given the Okanagan hasn't been producing wine that long. Full-bodied and with a really nice cherry and pepper finish. You should try it."

She did, and found the tannins smooth over her tongue, but she set the wineglass down, leaned forward, and placed her chin in her palm. "You're avoiding the question."

"Am I?" His lips curved slightly.

She straightened. "You are, and that's a concern to me." She looked around the yard, with its soft lighting and single tables set only for two scattered in secluded spots across the area. "Is this a date, Nathan? Are you wooing me?"

He eyed her speculatively over the rim of his wineglass. "Would it be so bad if it was?"

"Are you telling me that you came to the Okanagan just to find me?"

He reached across and caught her hand, so the bracelet glimmered between them. "I'll ask it again: Would that be so bad? We had chemistry between us way back when. Enough that you are still imprinted on my brain. I think we still have chemistry now—if we let it happen."

"Let it happen? Let what happen? A roll in the hay? We fall for each other and then you have to go back to L.A.? How would that benefit either of us?"

He squeezed her fingers and then released her. She pulled her hand away into her lap, but her flesh still tingled and the sensation arced right through her.

"Maybe...maybe if we thought it was worth it, we'd find a way? You have to admit that there was something between us back then," he said.

Why was her heart hammering so hard in her chest? Why did just looking at him make her flush? She'd felt like that on the set and had shoved the feelings back. Finally she nodded.

"There was something... Tender. Sweet. Unrequited. I was so young back then. I mean, how does a seventeen-year-old deal with suddenly receiving all that attention from grown men? I was so uncertain, and there was Simon. And then I met you. I was so attracted to you it should have been illegal."

"It was illegal—under California state law. I was twenty-four. Too old for a seventeen-year-old. But..."

"But what? Simon was thirty-five."

He sighed. "But the fact I was so attracted made it clear to me that my relationship with my then-girlfriend wasn't going to work. I broke up with her the day of the wrap party. I wanted to tell you there—spend time with you and see what happened."

"And instead, I left. Sort of ruined your plans. Sorry about that." Oddly, she felt sorry, too.

He shook his head. "Not too worry. I consider it fate. After all these years, it brought us here."

§

He was going to have to be very careful. Her reaction to the suggestion that they try out a relationship said this might not be as easy as he'd hoped. And that was a damned shame, given every time he set eyes on her he was more certain that he'd done the right thing by coming here to try. Especially now, when the twinkly lights brought the most beautiful glow to her skin and the darkness placed a smoke to her coils of hair and the soft green-brown of her eyes. There was something like an electric current between them so that just the sight of her sent a shock to the pleasure centers of his brain. At the moment it was almost overloaded with her presence.

Was he raising the same response in her? It was the kind of visceral response that he always tried to evoke in his movies, but this time the audience he was going for was an audience of one.

She didn't seem to be reacting to him. Or she was resisting it. He couldn't be sure, but he was sure that he made her nervous. Her fingers had worked that bracelet on her wrist continuously since they sat down.

The first course arrived—an amazing *amuse bouche* of endive, prawn, and chives with an oyster butter foam that filled their mouths with crisp and sharp and salty as the brine of ocean with a buttery overtone. Lila talked of the store and of the grand opening of a new sister store planned for this month, but all the time she spoke, her fingers were on that bracelet, work-work-working.

"What's with the bracelet?" he finally asked as a soup course was set in front of them—a chilled gazpacho of sweet garden vegetables.

Her spoon stopped halfway to her mouth and she met his gaze. "Bracelet?"

But her gaze fell almost guiltily to her wrist.

"You told me about the soul mate thing, but the way you play with it all the time, you look like you're worried."

She sighed and looked away. "Let's just say I'd give anything to get it off."

He frowned. "Are you saying that it won't come off?"

"Something like that." She held up her arm and jiggled the bracelet, still avoiding his gaze, and that definitely wasn't what he was going for.

"It's very unusual, isn't it?"

Finally she looked at him, her lips barely curved in a smile. "An understatement if there ever was one."

It was as if that was all she was going to say, and he wanted to get her talking. The soup course was swept away and a plate with a single, delicate round of egg tortellini was set before each of them. Lila smiled and cut into the almost translucent pasta, releasing a flow of perfect egg yolk to go with the brown butter and basil in which the tortellini had been cooked. Nathan tasted his own serving and the velvet flavor covered his tongue.

"So why don't you tell me about it?" He nodded at her wrist. "You already dropped the hint that Chloe and Kylee have odd ideas about it. What's the deal?"

She eyed him over the food and then seemed to decide. Taking a deep breath, she held out her arm to him. "Try to unlock it."

He hesitated. "What's it going to do? Shock me?"

She shook her head, a little devilish dare in her beautiful eyes. "Try it and find out."

He caught her hand—smooth, cool skin, slim palm, and long fingers with perfect French manicured nails, but without all the googaw rhinestones and glitter women seemed to be using these days. Her hand felt exactly right in his clasp. He looked back at her and her gaze was watchful.

The bracelet was the kind of unique piece he could imagine as a set piece in a movie. Seven tiny ornate doors made up the band, each one unique. "I can see it now in a movie—one door opens for a wearer and they're sucked through into an adventure."

"Close, but no cigar. Darn thing doesn't work that way. Try the clasp."

He turned her arm over, exposing the pale, smooth flesh of her inner arm and felt a tremor run through her. His fingers ran lightly over the sensitive place where her pulse beat and up to the silver.

A flash momentarily blinded him and he swayed where he sat, feeling hot-cold and hot again, before the moment passed. He found himself gripping her wrist—hard. His body leaned forward so he was hung over the bracelet clasp. Lila yanked her hand back.

He released her.

"What—what just happened?" He gripped the table, the remains of his luscious tortellini forgotten. "For a moment there, everything here just blacked out."

He caught a wary look in Lila's eyes that was swiftly smoothed away.

"Perhaps we should just call it a night, then. You're unwell and frankly I think the accident this morning has caught up to me. I—I can call a friend to come and get me and you can go get to bed—get some sleep."

"Lila, I'm fine. Now." But what the heck just happened? "Besides, we haven't finished our meal, and don't you want me to relieve you of that bracelet?"

She shook her head. "I don't need your help. The bracelet's fine where it is, isn't it? And as for dinner, I shouldn't have agreed to it—for far too many reasons. I'm not feeling well and I'd like to go home. Please."

She met his objection with firm, unrelenting regard and a rigid posture as if she was about to leap up and run. Clearly, something had erased the rapport he'd thought they'd had earlier and the evening was over.

"All right. I'm sorry you're not feeling well. I was just dizzy a moment."

Her throat worked and her gaze was worried? Afraid? Sad? A combination of all three? "Dizziness can be a sign of something greater—far worse. You should get yourself checked."

"Maybe I will. Tomorrow. But please, let's enjoy this lovely meal."

She shook her head and pushed to her feet. "I'm sorry, no. Thank you for the invitation. It was a fine idea to have dinner together, but I don't think it's going to work. The past is the past, Nathan, and I have too much in the present to worry about."

She held the arm that wore the bracelet pressed protectively against her and avoided him when he leapt up to stop her.

"I can find my own way out, thank you. It has been good seeing you, Nathan. It's nice to know that you're alive and doing well." She smiled sadly and turned from him, but he caught her hand.

"Lila? What the heck is this? I thought we were getting along and just feeling our way into whatever might happen."

She turned to him and laid a cool palm on his cheek as she shook her head. "It's a nice thought—terribly romantic—but we're adults—we both know better. Like I said, the past is behind us. We're both different people now. Besides, it's too dangerous for both of us."

She extricated her hand from his and started across the lawn again like Persephone retreating back to Hades.

"Lila, hold on. I'll drive you."

Thankfully, she nodded and waited just inside the living room as he hurriedly paid their bill. People were clearly staring at him from the other tables. Probably wondering what he'd done to send a goddess running. Hell, he wondered himself.

He left a hefty tip for the waiter and turned to Lila.

She wasn't there.

What the hell? He hurried out the front door to where shadows had congregated under the trees that lined the streets. Only the front door lights of the heritage houses leaked light. The air smelled of damp earth, lake water, and something burning. Where was Lila? How the hell had she moved so fast and where had she gone?

"Lila?" he called and ventured down the sidewalk to the curb.

A sharp cry came from down the street where the Mercedes waited.

"Lila?" He set off at a jog and caught movement ahead of him—two figures struggling. The faint light from a house porch caught on something cream with a flash of amber. "Lila!"

He dashed toward her as an attacker knocked her down. A knife blade flashed, and *holy shit,* what was happening!

He reached them in time to grab the attacker's knife arm, but the man twisted away. He stood ready to fight—strapping big, with muscled arms and broad shoulders, his face covered in a balaclava. Pale eyes seemed to study Nathan and the stench of smoke almost choked him.

Then the man turned tail and ran down the sidewalk, leaving Nathan to help Lila. She was on her side on the pavement, her copper curls a tangled mess around a pale face that was filled with too-large eyes. He knelt beside her, and before she could protest, he scooped her up; model thin, she was far lighter than her height suggested. Her heart beat like a frightened bird's as he carried her back to his car and settled her inside. Then he climbed in beside her and pulled out his phone.

"I'm calling the police."

"No." She shook her head. "No police. I'm fine. I'm safe."

"Like hell. I'm phoning."

She caught his hands. "Please. No. Do this for me. I know what I'm doing."

Sighing, he put the phone down. "Two attacks in one day, Lila? Something's going on and you're going to tell me about it."

She was silent a moment, then: "Do you really think sticking your nose in is going to make things any better?" She was a shadowed figure huddled in her pashmina as if it could protect her.

"I think you need someone to protect you."

"I have friends. I know the police."

"Then why not call them now? Or this morning, for that matter? It was me that helped you both times. So why are you shutting me out now?"

Her eyes flashed toward him. "Did you ever think maybe I'm doing this for your own good?"

"Well, that's stupid." He started the car and turned to look at her again. "I came here looking for you, Lila. I didn't know what I'd find. You could have been married with kids. You could have been dead. I didn't know, but I was going to find out, because what *didn't* happen between us all those years ago was a mistake and it's worried at me all these years. I was a fool for not coming after you when you left, but I told myself that you hadn't felt anything and that's why you'd left. Over the years I've come to think that maybe I was wrong so I had to check. This time I'm not leaving again until we give it a chance. Especially not now, when it looks like you could really use some help." He rested his hands on the steering wheel when he really wanted to reach for her and hold her in his arms. "So whether you want it or not, I'm going to be here for you. How about you tell me what I'm fighting against?"

There was silence from her side of the car. Her gaze was far away, peering out of the side window as if to avoid him. She was shutting him out and he wondered whether she'd even heard him. His fingers clenched around the smooth leather of the steering wheel. This was the kind of stupidity that drove him nuts with the scatty women of Hollywood. Lila, thankfully, hadn't been like that.

Until now.

Sighing, he dropped the car into gear and guided it onto the street and back toward the highway.

Chapter 5

The set of Nathan's jaw in the dashboard lights told Lila that he wasn't going to just let things go. He sat beside her on the buttery leather seats of the Mercedes, his hands clamped on the steering wheel as he maneuvered the car through the red lights of three lanes of traffic. Kelowna fell behind them and West Kelowna unscrolled as the car crossed the floating bridge over the dark water of the narrow waist of Okanagan Lake. Then they were up the hill into West Kelowna and heading south.

"Who was that guy?" he finally asked through clenched teeth. "You've gotta have some idea who he is or you would have gone to the police. Who are you trying to protect, Lila?"

Wrong. He probably figured it was some ex-boyfriend. So wrong and she just wanted him to leave things alone. If he got involved, there was too much chance he'd get hurt. Like Cesare had. Like Danny had. Both men were still recovering. And what if the thing, whatever it was, took over Nathan like it had Danny? But Nathan was the kind of guy who wouldn't take kindly to her trying to protect him.

She glanced in his direction, then looked away, back to the straggle of ponderosa pines still holding on as new construction erased the landscape. "No one. Everyone. Just leave it alone."

The car swerved to the side of the road, traffic horns blaring around them. It screeched to a halt and he turned to face her.

"Lila, give me a break. I know you're in some kind of trouble. Just like I knew you were in some kind of trouble way back when. Back then I was too young and stupid to do something about it. I knew Simon Grafton was a lech and I knew his *modus operandi* was to take advantage of the young women he had on set. I'd heard rumors about drugs and sex parties and I knew you were unhappy. I should have done something about it back then, but I didn't and I'm sorry. I'm not going to stand aside and let something happen to you now." He caught her cold hands, forcing them away from clutching her shawl and his warm grasp enveloped them. "Now you can tell me what trouble you're in, or I can make a nuisance of myself talking to your friends. I figure they'd be pretty good sources, wouldn't they?"

His blue eyes were like pieces of agate in the light from the dash. His hands were gentle, but unrelenting.

"Damn you, Nathan, I'm trying to do what's best. Don't you understand that?"

And suddenly he pulled her into him, his arms coming around her, her head fitting against his shoulder as if it was meant to be.

"What I understand is that I've been an idiot waiting fifteen years to come and find you. Now I have and I could have lost you twice today." His words rumbled up through his chest into her ear. "I'm not going to let that happen, Lila. We need to have a chance. We deserve it."

She felt his breath on her cheek, scented of fine red wine. His lips were on her hair as his palm smoothed her face. Then, ever so gently, he tipped her face to his.

"Do you understand what I'm saying? I'm not giving up. I'm asking you to give us a chance."

"I—I want to. At least I think I do." It was hard to meet his gaze because she truly wasn't sure. Nathan Moon had populated her dreams for years, but was he the man for her now? And the coincidence of his arriving now—was this something like with Danny, where the creature had taken over? Could she trust him? "But this is about the worst time ever and... and I won't be anyone's conquest. Not ever again."

She felt him stiffen. "What's that supposed to mean?"

"What do you think? I'm not about to be chased or wooed or—or drugged or coerced in some other way. I know what I want and if I don't want it—well, then it's over. Do you understand?"

He was so still, she thought he might be about to shove her away, but then his arms tightened around her. "That bastard Grafton hurt you badly. So no conquest. Deal."

As if to seal it, he dipped his head to hers, hesitated, and then their lips met, so lightly at first it was no more than a breath, a wish, a hope, a prayer that sent a soft flush of pleasure through her. So gentle she wanted more and lifted her chin. Another brush of his lips across her bottom one, and a more firm peck on the corner of her mouth. She turned her head to him. For a third time his lips grazed across hers, sending what felt like bright sparks across her skin. She reached for him, held his chin, and kissed him. Really kissed him.

More sparks filled her vision as his hands slipped up her back to hold her head. His mouth devoured hers, sending a pulsing heat through her, and her arms came around his neck of their own accord.

Nathan groaned and held her to him so she felt like something precious. "That was everything I hoped it would be."

"Kinda good, I'd say." She had to catch her breath. "Who knew Nathan Moon was such a good kisser?"

"Come on! You had doubts?"

She grinned up at him, feeling so much younger than her thirty-three years. "Not really. It would be unforgiveable for a guy who looks like you not to know how to kiss."

"So tell me. What makes this the worst time for us to get together?"

Oh God. She shook her head. "If I tell you, it means you'll get sucked into the same madness that's been dogging me and my friends all summer. I don't want that to happen, Nathan. You don't need that."

She pulled away to her seat, putting the car's console firmly between them. She'd practically been in Nathan's lap when they got into that clinch.

"But I'm not going anywhere, Lila. Given that, don't I deserve to know the trouble I'm walking into?"

She thought about it a moment. "It means you're getting yourself involved in some pretty weird stuff. Stuff that stretches the realms of credibility. Are you sure you want to walk on the weird side?"

"Tell me and let me decide."

She slumped back against her seat and leaned her head against the rest. Sighed. "Okay. But just drive while I decide where to begin."

She closed her eyes, but felt his gaze on her. Then the car eased back into traffic and cruised southward. Where to begin?

"It all started in June," she said. "My friend Kylee had just arrived and was staying with me. I'd just brought home a shipment of jewelry from an estate sale. We were sorting through the stuff and Kylee found a bracelet—this bracelet." She held up her arm and opened her eyes. In the amber dash lights, gold flashes appeared to run over its links.

She told how Kylee had tried the bracelet on and then, to her horror, had discovered it would not come off, no matter what she did. The clasp just wouldn't work.

"Then a stranger showed up named Johan Fehr and he said he was looking for a trinket that was a family heirloom but not worth much. He spoke to Chloe, and Chloe, who's a sensitive, sensed something bad about him. Worse, she found herself under some kind of compulsion to tell him whatever he wanted to know. He looked at everything in the store and was furious that whatever he wanted wasn't there. It was because Kylee was out for lunch at that moment.

"At the same time, the police were involved because the woman who had run the estate sale that the bracelet was from had been killed in a hit-and-run. Their investigation brought up a bunch of people—all men—who claimed to have been possessed by aliens—or something. Then Kylee was abducted and we barely got her back. She finally got the bracelet off when she and Brett, Chloe's brother, got together."

"You mean you weren't kidding today when you said that Chloe and the others think this bracelet connects you to your soul mate?"

She nodded as they started down the hill toward Peachland. "It's kind of hard to refute when it's happened again and again. Kylee, then Chloe, then my friend Ally, then Reggie, then Victoria." And now she wore it, but she wasn't looking for a soul mate. Didn't see it as in the cards for her life. She jingled the bracelet on her wrist. So pretty and such a problem. Like a silver version of the hope diamond.

"Each of them wore the bracelet until they reconciled with a man. Each of them was attacked and in danger. Now, supposedly, it's my turn."

He glanced at her speculatively. "So maybe we could just cut to the chase and agree to be in love. Then the bracelet would come off."

"You think?"

"It's a chance."

"Right. So have you got a door in your life that looks like this?" She sorted through the bracelet links and came up with the arched-top one that looked like it had a ornately scrolled hinges. She held it out to him as he drove down the hill.

He glanced at it and shook his head. "Not that I know of, but then the lighting's not good."

She brought her hand back to her lap feeling vaguely disappointed. It might have been good if it was Nathan and she could get this over with. Get the bracelet off her wrist, though who she would hand it off to, she had no idea. "Then supposedly we can't be soul mates and that's that."

"Well, pardon me for saying, but that's stupid."

He turned the car off the highway and down to the water, then pulled into the curb in front of the house. The lights of the town glittered in the waves, but across the lake was only darkness. Her grandparents' house was dark, too. So Victoria must have moved to the apartment she'd leased over her shop. That could make things a little more awkward.

Before she could say anything, Nathan was around the car and opening the door. She went to climb out but her left leg gave under her in the ridiculous heels she wore. Nathan caught her before she could fall and swept her up in his arms again.

"No! You are not carrying me into my own home." She batted his shoulder until he put her down. "I am perfectly capable of walking. I just need to get rid of these stupid stilettos." He steadied her as she slid them off, then stepped down onto pavement and wiggled her toes. Then she looked up at him and grinned. "Better."

But her ankle wasn't. She'd obviously twisted something and the pain shot up her leg every time she put weight on it. She bit the inside of her cheek and walked as steadily as she could manage around the side of the house, Nathan shepherding her.

The rear patio was dark, the flagstones glistening in the moonlight, the lawn furniture shadowed. Reggie's workshop hunkered down at the side, and the opening to the carport yawned darkly. She paused and reluctantly searched the shadows. It wasn't good that she suddenly didn't feel safe in her own yard. Steeling herself, she crossed to the kitchen door.

"Thanks for seeing me to the door." She looked up at Nathan, feeling short in her sock-feet even though she was tall.

"You're not sending me away right here. I'm checking the house first." The set of his jaw said his mind was made up.

"But that's not…"

He took her key from her and unlocked the door. The alarm started beeping.

She went inside to punch in the code. "See? All safe." She flipped on the lights and went to do a spin, but something caught her eye.

In the middle of the kitchen table sat one of her photos from the hallway—the one of Lila and her grandparents. On the glass of the photo, someone had used a black marker and had drawn a bull's-eye—right over Lila's face.

§

Lila Weber was no weakling, but the way the blood leached out of her face, Nathan thought she might faint. He grabbed her as she sagged against the counter, then turned to follow her gaze. A photo he recognized from the hallway sat on the table. A bull's-eye.

"But how the hell did that get here? Who would do that?"

Lila was shaking and he put his arm around her, took her over to the chair at the table, and slid in beside her. "Now will you let me call the police?"

She nodded, her throat was working. He caught her hand and felt her trembling. The she drew in a deep breath and pulled herself upright.

"Not 911," she said. "There's a pair of detectives that know the case. Heck, Jas matched with Chloe, and Danny's Victoria's soul mate. He's also the closest thing we've got to an expert on this thing because he's been possessed by the thing—twice."

Thing? Possessed? "Give me the number."

She recited a phone number. "That's Chloe's place. Jas is probably there if he's not on shift."

He dialed and the phone buzzed until it was picked up.

"Main residence," a deep male voice answered.

"I'm looking for Jas Stone."

"Who's calling please?" That would be a cop answer, not identifying himself.

"The name's Nathan Moon; I'm calling from Lila's place. We were out for dinner tonight, but a couple of things have happened. Lila said I should call you and your partner."

"Sit tight. We'll be right there."

The line went dead and Nathan set the phone down and caught Lila's hands. "He said he'd be here right away."

"I heard," she said, but her gaze was too large and too glassy, not at all the businesslike Lila he knew. She looked exhausted, too, even though she tried to hide it.

He slid out of the nook. "I'm going to check out the rest of the house."

"I'll go with you. You wouldn't know if anything was missing."

She went to get up, but he eased her back into her seat. "I'm not looking for anything missing. I'm looking for anyone here."

"No!" She grabbed his hand. "You wait here with me until Jas and Danny come."

She looked positively afraid, so he squeezed her hand. "All right. I won't leave you. Can I get you something? Maybe make you a cup of tea?" he asked.

"What a poor hostess I am. I should have offered." She went to stand, but he waved her away.

"I'm up. You tell me where things are. I can make tea. Renaissance man, remember?" He grinned.

A smile ghosted over her too-pale lips and she nodded. "Tea's in the cupboard closest to the sink. Kettle's already on the stove. There's a teapot and mugs in the cupboard next to the one the tea is in."

The shadows under her eyes said she was just about done in, this beautiful Valkyrie of a woman trying so hard to be strong, and he wanted to protect her. Had to protect her.

He selected a Canadian breakfast tea, comfortingly scented of maple, and brought the teapot and mugs to the table along with milk and sugar. Then he tended the copper kettle on the stove until a knock came at the back door. It pushed open and admitted Lila's friend Chloe and the one who must be Jas Stone because he had "cop" indelibly imprinted on him better than any character actor.

He was tall—tall as Nathan—and long and lean, with the physique of someone who did more than work out. This was someone who used his muscles. He had black hair that he wore longer over the collar of his yellow polo shirt and jet-black eyes that seemed to take everything in without letting anything out again. Typical closed off cop, and yet there was a warmth to him that flared whenever he looked at or touched Chloe.

"Nathan Moon, Lila's friend," he introduced himself and held out his hand.

Jas accepted it and demonstrated the power in his grip. Nathan let him win, but liked him a little less.

"Jas Stone, RCMP General Investigation Squad. So what's happened?"

RCMP—Royal Canadian Mounted Police. The man's gaze flickered over to Lila and his expression changed to one of protectiveness. "You okay, Lila?"

Chloe had already slid into the nook beside Lila's chair and had hold of her hands. "Tell us what happened."

"How about I tell you what's happened because I think Lila's just about had enough of everyone for the night. I'd frankly like to see her in bed."

Three sets of eyes turned to him and he realized what he'd said. He felt himself flush, and damn it, the double entendre was not his style!

"She's had a rough day," he finished lamely.

"Go ahead," Jas Stone said, but another knock at the door brought in a stunning blonde bombshell he was introduced to as Victoria and a rangy, red-headed cop named Danny Forester. So Lila really did have cops to call on. It was actually a relief.

"I just brought Lila home from dinner and when we came in the door, that was on the table." He nodded at the photo on the table with the Lila figure in the cross hairs of the bull's-eye.

"Ohmygawd, Lila!" Chloe pulled her into a hug and clutched her hand when she released her. Nathan stood behind Lila's chair and wanted to touch her.

"It's just like with Kylee—a warning and a threat. Its telling me that all my alarms are no good." Victoria had slid in on Lila's other side and had poured her a mug of milk tea.

Lila sipped and faint color gradually seeped into her porcelain features.

Danny and Jas both leaned over the photo. "Did anyone touch it?"

Both Nathan and Lila shook their heads, "no."

"You have a large plastic bag we can use?" Jas asked.

"In the drawer by the sink," Chloe answered for Lila.

Nathan retrieved a bag and he stood to one side as the police officers nudged the framed photo off the table and safely into the plastic. "There might be prints," Danny said with finality as if the show was over.

"We need to search the house," Nathan offered.

"We will," Danny said.

"This is just the latest thing to happen. This morning someone tried to run Lila down. I barely got her out of the way in time. It was like the driver aimed for her. Either that or he just plain didn't see her, but that seems impossible. I thought it was probably some stupid teenager, but tonight someone attacked her."

"What?" The group chorused.

Everyone looked at Lila, who suddenly looked smaller and more vulnerable than he'd ever seen her. She sipped her tea and had her eyes closed as if to hide from the inspection of all her friends. Lila Weber was not someone who liked being vulnerable and by the expressions on the others' faces, he wasn't the only one who hadn't seen her this way.

He stepped behind her again, and placed his hands on her shoulders. A tremor ran through her and the hand that wasn't clutching her teacup crept up to clasp his. An electric tingle ran through him.

"I think Nathan's right. Maybe we should get you to bed," Chloe said. "Maybe a nice warm bath to start."

"Hold on," Danny said, holding up his hand. "Can you give us the details?"

Lila looked up to Nathan. She licked her lips. "Nathan—Nathan took me out for dinner. I got stupid at one point and wanted to leave. He was going to drive me home so I stepped outside to wait."

Her expression said how sorry she was.

"I started down the street to the car, figuring Nathan was just behind me, and had just entered some tree shadows when someone leapt out at me. He grabbed me around the neck and started squeezing, but Nathan heard and scared him off. He rescued me. Just like he did this morning." Her eyes fell to their clasped hands as if the admission hurt her.

"What happened?" The two cops turned to Nathan.

"It was like Lila said." He described what had happened. "So I picked her up and got her into the car to keep her safe. She wouldn't call the police, so I brought her home and called you. Lila said you'd understand what was going on." And please, God, let them explain it to him, because Lila's connecting the attacks to the bracelet was just a little too farfetched.

"Did you see what he looked like?" Danny asked; a small black notebook had appeared in his hand.

"Not really," Lila said around a sip of tea. "He was wearing a mask—one of those balaclava things. But he was very tall and very strong, like he worked out, and when he touched me it took everything I had to keep fighting. I think—I think the fact that I could fight him at all surprised him." She closed her eyes for a moment and the room hushed around her. Finally she opened her eyes again. "I think his eyes were blue."

"Anything else?" Danny was hanging on her words and damn it, couldn't they see that just talking about it cost her? She was asleep on her feet.

"There was a scent of burning in the air. I don't know if that means anything, but I noticed it," Nathan said.

The way the others looked at each other, clearly it did, but that wasn't the most important thing.

"This just doesn't make any sense," Jas said. "If he wants the bracelet so badly, why didn't he just use a gun and shoot you? Sorry, Lila. I'm glad he didn't, but it doesn't make sense. Just like breaking in to leave Kylee a note or marking up your photo doesn't."

"He could have been worried about the noise from a gun. It would have drawn people," Danny offered.

"Or maybe he's toying with her like Clyde does with a bird," Chloe said quietly, as if lost in thought,

"Clyde?" Nathan asked.

"My cat," Chloe said. "He's a lovely cat, but he can be very evil when it comes to catching an unwary bird on my balcony."

Nathan closed his eyes, suddenly tired of all this and all these people. "I think maybe that's all the questions for tonight, don't you? Lila's beat. How about we search the house and you finish your interview tomorrow?"

"Johan Fehr had blue eyes," Chloe said with a shiver from her seat beside Lila. Her tanned face had paled. "I remember when he was in the store, it was like I couldn't move. Couldn't escape."

"Lots of people have blue eyes. I have blue eyes," Nathan said. "Now can we please let Lila get some rest?"

Everyone looked up at him. Four heads nodded. Finally.

Jas and Danny excused themselves and went off to inspect the premises, while Nathan came around Lila and helped her up. One leg almost gave, and Chloe and Victoria gasped when they saw the ruin of her dress. In truth he hadn't even noticed the tear of the side. He'd been too busy checking for injuries like she'd had this morning.

"Come on." He picked her up easy as pie and the room went silent. "Where's your room?"

"Upstairs," Lila said as her arms came around his neck. She looked frustrated and resigned and scared and desirable all at the same time and her scent of roses filled his head.

He turned to leave.

"Chloe, maybe you can come and give me a hand?"

"I'm right here for you."

He heard the other woman's movements behind him as he carefully carried Lila up the stairs to the second floor.

Her bedroom shouldn't have surprised him, and yet it did. All white and blue with a feel of cool breezes, while the Lila he knew was warmth incarnate. The room might be beautiful—like something out of a magazine—but it felt like she'd locked away the best part of herself, the warmth he remembered.

He set her down in the chair by the bed as Chloe bustled around the room tugging down the bed covers and fluffing pillows.

"I'm going to run you a bath and then I'll run home and get a nightgown. I'll stay here tonight."

"No, Chloe. Thank you, but no." Lila shook her head as he leaned down to kiss her forehead. Then she caught his face and kissed him full on the lips; her hazel gaze had gone mossy green in the bedside table light.

"Would *you*—would you consider staying here tonight? I know it's a lot to ask, but I've got the spare room and I—I don't want to be alone."She bowed her head as if embarrassed at her vulnerability. "I'm sorry. I should be angry that he makes me feel scared in my own home."

He pulled her into him and stroked her head, amazed at the protectiveness he felt for this lovely woman. "Hold onto that anger. It'll keep you strong. And of course I'll stay. As long as you need me."

"Lila, I hate to be a wet blanket, but is that really the best idea?" Chloe asked. "Think of what happened with Danny."

He looked a question back at Chloe, but she just shook her head. "I'm staying. That's all there is to it," he said.

"But Lila…"

"Chloe, let it be. We'll be fine. Nathan's protected me three times today. Nothing's going to happen in my own home. Besides, if the guy who attacked me came here, you wouldn't be enough help to stop him."

Chloe's gaze flitted from him to Lila and back, uncertain. Finally she nodded, but muttered something that sounded suspiciously like "Damn bracelet."

"Thank you," he said and turned back to Lila. "Now I'm going to leave. Chloe can help you have a bath and get ready for bed while I talk to the others downstairs. I'll be right here if you need me."

He released her then, and left the room.

It was the hardest thing he'd done in a very long time.

Chapter 6

It was like a wind slammed a door closed in her heart when Nathan walked out of her bedroom and Chloe closed the door behind him. She wanted to call him back and throw her arms around him because for a little while this evening all the years had rolled away. She'd remembered just why she'd been so attracted to one Nathan Moon. Now the room felt empty. Lila struggled up out of the blue chair and started to remove her dress.

"I could stay, too, you know," Chloe said as she turned from the door. "I could sleep on the couch downstairs."

"I know you could. But why should you when you have Jas waiting for you at home? No, it's better this way. The two of us wouldn't be worth much more in a fight than just me. The guy tonight was powerful. Big and powerful and able to make me feel totally weak." She shivered at the memory. Being helpless was not a feeling she liked. It brought back memories of her time in L.A.

She couldn't seem to reach the darn zipper on her back and her legs felt so wobbly, she finally sank onto the bed in frustration. Even the room's calm blue walls couldn't soothe her and she loved this room. She'd decorated it herself, like a cool room in the

Bahamas. But it didn't feel cool and calm right now. It felt cold—chilly, even. The shivers of shock were setting in.

She tried for the zipper again, but her arms were apparently too short for the job. "Damn. I'm so stiff I can't even get the dress undone."

Chloe bustled across the room and helped her up again, then smoothly tugged down the zipper. She helped Lila slip the dress off her shoulders.

"Oh my God, Lila! Look at you!"

The cream silk dress slipped down to pool on the floor leaving Lila in cream lace underwear and bra. She looked down at herself. Aside from the scrapes healing on her knees, there were huge black-and-blue bruises running up her side—thigh, hip, and shoulder. The latter had been hidden under the strap of her dress and her pashmina, and formed the perfect crescent shapes of forceful fingers.

"I guess the guy held me there. I don't remember. It's a blur, it happened so fast." She rubbed her gritty eyes. "I feel so stupid getting everyone out like this."

"Not stupid at all. Someone attacked you, Lila. Twice, I'd say. Thank goodness Nathan was there." Chloe had scooped the dress up, tsked at the damage to the fabric, and hung it on a hanger on the closet door. "And you still gave Jas and Danny something to go on."

"Not much." She studied the unlovely scabs on the heels of her hands. They looked like she felt.

"Well... I'll bet Nathan is glad he was around."

Lila looked up. Chloe stood before her, her long braid over her shoulder, her caftan of midnight blue glittering around the neck from tiny sequins.

"What's that supposed to mean?"

All business, Chloe's warm hand came around Lila's shoulders and steadied her as she limped across the floor to the bathroom. "It means that what red-blooded man wouldn't be happy if he got to spend the night alone with you in your home? That's a very different direction from where you were sure things were going between you and said man this morning. My goodness, you're shivering."

"Everything aches so I feel like an old woman."

"A warm bath'll make you feel better." Chloe settled her on the toilet in the white-and-cream bathroom and bustled around getting the bath running and finding a lovely water lily bath salt to foam the water. Lila had had the room renovated before she moved in so the bathroom had not just a lovely deep soaker tub, but also a glassed-in shower tiled with white Italian marble that matched the bathroom counter. But it, too felt cold, regardless of the plush white mats and the thick white Egyptian cotton towels.

She hugged herself against the chill, suddenly wondering why she'd decorated the bathroom in these non-colors when the face she turned to the world in her kitchen and on her porch spoke of light and life and laughter. She missed the warmth of Nathan's arms around her, but that was just plain stupid. Maybe she just needed to turn the furnace on early this year.

"You're wrong, you know. Nathan took me to dinner for old-time's sake. That was all."

"Yeah. Sure. And old friends put their arms around you like that. They hover over you like they're afraid that you might blow away. And, of course, old friends kiss you like that. I know all mine do."

Chloe turned her grin from the now-partially filled tub. "I think the water's ready. Do you need help getting in?"

"You know, you can be really snide for a friend."

Chloe nodded. "That's what real friends are for. To hold the mirror up and save you from yourself. Now can you get in, or do you need my help?"

Lila waved her away. "I'm fine. Really I am."

She tried to stand but couldn't quite make it work. She thumped on the toilet lid and groaned at the protest in all her bones and muscles.

"Come on. Let Aunty Chloe give you a hand."

Chloe slipped an arm under her shoulders and helped her up. Feeling mortified, Lila let Chloe help her finish undressing and then help her lower herself into the tub. Warm, lily-scented water and suds covered her body and she moaned in pleasure and leaned her head back.

"Maybe I'll just stay here until I feel better." She opened her eyes to Chloe, who again stood with her hands on her hips.

"That water's not going to stay warm forever, but I'll leave you to soak while I take care of your clothes and get you your pajamas. I thought maybe warm milk would be nice. You interested?"

Lila closed her eyes and leaned her head back. "That sounds heavenly. Maybe add a dash of vanilla?"

"Done."

Chloe's footsteps retreated into the bedroom and then down the stairs, leaving Lila in peace. The lovely warm water supported her aching body and the warmth seeped into her frozen limbs. How she'd gotten so cold, she didn't know. Shock, probably, the logical part of her said. But it was something more, too. As if a chill had bled into her from her attacker. Or maybe it was that he'd sucked all of her warmth away?

Yes, that was what it had been. It had fed on her.

Her eyes flashed open and for a moment she didn't know where she was. *It should be desert and she was drowning in eternal sand.*

What the heck?

She sat up, the water sluicing off her skin, her heart pounding. *Desert and sand had been a long time ago.*

No. There never had been desert and sand—well, maybe when she'd visited Morocco. And in India, but that had nothing to do with drowning.

She scrubbed at her face and then washed off her makeup, then lay back again hoping that blissful feeling would return.

But the water had cooled even though the bracelet burned and it was *so hard* to reach the faucet at the other end of the tub.

She was shivering when Chloe returned. Thank God.

She couldn't get out of the tub soon enough. At least the initial warmth had helped her aches.

After drying off with thick Egyptian cotton bath towels, she pulled on a pair of flannel pajamas that Chloe had dug out of her drawer. Usually she only wore them on the coldest of winter nights, but the way she was feeling, they were what she needed tonight.

"How did you know?" she asked as she finished buttoning the pajama top.

"You were shivering. I figured the warmer the pajamas the better." Chloe shrugged and helped her to the bed.

Lila climbed in and settled against the pillows. Chloe handed her a mug of warm, vanilla-scented milk and fussed about the bed, pulling the covers up, getting her a book. And producing a pill bottle from her pocket. "I sent Jas home for these. Valerian. Good to help you sleep. I figured you'd be so achy you might not be able to. It's totally herbal."

"Thanks." Lila accepted the pills and set them beside her along with a glass of water Chloe brought to her.

Chloe settled, grinning, on the edge of the bed. "So aside from getting attacked, how was dinner? Last I heard, you still weren't sure you were even going."

Just why had she gone? She hadn't thought it was a good idea, and yet it was Nathan—the one she'd always wondered about. What might have happened between them if things in LA had been different? The warm strength of his arms around her and the hard breadth of his chest had felt good. And his lips...

"I blame it on Victoria," she quirked her lips. "The woman caught me trying to dress and turned a perfectly functional outfit into something come-hither. Then she kicked me out of the house."

Chloe's brow arched. "And you let her?"

"Well..."

"Nuff said. Your subconscious knows what you haven't admitted yet—he is one hot man. I'm surprised he never made it in front of the camera. A man like that would have fans."

Lila rolled her eyes and sighed. "That's what I'm worried about. Hollywood guys are eternal playboys. They pursue, they capture and then they move on. I don't want to be a notch on someone's bedpost."

Nope. She'd already done that a long time ago and wasn't about to repeat it again.

"But you like him." Chloe's gaze demanded an answer.

"That doesn't matter, does it? The Hollywood life isn't for me and I can't see Nathan ever wanting to live in a small town like Peachland. Therefore the relationship is doomed from the start, so why even bother?" She shook her head. It was the logical truth and it might make her sad, but there was nothing she could do about it. They'd missed their chance all those years ago. The infatuation had had its time and place, but both of them were over it. They'd both moved on and become different people with different lives.

The realization left her feeling old, sad, and incredibly tired. She yawned.

Chloe patted her hand. "I think I better let you sleep. You look totally beat."

"Beaten, is more the way I'm feeling." So that even her eyelids ached.

Chloe stood and turned to go.

"Could you do something for me?"

Chloe turned back to her.

"On the shelf at the back of my closet is a box of old photo albums. There's one marked Hollywood. Could you get it for me?"

"I'll be right back."

Chloe disappeared into Lila's walk-in closet. Lila leaned back against the pillows, listening to the thumps and bumps as Chloe found the box and dug through it. Why the photo album had never made it into storage, she couldn't say. But every time she went through her things looking to store or throw away, for some reason that particular album made the cut to stay in her closet. It made no sense at all after all the intervening years. Especially when she considered all the things she *didn't* want to be reminded of.

"Aha!" came from the closet, and more bumps and thumps. Then Chloe returned showing off a cream-colored album that had a post card of the Hollywood Hills pasted on the front. "This what you wanted?"

It was what she'd asked for, though she wasn't sure if she wanted it. "Maybe just leave it here on the bedside table. If I can't sleep, I can look at it."

Chloe did as requested, but tilted a brow as if she didn't quite believe Lila. Then she headed for the door. "Lights on or off?"

"Off, please. I think I'll try to sleep."

Chloe stepped into the hall and flicked the lights off as Lila slid down deeper under the covers in the blue-black darkness and closed her eyes.

Chapter 7

On the sidewalk outside *This and That,* the moon had risen, lacing light across the waves on the water. A brisk wind blew up the lake, cooler than Jas Stone had felt in a while. It suggested summer was long gone, even though Labor Day was just over. He pulled Chloe into his side and leaned down to kiss her.

"I'm glad you got rid of that damn bracelet. I've got a bad feeling about this."

"So you do think the attack is related?"

"I don't know, but it was an attack and assault. Whoever it was shouldn't be left on the street. The trouble is, we'll be working across jurisdictions because the attack took place in Kelowna."

He sighed and rubbed the back of his neck, feeling the fatigue of a long summer of not many results for all the investigation of the strange goings-on related to the bracelet. "Hold on a sec."

He jogged up to Danny Forester, who was walking hand-in-hand with Victoria back to her apartment.

"Danny!"

The couple broke apart as Jas came up to them, Victoria's curvy form swathed in shadows while Danny's pale, red-head complexion seemed to catch the moonlight.

"I don't think we should leave this. I think we need to get into the office and figure this out. Maybe check out the scene where Lila was attacked."

Danny sighed and looked back at Victoria. "Told you." He looked back to Jas. "I was just saying goodnight before I came back to you."

Jas nodded. "How about we give Chloe a ride home and then slide into the office together. Victoria, you'll be all right in the apartment alone, won't you?"

"Of course. I am not a little girl. You go solve the mystery so that Lila can find love with that very nice Nathan."

Jas met Danny's gaze in shared dismay. Was that what they'd been doing all summer—setting men up with Lila's lovely friends? Not that he was regretting what he'd found with Chloe, but a guy should have a choice.

"I think we'll be focused on the crime," Danny said. He placed a peck on Victoria's cheek and walked her to the condo door. When she was safely inside, Jas led him back to his SUV and they climbed inside.

After dropping Chloe off at her apartment down the lake, Danny climbed in the front.

"Feel like taking a drive?"

"You thinking the crime scene?"

"It's a place to start."

They rumbled up Drought Hill and then through West Kelowna before wending their way across the floating bridge and into the genteel streets of old Kelowna.

Jas rolled down the windows and inhaled the cool night air, moist with lake water and the scent of newly sprinkled lawns. The moonlight caught on the chrome of the cars parked along the curb and glistened off the leaves of the maples and elms as the SUV cruised slowly down the darkened street. Porch lights lit the front of the heritage houses, neat gardens, winding walks, and hanging baskets of flowers. He slowed in front of the house that had hosted the pop-up restaurant according to the address Nathan had provided. There was still a light on and a white panel van was backed in close to a door at the side of the house. Cases of china and crystal were being loaded and clinked quietly in the darkness. Jas pulled in, in front of the next house down, and climbed out. Danny met him on the curb.

"Whaddaya think? Talk to the staff?" Jas asked.

"They're going to love us for interrupting their cleanup."

"Yeah, but we'll hate it if we have to go chasing after individual waiters tomorrow." Jas checked his watch. "If they haven't let all the wait-staff go already"

They headed up the driveway, but were disappointed to learn that the only one left at the site was the organizer. All the staff had gone for the night. Jas asked for a complete list of everyone involved and they found themselves back on the street.

"Nathan said the attack took place just over there." Danny pointed across two front lawns to where a large elm leaned over the sidewalk.

Jas pulled a Maglite out of his pocket as they approached. If there had been a struggle, there might be some sign left. He swept the flashlight beam over the concrete—scuffed and pebbled from many feet over years of use. Not much of use. But there was something in the air. He sniffed. An acrid bite. Sniffed again.

"You getting that?"

Danny looked up from where he was kneeling beside a Lexus parked at the curb, a question in his eyes.

"The air. You get anything?"

Danny inhaled and closed his eyes. Then he shuddered. "Like something's burning, with a touch of incense. It's him, all right. God, just sniffing that scent makes something inside me want to howl at the moon and turn tail and run."

Danny had been through hell both times the creature had possessed him. He stood up, shaking his head. "Can you flash the light over here?"

Jas came up beside him as Danny pointed down by the wheel of the Lexus. The light caught on something metallic.

"What the hell?" Jas said.

"I think it's a broken zipper pull. See the bit of leather? That's the pull. It hasn't been here long, either, or the car would be parked over it."

"Good catch." The little leather pull leaned against the wheel's wall, almost invisible.

He fished his phone out of his pocket and photographed the position of the item, then fished the zipper pull out with the tip of a pen through the leather loop. "You got a baggie on you?"

"Always," Danny said and fished a small one out of his windbreaker pocket. Jas slipped their find into the plastic and then held it up to the light. Flat black metal pull, about a quarter inch across, with the leather looped through the end.

"Looks like the kind of thing you'd find on a good quality fleece or high-necked base layer—the kind hikers, mountain climbers, and skiers might use."

"Wrong kind of weather for that around here these days." Danny said. "The zipper piece is large enough there could be a print, though."

They looked at each other. As if they could send this in to Ident without a file number.

"So we get Lila to file a complaint?" Danny asked.

"She might not, but Nathan will. He was pretty pissed off and worried that someone attacked her." He flashed the flashlight along the curb between the other cars and the sidewalk, then went to the flower beds that lined the other side. It was thick California lilac, the small, glossy leaves effectively obscuring anything that might have fallen there. He brushed the branches aside and flashed the light underneath. Candy wrappers that could have been blown there any time this summer, a dime, a quarter, wadded tissues, and a plastic bag of discarded doggie-do. He pulled the flash back.

"I think we've found all we're going to. We should head back to the office."

Danny shook his head. "I don't know. Our guy—if this is from him and he realizes the zipper pull is broken, he's likely dumped the jacket somewhere between here and wherever he'd staying. I'm thinking maybe we should start a Dumpster search just outside the residential area."

Jas sighed. It was true. And a jacket dumped could hold a lot of forensic evidence. "All right. We'll get in touch with Lila and Nathan in the morning. In the meantime we conduct the search."

So much for snuggling up to Chloe for part of the night. But if they could catch whatever poor bastard the creature was riding before he did more harm, it would be worth it.

The two of them started down the street together, but at the first corner they split up with Danny heading further north toward the commercial areas just north of the neighborhood while Jas turned toward the downtown core. It was a big city to cover with just the two of them, but it was worth the work if they were able to find the jacket. It would at least give them a sector of the city to look in. Then they'd stand a chance of finding the proverbial needle in a haystack. He hoped.

§

Worried and just a trifle out of his element, Nathan lay in his skivvies in the crisp pale lavender sheets of Lila's guest room and tried to focus on the book he was reading—not that Jane Eyre was anything that he would ever read on his own. But he had to do something to try to tame the wild-mind that had been prowling around in his head since he'd seen Lila being attacked this evening and then after Jas and Danny had interviewed him. So, after scouting the house, he'd grabbed a poker from the fireplace and a book off a shelf in the kitchen. Heck, his mind hadn't been much better before this evening, either, what with finding Lila again and all the old feelings that had rekindled at just the sight of her.

He glanced at the little brass clock on the white enameled bedside table. Three in the morning and he was wide awake in this room that seemed to personify the Lila he'd just met, with its smoke and lavender colored walls and gossamer curtains, sort of will-o-the-wisp and beyond taming. Lavender bedding, too, and the bouquet of some kind of white flowers on the dresser that made the room smell like a bower for a goddess.

Get over it, Moon.

In disgust he set the book on the table, intent on giving sleep a try one more time, but he felt rather than heard something stir in the hallway.

Shit! The guy had come for Lila again? He'd circumvented the alarm and broken in to finish what he'd started.

He slid out of bed onto the cool hardwood floor and pulled his trousers on. Call the cops? Not the right option according to Jas and Danny, and damn it, he hadn't thought to get their numbers.

But the guy who had attacked Lila had bolted when he'd seen Nathan. Maybe he thought Lila was alone. He hefted the fireplace poker and hoped it was a solid enough weapon. The good thing was, the element of surprise was on his side.

Stealthily, he padded to the door to listen.

The faint sound of movement came from the hallway. Was the guy steeling himself before the attack on Lila? Was he slowly opening the door to the room where she slept? Nathan could imagine her asleep, with her curls splayed over her pillows. Her chest rising and falling with each breath and the man—the hunter—creeping across the room to hurt her.

He yanked the door open, roared, and leaped into the black hallway, the poker raised, but something stopped him from swinging.He slammed the figure swathed in darkness back into the wall.

The figure was soft. It was scented of roses.

The feminine *oomph,* left no question as to the "attacker's" identity.

"Shit! Lila?"

"Yes." It was more of a groan.

He pulled back from her a little. "Sorry about that. I didn't expect you to be up. Chloe said she gave you pills to help you sleep. Didn't you take them? Are you all right?"

In the dim light from the guestroom, her large hazel eyes were almost black. Her hair was a tumble about her pale face, her lips full and eminently kissable. She looked young and vulnerable in thick flannel pajamas—except the curves of her body and the décolletage of breasts at the open collar made the outfit almost sensual. She held a large book or album clutched to her chest.

"Chloe said to take two. I took one. I don't like taking pills— even herbal ones—but it didn't work." She lowered her gaze like she was ashamed of something.

"So what's got you out here in the hall in the middle of the night, then?" He tried to tip her face back up to him, but she twisted away and sighed.

"You. This." She shifted the album she carried. It *was* an album, by the look of it—a padded cover held thick, plasticized pages of the kind that held photos. "This is stupid. I'm sorry I disturbed you."

She went to turn back to her bedroom, but he blocked her with one arm. "Lila, what's going on?"

She looked up at him, from somewhere drawing the strength to be clear-eyed and strong. "Do you believe the saying you can never go home again? Or do you believe all the hype about home being where the heart is? That you can always go back?"

"How the hell do I know? My parents sold the house and went traveling as soon as I went off to college. There never was a place to go home to."

Lila frowned. "So how do you give yourself a place in the world?"

"My work. Wherever I am. The people I'm with, I guess." He shrugged.

"But if you're never with anyone or in a place for very long, how do you ever develop a deep relationship with a place or a person?" Her voice quavered a little as she studied his face.

"Lila?" He had to pry one frigid hand off the album. "Are you afraid of something? Of the guy who attacked you? Of me?" God forbid.

She shook her head, her eyes glistening like pools, the light catching her at the perfect angle for the camera. She was beautiful and vulnerable and strong and positively the goddess she had once played so well on screen. Her throat worked as if it took everything to find the words. Finally she nodded.

"It's you," she said, her voice terrifyingly certain.

He felt like a breath of air could knock him over.

"Me? I'm here to protect you, aren't I?"

"I know." She closed her eyes and shook her head. "I'm being incredibly stupid and I hate it. I don't know what's gotten into me." She squared her shoulders. "I'll leave you to your sleep and deal with my insecurities and insomnia myself."

She went back into her room and the door closed with a soft click behind her. Let her go? But she clearly needed something and whatever it was, he would help her however he could. He caught the door and pushed it open. A bedside table lamp placed a pool of light on the far side of the bed. He followed her into the blue and white room. Cold, so cold, as if all the windows were open on a chilly winter night, instead of heated summer. His feet felt frozen as he padded across the hardwood to where she stood by the bed.

He tried to set the album aside, but she held on tight, so he caught her elbow and eased her back into her bed, sitting up against the pillow. He tucked the covers in around her and she smoothed her palm over the album on her lap as she looked up at him.

"Do you remember this?" She turned the album over and it was as if the room and time telescoped around him and he was back seated in a square-sided tent against the harsh sun of the California desert, beside a young woman who was waiting for her next turn on set. She was young and still not convinced she would be the star they thought she could become, so she took pictures of everything to create a "memory book," as she called it.

"I helped you choose the photos. I'm surprised you still have it."

She let him take it from her and open the cover. There was Lila's so-much-younger self, standing in a long skirt and blouse in front of the studio like a proud fisherman who had just caught a whale. He remembered taking the photo when he'd been asked to show her around by Simon Grafton.

He grinned up at her. "Now, that's a flash from the past."

He turned the page. Lila in front of the Chinese Theater. Lila with her foot beside Marilyn Monroe's dainty footprint, her head thrown back laughing at the discrepancy in size. More photos of their early days together when he'd been so blown away by the maturity of the lovely starlet that was Simon Grafton's latest conquest. He'd known he should stay away, but circumstance and his own weak will had kept him coming back to her. His heart did a slow thump-thump and all the fifteen-year-old emotions flooded back as he remembered the arousal that had come with rubbing shoulders, just catching a whiff of her scent of roses. His body stirred in remembrance, and even in trousers, his arousal was going to become apparent pretty darn quick.

"I was looking at the photos. They brought back so much. Do you want to go through it with me?" She shifted on the bed to make room for him beside her.

Did she think he was a hermit? Asexual? That she would invite him into her bed?

"That might not be the best idea."

But the way she looked at him, the way she reached up a hand for him changed his mind. He sank down on the bed beside her, her swathed in flannel and bedcovers, him almost naked, and he felt her gaze like heated tracks on his skin.

Then her fingers traced up his arm and sent hot flames rushing over him. His groin tightened and he hissed air through his teeth.

"Touch me like that and I might get the wrong idea," he growled.

"You're in my bedroom, aren't you?"

It was a surprising, almost blatant invitation, and for a moment he was confused. She'd rejected him so firmly earlier. This kind of reversal was more like the flirtations of Hollywood women. But this was Lila, the woman who had haunted him like an old song that ran on auto-repeat through his mind. He couldn't help himself. He caught her chin and leaned in for a kiss.

Her full lips parted for him.

Hungry. He felt as ravenous as a starved man before a table of delights and not just because he'd only eaten appetizers the night before. He held back, but trailed his lips along her jaw, under her hair, tasted the rose-scent there and then returned to her lips. Oh God, her lips. Soft, full, swollen as if he had already feasted there.

"I want you," he whispered into her hair. "I've wanted you since the first time I laid eyes on you, and I only wanted you more as I got to know you."

In answer she ran her hands up his naked pecs, her palms trailing more fire so his flesh felt filled with sparks. The bracelet gleamed in the lamplight and almost seemed to shimmer and twist. But this wasn't about the bracelet, this was about Lila and him.

He kissed her again and trailed kisses down her neck to the collarbone exposed by the pajama neckline. He tugged the collar aside to get at her shoulder and Lila shivered. He shifted position so he faced her, pushed the album aside to lift her into his lap. He cradled her against him.

"Maybe we should just stay like this. Give the whole thing time."

She shook her head against him. "Who knows how much time we have. Life—life is uncertain, isn't it? I realized something when I looked at that album—I've been too cautious—too concerned about self-preservation, even back then. Did you know that this summer I almost abandoned one of my best friends because of what it would cost me? Some important design files of Reggie's got stolen and then someone put in a claim saying she had used stolen designs in her work all these years. Whoever stole her design files sold them to Milan, saying Reggie had used them illegally. It ruined her deal with a Milanese designer and things still haven't been fully worked out, but I almost cut her out of my life out of fear of what I might lose if I supported her."

She looked up at him. "Looking at those old photos, I remembered how I wanted to be with you, but I was too afraid of what would happen if I didn't go along with what Simon wanted. I felt like I sold my soul for the part in that picture and I wasn't true to myself. I felt like I was doing the same to protect this house. I love it, but it is just a house. Friends are more important, and dear friends most of all." She drew in a breath. "And you. I don't know where this will go, or even if I'm doing the right thing, but you're the passion I never acted on. Until tonight."

She climbed off his lap and performed a limping strip tease as she unbuttoned her pajama top. Through the shirt opening, her belly was a smooth cream expanse of taut muscle. The insides of her breasts were twin mounds of temptation. He stood to meet her, placed his hands around her naked waist, and a reverberating gong seemed to go off in his soul.

Her flesh was smooth over her toned back. He ran his hands lightly up her sides and she shivered right down to her core and stopped her foolish dance.

"You don't need to dance to tempt me, Lila. The fact you exist is enough."

She quirked a brow up at him. "You're not one of those fan boys, are you?"

"And if I were?" He parted her shirt and tugged her against him, smooth against hard, the warm mounds of her breasts, the taut nipples sending his body to attention. He shoved her shirt off her shoulders and trailed kisses down over her collarbone. His hands came up to cup her breasts, tease the nipples, and he felt her tense. Her breath hissed in her teeth and she caught his head as he sank to the edge of the bed and pulled her into him.

He caught the dark nubbin of her nipple in his teeth and bit down lightly so she groaned and her head lolled back in pleasure. One hand slid down the small of her back and into the elastic waistband of her sheep-print pajama bottoms and down farther. Smooth, muscled buttocks and warm dark spaces. He tugged her pajama bottoms down and shoved them down her hips so she stood naked before him inside his splayed legs. The cream of her skin flowed down from her breasts to her flat belly, to her hips, a small strip of tight-coiled copper hair between her legs.

He took her with his mouth and her breath came in short, sharp gasps. His head swirled with the scent of roses and damp earth as he sought and found her sweet spot. Her gasps became a low moan as he worked, as her body tensed and then released with a soft cry and muscles rippling across her belly. She collapsed against him, her heart pounding against his cheek.

"That—that was very good, but a little one-sided, don't you think?" she said when she had caught her breath.

She hauled him up in front of her, undid his trousers, and shoved pants and boxer shorts down until he stepped out of them. Then she pressed against him.

"Better. So much better skin to skin." She leaned on tiptoe to kiss him and together they lay back on her bed.

The light from the bedside lamp sculpted her skin with light and shadow as she rose above him to slide down his body. She kissed his length, her coils of hair masking her face. Then the warmth of her mouth enveloped him and he thought he might go crazy. He fisted her hair as she worked and arched his back into her. Each stroke brought him closer, as just the feel of her flesh did. He pulled her up to him, kissed her deeply as she straddled him and rubbed herself against him.

He flipped them over so he trapped her beneath him. "You seem to have forgotten, Madam, that this is all about you."

He stroked hands down over her perfect breasts, lightly, like feathers, down over the mound of her pubis to stroke the insides of her thighs. Her face became a mask of pleasure as he reached higher to stroke her, strum her as he felt the hum of her tension. He slid his hand down her moisture and inserted two fingers.

Her eyes flashed open, her hips lifted to match his slow and easy movement.

"More," she gasped.

He chuckled. "Greedy girl. Let's see what we can do. Hold on a moment."

He reclaimed his trousers and dug in the pocket to come up triumphant with a condom.

He swept her up off the bed and into his lap again, this time straddling him. Together they got the condom unwrapped and Lila used light fingers to roll the latex on. He was so hard he thought he might explode at her touch, but when she was done he pressed against her and she shifted to admit him.

"You're sure?" he whispered into her hair.

She nodded her answer.

He caught her buttocks to lift her as her heels wrapped his hips. She guided him inside into slick darkness. For a moment they simply looked into each other's eyes. Hers were huge, black with a want that mirrored his, and filled with shock. It had finally happened, but it felt like home. He held her steady as he began to move, her hips quickly catching his rhythm. Held her gaze and watched the surprise fade, watched the pleasure build, the awareness of him as he slid deeper and deeper toward her core.

Toward her heart? Her soul?

For the moment it didn't matter. There was just the sensation of slick flesh on slick flesh, the filling, the being filled, as each stroke took him deeper. Her hands gripped his shoulders and she met him, stroke for stroke, but this was only a beginning. There was so much more they could do.

"Hold on," he said and her long legs wrapped about him, her arms clinging to his shoulders as he swept them both onto the bed, Lila beneath him.

For a moment he went still, just to look at this beautiful woman—hair wildly tangled, eyes dilated, lips bruised and half open with desire. The sweet curve of her shoulder and waist, the delight of her breasts. How could this finally have come to pass?

"Lila," he groaned and started to move, deep, slow strokes that spoke of all the emotions that were trapped in his chest all those years ago when it came to this woman. Tenderness. Caring. Love?

The thought shuddered through him and he almost lost control. No, love wasn't anything in his repertoire. Love was a commodity where he came from. This was lust, this was pleasure, and if it led to companionship for a while, that was the best that anyone could hope for.

He drove into her and Lila cried out. Drove into her again and she met him as fiercely as he felt. They plunged together like torrents released, like enemies in battle, like ravening beasts. Each was starved and each was determined. She caught his rear and held on, driving up to him, their breath coming in gasps.

He rolled over, pulling her on top of him and there she was, breasts jutting as she thrust her pelvis against his hips, as she let gravity take him deeper, as she opened herself completely and threw her arms up.

So close. He lifted his torso to hold her. To suckle her breasts as she rode him. To pull her hips more tightly into him.

Uh and uh and uh. The room filled with their efforts. His senses filled with her sweet scent, her silken skin, her tension, and the utter bliss of her tight slickness.

"Wait a moment." He slowed her, though she kept thrusting her hips.

"We're going to do this many more times. We can take ourtime."

He rolled her beneath him one more time, took the time to rain kisses down her face and breasts and then began to move slowly, one more time, watching the slow plunge of his flesh into hers. Sensual, exciting. He looked up and caught her sharing his view. He raised himself above her and kept the long slow strokes going, then gradually, gradually increased the tempo. He hooked her legs over his arms and curled her buttocks up to expose her. Her hands found his hips and urged him home. He drove into her. Again. Again.

The room exploded around him as Lila shuddered. She gave a soft cry and pulled him against her as they collapsed on the bed.

He raised his head, stroked her tangle of hair off her face, and kissed her long and deeply.

Lila.

God help him, he already wanted her again.

Chapter 8

She had done it.

Four a.m. and Lila lay in the tangle of sheets and limbs, inhaling the warm male-musk and cedar scent of the man sleeping beside her, the room in darkness except for the pool of light from the bedside lamp. She felt wanton and free and afraid all at the same time—not afraid for her person, but for her heart. There was no question but that she'd fallen for Nathan. The question was what would he do to her heart now that he had it? The air through the open bedroom window felt too hot and sultry.The gossamer curtains rippled as if the wind had changed and came from the south. It brought with it the scent of wood burning—from the campground down the lake, probably.

Nathan's soft breathing filled her ear. He lay spooned around her, his arm possessively over her side, his hand cupping her breast, his groin pressed into her backside already half aroused. And she wanted him right back. Good Lord, she did, and the way her heart pounded, the way his musk made her stomach flutter and her insides moist—she was—it was as if—good God, she was a blithering idiot who couldn't even tell what was in her own mind!

"Nathan? Are you awake?"

"Mmm...?" And a snuffle, then his breathing steadied out again. He nuzzled her neck.

Not really awake, but aware. If she turned toward him—if she gave into the lust he evoked in her, he'd be awake in an instant, but maybe that wasn't such a good idea. Maybe she needed to think this through first.

She eased out from under his arm toward the side of the big white bed and instantly missed his closeness. Slowly, so the bed wouldn't transfer her movement, she stood and looked down at him. There was only the lamplight to show the shape of the man under the single white sheet carelessly pulled up to his waist. Nathan Moon in her bed.

A surprise. A mystery. Once upon a time, a fantasy, but now it had happened. She had asked for it to happen—had lured him into her bed.

The way her body tingled, the sex had definitely been worth it and she wanted more.

But was that the right thing to do? He was not a man who would or could be here for her. He would always be off shooting another movie and she would be here taking care of her business. Both of them had their lives in order. Together, though? Well, it just didn't look like much more than a muddle and a mess, and she couldn't imagine either of them needed that. God, what had she done even starting this? Maybe there really was something to this idea that the bracelet affected the wearer. She'd seen it in the others; she'd just refused to think that it could happen to her. She was Lila Weber, businesswoman.

"Yeah?" she could hear Chloe's voice. "And what are we? Chopped liver?"

Sighing, she pulled on a peach silk robe decorated with hand-painted oriental flowers and stylized cranes that she had purchased in Bangkok. Then she scooped up the photo album from up off the floor where it had fallen and padded out the door. She closed it behind her.

The dark house ticked like a time bomb as she went down the stairs and into the kitchen. She flipped on the lights and set about making a chamomile tea. Something to settle her—she hoped. Something to help her sleep—she prayed. The album she left sitting on the counter as she fussed and filled a tea bulb with loose leaf tea, then poured boiling water over it. When it had steeped enough in her mad-hatter teapot—fitting or what?—she poured herself a cup.

Photo album and cup in hand, she flipped off the lights but left the range hood light on, and settled into the nook beside an open window. The warm dry air was heavy with the scent of lake water and honeysuckle from the neighbor's garden, but still carried that wood smoke scent. She slid into the nook and pulled her feet up onto the seat, then laid her head back to peer up at the stars and the westward mountains. There used to be so many more stars in the sky, but now the lights of Peachland development drowned out so many of the lesser stars. It was a lot like life—so many things happen in life that it drowns out what makes a person who they are and what they really want.

Once she had thought the man in her bed upstairs was what she really wanted, simply because they were so able to be friends. When she left Hollywood, she'd told herself it was the right thing to do because she'd needed to leave to save herself from turning into just another starlet being used to feed the old men who ran the machine. But even fifteen years hadn't been able to erase her attraction to Nathan.

Now that she was older, could she preserve herself in a relationship with him? Did he just bring with him all the things she hated about Hollywood? Was there even a relationship to have? It had been good sex—even great. But that didn't mean that Nathan meant anything else by it. Sure, he'd come looking for her, but that didn't mean she was anything more than a notch in a Hollywood bedpost for him.

The way he'd looked at her—the way he'd held her hand—she didn't think that was the case, but how can one person ever know what's in another person's heart?

She smoothed her hand over the album cover and flipped it open. The photos, taken so long ago, still had the power to evoke so much in her. She felt old and jaded looking at her much younger self in the early photos. Shining eyes and so much hope. God, she'd been so young.

But as she flipped through the pages, she could remember the doubts creeping in. No longer feeling like an adult because Simon Grafton wanted her in his bed. Instead starting to feel uncomfortable with the things he wanted her to do—another woman—another man. Not her style now and not back then.

And then there'd been the drugs he wanted her to use—to give her more pleasure, he'd said. She'd tried it once, but resisted after that because she didn't like the out-of-body feeling. Her refusal had led to some of their fiercest fights and the threat that he could ruin her career any time he wanted. She'd realized he was right, and from that point on she had spent her time in Hollywood hanging on by a thread until her contract and the movie shoot were over. Nathan Moon had been the one bright light that had held her together.

"Oh God, Nathan. I wish I understood why now? What you really want?" Could she trust that he was really here looking for her because of old times, or was this a product of the creature seeking the bracelet?

The mountaintops were rounded humps—dark against the darker night sky, the scattering of house lights through the pine trees on the hillsides like fallen stars.

A sound from in the house brought her back from her ruminations. Nathan, hair rumpled like a child and bleary eyed, entered the kitchen. He looked around, spotted her, and relief flooded his face.

"There you are!" He settled beside her wearing only his boxers.

"Sorry. I couldn't sleep. I made myself a cup of tea."

"When I woke and you weren't there, I came looking for you. I called you and got worried when you didn't answer." He leaned in to kiss her, his lips a hot flame that trailed across her face and left her needing him.

She clamped down on the need to open her robe and have him take her right there and then. No, she needed to decide what this was before she let herself go again. Once was an act out of character—a response to old unrequited feelings. Twice was risking too much of herself.

"I needed to think," she said.

His brows rose slightly and she felt the weight of his consideration.

"What is there to think about? We finally found each other."

She shook her head. Nothing was ever that simple. "So that's all there is to it?"

"Yes." He caught her hands. "After all these years, the attraction's still there."

She had to smile at that. "Even now that we've done the nasty? Doesn't that get it out of your system?"

"Hell no." He stroked her hair back from her cheek, then rested his palm there. "If anything, it's made it worse. I feel—I—I want you, Lila. Plain and simple. I feel like an addict."

"Come on. We made love once."

"And I want to make it twice and three times and a dozen."

Well, it was nice to face that kind of interest and he was echoing what she was feeling—but... "We don't exactly have compatible lifestyles, Nathan."

He frowned, all his infatuation suddenly fleeing his face. "What is this? You were into it—me—us—upstairs and now you've gone all ice-maiden on me."

It wasn't ice-maiden, it was just an effort to be logical, but it hurt that he thought so and his tone was too reminiscent of discussions with Simon all those years before. "I—I'm sorry I led you on. I don't understand it myself, except I needed you badly, then. I used you, Nathan, and I'm sorry I did." She looked up at him, a part of her wailing what was she doing? This was Nathan—the man she had dreamed of for so many years.

"Dammit, Lila! Lifestyles be damned. We've got history and we've got this."

He surprised her by suddenly shoving in beside her and hauling her into his lap, cradled against his chest, the album on the table before them. "Now tell me what your reservations are?"

His strong arms were around her and his presence filled her senses. Warmth in the cool night air. Strength and protection. His scent of musk and cedar. The solid beat of his heart against her.

"God, Lila, I missed you so much all those years and I didn't even realize how much until I saw you again. It was like there was something seriously missing—a hole in my life, and the only thing I could imagine filling it was you. Don't end this before we've even had a chance." He leaned down and kissed her ear, her cheek. "Now why don't you tell me what's got you so spooked?"

She looked up sideways at him. "First answer me this. Why are you so sure this even deserves a chance? That it's more than just lust? It—it's been a while since I've been with someone. Maybe that's all this was…"

In answer, he hugged her in closer to him and bent down to her ear. "Well, for one thing, there's this." He shifted so she could feel how he still wanted her.

A tingle of lust ran through her, but she still rolled her eyes up at him. "Tempting. Very tempting, even, but not exactly what relationships are built on and I'm not the kind of person who just does casual sex."

There. She'd put him on notice. She wasn't some one-night-stand, or looking for a fling. That was too similar to the Hollywood life she'd run away from. When she left the shoot all those years ago, she'd been determined that if she was looking for anything it was long-term monogamy. She still held to that goal. Though she'd had relationships since then, none of the men had ended up wanting something similar.

"Did you really think I came looking for you just to get a roll in the hay?" His breath was warm on her neck and he smoothed her hair back behind her ear to nuzzle the earlobe. "'Cause I could have stayed in middle America if that was all I was after. I came looking for you because that wasn't satisfying anymore."

His lips on her neck sent her body shivering. It was moving too fast. Had moved too fast, and now she needed to slow everything down for a time. Just let her get her head on straight, because this turmoil of emotions wasn't like her. She felt tender, raw at her nerve ends so she was afraid and wanton at the same time. That was so not like her. It was as if something was destroying her logic, her mind.

She hauled the photo album open. "Let's look at it together. All the old times."

Nathan stiffened and stopped his patient nuzzling as if she'd shoved him away, and she knew she was perilously close to pushing him away more permanently. Was that what she wanted?

Clearly the answer was no. If that was the case, why all the reservations? Damn it, what was happening to her?

"I—I'm sorry, Nathan. I—think I live in my head too much. I need to get used to all this." She made a show of pulling his arms around her. "When you've been on your own for as long as I have, it's hard to believe there can be something more."

"So give you the space you need to believe it."

She felt stupid as she glanced up at him. "Please?"

"Consider it done. You're worth the wait."

"And you're worth—I don't know what. I just don't want to ruin the precious thing that we had between us."

"So let's look at those photos." He wrapped his arms companionably around her against the cool air through the window, and in the light from the stove, they revisited some of their ancient times together. The two of them seated, talking in on-set chairs. Lila with Simon, a forced smile on her face. Her on set in a scene, the hero of the story kneeling before the goddess she played. She and Nathan in the food tent, seated side by side, talking intently. The way their bodies leaned together, it was pretty clear that they'd been attracted even back then. Image after image, and most of them were her and Nathan. The few where she was doing something without him, he was still in the frame; and on some of those images his expression of longing was like a brand. The last photo in the book was taken the day before she left. It was taken in front of the set of the goddess's palace, she and Nathan with their arms slung around each other, smiling for the camera, behind them the smooth stone façade of the exterior set and the heavy, ornate doors of the entrance.

Lila stopped and brought the album closer, a frisson of cold running through her.

"What is it, Lila?"

She shook her head, unable to find her voice.

"That was such a sad day and we were trying so hard to be happy," Nathan said softly. "You can see it in our faces—so much strain."

"The door," she finally gasped and sat bolt upright. "It's the same."

She held up the bracelet and turned it on her wrist until the door with the ornate, scrolled hinges caught the light. "Here. Look."

She held her wrist and the album up to catch the light for scrutiny. Nathan frowned.

"Sure. They look about the same. That's a bit of a coincidence, isn't it?"

She scrambled out of the nook, the silk robe falling around her like a second skin.

"Don't you understand? They're the same." God, her hands were shaking. She sank down on the chair at the end of the table to hunch beside him, her face in her hands. This was a disaster. She didn't want to be linked to a man who would take her away from her home. She didn't want anything to do with Hollywood anymore. She had her life here. Just the thought of leaving Peachland left her breath trapped in her chest.

"Lila, what is it? What's got you so upset?"

Darn it, she was crying and Nathan's arms were around her, pulling her into his shoulder. "Tell Uncle Nathan, what's got you so upset."

She shook her head, but buried her face in his shoulder. Those strong arms of his. The intoxicating pheromones—this was bad.

"Lila?"

So gentle, so insistent. She palmed her eyes dry and looked up at him, then pulled back to pull her bracelet-encircled wrist between them. "This. Soul mates know they've found each other when they find the other person associated with a door that matches one on the bracelet. You've been matched with me for fifteen years."

It was strange to feel so uncertain. When she'd put the bracelet on, she'd known what she was doing and what awaited, but she hadn't really believed it could happen to her. And here it had already happened years before. Looking at the photo just confirmed it. Nathan's face in the photos had spoken volumes. So had hers.

She turned to him. "Did you know that I thought I loved you back then? It was part of what made me sick at what I was doing with Simon. But I didn't know what to do about it and you were already taken, so I played along as your gal pal friend."

Nathan was a dim figure beside her, but his eyes caught the light as he grinned. "Not something to cry about. I felt the same way, but I was hands-off because you were with someone. And as for this bracelet thing, I wouldn't believe it for a minute; but if it'll help my case with you, then I'm all over it."

He pulled her in against him again and soothed her shoulders, the back of her head. "I guess we're both just slow learners. But we're together now."

It was true. Almost like a fairy tale. Almost too good to be true. Nathan looked down at her from those deep turquoise eyes with such certainty she could almost believe that everything would be all right.

But she knew better, didn't she? Even now, in his arms, a lingering scent of smoke spoke of danger. A gust of wind through the window caught her hair as a light coating of snow caught against the metal screen.

Snow? In September? Another wind gust and more of the stuff fell on the window sill. In the light through the window, it swirled in the air.

Not snow. Ash.

She pulled away and stood to open the door, looking up at the mountain above Peachland. There were only the twinkling nighttime house lights, and above that, the sea of stars. But instead of the clear light of galaxies she'd admired earlier, a gray veil obscured the sky.

Smoke.

Forest fire. After a summer of little rain, it was every town's fear. Not right above the town on the mountain, that was clear.

But close. Too close, by far.

§

By morning it had been dubbed the Brenda fire, after Brenda Mine, the old copper and molybdenum mine that was just over the Coldham and Lookout Mountains from the town. It had started in the middle of the night as a grass fire, presumably lit by some late night driver tossing a cigarette from his car. It had caught in the grasses along the verge of the highway and burned up over the lip of the mine in short order. Then the wind had caught it and sent sparks blazing into acres of tinder-dry forest.

The Pacific winds drove the fire toward Lookout Mountain, following the route of the Okanagan Connector of the Coquihalla Highway. The Forestry Department had men and women and water bombers on-scene, but the winds were unrelenting and, thanks to the tinder-dry forest, had already driven flames as far as Mount Wilson. The trouble was there were no natural fire barriers to even begin to slow the burning.

Two mountains away slumbered Peachland.

Morning broke with Lila in her bed, Nathan's warm arms wrapped around her, her head on his shoulder. Dim light seeped around the edge of her window blind, slowly illuminating the blue walls, the tanned angle of Nathan's shoulder, the handsome angles of his face. In sleep he looked as young as he had when she first met him. Young, but talented, both in and out of bed.

His faint, warm scent of male musk and cedar filled her senses so she wasn't sure she would ever get rid of it. It made her want to touch him. It made her body tingle with the recollection of last night and how their bodies had come together again after they returned to her bedroom. Or quite possibly it was anticipation that it would happen again. A bad sign if ever there was one.

She squeezed her eyes shut. Darn it, she was not going to fall in lust or love with this man.

No, that deed was done a long time ago. She'd just been too intent on burying the Hollywood part of her past to recognize it.

She screwed her face and fisted her hands. It didn't matter what had happened. There were other things to worry about now.

"You know, if you go all tense like that, I might just have to do something about it. I like you much better when we're satiated and exhausted together," Nathan's low growl purred in her ear.

She opened her eyes and found tropical turquoise peering back at her. "I thought you were asleep."

"I was trying to be, until you went all plywood on me. What gives, Lila? What's going on in that too-intelligent brain of yours?"

She looked away from his concerned expression, down to his smooth chest, and felt the heat rise. Damn it!

Not about to admit her feelings, she looked away to the window. "Worried about the fire, I guess." And other things that would remain nameless.

A finger tilted her face toward him. Those darn turquoise eyes again, drilling right into her. "Lila?" said with a warning.

The man just wasn't going to let it go. She pulled away and sat up, hauling the sheets up over her breasts—a movement Nathan apparently felt humorous given the way a smile tugged at his lips.

"All right. I'll come clean. I've done the math, Nathan, and I just don't see how we can make this work. You have to travel for your work. Other than going on buying trips, my life is here. I—I just don't know if I'm prepared to go into this simply for the pleasure of the moment."

He studied her gravely, then pulled her back against him. "The key word in all you just said is 'pleasure.' That's what we need to focus on."

"No! It's not!" She sat up and threw the covers back. "That was what Hollywood hedonism was all about. That's what I left behind when I came home." And what she had clearly thrown herself into again. Nathan hadn't even been here a day and she'd gone to bed with him! Something was clearly wrong with her.

She stood up before he could stop her and pulled on the apricot robe that she'd tossed on the chair when she came back to bed.

Then she shook her head, feeling sheepish at her reaction. "Sorry. I just know my limitations. I'm going to go make breakfast if you feel like getting up. Just so you know, I make a mean omelet. Espresso, too."

She hustled out of the room, wondering what she was going to do. Love him or leave him? There was so much more than just the two of them to consider.

Downstairs, the kitchen was as she'd left it, with the kettle still on the stove, chamomile teacup on the counter by the sink, but everything looked washed up and faded, the usually bright light through the bank of windows gone flat.

Outside, the yard was filled with a mottled white light. She opened the back door.

The stench of burning vanquished the clean air of her home, a bank of smoke covering the sky, her neighbors, by the thickness—everything.

§

After pulling an all-nighter conducting the search for any sign of Lila's attacker, Jas and Danny sat in their office in the West Kelowna Royal Canadian Police Detachment in the early morning, the fruits of their labor on the desk between them. The RCMP building was the pride of West Kelowna for its modern lines and environmentally friendly architecture that used the Okanagan sun to light most of the building. Open walkways in the interior connected offices strung around an open courtyard atrium. As the only plain-clothed investigators in the detachment—most major cases being assumed by the much larger Kelowna detachment—Jas and Danny occupied one of those offices.

Jas eyed the three plastic bags on the desk. One—much smaller—held the broken zipper pull found beside the curb where Lila had been attacked. The other two bags held pieces of clothing he'd pulled from a Dumpster in town behind the restaurant at the corner of Bernard and Abbott. One was a windbreaker, black, that had been stuffed down among the trash in one corner of the rotten food in the bin. That had been fun to recover. His pant legs and jacket reeked from the Dumpster-diving he'd done. Not that Danny was much better; after slipping while he checked one of the Dumpsters on his route, he wore a vile smelling smear of what looked like rotten peaches and yellow mustard across his shirt front.

"A good night's haul," Danny said and went to rub his eyes. He caught himself, smelled his fingers, and grimaced. "How many times am I gonna have to wash to get this stink off my skin? And I was wearing gloves, fer God's sake."

Jas shook his head and felt the fatigue like a load on his shoulders. "I don't think it's your hands. I think it's your nose—as in the stink is indelibly imprinted on your olfactory senses. I know it is on mine. At least that's what I keep telling myself, because if I smell as bad as this, my clothes are going in the garbage; and I happen to like this jacket."

He hauled the evidence bag to him. "Windbreaker, size extra-large, with a broken zipper pull that matches that recovered at the scene. That would confirm the connection. So would that." He nodded at the last bag on the desk, its contents a black ski mask, its vacant eyeholes peering up at them.

Danny followed his gaze and shivered. "Reminds me of the empty shell of the men the creature leaves behind—most of the time."

Jas read the uncertainty in his partner. "You're all right. I wouldn't have you working with me if you weren't. I just wonder what it was that let you get away with your mind intact."

Danny shook his russet head and ran his hands through his hair. "You and me both. It sure as hell wasn't my good looks." He grinned, but then turned thoughtful. "I'm not sure it was anything about me, exactly. I think—I think the thing was scared at the end. It had a choice: stay in me and be caught or leave. What surprised me is that it didn't leap into someone else—like you, for instance. Why didn't it take you?"

Danny's green eyes were filled with questions and not a little self-doubt.

Jas thought a moment. "Maybe it was *my* good looks. Or maybe I wasn't good enough for it—ever think of that?"

Danny picked up the ski mask bag and examined the garment through the bag. "Maybe, but when it took me the first time, it had clearly been head hopping—the truck driver, the homeless guy, me. This time it wanted Victoria and the bracelet and was prepared to do anything to get it. So why not go for you?"

"My skull's too thick?" Jas quipped, but Danny just ignored the joke when usually he wouldn't leave an opening like that unused.

"Something was different this time. I can't put my finger on it, but there was something. The first time it had me, there was no room for me to move at all. I don't even think I was aware until just before it released me, though I remembered what my body had done when I was under its control. But it was like a memory through a haze. This time, though—this time I could clearly see what was happening and the thing was taunting me with it— taking pleasure that it had control and there was nothing I could do about it."

Danny's expression had gone distant and haunted as if he relived those horrible hours. Then his green eyes focused on Jas. "But this time I did do something. There was no way Victoria was going to get away from me. But somehow I slowed myself down and she was able to escape." He rubbed his head where Victoria had clubbed him.

"To be honest, I think either it was toying with me or it was weaker." Their eyes met over the evidence bags.

"Weaker. What the hell does that mean? Weaker how? Why?" Jas looked at the extra-large size tag in the jacket. It was a common enough brand that could be purchased at any outdoor store. Nondescript and nothing special—except for the zipper pull. That was something they were going to pursue.

The vacant, half-dreaming expression on Danny's face sent a chill up Jas's back.

"It's something about the bracelet," Danny said. "It wanted the bracelet before, but it had confidence—as if it had always been able to get what it wanted. This time it wasn't the same. Something has definitely changed. Either with the bracelet or with it or maybe both."

Danny smoothed the mask evidence bag on the desktop, then stopped to lean in to examine it more closely through the plastic.

"What is it?" Jas asked.

"Something's caught in the wool fiber." Danny shifted the bag to adjust one of the eyeholes to expose what he's found. He sat back in his seat and turned the bag around for Jas.

Caught in the dark knit fibers was a single short hair—blond.

Jas and Danny looked at each other.

"Who in this case has blond hair?" Danny asked.

"Does it matter? It could be anyone—the thing jumps heads, remember?"

"Ye-ahh... But like I said, it didn't—at least not from me to you or Cesare. It left and went somewhere else, even though a perfectly good male brain was standing right there. It could have leapt heads and still be sitting there plotting how to deal with Lila."

He stopped and pulled the mask back to him. Sighed, but wouldn't meet Jas's gaze.

"I'm gonna say something pretty wild here, but I want you to give it a chance. This whole case has been some weird-ass shit, so maybe this is just what makes it weirder. What if the thing has gotten weaker? What if it started out strong, confident, and overwhelmingly able to take over someone. I know. I was there. But what if each time it's failed, it used up part of itself? Like its energy, maybe. What if what was so easy at the start—jumping heads—isn't so easy anymore."

It was wild speculation made wilder by the topic, and for a moment Jas felt like the entire world had come unhinged. A head-hopping creature? Jesus Murphy, how had he ever come to let himself believe? If the superintendent of the detachment overheard this discussion, he'd have both of them in the looney bin.

But he had come to believe because, against what he liked to think was the natural order of things, the evidence had pointed in that direction. Hell, he'd even thought he'd seen *something* leave the body of a dying man. He scrubbed his hair and looked at Danny. "You're asking me to believe a hell of a lot of wild speculation, but I figure if anyone in this case is going to have some insight into what we're dealing with, it's you."

He sighed. "So if, like you said, jumping heads isn't so easy anymore, that could mean that the creature is sort of stuck where it is? That might mean it can't take you over again—nice to know."

Danny nodded. "If it's true, it is. But it might also mean that if there is a 'head' that it runs back to—and I can't help thinking something like this would have a home base of some sort—then maybe it has to stay at home base."

He tapped the ski mask bag with his forefinger, a familiar predatory gleam catching his eyes. "So I'll ask it again: who attached to this case, beyond the victims, is blond?"

"Well," Jas hesitated. "There is Nathan Moon."

Danny shook his head. "Nathan Moon fought off whoever was wearing this mask and he's a relative newcomer to this whole case. So who else?"

The people previously attached to the bracelet case were many and varied: an accountant, still in Kelowna Hospital Psych ward. A petty thief in the same place. There'd been others as well, but each was either dead or indisposed in some way. That left one answer.

"Johan Fehr." The elusive CEO of *Schwarzenacht* corporation had shown up at *This and That* very soon after the bracelet was discovered and had scared the hell out of Chloe. Could he be behind the series of misfortunes that had plagued the women of the store over the past three months? Could he be the "home base" of the creature? "Shit, with the resources that man has at his disposal, he could be behind everything that's gone on. He could have paid people to steal Reggie Lewis's files."

"To act as a wedge between Reggie and her friends—to isolate her and make her more vulnerable."

Jas nodded. "And when all his subterfuge didn't work, he took a more direct approach—and became a man the women trusted—you."

"It must have figured out that I was the love interest for Victoria, so it used me."

"And then that didn't work." Jas shoved back his chair and stood. He needed to move, needed to walk this out or he might not be able to believe. He started pacing. "But if what you're saying is true, the creature has worn itself out taking over people and might be stuck in the head of the person it uses as its home base."

He stopped beside the desk and the jacket evidence bag. "Extra-large. From the way Chloe described him, that would fit."

Danny nodded up at him. "Yup. Johan Fehr is here. We just need to find him and figure out why he wants the bracelet so much."

Chapter 9

Nathan's shower in Lila's bathroom felt great, but it would have felt better if a certain auburn-haired woman was there in the marble tile and glass-sided shower with him. Even soaped down and with water running over his face from the rain-shower faucet, he could still smell her roses on his skin, was still aroused by memory of the silken feel of her next to him, around him. He hoped she felt the same.

It should have been like that. Hell, he should have been able to lure her back to bed with the promise of more time together. But instead she'd bolted out of her room as if the shades of hell were after her. As if what they'd had together really didn't matter. He didn't think that was the case, but he wasn't sure.

He shut off the water and stepped outside the shower stall onto a cream, plush mat. He helped himself to an off-white bath sheet folded on a chrome rack shelf, resenting the fact that she'd left him feeling uncertain. So they had different lives—at their ages, everybody did. Was that reason enough to toss away their feelings?

Or was that just an excuse when she wasn't really interested?

"Dammit, Lila!" He used the towel to clear the mirror and leaned on the marble counter to consider his reflection. He still looked reasonably good. Women back home still... well, maybe not flocked, but he was never short of a partner if he wanted one. The trouble was he hadn't wanted those partners anymore. They were too flaky, too needy. One moment clinging to him like a Pacific limpet, the next walking away because his preference for monogamy was too cloying. Or he didn't cast them in his next movie.

He'd hated that inconsistency—the way he never knew what the woman was going to be like when he woke up in the morning. Sure, being with him might cause a woman to change, but from demanding to limp to a banshee and back again in the space of twenty-four hours? He just couldn't see where he was responsible. The last, the starlet Kaitlin Preston, had been the worst. He'd fallen hard for her, maybe because in some ways she reminded him of Lila, but one moment she'd be clinging to his arm like one half of a happy couple for paparazzi cameras, the next moment, at home, she'd be distant and brooding and preferred not to be touched. And then there'd been the magnificent fight because he'd refused to use his influence when a director cast an unknown as the star in a movie instead of her. It seemed like there was no real emotional basis for their relationship.

He glanced at the bathroom door. Unfortunately, the way Lila had left him this morning felt an awful lot the same. The way she had looked at him last night, the way she said she had always loved him... If she didn't want to be with him, what had last night been about?

"That is what the hell I am about to find out."

Towel wrapped around his waist, he grabbed his discarded boxers and trousers and headed across the hall to the guestroom. He pulled on his clothes and then went downstairs, where the wonderful scent of eggs and maple bacon met him in the hallway to the kitchen.

Not going to distract him. Not at all.

The kitchen was a pool of light at the end of the dark hallway, but it was a muted light today. The broad bank of windows at the rear of the room gave onto a backyard filled with—fog? He glanced at Lila standing at the stove in the alcove. Her copper hair matched the copper range hood.

"Hey, good lookin'," he said in his best Humphrey Bogart voice as he came up behind her and nibbled the nape of her neck.

She leapt like he'd bit her and whirled to face him, leaving a perfect-looking omelet half-folded over fresh tomatoes, green onions, wilted spinach, and a white, crumbly cheese.

"You startled me," she said, her hands on his chest, keeping him at bay. But her gaze wouldn't meet his.

"Lila, what's going on? I need to understand this change of heart."

She turned back to the omelet, finished folding the sides and then expertly slid it onto a plate. She turned back to him then. "Coffee? I have espresso made, but I can put on regular if that's what you prefer. Or I can steam milk if you'd prefer a latte or cappuccino?"

"Damn it, Lila! Talk to me!" He grabbed the plate from her and slapped it on the table, then faced her.

She silently pulled another plate out of the oven with a second omelet—smaller—and passed by him to set it on the table—avoiding talking to him exactly as Kaitlin had done and something twisted inside him.

"You know what? If you can't even talk to me, then there really isn't any point to me sticking around. There's not much chance for a relationship to work, is there? Too bad, because once upon a time that was what we did best together. We talked like friends. That was one of the best things about the Lila I knew."

The damn woman wouldn't even look at him. Instead she slid into the nook and stared at her plate like a beaten puppy. Well, Kaitlin had done that, too, hadn't she—after she'd driven him to distraction by also refusing to talk about whatever had her upset.

"So long, Lila. Sorry I imposed on your life." He went out the back door and what he'd thought was fog turned out to be smoke that immediately overwhelmed him. It stung his eyes and reeked of burning trees. Fitting, given all his hopes were going up in smoke. He'd last seen it like this in Los Angeles with all of the brush fires. He'd even spent some time with fire crews on the front lines, volunteering on the fireline as research for a script he was working with. He stepped around the patio furniture and then headed for the corner of the house. Get out of here, get back to his hotel, and get the first flight he could to anywhere but here. Relegate Lila Weber to a youthful fantasy. Whoever had said you can't go back had got it right.

"Nathan, wait."

The strain in Lila's voice cut through him like a knife. He stopped but didn't turn back, waiting.

"I'm sorry. I am. I'm not usually like this and, frankly, I don't like this Lila anymore than you do. I don't know what's come over me. I'll talk. I will. Just come inside and eat your breakfast. You gave up your night for me—to help me feel safe. The least I can do is explain myself. I'm sorry for acting like some distraught teenager."

Well, that was not something Kaitlin would have done. He turned around and she looked almost like the goddess of the old film, with the pale apricot robe belted around her soft curves, the smoke like an ethereal cloud around her. She looked earnest and afraid.

With a sigh he turned back and met her at the door. He tilted her chin up to him and looked her in the eye. "We sort this out now."

She nodded and he lightly grazed her lips with his thumb, then bent down to briefly taste them. When he pulled back, he grinned. "Not bad. Probably not as good as that omelet, but not bad."

She batted his shoulder but ushered him inside, then poured espresso into their coffee cups as he slid into the nook. She sat down in the chair beside him and he cocked a brow at her.

Heaving a breath, she nodded. "Please eat, while I figure out how to do this."

He took a bite of the omelet, still warm, with the tang of feta cheese and green onion. "Good." He nodded and sipped his espresso. Also good. Just like pretty much anything Lila did was good. Even seemingly lost for words, she was good. But he finally set down his fork and waited. "So?"

She looked up at him from pushing a forkful of food around her plate. She hadn't eaten anything, though she'd sipped her coffee.

"All right. You know about the bracelet—how it won't come off a woman's wrist until she's met her soul mate, and how there have been attacks against each of the women who have worn it."

"You were attacked, Lila. I don't care about the other women. It's after you."

"Sure." But she shook her head. "Yes. Maybe. But that's—that's not what I'm worried about. You see, I've been a bystander in all of these cases. I've had the chance to see what's happening and I like to think I can be objective. What I've seen is an escalation. I haven't talked to Jas and Danny about it, but it seems that in each case the attempt on the woman's life has been more direct and more lethal. There've been differences in other ways, too, as if whatever it is that wants the bracelet has tried different tactics—abduction, misdirection and luring, threats and coercion, and then a direct attack when the thing took over the very man who was Victoria's soul mate. At first, the man the woman was involved with didn't seem to have the attention of the creature." Her throat worked. "When it took over Danny, it showed that it does. Now."

She dabbed her fork in the remains of her omelet, but would not meet his gaze.

"Are you telling me that you don't want me around because you're worried about me?" Okay, that made rejection a little easier. A very little.

"Maybe. A little." She finally smiled and it was like sunlight found its way through the smoke outside. "Do you know how I'd feel if anything happened to you because of me?"

He leaned his chin on his palm. "I'm prepared to be amused. Tell me."

"Typical Hollywood. It's all about him." Lila rolled her eyes. "Yes, I'm worried about you, but there's more. This thing has tried to screw with our lives. Everything from direct threats, to trying to force us to do things, to screwing up business deals. It even tried to drive a wedge between my friends by threatening a lawsuit against Reggie and me. That one, we're still sorting out— the lawsuit, I mean. Reggie and I are fine." She smiled weakly at him.

"You still haven't given me a reason for acting like you have. Frankly, Lila, I've got no tolerance for this on-again, off-again passive-aggressive thing. I've ended relationships for less. If I enter into a relationship with you, I want us both to be all-in. So I need to understand what's stopping you—and don't tell me you're afraid for me. I'm a big boy. I can take careof myself."

Her eyes seemed to try to read him, but finally she shook her head. "I think Cesare probably had something similar to say and he nearly lost his life trying to protect Reggie. But just say I give you that—I'll accept that you can take care of yourself. There's still an outstanding issue."

She lay her arm on the table and the silver links shone dully in the muted light through the window. She tapped one finely shaped fingernail on a small arched door that had tiny leaves around it. "This was Kylee's door. She found its match in the front door to Brett's house."

She tapped what looked like a heavy door strapped and bolted with iron. "This was Chloe's. Jas Stone had a matching door hung over his fireplace." She went through three other doors, reciting how they were matched with something in real life as a symbol of the meeting of soul mates.

"This is me." She tapped a little door with narrow ornate hinges. It was the same door that matched the image in the old photo of when she'd been so much younger.

"So isn't that proof enough that we're meant to be together?"

She smiled wistfully. "Maybe. I wish it were so."

Her gaze dropped to the bracelet and her fingers eased over to reveal another small door, this one with leaf-shaped door hinges that reminded him of something ancient and elfish. A small lock and chain encircled the door. "This is the problem, Nathan. Two problems, actually. First of all, there's one more door and there's no one else in my circle of friends to wear the bracelet. That means that if the bracelet comes off me, there's no one to defend it, or if there is, it's a total stranger who might not understand the extent of the danger."

She looked at him then and there were tears in her eyes. "We can't let the creature get the bracelet. That means that I can't let the bracelet off my wrist, and that means that I can't afford to have a soul mate—no matter what my heart might feel. As long as I keep the bracelet on, no one else has to be dragged into danger."

§

It was painful saying the words. Lila's throat hurt. Her eyes hurt worse, and she had to blink to keep the stupid tears in from falling. She was not going to cry. She was going to deal just like she dealt with everything else—with logic.

The kitchen smelled of the omelets and bacon, good, but the acrid smell of forest fire had also weaseled its way into the house. The mélange turned her stomach. The radio this morning had broadcast air quality warnings suggesting that people should stay inside unless they had to go outdoors. The pall of smoke out the window might as well have filled the kitchen for all the cheeriness of the white and yellow room helped. At the moment, the bright paint on the cupboards and the turquoise accents just looked like it was trying too hard. Like Nathan was trying too hard to win her back.

He set down his fork, his sun-blond hair falling into his face. Then he pushed his plate away and caught her hands. "If that's all that's stopping you from giving us a chance, then I figure the best thing we can do is deal with this thing. If we can get it safely off your wrist and stop whatever this is without endangering anyone else, then you'll give us a fair chance?"

His face was so hopeful, but there was so much he didn't understand. Even if there was something about this man that made her want to be with him for a very long time, there was just so much to overcome.

"There's still the matter of the different lives that we live."

Squeezing her hand, he nodded. "But if we can overcome the bracelet creature, then surely the other incompatibilities should be a snap to overcome. It's the hero's journey all over again."

"Hero's journey?" She frowned at him.

"Something from Hollywood—a scriptwriter's tool. The hero of a story has to accept a challenge and then overcome it, but then he has to have the chance to prove that he learned the lessons he learned in the battle by overcoming a final obstacle. You see it in movies all the time."

"So you're saying our relationship is a melodrama?"

"Nah. From what I've heard about the bracelet, it's more like a fantasy adventure with a strong romantic love interest. Not sure we could capture it in a ninety-minute script, though." He caught her hand and lifted it to kiss its back. "Now come on, Lila, smile and eat some of this terrific breakfast. It's really good."

It was that kind of charm that had always attracted her to him and had kept him in her mind for so many years. Was it also what had made every other man she had dated seem like a drab facsimile of the partner she was seeking?

She freed her hand and tried to eat again. Surprisingly, though the eggs were cooling, they tasted better this time and she realized she was famished. She finished the eggs and smiled up at him. "Surprising how hungry I was."

He shook his head, a gleam in those lovely turquoise eyes. "Not surprising given you hardly ate anything at dinner and the workout we had last night."

Warmth streamed up her spine to her face and Nathan chuckled. "Rose is a lovely color on you, woman."

He leaned over the table and kissed her, full, lingering, tasting of eggs and coffee and the cedar of his scent.

"So tell me everything about the bracelet. If we stand a hope of getting this over with, I better understand what we're dealing with."

She shook her head and held her hand up to stop his protest. "I'll do you one better. How about if I try to get everyone together? We've all had different dealings with this thing and Jas and Danny have been conducting an investigation at the same time that Kylee, Chloe, and I have been trying to dig into the bracelet's history. I can even contact Ally and Séamus about what they found out about *Schwarzenacht*."

"*Schwarzenacht*?"

She explained that it was a German company that had been implicated through a limousine rental and through the man named Johan Fehr. Then she checked the clock. Still very early—barely seven a.m.—but most of the people she wanted to invite were early risers. She shoved back from the table and stood.

"I'm going to go have my shower and then make some phone calls. How about we meet at five for dinner? That gives you all day to do whatever it is that movie producers do, while I gather the gang together."

From his place at the table, he shook his head. "I'm not leaving you here on your own. I had that conversation with Stone and Forester last night."

She opened her mouth to argue, but realized that he was probably right. Nodded. "All right, but let's get things straight. I am a private person and I don't need a guard—or a guardian."

Nathan went to argue, but she held up her hand. "I know: You're not my guard. You're my friend, and lover. I get that."

She leaned down to kiss him. "But let's still get one thing straight. If this is going to work, I need my space. If you are going to expect me to be where you want me every minute, this won't work." She swung a hand between them. "If you expect to be with me every minute, this won't work, either. Understand?"

He grinned. "Understood. The woman needs her space and she doesn't want someone ordering her around or a puppy that gets underfoot. Tell you what: If you've got a pen and some paper, I can occupy myself here with some ideas I've been noodling around."

Not what she was expecting.

"Really?" Wouldn't he just be in the way of the things she wanted to do?

When he nodded, she pulled paper and a pen from a drawer in the counter. "You'll really be happy right here?"

He waved her off. "Lila, I'm a big boy who's been on his own for a very long time. Now go do your thing, and when your friends arrive, I'll get out of your hair."

She got, but not without checking over her shoulder. Nathan was already writing something. In the muted light, he looked terribly handsome and it should make her so happy that after all these years he was here.

Instead his presence just made her danger more real.

§

She spent an hour doing yoga in a converted bedroom filled with plants that was also used for Chloe's crystal healing. The yoga hadn't gone well. She couldn't seem to center herself as she always had before. Even the room that had always been a source of tranquility for her seemed filled with uneasy rustles and creaks and groans of the floorboards. Everything about her felt warped out of shape, as if a different woman existed just under her skin.

Then she showered—the water sluicing off her body. But it didn't remove Nathan's scent—if anything, the caress of water just reminded her of Nathan's hands and an old tenderness welled up inside her. Smart, strong, committed, and good-looking—everything a woman could want in a man—except for the Hollywood connection, he was perfect.

Was this just the fulfillment of a teenaged fantasy? What woman wouldn't like the one that got away to come looking for her after all these years. The pursuit was a compliment of the highest order.

There was no question that she still cared for him a great deal. What she'd told him about needing her space was just as true for the rest of her life. Did she care enough to consider leaving Peachland for him? She was surprised to realize she was no longer sure.

Enough to drag him into danger? Definitely not.

Out of the shower and dressed in black Capri trousers and a man-cut white shirt, she made the calls to Jas, Danny, Brett, and Cesare and tried calling Ally and Séamus all the way in Ireland. The men said they'd be here. She knew her friends would be. Ally and Séamus weren't at home.

She couldn't get her mind to settle into the tasks needing attention in her office, so she took a page from Nathan's book and spent time with a pad of paper, listing what they knew or suspected about the bracelet. The list wasn't as long as she'd like it.

The bell tinkling above the shop door at the front of the house made her heart leap.

"Lila?" Chloe's voice.

Lila's alarm faded. "Hold on amoment."

The rain sound of the bead curtain being pushed aside and then Chloe's footsteps came down the hall. Lila met her at the kitchen. Chloe was shaking her head. "That smoke is thick enough you can barely see to drive. I had to keep everything locked up tight last night and Clyde was going nuts because I wouldn't let him out on the balcony. I swear there isn't a bird anywhere, either. Walking here, it felt like I'd stepped into a bad Stephen King movie. I should have taken my car." She hefted her long braid to sniff it and frowned. "And now I stink like a survivor from a fire sale. Darn smoke. It's a heck of a thing the way the winds can bring the smoke so far and then leave it trapped here in the valley over the lake."

She wore a teal-colored caftan and matching leggings that set off the cluster of long, silver chains and string of jet beads that she still wore for protection against whatever Johan Fehr had used on her. According to Chloe, the one and only time that Fehr had come to *This and That,* it had been like the man exerted mind control.

She plunked down at the table across from Nathan. "Hey, handsome. You're still here. That's a good sign."

Lila rolled her eyes. "And he was just leaving, weren't you, Nathan? Now that the next shift of my guardians has arrived?"

He shook his head at Chloe. "Watch her. She's not exactly the cooperative type."

"Didn't I tell you something similar way back when? Bitchy. Way too bitchy, by far. Temperamental, even."

"Hey! I'm wearing the bracelet and I deserve a little understanding."

"A little!" Nathan and Chloe spoke in unison.

"Out! Out of my house. I will not be ganged up on!" She stood with one hand on hip and the other pointing at the door.

Nathan dutifully tore his scratch pages off the pad, folded them and stuffed them in his inside jacket pocket. Then he was up, and paused long enough for a lingering kiss before ducking out into the smoky backyard.

"Whew. I swear there was a little fire in that kiss to go with the smoke." Chloe fanned herself.

With a little flutter of her heart, Lila watched Nathan disappear around the corner of the house before turning back to her friend. She eyed Chloe. The woman's blue gaze was almost violet this morning, highlighted by the redness from the smoke irritation. She had the same glow about her that had been there since she and Jas started dating.

But Chloe was clearly sizing her up, too. Uncomfortable about it, Lila went to tidy up the table. "Coffee? I know my espresso isn't quite your standard, but I'm going to make some for myself."

Twin small lines formed between Chloe's brown brows. "You okay?"

Lila shrugged. "Of course. Why wouldn't I be? I made it through the night, didn't I?"

Chloe's eyes widened. Then she grinned. "My God. Something happened, didn't it? Between you and Nathan? I hoped it might what with him staying over for protection and all." She shoved out of the nook and enveloped Lila in a hug. "He's a good one, Lila."

"Would you just cut it out?" Lila shoved her way free. "You want coffee or not?"

She crossed to the counter without looking at Chloe and filled the water reservoir of her espresso maker. She didn't need anyone pushing her at Nathan. She liked the man enough as it was. She ground beans to fine powder and then filled the portafilter, screwed on the top, and set the pot on one of the gas burners on high.

When she looked back, Chloe still stood where she'd left her, a look of compassion on her face. "Scared you, did he?"

Four simple words and it was like an emotional dam crumbled inside her. She felt the tears well up and grabbed a tissue and covered her emotions by feigning blowing her nose as she stared out the back windows. She was not going to cry. She. Was. Not.

"Oh, honey. It's okay to love somebody." Chloe's warm arms came around her from behind. "I've never seen someone get under your skin like this. You've held out a long, long time."

"It's not Nathan. It's the bracelet. It's got to be why I feel like an emotional wreck."

"Sure it is, Lila. Come on. Come back to the table and tell Chloe all about it."

She let herself be led back to the table and Chloe took over fussing over the coffee. She hauled milk out of the fridge and set to steaming it in a pot. "You really need to get a proper espresso maker, you know."

Lila shook her head. Why was everyone pressing her to change things in her life?

"Chloe, what am I going to do? I like Nathan—no question— but I don't think he's the right man for me. He's a Hollywood producer/director. And he does independent films. That means he's traveling all the time. I can't do that. I have a store to run and a life here. Besides, given everything that's happened, liking him just puts him in danger. I don't want to do that."

Balancing two overfilled latte cups and saucers, Chloe returned to the table and slid into the nook beside her again. "Like him? Is that all? I like it when the air's not full of smoke. I like it when I can sleep in Sunday mornings."

Lila wrapped her hands around the bowl of latte. Was she kidding herself? "How about really like him?"

Chloe's violet eyes just held steady on her.

"All right—how about I don't know how I feel? I really like him—or—or something more that feels like a balloon about to burst in my chest. But that's the trouble. I can't afford to. It's not just the difficulty of our two lives not meshing, it's this damn thing."

She jiggled her bracelet wrist.

"Didn't come off, I see," Chloe said. She had a moustache of latte foam that she licked off her lip like a cat.

"No. It didn't come off, and that's a good thing."

"It is? I thought each of us wanted it off our wrist. I thought you did, too?" Chloe took another sip of latte while Lila considered.

The bracelet was lovely. Unique in every way with its seven small doors. She did want it off her wrist so she could have her life back, but...

She tapped the last two doors. "What happens if it comes off? Who does it pass to?" She met Chloe's searching gaze.

"Is that what this is all about? All these reservations?"

"I don't dare let it off my wrist. Who would it pass to? How do we even know if the next wearer would take care of it? Or be protected?" She shook her head. "There's too much uncertainty to let it go. No, the bracelet is far better off where it is. We at least stand a chance of maintaining control over it."

Chloe's cup clanked too loud in its saucer as she settled it back in the nook. "Are you telling me that you're going to keep that thing on forever—give up your chance at love?"

Lila looked away. Hopefully Chloe wouldn't see how hard this was. "It's better that way. We've been able to block the creature until now."

"Yeah. With the help of police and at the cost of attempts on our lives. A number of us very nearly didn't make it. Cesare nearly died. So did Ally. All of the cases were near misses. You're not going to live your life alone and hunted."

"Maybe." But she couldn't look Chloe in the eyes.

Chloe's sigh seemed to fill the kitchen. Then she pushed up from the table. "Hold on."

She left via the hallway and then came the rain-sound of the bead curtain falling behind her. When she returned she carried a fine chain of jet beads interspersed with amethyst.

"Here. I've been remiss. I gave Victoria protection when she wore the bracelet, but I guess I just thought you'd take something from the shop. I made these for sale, but I want you to wear them. The stones will help protect you. And there's this." She held up a silver chain with a pendant of blue-white stone that shimmered in the kitchen light.

Lila arched a brow. "Moonstone, Chloe? I'm not seeking fertility—or love, for that matter."

"It has other properties," Chloe protested. "It's good for anxiety and brings inner harmony."

"No." Lila shook her head and stood. "I'll wear the jet. I can wear them under my clothes if I have to, I suppose, or twist it on my wrist as a bracelet, but I am not wearing a moonstone."

"But Lila, it could—"

"No! And that's final. Now we've got the others coming over at the end of business to discuss what to do. When I spoke to Jas, he said he and Danny had news. I'm going to spend today doing more research into that fairy tale Victoria's old nanny provided. I've got a line on a folklorist down at University of Washington. I sent her an email the other day and I've arranged to talk to her this afternoon."

Chloe shook her head, glanced at the turquoise clock on the wall, and drank the rest of her latte back. "I hope you know what you're doing, Lila. I had reservations about Jas, but he was the best thing for me. I feel like I'm flying these days I'm so happy—even if I don't get to see him all the time. Now I've gotta get busy with the shop, but promise me you're not going to do anything stupid like go out in this stuff?" She nodded at the murk through the window.

"I can't promise that, but if I do plan to go out, I'll let you know, okay?"

Shoving out from the nook, Chloe gave her a big hug and kissed the top of her head. "Just remember that love is the best way, Lila. You are far and away too deep in your head. And one final thing to think about: maybe you're coming up with all these self-sacrificing reasons you can't love Nathan because you're afraid of not controlling what love brings. Think about it."

Then she was gone, sweeping back out of the room, her myriad silver chains and pendants tinkling music as she moved.

The kitchen felt empty after she'd left. Chloe always was a force of nature. Lila finished her coffee contemplating her friend's disapproval.

She thought of Nathan and had to smile at the image of his lopsided grin and the way he had been so tender with her. It would be so easy to close her eyes and feel his hands, his movements inside her, but that would get her nowhere in dealing with this thing. Afraid? She was afraid of meeting Johan Fehr. She was afraid of dying. Afraid of love?

She shoved away from the table and swiftly cleared the cups into the dishwasher. There. The room was clear and clean again, just like she wished her life was.

Chapter 10

To Nathan it was amazing that after the long days of summer, early September mornings arrived later and later until it was dark until almost seven. As the morning light rose, it filled the smoke-inundated valley with a weird, amber murk that dulled to tarnished pewter as the sun pushed an angry red ball above the invisible space where there should be the eastern mountains across the lake. It had been a long two hours in that house staying away from Lila. The woman was like honey and he was the fly. He grinned to himself as he pushed out of the gate in front of the red-and-white house and wished for another strong coffee like the one Lila had made.

The lake carried a ripple and was as dull as the sky. The beach lay abandoned—who wanted to lie out in the smoke? It was hard to breathe and brought tears to the eyes just walking to his car. He liked to think that it wasn't as bad inside the rental car, but more than likely it was that his nostrils had been burned out by it. He couldn't even smell the smoke on his clothes and that had to be wrong.

From where he sat, he could just make out the red-and-white house. Lila's house. All that fine silken skin. The tumble of her rich copper hair. The vulnerability in her hazel eyes, though she was determined to hide it.

It was so damned like Lila to decide that she'd give up her—their—chance at happiness to save someone else the trouble of the bracelet. It was that selflessness that he loved about her, but on the other hand he was not going to accept it. If that was the reason she'd acted as inconsistently as she had, well then, the situation demanded that he help clear that barrier away. He'd dreamed of the day they could be together. He was not just going to walk away.

Yawning at his lack of sleep, he started the car.

Lila might have invited people over for five, but he needed to talk to someone about the situation now. He wasn't going to wait. He started the car and pulled out from the curb with his lights on. The sun burned an angry red hole in the sky across the lake, but the smoke ate the light until he was driving through a perennial dusk. The bakery café was crowded inside as he cruised past, but the patio seating was empty. A few joggers foolishly ran past and vanished into the smoke. A V of Canada geese flew like wraiths on the water. He turned away from the lake and onto the highway.

Previously the lake had lain like a cool blue oasis just below a string of expensive houses and old orchards that ran below the road. Now it was invisible in the smoke. He drove up the long hill out of Peachland and curved through the bluffs that separated the small town from the sprawl of West Kelowna. He pulled into a shopping center parking lot and searched police and West Kelowna on his phone. Jas Stone and Danny Forester had to work around here somewhere. He needed to talk to someone and they seemed like the best candidates.

Following the online map, he found the police station easily. Located between the two directions of highway traffic that now bisected the town, the RCMP building hunched in the murk and didn't look like much. A roofline that was concave as if the ceiling was giving in. Yellow walls and glass—probably to let the light in, not there was much of that today.

He parked and jogged inside through the warm smoky air. In the unseasonable air-conditioned cool, he asked for the two detectives at the front counter.

By luck they were there, and soon Jas Stone buzzed through a locked door to greet him.

"Nathan. This is a surprise." Jas Stone had the perfect, stern cop persona in place. Dark hair, dark, unreadable eyes. Even in jeans and a polo shirt, Nathan could positively see the stripes up the sides of uniform pant legs and reflective sunglasses. But by the rumple of his clothes and hair and the faint stink of garbage that clung to him, Stone clearly hadn't just arrived at work.

"Sorry to bug you, Jas. If this is a bad time, just tell me." Nathan shook Jas's hand. "I know this isn't exactly your jurisdiction, but I needed to talk to someone."

"I thought we were getting together tonight."

"We are, far as I know. I just need some advice."

Jas was still for a moment. "About Lila?"

When Nathan nodded, Jas hooked his head at the door behind them. He used a key card to get them inside the secure area and led him up through walkways suspended around a central open area filled with the strange natural light. The air smelled metallic with a faint hint of urine.

Aside from the strong scent of garbage, the office he entered was the stereotype of every police office he'd ever put on film. Two desks pushed together back to back. Computer monitors flanking each other and locking file cabinets. A couple of plastic bags with dark pieces of clothing sat on the desk. A swivel chair sat in front of each desk, one a battered old oak affair that looked like someone had rescued it from a government office furniture sale. A single, hard-backed chair sat against one wall. Jas hooked it to the side of the desks with his foot.

Danny Forester sat back in the oaken chair so it let out a groan. By the fatigue on his face, he could have made the sound himself. "Nathan. Hi. How's it hanging, brother? Grab a stool. You want a cup of very bad coffee?"

"Here's a better idea," Jas said as he picked up the plastic bags and locked them in a cabinet. "How about we hike over to Betty's for that coffee? She might not be open, but she'll be there; and for us she'll find coffee." He grinned at Nathan. "We're her favorite customers now that we've got girlfriends, and her coffee beats this swill hands down." He motioned at the deeply stained coffee cups on the desks.

It didn't take long to get there. Nathan drove after Jas and Danny discovered the extent of the smoke outside—it hadn't been that bad when they got back to the office.

The small café owned and run by Elizabetta di Maria sat in a small strip mall in the old part of West Kelowna, but in this case the strip mall was obviously cared for with fresh cream paint and lush hanging baskets hanging from the light standards along the store fronts.

As predicted, the front door was locked, but a light was on inside in what must be the kitchen. Jas knocked on the door and a diminutive figure appeared from the back. Older woman in her sixties at least, with close-cropped curly hair and a smile on her face that quickly broadened when she saw it was Jas and Danny. She came to the door wiping her hands on her apron.

"My favorite officers. Come in. Come in. Now what can I do for you fine gentlemen and who is this? Another policeman?" She looked Nathan up and down, her bright bird eyes assessing. Then her nostrils curled. "What is that smell?"

"Hazards of the job, I'm afraid," Danny said and motioned at the marks on his clothing. "Promise we won't stay too long, okay?"

"Betty, This is Nathan Moon, a friend of ours visiting from the States," Jas said. "A friend of a friend, you might say. Nathan, this is the maker of the best coffee and Italian food in Westbank."

"It is the only Italian restaurant in Westbank," she said archly and raised one thinly penciled brow at Nathan as she led them to a table in the rear of the cafe. "Whereabouts in the States?"

"All over, actually. I travel a lot. But I guess you could say my home base is California. L.A. to be specific."

"He's a Hollywood mogul, according to Chloe," Danny chimed in.

Not exactly the word he wanted getting around.

"Not a mogul. I make independent films now."

"Anything I might have seen?" she asked, her hands on her hips. She was a tough one, this little woman.

"I doubt it."

"Oh, come on, Nathan. Everyone's seen *Battle for Olympus*. Lila was in it. That's why she still has a fan base."

Betty's eyes had widened, so she knew the movie, too.

He sighed. "That was a long time ago. Not what I do anymore."

"And what brings you to the Okanagan?"

He looked at Jas and Danny, who weren't doing a darn thing to protect him from the interrogation. In fact, the two of them practically smirked.

"If you must know, it was a woman. A woman I let get away a very long time ago. I came looking for her. Found her, too." He couldn't help himself. He smiled.

A beatific smile filled Betty's face. She clapped her hands. "For love! Now that is a worthy reason for coming. Not one of these foreigners up to tear down our orchards and build mansions." She looked around the table. "Now what can I get you boys?"

They told her and she bustled off. Nathan watched her go, shaking her head. "She could be a character in a movie. The trouble is, I can only think of maybe one character actress who might do her justice."

"Betty's a character, all right," Jas said, low-voiced. "She immigrated to Canada with her family and grew up on her father's orchard here in West Kelowna. She was Miss Westbank way back when, before she got married and raised a family. She bought this place a few years back after her husband died because she couldn't stand sitting around doing nothing. She's gangbusters."

Soon she came bustling back with an Americano for Danny and two espressos for Nathan and Jas and waited as they sampled.

"You know this is stupid, right? Caffeine jolt when we should be heading home to bed," Jas said.

Nathan nodded but didn't let that stop him from sampling the coffee. Dark, rich, and covered in crema. He savored the nut flavors and let it warm him from the inside. He hadn't realized how cold he'd felt since Lila banished him from her house.

He nodded up at Betty. "It's very good. Best coffee I've had except perhaps in Italy. And that's only perhaps."

Betty beamed. "So tell me—this woman you chased after—how is it going?"

He glanced at Jas and Danny. "Well, I guess that depends on who you're asking. There seem to be a few obstacles to our happy ending."

She frowned. "But you are a good boy. You at least know you want a happy ending. You do not try to hide it like these two *sciocchi.*" She patted his cheek and disappeared into the kitchen.

It was like a small dog had just had at him. Jas and Danny just grinned.

"Keeps us honest, coming in here," Danny said. "Course the coffee and the food brings us, too. You should try her lasagna."

"So what brought you to us, Nathan? You've been pretty tight-lipped since you got here."

He rubbed his gravelly eyes and took another sip of coffee. "Like I said, I'm looking for advice. I thought things were going pretty well with Lila last night. Then this morning she dumps on me that it can't possibly work because she's not prepared to take the bracelet off and risk someone else being in danger, or who-or-whatever it is getting the bracelet."

Jas looked thoughtful. "That sounds like Lila, always playing the caretaker. She's done it for each of her friends when they wore the bracelet—sort of the voice of reason into the madness the bracelet brings."

"Madness?"

Danny shook his head. "Not really madness, but Chloe and Kylee each have talked about how wearing the bracelet clouded their judgment."

"So are you saying that this decision of Lila's is all based in the effects of the bracelet?"

"Maybe." Danny shrugged."I mean, what do we know about the bracelet, really?"

"Shit. What you're telling me is that I can't believe anything Lila has told me—in fact, everything between us could just be a lie brought on by the bracelet." And she'd said something like that to him, too, but he'd chosen not to believe. It left him feeling deflated and a little angry at himself for wasting not only his time, but that of everyone else, too.

He scrubbed his fingers through his hair and felt the caffeine jolting through him when he knew he'd be better off sleeping. Too late now. He looked up and found two sets of eyes waiting.

"Been there, buddy," Jas said.

"So what do I do?"

"Make a choice, just like we had to. She's either worth it or she isn't. If she isn't worth it, you walk away."

Nathan held Jas's gaze. Could he walk away? He'd done what so many men had dreamed of—he'd slept with Lila Weber. The trouble was, it wasn't enough. There would never be enough time to be with her.

"Okay. So you're not walking away."

Jas had read him right. "So what do I do?"

Danny stirred uncomfortably. "I'm not usually an advice kinda guy, but the things that happened with Victoria... She's no weakling, but she was really afraid. It was like someone was stalking her. Thing is, I'm afraid it might have been me."

"O—kay. I think that needs explanation," Nathan said.

Jas sipped his espresso. "What Danny's saying is that the creature possessed him and he's feeling pretty guilty about what he put Victoria through. In all of the cases, there was a man who led the attack on the bracelet wearer. After what happened yesterday to Lila, I think we need to be concerned for her safety. It was good you stayed the night to keep her safe."

Nathan looked at his cup, dealing with the tiniest pang of guilt. Had the sex just left Lila in a more difficult emotional condition? If she was under pressure from her attacker, she probably didn't need pressure from him. "Yup. Good. It was."

Jas and Danny's regard felt like it had telescoped in on him. He shifted in his chair—for all the charm of Betty and her restaurant, the chairs were definitely not made for comfort. He felt like a suspect undergoing questioning with a spotlight in his eyes.

"So—Nathan—that response sort of begs the question of just what went on last night."

He met their gazes trying to hide his qualms, and Danny's face split in a grin.

"You dog. Lila Weber. Who'da thunk it?"

"Congratulations, man," Jas said. "Welcome to the land of the fully hooked."

Jas nodded at Danny and motioned to himself. "Something about the Peachland women, I guess. Chloe's everything I could ever want, even though she was about the farthest thing from what I thought I'd end up with. And can you imagine this slob with an Italian fashion designer?" He shook his head. "Whoever said love works in mysterious ways had it right."

Love? Was that what this caged-mouse feeling around his heart signified? He'd barely found Lila and she was trying with all her might to send him away. That didn't exactly indicate that the feelings were mutual. He shook his head and studied his almost empty espresso cup. "Thing is, I don't want to leave her but she seems pretty determined that we not get involved—at least not as long as she's wearing the bracelet."

"Then I guess you just need to get the darned thing off her wrist, don't you?" Danny said. "Seems to me that could be a pleasurable task, but you'd know that better'n me."

"I don't think Lila's going to let me near her again until the creature—whatever it is—is caught or stopped. She was pretty adamant about that."

Jas looked thoughtful. Danny just shook his head. "That's bad luck."

Bad luck, bad news, bad karma—this wasn't helping. "You know what, guys, I'm sorry I bothered you. I think I'd better be going and let you both get some rest."

While he felt like electrodes sent pulsing jolts through his brain and body. He needed to be up. He needed to be moving.

Jas shoved back from the table and stood. Danny hiked himself up from his slouch in the chair. "Listen, Nathan," Jas said. "We're just looking into something about the guy who attacked Lila last evening. Let us do our job and hopefully we'll have some news when we meet over dinner this evening. Okay? Just give us the day."

"And in the meantime? How do we make sure Lila's safe?"

"She's got people around her—Kylee and Chloe."

Not good enough. Not good enough, by far.

"I think I'll head home for a run where I can breathe and a change of clothes. Then I'll go keep an eye on things."

Jas shook his head. "You're not exactly going to be inconspicuous in this murk. There aren't going to be too many people on the promenade today."

"Inconspicuous isn't my concern at the moment." Nathan tossed bills on the table to pay for their coffees and called thank you to the diminutive owner as he headed for the door. "I'd rather put whomever it is on notice that he has to get through me to get Lila and that damned bracelet."

Betty poked her head up through the kitchen window. "Nice to meet you, Nathan. You boys—you go take a shower!"

§

In the muted light through the kitchen windows, the bracelet gleamed softly with the patina of age. Lila ran her thumb pad over the two silver doors that had not found their match in real life—well, maybe make that one door. On the kitchen table beside her was the photo album of the Paleolithic era of her life, open to the epoch when she and Nathan had had their photo taken in front of a door that was supposed to be the entrance to her palace of heaven. Symbolic much? But she didn't have to believe it—or do anything about it.

From the front of the house came the soft voices of customers who had braved the smoke to come to the store. The kitchen smelled of oranges and cinnamon that she had thrown in water in a pot on the stove to dispel the smoke scent that was gradually permeating the house. She scrubbed at her itchy red eyes that she was pretty sure weren't the product of the smoke, though she'd tried to convince herself that they were. Nope, these itchy red eyes went with feeling like crying and that was just so unlike her. She was always the strong one—at least she'd always thought so. But maybe this clenched, vulnerable feeling in her chest was just the fatigue after a night spent virtually awake. Not that it hadn't been pleasurable—it definitely had been—but women of a certain age needed their sleep.

She clamped down on the emotions and thunked the photo album closed. She'd wasted enough time worrying about what was the best thing to do. Better to just get doing it. She stood, the string of jet beads Chloe had given her cool against her skin under the crisp, collared white shirt she wore over black capris.

Leaving the album on the table, she headed up to her office. At least there the surroundings were conducive to focusing on facts, figures, and spreadsheets. And she needed to call Ally and Séamus in Ireland and also make the phone call to the folklorist. She shoved the business of *This and That* aside and pulled out a sheaf of paper that had the Italian fairy tale about a bracelet. Not that she hadn't read it before, but maybe she'd get more out of it now that she was wearing the bracelet. Stupid thought, but the bracelet had an effect on the wearer.

Well, after watching almost four months of drama, she was darn well not playing the part intended for her. She was not going to swoon into Nathan Moon's arms simply because there was a photo with a door in it.

Who was she kidding?

In self-defense she tried Ally and Séamus's number, but the phone just rang through to an answering machine. She left a message asking what they'd learned about *Schwarzenacht Corporation*, then hung up and gathered the papers that Victoria had transcribed. They held the record of Victoria's Italian nurse's telling of the fairy tale. She picked up the phone again and dialed the number for Professor Sheila Orr. The call signal hummed.

"Hello?" The voice at the end of the phone asked with a slight Scot's burr.

"Professor Orr? This is Lila Weber calling. I'd arranged to phone you to discuss an old story that seems to be involved in some strange goings-on here in Peachland."

"That sounds a mite ominous. Call me Sheila, please. How did you come by this story of yours?"

Lila sighed. "It's a rather long story in terms of what brought us to even looking for the story, but let's just say that an item—a bracelet—came into our possession. Strange things started to happen so we went looking to try to find out more about the bracelet's provenance. The previous owner's diary said it was discovered in the North African desert, but Egyptologists say it isn't Egyptian. They suggested Mesopotamian or Southern European. Anyway, some friends mentioned that their Italian nanny had told them a story about a bracelet when they were children. Thankfully the nanny was still around and provided us with the story. I was hoping you might help us understand it."

There was silence a moment on the phone. "You've quite the story of your own, Ms. Weber. I'm between meetings at the moment. Could you tell me the nanny's story?"

Lila scanned the stack of papers before her. "All right. The story goes that there once was an Italian tinsmith. Of course this was in the days long before there was an Italy, but in the area known as Lombardy there lived a man who worked tin and silver and who was known to dabble in the art of magic. He wished to improve his art and so had sought an apprenticeship with a great man who lived somewhere else around the Mediterranean. Although the story doesn't say it, I get the sense that this great man's location was a great distance away."

"That may be, but you must remember that distances would have felt much greater in those days when everything was dependent upon foot travel or horse."

"Good point." She noted it down and continued. "The master lived in a great palace. He had many servants and initially refused to apprentice the tinsmith, but finally agreed to teach him in return for service."

"Sorry to interrupt you again, but is the great man, as you call him, called a king? If not, then it is odd that they speak of him living in a palace."

Lila worked her neck and shoulders and made another note. A yawn threatened, but any fatigue was her own darn fault. Acting like a randy teenager at her age. Come on.

The tinsmith had gone a long way to improve himself by learning from someone who must be very wealthy, but not royalty. A merchant? She kept reading.

"Within, the palace was also a lot like a fairy tale, with a maiden held virtual prisoner who the tinsmith fell in love with—what would these guys do if said maiden turned out to be a monster?—and many beautiful and magical things. The great man—the master—wielded magic, but apparently he would not teach the tinsmith, but instead used him as a servant. The tinsmith brought food to the imprisoned maiden every day and fell in love with her. He conspired to free her so that they could be together and, in secret, somehow stole the master's secrets. He made the key to her escape and escape they did. The two of them ran, pursued, across many countries and eventually found safety in the tinsmith's own country. They had a small villa and were apparently happy. That's where the master found them." Lila paused to ease her back.

"Interesting," Sheila Orr said. "Usually a fairy tale would end with their escape and that they lived happily ever after."

"That's what made me look you up. I saw your paper, *The Myth of Happily Ever After,* on-line and that made me call you because the story doesn't end there. It goes on, telling about the unhappy demise of the characters. Let me read it to you."

She turned the pages to the end to study what Victoria's nurse had told them.

"It was in the third year after they thought they had reached safety that their peace was disturbed. In the middle of the night, the silversmith came with soldiers. They surrounded the villa and tore down the door. The woman wished to just return to the silversmith to save her beloved husband, but the tinsmith would not be protected. He was a man. He would protect his wife and he had hatched a plan.

It was then that the silversmith revealed his true self—of great power and smokeless fire, he rose up and up and yet the tinsmith still defied him, for the tinsmith had studied the great man closely and wished to rid the world of him. In answer the silversmith told the tinsmith that he would always be a little man—too paltry to ever amount to anything. The silversmith struck the tinsmith down and stole his essence. He trapped it inside a silver bracelet for a thousand thousand years.

But as the silversmith struck, the woman screamed and ran. She so distracted the silversmith that the tinsmith fought back and drew much of the silversmith's power to him.

In fury, the silversmith pursued the woman, for he knew she had distracted him purposefully. In the disruption the silversmith left the bracelet, for he did not yet realize what the tinsmith had done. A serving girl took the bracelet and ran. But the tinsmith's wife was caught. In vengeance, the silversmith turned her into a door in his palace—to exist there until the palace was destroyed. When he realized what the tinsmith had done to his power, he pursued the bracelet, but the maid had by then crossed many countries. To this day the bracelet has never been found, and though the palace of the silversmith has long ago blown away to dust, the Beauty still wanders the world as a ghost until she reunites with her soul mate.

"That's it. That's the ending of the story my friend's nanny told."

"Most interesting," Sheila Orr said. "Did you notice how there are more details in the telling of the death than of the love story? That suggests that there is a difference in importance. Most fairy tales are either teaching tales or records of historical events. You can look as far back as the Epic of Gilgamesh for the story form. This story has the ring of history to it, though it's odd for magic to figure so prominently and so overtly. Usually, if something magical occurs, it isn't presented in quite the same way that your story presents it. It's almost a natural order of things. But your story clearly makes the magic a devastating thing that destroyed the lovers. That's no fairy story. Well, maybe it is if you want to look at the old Brothers Grimm tales."

"So just what does that mean?" Lila looked at the phone, concerned.

"Well..."

She could picture the professor in a book-filled, dusty office mulling over her answer.

"I'm not sure how much help I can be, Ms. Weber. Clearly the story concerns me because the ending is so dark. It is not a teaching tale, so I have to think that it is a rendering of a bit of history, even if that seems farfetched. Tales can mutate over the years, but this is not one of the common tales that has spread through Europe; no, this seems to be something local to wherever the story was told."

"Northern Italy," Lila offered.

"Aah. The Lombardy of the story, then. That only makes the truth more evident. You say you have this bracelet?"

Lila's hands went to the cool silver links. History. The professor was suggesting the story had really happened. "We don't know if it's the same one..."

"But something has you linking the bracelet in the story to the one that has come into your possession."

"Well—yes. But... Is there anything else that you can tell me from this story? We're particularly interested in anything you might be able to tell us about the nature of the silversmith or anything about how the bracelet might be destroyed." Lila found herself holding her breath, waiting for the ridicule to come over the phone.

There was silence again. "Ms. Weber, I don't know what you've gotten yourself tangled up in, but old magic is never a good thing to play with. I would suggest that you might be better to walk away from the bracelet. Lose it or lock it away, perhaps."

The links felt heavy on her wrist, a shackle to a task she suddenly did not want to deal with. "I—I'm afraid that's not possible."

"Then I suggest that you be very careful. There was one phrase that you used that concerns me because there are so many tales associated with it. Smokeless fire. That's a phrase from the Koran. It is used to describe something dark. A demon. The Djinn. And one last thing: if this bracelet is the one in the story, be very careful of it, for magical items have a will of their own and are always trouble in whatever fairy story I've ever read."

She didn't know the half of it. Lila thanked Professor Orr, hung up, and closed her eyes. Djinn? A demon? The maid stole the bracelet and she would bet anything that the maid was one of the bodies the colonel had found in the cave where he recovered the bracelet. Had she been blasted out of existence by a demon? How had the bracelet remained hidden until a British colonel found it? Or perhaps, given what she knew of the bracelet, it had waited until its first opportunity to be found and the colonel was it.

A silly thought, almost as silly as saying the creature causing them problems was a thousand-or-so-year-old demon, but all the evidence pointed in that direction. But didn't the tale say the essence of the tinsmith was trapped inside the bracelet and didn't the professor say that magical items have wills of their own?

Eyes still closed, she traced the bracelet doors with her fingers. Are you really there? Could it be true? Was that why the bracelet seemed to influence the wearer? And if the tinsmith trapped the demon's power with him in the bracelet, then that might explain why the creature wanted it so badly. It wanted its power back and the tinsmith wasn't allowing it. She and her friends had become unwilling pawns in an ancient battle!

Stretching and yawning wasn't enough to deal with her fatigue. She stood up to pace the small space in her office. So what did it mean for each of her friends to find their soul mate with a matching door? Why was that important? Why should she have to love Nathan?

She stood at the window, peering out into the murk. Smoke swirled outside the house, the lawn was ash-white, the lake a dull steel surface beyond the almost empty street. It was like the world had ended and ended badly.

No light, no life, no love.

Her chest clenched and she felt like crying.

It had been so many years since she had lived the disaster. The world had ended for her then, as the demon had come for them; her brave mistress taken, the brave householder fallen in the courtyard, his body a discarded husk, the best of him swirled up and entrapped in the bracelet links and the key he'd created to free his beloved. She knew. She had seen. Her throat tore with the depth of her scream as she had escaped the destruction of that horrible night. And he, the evil one, had pursued her back across the land and ocean to die in that desolate place. Thus was the evil one's curse: that the door the woman became and the key that would open it would never meet again, until each door was opened by the soul mate of the bracelet wearer. The bracelet she had hidden.

Lila staggered against the windowsill, her cheek coming against the smooth glass, her heart pounding, her mouth sour and her knees weak. It was as if the swirling smoke played out the panoply of ages and she could see it happening. Almost grasped the full meaning, but it was just beyond her reach.

She laid her forehead against the cool glass and fought to steady her breathing. A waking dream? Her imagination? She was no sensitive like Chloe, but this feeling was less like something out of a fable and more like—well—a memory?

So much to think about. So much to talk over with the others tonight. And Nathan?

Nathan would just have to understand that there was no place for him here until a thousand-or-so-year-old drama played out.

Chapter 11

By five p.m. they had all arrived but one, and Lila had shooed Kylee and Chloe into the dining room from the kitchen to play hostess for a moment while she gathered herself. The yellow and white room ticked around her, and through the broad expanse of window the gray smoke in the backyard swirled in an unseen breeze as if it was seeking a way inside. She closed her eyes against the squeamish thoughts. Since the episode in her office earlier that day, she'd felt like she was seeing everything through deep water. Sounds echoed in her head as if she dwelt inside a bell and her legs felt hollow. She closed her eyes and squeezed the bridge of her nose against the headache that had slowly been building all afternoon. She just needed to get through this and she could sleep.

After shutting the store early because no one was out in the murk of forest fire smoke, Chloe and Kylee had stuck around to help pull together a meal of bruschetta of pesto with fresh tomato and feta, followed by prawn skewers—flash-fried on the stove because of the murk outside—and three different salads: creamy potato, spinach with cranberry and pecans in an apple-cider dressing, and quinoa with a medley of lightly toasted vegetables in a cilantro vinaigrette. While they'd worked, they'd listened to the radio: Reports of the fire said it was moving fast toward Peachland. It had already inundated the old Brenda Mine Road when it circumvented Mount Wilson; now it was trying to climb the rear of Mount Coldham. If Coldham was inundated, that left only Pincushion Mountain between the town and the flame.

To take her mind off too many things, Lila had readied the mostly unused dining room that sat between the shop and the kitchen at one side of the house. The room had high crown moldings and dark wainscoting and a darker, rectangular oak table that could seat eight easily and ten with the barest of squeeze. The dining room had been left largely unchanged since the loss of her grandparents. Just stepping inside still brought an instant of drawn breath as if Lila's grandmother might look up from saying grace at her end of the table and smile at her granddaughter.

A soft knock on the window of the back door brought her upright and blinking. Nathan, looking dapper in a navy sports jacket, pale blue polo shirt, and jeans, waved through the window at her. In his other hand he carried a brown paper bag over a wine bottle. She started for the door, but a bout of vertigo hit her and she staggered. A billow of smoke and Nathan was through the door to catch her arm.

She pulled away and straightened, catching herself.

"Are you all right?" he asked.

She shook her head, feeling stupid. "I'm fine. Just close the door."

Long fingers of smoke had twined into her cinnamon- and orange-scented kitchen as if they reached for her. She shivered.

"I'm fine. I am," she said more to convince herself as she waded back to the counter and tried to sort out what she'd been doing.

"Lila?"

Nathan was standing too close—close enough she inhaled his musk and cedar, felt his breath as he leaned down, prepared to kiss her. His nearness evoked an electric pulse down deep in her belly and between her legs. She looked up at him as he stood beside her, his expression clearly one of concern.

"So I hope you know you have a bad effect on me."

He cocked a brow and the corners of his lips turned up. "I'm going to consider that good news."

Typical Nathan. "Don't." Before he could complete the kiss, she grabbed the platter of prawns from the oven and led him down the hall to the dining room that sat off to the side of the hall.

Bright yellow placemats were counterpoint to the room's teal-blue walls.The gaily-colored Portuguese salad bowls were set between her grandmother's silver candle sticks. At the end of the room, an antique mirror with a silver, leaf-shaped frame sat above an antique sideboard. The misty reflection made it seem as if she looked across time. Unfortunately her friends had conspired against her; Victoria sat with Danny, Cleopatra-haired Reggie with Victoria's bad-boy brother, Cesare. Chloe sat beside Jas, and Kylee sat between Jas and Chloe's brother Brett. They had left her grandmother's chair for her and the chair next to it for Nathan. She shot "traitor" gazes at Chloe and Kylee. They both smiled back innocently.

So much for friendship.

She went to slip into her chair, but darned if Nathan didn't hold it for her. Everyone around the table awaited her reaction.

She looked up at Nathan. "Thank you, and thank you all for coming. It seems to me that we've done this a lot over this summer. For all the bad things that have happened, it's wonderful the way our family of friends has grown. This room was one of my grandmother's favorites and now I can see why. Having a table full of friends to share a meal and conversation is wonderful. So far I've kept those wonderful gatherings to the kitchen and the patio, but it seems we've almost outgrown the kitchen and, well, the patio is no place to be today. So welcome to all of you—bracelet wearers, protectors, friends."

Just where all that had come from, she wasn't sure, but it fit the occasion and the room, except she couldn't look at Nathan. He no longer fit the description "friend."

"Please help yourself to the food. It was the least I could do given all the trouble I've caused by bringing the bracelet into our lives. You can thank Chloe and Kylee for a lot of it and the smoke for giving them nothing to do in the shop." She passed the platter of prawns to Nathan and sipped white wine from the goblet that someone had filled. Brett, probably. He'd come armed from Elkhart Winery with some of last year's finest.

The mellow taste of pear and apricot settled over her tongue, refreshing enough to make the smoke outside seem like an evil dream. "Is the smoke as bad up top?" she asked.

Brett's winery sat at the top of Trepanier Creek bluff, where it might possibly get more wind.

As he helped himself to potato salad, Brett shook his head. "There might be a bit more breeze but all that does is swirl the smoke around. It's still thick, though. It looks like it fills the entire valley from Kelowna southward."

Danny nodded and Reggie did too. "West Kelowna is socked in," Danny said. "The wind is picking the smoke up from Brenda Mine and lifting it right over the two mountains between us and them."

"I heard on the news that the Kelowna airport's shut down, too. The visibility is too bad," Reggie added.

"I wish they'd get this fire under control. I know it's still a good ways away, but I remember too well the evacuation orders of before," Lila said. It was true and maybe that was the source of her ill-ease. All those scenes from the great Kelowna fire of people leading their horses through smoke like this trying to escape the pursuing flame. She thought of the deer and bear who lived on the mountains above Peachland. Of the fiery death coming for them. For a moment it was like the room went away and all was flames.

She slumped in her chair and came to herself when a warm hand covered hers. A concerned gaze the color of warm tropical waves met hers. "Lila?"

"I'm fine. Nothing a good night's sleep wouldn't cure." She forced a smile as she slipped her hand away, but the interaction hadn't been missed by her sharp-eyed friends. Chloe and Reggie looked positively smug at their end of the table.

Lila shook her head. "So Victoria, how are things coming with the store? Have you had many R.S.V.P.'s for the grand opening?" Victoria looked up from a discussion with Danny— or Daniel, as she called him. It was sweet actually, the way the blonde Italian bombshell had found her love in the slightly rumpled Danny Forester. Oddly, even though she was a fashion designer, she hadn't tried to change Danny, but the man seemed to stand a little straighter and just maybe his clothes weren't quite so rumpled.

"It is good, Lila. The shelves are filling. The seamstresses have been *perfetto*. Very quick. Very clean with their sewing. The garments are beautiful, but I am worried about the opening. Should the air stay like this, what will we do? All the people we have invited cannot fit into the store at once and we planned for all our tables and food to be outside. In this smoke, that will not work." She shook her blonde mane, obviously troubled.

"It is a concern," Lila nodded. "But surely to goodness the winds will change or they'll get the fire out by then."

"It's a real issue." Brett shook his head. "With all this smoke, the air tankers can't fly and that means firefighting is left to the ground crew. I've been keeping a close eye and this fire is moving fast. There's just Pincushion before it'll be right above us." His frown said he was clearly worried because Elkhart Winery sat just below Pincushion Mountain.

"Won't the old burn from the previous fire act as a barrier?" Chloe asked. There had been a fire above Trepanier Creek a few years ago.

Brett shook his head. "Don't know. Cesare and I are hoping."

"And me," Kylee added. "And about anyone with any links to the Trepanier Creek area. It's so beautiful up there."

"What we need is a change in the wind's direction. Something from the east would blow the fire back on itself and allow the tankers to fly so they can knock the darn thing down,"Jas said.

"Then let's all ask the weather gods for exactly that," Lila said.

Around the table people nodded. The prawn platter was almost depleted and the salad bowls were emptying. Everyone seemed to be hungry except her. Lila toyed with the spinach leaves on her plate but couldn't find the energy to eat it. The pink-fleshed prawns just turned her stomach. She sipped her wine and turned her attention back to the table.

"I asked you here so we could compare notes about the matter of the bracelet. I'm concerned that, if it comes off my wrist, it leaves the bracelet at risk because there isn't anyone to put it on after me."

"So are you suggesting that we need to recruit another victim?" Kylee asked, setting her fork down. "Because given the way people have admired that bracelet, it shouldn't be a problem." Her laughter tinkled in the room but no one joined her. She stopped. "Hey, just kidding, all right?" She turned back to her dinner.

"I think we need to find a solution to this thing. I'd like the buck to stop here, with me. There's been too much danger to my friends. I don't want that to continue. Not to anyone, and I certainly don't want whatever is out there to get the bracelet."

Danny and Jas looked at each other. "We're not sure what it means, but we followed up on last night's attack on Lila," Jas said. "We went into Kelowna to examine the scene and found something. Do you remember anything from your fight, Lila? Did you do any damage to your attacker?"

Her fork rattled against her plate as her fingers went slack. The room disappeared and *the night was dark except for porch lights through the trees but she was not going to have dinner with Nathan Moon and face his intentions. It wasn't going to work. It couldn't, and she wasn't going to see him in danger. As she marched toward the Mercedes the sidewalk was hard and unsteady under her precarious stilettos. She'd really rather just take a taxi and not have to face Nathan, but she'd told him she'd accept a ride and she wasn't going to act any more scatty than she already had this evening. Fuming at her predicament, she passed a Lexus gleaming in the dim light and stepped into the deeper shadows of a tree.*

The hand came around her neck and she smelled fire and burning and her vision dimmed. She twisted in her attacker's arms, trying to get her arms up, but her rings caught on something as she fought to get her elbows between them. Whatever held her ripped loose.

"Help!" she yelled, but then it was as if a freezing fog descended and she couldn't move. Could barely breathe. Her tongue felt frozen in her mouth. Then Nathan yanked her attacker off her and she could suddenly move again.

She blinked and found herself back in her grandmother's dining room, nine sets of eyes on her.

"What? I was thinking—remembering." She told them about her rings catching.

Danny and Jas nodded. "That makes sense. We found some evidence of that, so we spent the night seeing if we could recover the jacket. Let's just say we did a search and came up with a jacket and a mask that matches the evidence and your description," Jas said.

"And a blond hair," Danny added.

Everyone turned to look at Nathan.

"The hair was on the inside of the mask, so we don't think it was Nathan's," Danny added.

"Given everything that's been happening, we asked ourselves who we know who is blond that might want to do Lila harm," Jas said.

A small gasp sounded from Chloe's end of the table and her face went pale. "Johan Fehr. You think he's here?"

The sounds of cutlery on plates and the conversation ceased. Everyone turned to Chloe.

"Johan Fehr was blond, and if there was anyone I was afraid of in this whole thing, it was him. Since I've remembered him, I've had the chance to realize that when I was attacked in my apartment, the air reeked of the same scent as Fehr. At the time I thought it was a cologne or something, but now I don't think so. As a matter of fact, thinking about it, I'm certain. Whatever made Johan Fehr so terrifying when he came into the store was also in my apartment that night." She shuddered and Jas caught her hand.

He shook his head. "I don't believe in all that psychic stuff, but I believe in Chloe, and unfortunately I think she'd right. Danny and I are quietly checking the Kelowna hotels to see if we can find where he's staying. The trouble is, all we have is a very old photo of him when he was the bad-boy son of a Berlin industrialist. It's a tabloid photo from before he took over the company. There's a good chance people won't recognize him, but we've got to try. We already checked the airport and there were a few private jets that came in this week. One of them originated in Tegel airport by way of Vancouver. Tegel's in Berlin."

"*Schwarzenacht,*" Kylee breathed. "It is him." The bright openness of Kylee's pixie face seemed to crumple in on itself. Lila felt a cold wind down her back.

"That's all well and good," Nathan said, "but we need to know more—like what the hell this is all about? Why the bracelet? Why the heck does he want it so badly, and if he wants it so badly, why hasn't he just come in here and shot the wearer and taken it?" He glanced at Lila. "Sorry, but I just don't get it. You've had women in danger all summer. What the hell is going on?"

"Motive." Jas nodded. "Understanding it would be helpful."

"Heck, yeah. Something to make a case hang together," Danny agreed. "Course, I'd also like to know what the hell the thing is."

Lila took a deep breath. "I've been thinking about that today, trying to put the pieces together after I talked to the Seattle folklorist. I think we should run through what we have."

"We've got a bracelet that comes from points unknown that's causing problems for a group of women and now it's on your wrist and you're in danger. Is there much more to know?" Nathan asked.

Lila shook her head. "We know we have a bracelet with seven doors. We know something wants it. We know for sure the bracelet was found in North Africa and held securely until it came into our hands in an estate sale. We know somehow the thing that wants it tracked it here and we know that it won't come off its wearer's wrist until she resolves things with her soul mate." She felt Nathan's presence like a magnet to her glance. She refused it.

"We know the bracelet contains silver from northern Italy, and that it was smelted in a style consistent for that region. That came from the university chemical analysis. We also have a date somewhere back at the start of the second millennium—the eleven hundreds or something," Cleopatra-haired Reggie supplied.

Nathan sat back in his chair. "You're saying this thing on Lila's wrist is something like a thousand years old?"

For a moment the room went silent as people dealt with that realization. Lila uneasily played with the bracelet links. Nathan's words made it somehow different from just thinking about the date.

"I suppose that would fit with the fairytale, wouldn't it." She scanned her friends. "An artisan—a tinsmith, a lesser man—wishes to better himself and seeks learning from someone much greater—someone evil. In the process he learns skills and rescues the woman of his dreams. But this isn't one of those stories with a happily ever after ending like we see in Disney movies.The evil pursues. That was something the folklorist pointed out. She said it wasn't a teaching tale like many fairytales. She said this one likely was presenting a historical story."

"The evil found them, too," Chloe picked up the story. "They were happy, had been happy. They lived in a villa with a courtyard, but the thing—the silversmith—came for them. The woman said she would go with him if the tinsmith was spared, but the tinsmith had other ideas. He thought he could fight the silversmith with the skills he'd learned sneaking into the silversmith's workshop. Instead he was consumed and transformed into the bracelet. At least that's what the fairytale says. Right?"

"But not before he did something to the silversmith," Reggie added. "Didn't the story say that, too? That he stole something from the master?"

Everyone turned to Victoria, who had last worn the bracelet and who had translated the story told by her childhood nanny.

"The story speaks of the tinsmith—as if he stole strength from the master while the master destroyed him. As if it was the last thing he did."

"What does that mean?" Chloe asked.

"That it took everything the master had to destroy the tinsmith?" Danny said as he laced fingers with Victoria's.

"No." Victoria shook her head. "Maybe. It is not clear, but that is not the sense I get from the story."

Swiftly she spoke in Italian to Cesare, who frowned.

"It is interesting," he said. "The story as our Nonna told it suggests that it is more than just requiring all the silversmith's strength to destroy the tinsmith. It is more as if the tinsmith actually did something to the silversmith—as if he stripped strength from the silversmith to be confined in the bracelet with him, but in this case it may be not strength, but power."

The room ticked around them for a moment, and from outside came the sound of a car traveling along Beach Avenue. The car pulled in a few doors down and Lila heard the engine idling.

"So you're saying the story could be telling us that the bracelet not only contains the tinsmith but also holds the creature's power?"

"It is possible the story means this." Cesare inclined his head.

Lila looked down at the bracelet that glimmered on her wrist. Five of the links seemed to catch the light more brightly. "Reggie, a ways back you remarked on how some of the bracelet links looked different."

Reggie frowned, then nodded. "I remember. It was as if an oily patina had been removed from two of the doors—the ones associated with each of the bracelet wearers who had found their soul mates. That was when Ally was wearing it, wasn't it? Why?"

An idea swirled in Lila's head, and she floundered trying to contain it. "What if—what if that patina was something to do with whatever it was that the tinsmith stole? What if each bracelet wearer finding their match cleared the patina off?"

"The power," Chloe said. "You're suggesting that each time we complete a match, some of the power is released." She looked around the table.

"Is that a good thing or a bad thing for us?" Cesare asked, fishing another prawn skewer from the platter. "Does that mean that we give the thing more strength when we fall in love?"

"No," Of that Lila was suddenly sure. "Exactly the opposite. It—it's like each time one of you accepted your match, the power was gone—bled into nothing!"

"Shit," Jas murmured and pushed his plate away from him. "There's our motive, Danny. One hell of a one, if it's true. If the interpretation of the story is right, and we're right in figuring that whatever is in Johan Fehr is a millennia-old monster—I can't believe I just said that. But if it is all true, then the reason it wants the bracelet is that it wants what's left of its power back."

Danny straightened from his laid-back slouch beside Victoria. "You're right. Like I said the other day, when the thing was in me last time, I had the feeling that it wasn't as strong as it was the first time. What if it's been using too much strength taking over all these people trying to get the bracelet? That would likely make it a little desperate to get the bracelet and its power back."

It made perfect sense. *The thing had pursued her for years...*

...until it found her in the end. A blast of flames...

Lila shuddered and blinked, the dining room reforming around her and the stench of flames and death receding.

"Lila? What's happening to you?" Nathan's voice, his hand on her wrist.

"Nothing. Well—maybe there's something. I keep getting these impressions—as if I'm the serving woman who hid the bracelet. Stupid, I know. It has got to be the bracelet stirring up my imagination." She shook her head, but clung to the edge of the table. What the hell was happening to her? She'd seen Chloe become unsteady under the bracelet's influence, but it darn well was not happening to her. She was no psychic, nor did she want to be one.

"You've gone pale as the proverbial ghost," he said.

"He's right, Lila," Kylee said, pushing up from her chair and coming around to her. "My goodness, you're shivering."

Nathan swung his jacket off and placed it over her shoulders, while Chloe left the room and returned offering a pashmina.

Lila waved them all off. "I'm fine. I am! I don't need all of you acting like I'm sick or something. I've got the bracelet on my arm, that's all."

Chloe raised a single brow. "Sounds suspiciously like I did."

"And me," Kylee echoed.

"And me," Victoria said.

Reggie just held up her hand and nodded. "The bracelet strikes again."

All those concerned faces and Lila really just wanted to turn and walk out of the room. Do her own thing—wasn't that how she'd always done things? Focus on practical things that she could control. That was how she'd gotten this far with the business. Sure, she had partners, but that was through good logical thinking and she *was* the businesswoman among them. She just needed to think things through.

The trouble was, it seemed so darn hard to do so these days. It was like an emotional basket case had been released inside and she didn't like it—*at all*. Chloe might have had problems, but Chloe was a far more emotional person.

She shook her head. "It's silly, really. I'm sure it's just my imagination suddenly run amuck. I mean, I'm not Chloe with her sensitivities. I don't get visions—but I might have. I think—I think I saw the ending. There was darkness and torch smoke and then a horrible blast. The woman screamed and ran—or maybe that was me. I'm not sure. Either way, it was terrifying." Just thinking about it made her shiver again. She pulled Nathan's jacket around her, thankful for its warmth. Unfortunately it released the comforting scent of musk and cedar. She felt his gaze on her like the warm caress of the hand.

No. She settled back in her chair.

"Are you sure you don't need to rest?" he asked.

"What I *need* is to figure this out with the rest of you." She felt bad for snapping, but she didn't need his help, only his jacket. "Would the rest of you quit hovering over me? I'm a big girl. I can deal with this."

She tapped her finger on the bracelet. "So we have a bracelet that might contain power but that power is leaking away every time one of us meets his or her match. That's got to make the creature pretty desperate if it's like Danny said and it's used up its power."

"And we've got a couple of people who could weaken it further if they'd just let themselves fall in love," Chloe offered looking anywhere but in Lila and Nathan's direction.

The room went quiet. Lila felt the flush run up her neck as the others stood considering.

Lila forced a chuckle. "Well, there is that, I suppose. But that still leaves another door to open." She had kept her tone light, but the others weren't reacting in the right way. They shuffled to their chairs, but kept eyeing her as if something was wrong.

Danny and Jas were in the midst of a quiet conversation. Finally Jas looked at her. "This explains a lot, Lila. Like why Johan Fehr is here in person—maybe the thing inside him is too weak to leap heads anymore, especially after its last attempt on Victoria. It also explains the attacks on you. There's only two doors left."

All eyes in the room seemed to center on her wrist. She wanted to rip the bracelet off, hide it under the table, or leave the room. Instead she took a deep breath and held it up. "So we know what it wants and why. How does that help us? How does that help us destroy it?"

"Other than it's got to be really pissed off, I've got nothing," Danny said with a grin that tried and failed to lighten the gloom on the room. "Hell, we don't even know what it is."

The room went quiet. Lila thought of Professor Orr's suggestion of the nature of their foe, but for some reason could not bring herself to tell the story. Surely the good professor had been pulling farfetched ideas from nothing. She *was* a folklorist. No normal person would ever likely come to a similar conclusion.

"I—I might have something." Victoria pushed her lush blonde hair back behind her ears. "I know it might be foolish, but after translating Nonna's story, I thought I would do a little research. Because the story talked of the palace and the desert, I thought of Arabia and so I read the Thousand and One Nights to see if the bracelet story is perhaps there."

She shook her head. "It is not, so far, but it is filled with stories of fantastical beings and amazing things."

From the front of the house came the sound of someone knocking insistently on the front glass door. Lila took it as the excuse she'd needed to escape the sympathetic glances and the scrutiny, not to mention Nathan's attention. She wavered a little as she walked the hall and trailed a hand on the wall. At the front door stood a man in a District of Peachland shirt, the smoke swirling around him. She went to the door.The lake was barely visible across the street.

"Yes?" she asked through the glass.

"From the Fire Service, Ma'am. The District's trying to get the word out to everyone." He held out a piece of paper.

She opened the door a few inches and accepted it from him. With a nod he turned, leapt off the porch, and loped out of the yard and continued down the block.

Scanning the paper, she locked the door behind her and headed back to the dining room feeling an even heavier weight on her chest. She waved the paper at them. "Fire evacuation alert. I guess we're all probably getting one in case the fire gets closer."

Nathan looked up at her. "Now, isn't that fitting? Victoria was just telling us about how reading Arabian Nights led to her reading the Koran."

His words were sharper than they needed to be and the mention of the Koran brought back Professor Orr's concerns. Lila turned to her Italian friend.

Victoria gave one of those lovely little feminine shrugs that seemed so Italian. "From everything I have read and from the description of what the creature has done, it may be that the creature is a djinn. They are described as creatures of smokeless fire. At least that is how the Koran describes them."

Lila sat down hard in her chair.

Chapter 12

A djinn? A part of Nathan listened incredulously to the conversation swirling around the wainscoted dining room. It was all too surreal—the normalcy of the scene—spent dinner plates and platters, the antique mirror on the wall, the voices and the sweet, dry taste of the very good wine—but it was juxtaposed with the subject of the conversation just as he would do in a movie to raise the tension.

A djinn—better known as a genie, but not the kind that had been presented on that 1960s sitcom. Nope. This was a far different being, more akin to tricksters and demons—at least according to Victoria's Arabian Nights readings. Kylee pulled out her cell phone and read them excerpts of the Wikipedia entry on djinn, which confirmed Victoria's description of the creatures as made of smokeless fire. How the hell was this going to help him get through to Lila to give their relationship a chance? Hell, the whole conversation, spoken in such reasonable tones, was demented!

"At least the smokeless fire thing explains the smell," Reggie said. "Dietrich had the scent and the air reeked of it when the creature escaped."

"I smelled it, too, when I was abducted." Kylee said.

"Daniel smelled of it. It was part of what told me that something was wrong." Victoria caught the red-headed policeman's hand and smiled up at him.

Damnation, this was making no sense! These seemed like perfectly normal people. Nathan finally shook his head.

"Come on. This is a joke, right? At my expense? Surely to goodness, you don't believe in crap like this."

The room went silent. Everyone looked at him as he stood. "Come on, people. I may have cut my teeth on movies like Lila's, but I know that's fantasy. Now I focus on real life and I'd like you to, as well. Lila has been attacked twice. I don't see how discussion of creatures from middle-eastern mythology is going to help her now. Wouldn't it make more sense to track down this Johan Fehr and deal with him?"

"The only way we'll be able to deal with the man is to understand what's inside him." Lila said quietly. Still white-faced, her expression was one of patience and... pity? For him?

He shook his head. "He's a man, Lila. There's no such thing as djinn or genies or whatever you want to call them. Men can deal with other men." He scanned the room's occupants, all the hope he'd had when he came here this evening evaporated in the presence of the conviction in all the faces. He looked back to Lila, and the same belief lay there. Just like Kristienne and her belief in the wack-job Hollywood soothsayers who had told her she was going to be a star.

"You really believe this crap, don't you? What the heck happened to you, Lila? You were such a straight shooter—a clear thinker, even at seventeen."

Her hazel eyes turned cool green as she considered him. Then she sighed. "Like I said. Things change, Nathan. I've learned that life isn't like in the movies. It's not black and white with clearly marked heroes and villains, it's all the spectrum of grays in between. That has to leave room for strange possibilities like this. I like to think we've all come to similar conclusions." She nodded at the table and then down at her hands. "But I totally respect your choice not to believe."

He willed her to look at him, to at least make it seem like this—and he—were important to her, but she just stayed as she was, as if her future really was written in the palms of her hands.

"Damn it, Lila, I came here looking for you to give us the chance we never took all those years ago. If this—this fairy tale is more important than us, then it's really not worth my while to stick around." He nodded to the others—all those faces embarrassed at the scene he'd just performed. "Thank you for dinner. It was a pleasure meeting you all. Lila, it was good seeing you again, but I think this is where I take my leave."

He turned on his heel and left, heard murmurs behind him as he headed for the kitchen door. What a boondoggle this had been, for all he'd come with such hope. These people—they weren't concerned about Lila, they were concerned about literal smoke!

He shoved into the kitchen and headed for the door. The smoke swirled beyond the windows and in the dusk he could barely see the carport at the rear of the yard. Even the wicker lawn furniture were indistinct—like his future.

Shit.

"Nathan?"

He spun around. Lila stood at the hallway entrance, her face pale, her eyes huge.

"I know you want to go and I know you don't believe, but these are good people doing their best in an impossibly strange situation."

"So... what? You want me to stay? Isn't that a bit inconsistent with the woman who just wanted me to go away?" It hurt to say it. He didn't want it to be true, but it was, and wasn't inconsistency the thing he'd hated the most about all of his girlfriends?

Head bowed, Lila nodded. "You're right, of course. It never could have worked between us. Too much or too little history and not enough recent contact. Too different lifestyles to ever be able to make a go of it."

She crossed the room to him and, more swiftly then he'd expected, leaned up to place a soft kiss on his cheek. Her scent of roses filled his senses, and just as swiftly was gone as she stepped to the door and opened it for him. Smoke pillowed into the room.

"Thank you for coming, Nathan. It was—nice to see you again." She lifted her chin to him as if daring him to leave. There was nothing left to do but either take her in his arms and start again or go.

His heart urged one response, but this time he was going to follow his head. His heart had betrayed him with bad choices before. This time would be different.

With a nod, he stepped past her into the smoke.

§

The heavy smoke billowed into the kitchen and gathered around Lila's feet. The stench of burned wood and ashes filled her nose as she watched Nathan turn the corner to the side of the house.

He was tall and strong and ever since she had known him had provided a template for everything she had ever looked for in a man. He had been that when she first knew him and ever since. She realized that now. And here she was letting him go again, except this time it was him walking away. For good.

A shiver at the cooler outdoor air made her pull the jacket closer around her throat. The jacket. Nathan's.

"Damn." Or maybe it was meant to be. Suddenly she desperately wanted to see him again.

She ran out the back door after him. Around the house and to the front yard. No sign of Nathan. He'd been in more of a hurry to leave than she'd thought.

At the front gate she paused and looked left and right. Where was he parked?

"Nathan?" She called. "Nathan, you forgot your jacket."

Still nothing, or was that a dark figure moving toward her through the smoke along the lake promenade? She stepped through the gate to the sidewalk.

"Nathan, thank God. I don't want you to go."

Did the dark figure increase its stride toward her? Down the street a car started and pulled out from the curb and she was suddenly certain that Nathan was driving. The dark figure was in a lope and had come even with her. It leapt through the ornamental grasses into the street toward her.

If the car contained Nathan, then who was this? The reek of smoke and burning filled her nose and suddenly she was sure that she did *not* want whoever this was to reach her. She turned tail and ran, leaving the gate swaying open behind her as she dashed down the side of the house.

Was that feet thumping on the grass behind her? She bumped into a patio chair scraping it over the flagstones. She almost tripped over the chaise before scrambling through the still open kitchen door. Slamming it behind her she stabbed the security alarm on and stood there shaking.

Outside the dusk had eaten the light from the yard, except where the kitchen window light revealed the roiling smoke. It parted for an instant to reveal a black-clad figure. Male. Darkness concealed his face.

Chapter 13

The smoke closed around the figure and when the ash thinned again the figure was gone. Lila stood frozen at the kitchen window. She might not have seen his face, but he'd been looking at her. Of that she was certain. And he was out there, still. Not Nathan. Nathan was gone—for good this time. But this man was out there waiting for the opportunity to get her and she'd nearly given him one. If she'd run down the street to try to catch Nathan's car, whoever it was would have caught her.

And then what would have happened?

Her shivers increased and she was colder than she'd been all evening, her skin gooseflesh, her muscles like ice.

"Nathan's gone then, is he?" Chloe came up beside her and slung an arm around her shoulders.

Lila nodded, uncertain whether she could speak.

"I'm sorry this whole thing is so weird. I really thought Nathan was the kind to stick around. He really seemed to like you."

Another nod, and would Chloe please stop talking about Nathan, because it brought up emotions that she'd thought she'd left behind when she was seventeen and running for her life, or at least the life of her self-respect, and right now she really needed to come to grips with what had just happened.

She swallowed. "I—I think that—that Johan Fehr is here."

"What?" Chloe grabbed her shoulders and turned Lila as if she were a child.

Damn it, her own voice sounded too timid and halting, not like the confident woman she was. She sucked in a breath and straightened her shoulders to pull back from Chloe.

"I went after Nathan but the smoke's so bad I couldn't see him." She told what had happened. "And then the smoke in the yard parted and I—I thought I saw something. A man clad in black, but I couldn't see his face." Another cold tremor ran up her back, flooding her body, and she hugged herself against the horrible chill. "I put the alarm on," she said weakly and felt like a fool. A lot of good that would do.

Chloe leaned over the counter to peer out the window. Then she pulled back. "Sweetie, you did fine. You got back in the house where people are here to protect you. You're safe. Now come on. Let's get you back to the dining room and let them know what's happened. We've been talking about what we know about djinn and how to kill them. Kylee's got her tablet out looking at websites."

Arm linked with Chloe for warmth, or maybe support, Lila returned to the dining room. The others must have read her face, or maybe Chloe's, but Jas and Brett were instantly on their feet.

"What's happened?"

"Where's Nathan?"

"Nathan's gone. Apparently Lila couldn't catch him. He must have wanted away from us pretty darned badly," Chloe explained. "But something happened to Lila."

Jas caught Lila's hands, not warm enough against her cold. Someone living, but not the one she wanted.

"Tell us," he said as he urged her into her chair and crouched before her.

She did. Feeling stupid for not stopping Nathan before he left and stupider still for going after him. "I don't think I really believed he was after me until this moment. I thought it might be chance. Coincidence." She rubbed her brow, a headache settling in behind her eyes. Everything smelled like smoke, maybe because she'd allowed the smoke to permeate the house, or maybe because it had gotten into her nose. Her throat still burned from it. She coughed.

Kylee handed her a glass of water to sip and the coughing passed. She looked up at the others—all those concerned, pitying faces, and she didn't like it.

"I'm okay. It was just a surprise. If I thought I was going to coast through wearing the bracelet, apparently I was wrong. I'm not doing do any better with the bracelet than any of you." She chewed her lip. "I suppose letting Nathan go was one of the stupid decisions the bracelet influences?"

"It *was* pretty stupid," Danny allowed. "He seemed like a pretty stand-up guy for someone from Hollywood. I would have thought he'd have been a little more open-minded."

"He seemed pretty crazy about you, Lila. From the little I've seen, he was sticking by you," Brett offered.

"I—I think he would have stayed if I'd asked him to. But I missed my chance." Lila squeezed her eyes shut against a sudden surge of pain next to her heart. She grabbed the arms of her chair and hung on because she wasn't going to let this get to her. There were other things to worry about.

She opened her eyes to the concerned faces and managed a smile that felt more than a little crooked. "I guess getting chased really spooked me. But maybe it was just a jogger and it could have been my imagination that I saw someone in the yard. I *had* just thought I'd been chased. Why would he just stand there?"

"Lila, listen to yourself." Chloe had her arms crossed over her chest like a schoolmarm. "You're doing it again—trying to rationalize away something that is a real danger."

The others were nodding, all except Kylee.

"Can't you see she's trying? Lila's trying to protect herself because this whole thing has her scared to death. Isn't that right, Lila? I know I was," Kylee said, sympathy in her wide blue eyes.

Lila had never been one to want sympathy, but Kylee's understanding helped a little. "I guess I am scared. More than I want to admit."

"So you guys just give her the benefit of the doubt. She was there for all of us. Heck, she even went out in the woods for Victoria, and we all know Lila is not a woodsy sort of girl." Kylee pushed past Jas and leaned down for one ferocious hug. "I'm with you, Lila. Anything I can do, I will."

Lila hugged her petite friend back and felt some of the frozen fear release from her heart. It left behind an ache and she was pretty sure she knew the cause. Well, there was no recourse with Nathan, though she might try calling him tomorrow. Maybe. All the feelings in the world for the guy still weren't going to deal with the fact that their belief systems and lifestyles weren't compatible.

"All right. Enough, everyone. You were in the middle of a conversation about how to destroy a djinn. Anyone have any information about how I might protect myself from one?" She turned back to the table.

§

It was a joke—the whole damn debacle—and the worst part was, the joke was on him. Lila Weber had turned just as flaky as his prior Hollywood women. So maybe it wasn't Hollywood that did it. Maybe it was something written in all women's DNA. And yet his mother hadn't been like that, had she?

Nathan peered through the windshield of his rental Mercedes, the smoke and the darkness making it hard to see. The headlights were dim tunnels in the murk, the headlights of cars swimming like faded yellow lights in a dark sea. It was a wonder the vehicle engines continued to work with all the ash flying around in the air. Not his problem. Not anymore. When he got back to the hotel, he was going to book a flight right the hell out of here. He'd wasted enough time as it was. Time to find a new project, get back to work, and put this debacle behind him.

It would have been better if he'd never come. Just held onto the memories of what Lila Weber had been and not tried to confront the woman she'd become. Strong. Still beautiful—actually more so because now she had the maturity of years and the grace. The fine lines caused by smiling just added character to her face.

Too bad the inside wasn't just as pretty.

He swore as a car darted out from a side road onto the highway and he had to slam on the brakes. Ahead the road swooped down toward the lake and Kelowna. The lights of the city gave the roiling smoke an eerie yellow glow from across the lake so it looked like the city boiled.

The road rose into the arch of the floating bridge across the lake, a slender bracelet of light across darkness. He shook his head. Damn bracelets. Bracelets on the brain—that's what Lila's crew of friends had. Well, he wasn't having anymore of their idiocy. They might take him for a fool, but he was *not* the kind of person who believed in all the mumbo-jumbo and conspiracy theories that played on late-night radio.

Just off the bridge, he turned along the waterfront and pulled into the parking lot of his hotel. He left the car with the valet, held his breath in the smoke, and pushed through the doors to the lobby. It was a cool space with high ceilings and thankfully, very little smoke. It had marble floors with an arcade of stores, a casino, and a fountain of three leaping black dolphins—not that there were dolphins in Lake Okanagan, but the tinkling water helped smooth out the echo of voices and accompanied the soft tunes of the grand piano being played in the corner. The air smelled of damp soil from the potted palms that nodded in the air conditioning.

Nathan strode to the registration counter and waited for a clerk. Another man joined him and nodded in his direction as fellow travelers will.

"May I help you, sir?" asked the lovely young blonde with the equivalent of a California tan. She looked up from her computer.

"I'm Nathan Moon in suite 501. Could you please do up my bill. I plan to check out tomorrow. Oh, and could you please have the concierge book me a flight to Vancouver for tomorrow?"

The woman looked up from typing efficiently into her terminal. "Sir, there may be a problem. The smoke had closed the airport. If you must travel tomorrow, you will have to make other transportation arrangements."

Nathan closed his eyes against the frustration. It was like this whole trip was a boondoggle right from the beginning. He never should have come here and he was pretty damned sure he wouldn't ever return—regardless of the area's beauty. Certainly not as long as his anger at Lila made his stomach churn.

"So what other transportation options are there?"

The woman looked him up and down. "Greyhound Bus. Or car rental. You could drive to Kamloops and catch a flight there, or chance that the Coquihalla Highway is open and head straight to Vancouver."

He sighed. "All right. I'll think it over. Better not cancel me out of the hotel just yet."

He found a smile for the clerk and headed for his room, but somewhere along the way must have changed his mind, for he found himself in the bar, alone at a table with three fingers of scotch, neat, and a moody glare at his reflection in the night darkened window glass. The scotch burned going down, exactly as he wanted. Outside the night seemed to seethe as the smoke swirled around lights on the resort grounds and the marina beyond. A bank of abandoned tables sat barely visible like a shoal around the breadth of the bar patio.

"It is problematic, yes?"

Nathan looked up from his moody regard of the window. In the reflection, the stranger from the registration desk stood beside him. Nathan shifted in his chair. "Pardon me?"

"The smoke. It is a problem. I had thought to leave myself, but it is not to be."

The man was likely in his early forties, but fit, with blond Teutonic good looks belied by a pair of ice-pale eyes. The kind of man who always looked like he was in charge, or who took charge when he could. Nathan wasn't sure he liked him.

The man smiled down at Nathan. "Sorry. I disturb your reverie." He half-bowed and went to turn away.

"Hold on. You didn't disturb me from anything worth worrying about. I was just sitting here feeling sorry for myself. Would you care to join me in a drink?" At least conversation would get his mind off things. It wasn't like him to feel so—so twisted up inside.

"That is very kind." The man sank into the leather chair across from Nathan's and motioned the waitress over, then ordered a scotch as well. When the waitress retreated, he eyed Nathan.

"If you do not mind me saying, you do not strike me as a man accustomed to feeling sorry for himself."

Nathan shook his head. "I don't usually. What's done is done, is my usual motto." But he just hadn't been able to let Lila go, had he? She'd been like a worm in his brain for too many years. Surely to God he could dig the worm out now.

"By the look in your eyes, Mr. Moon, I would guess it is a woman who causes you pain at the moment."

What the hell? The use of his name brought Nathan fully back to himself. "I'm sorry. Do I know you? Because I sure as hell don't remember ever being introduced."

The stranger just looked at him, his pale gaze as beguiling and treacherous as spring ice.

Head spinning, Nathan heaved a deep breath. His vision blurred for a second and he realized that he had been rude. "My apologies. It's been a rough day. You seem to have me at a disadvantage. You are...?"

The waitress brought the stranger his drink and he knocked it back and stood. "The name is Johan Fehr, Mr. Moon, but there is no need for you to remember that. Interesting that you plan to leave Lila Weber's side even though it kills your heart, but that is no matter. Now I thank you for your company and bid you good night." The man waved a hand in Nathan's direction...

§

"Are you done here, sir? We'll be closing in a few minutes."

The smoke roiled outside the bar window, but the voice hauled Nathan back from wherever he'd been mentally wandering. He came to himself, blinking at the waitress's words and thinking of all the things he needed to do that would put Lila behind him.

The trim, young, red-headed waitress with the alabaster skin was motioning to his almost empty glass.

Done? He felt—groggy—as if he'd run headfirst into a wall or something.

"What time is it?" he asked at the same time as he checked his watch. Eleven fifty-five? What the hell, it had been around eight p.m. when he'd sat down. Where had the time gone?

Floundering to remember his evening, he nodded. "I'm done. Yes. Wait." He fished in his pocket. "Let me pay you for my drink."

The waitress shook her head, her red hair bouncing against her shoulders. "The other gentleman took care of it a while back, sir. You're good." She gave him a professional smile primed with pink lipstick, scooped up his glass, and left.

Nathan watched the swing of her hips as she walked away and then went to stand. Damn, both his legs were asleep. So were his arms. In fact, his whole body felt like it had been pressed between the leaves of a book like a leaf—desiccated and depleted. He staggered up and, almost as if he was drunk, wove his way across the bar to the door. It took him a moment to spot the bank of elevators but he made his way there, climbed inside and, still fighting the feeling of disorientation, stabbed the button for his suite on the top floor.

Chapter 14

After an uneasy sleep, with nightmares of something pursuing her across miles of stone and sand desert, and dark hours spent mentally listing everything she should take if the fire evacuation order came, Lila rose earlier than normal, her eyes gritty and her mouth tasting of iron. At five in the morning, her room was in total darkness when throughout the summer light had always leaked in around the blinds. Now the days were shortening and the smoke had eaten the early morning light. The white duvet with blue flowers seemed to weigh a ton on her body. She threw it off and stood, pulled her apricot silk robe around her, and padded silently downstairs hoping not to disturb Chloe and Jas, who had stayed the night in her guestroom. Jas and Danny had insisted that someone needed to be with her at all times.

Quietly thankful for her friends and determined not to wake them, she went into the kitchen, the cool tile floor and metal surfaces a welcome relief from the overwhelming soft warmth of her bedroom. Her gaze strayed to the bank of windows above the counter. Darkness and smoke effectively masked all view of the yard.

Did someone stand there, watching her?

No. She was not going to let herself be spooked. She had things to do and this was her house. She busied herself with her little espresso maker and dug in the freezer for a package of crumpets. The white spongy bread rounds had always beena special treat that she and her grandmother had enjoyed on occasions when Lila had required cheering up. Grandma would toast them up and then, with butter and fresh raspberry jam melting through the chewy rounds, they'd sit in the nook and drink tea and talk out the problem.

"I could use your help now, Gran." She could. She felt small and vulnerable and, at the moment, a tad stifled by her friends, not to mention the cushioning billows of smoke that pushed at her windows.

The crumpets toasted, buttered,and with homemade jam, and the espresso straight out of the pot because she needed the jolt this morning, she slipped into the chair at the end of the nook and pulled a pen and paper to her.

They might have bandied about wild theories of how to deal with the creature after the bracelet, but she had more mundane things to worry about.

First off was the evacuation alert. Not an order, the alert put her and presumably the entire town on notice that the fire was coming their way and there was a chance that it might not be stopped. It gave people notice to be ready to leave quickly if the evacuation order came. She needed to put all her midnight thoughts down on paper. She would take the jewelry, of course— the inventory that, if all else was lost, could still be sold through the website until they could rebuild. So they were going to have to set a case next to the safe so that if the order came she could just tear out the displays and the contents of the safe and be gone.

She thoughtfully bit into the succulent crumpet oozing with sweet, melted butter and jam.

But beyond the jewelry, what would she save? She picked up the silly little tangerine fish salt and pepper shakers, their ceramic cool in her hands. She'd bought the frivolous little things in a small curio shop in the backstreets of St. Martin on a whirlwind cruise holiday that she and Chloe had taken. They were the perfect memento of the venture—small, inexpensive, and best of all, functional. But not worthy of a precious spot in the box she felt she had to pack. She set them back on the table, took another bite of crumpet, and stood. She left the kitchen for the hallway.

Photos. Those were the things that she'd decided couldn't be replaced. She really should have all of the old family photos digitized, but in this, just like Reggie with her jewelry files, she'd been remiss. Thankfully Reggie's situation had died down. The lawsuit from the jewelry firm had seemingly evaporated when Cesare challenged them to produce proof of theft. When Erminio Biondi, the fashion designer, had tried to reopen the suit against Reggie, Victoria's sworn affidavit of what she had found at Biondi's office had found its way into the media and caused a furor in the Milanese fashion industry. Thankfully for Reggie, it had worked in her favor. The newspapers had carried photos of Reggie's jewelry and the story of the attempted theft. The result had been a series of surreptitious phone calls from other designers enquiring about Reggie's interest in designing for them. Things were looking up.

Lila plucked the most precious photos off the wall and carried them back to the kitchen and her coffee. Yes, these had to be taken. Actually, all of the pictures in the hallway did. And her photo albums. Those were precious, too.

Including the one from Hollywood?

She squeezed her eyes shut against a sudden surge of tears. Damn it, she'd been doing so well not-thinking about the one person who kept reappearing in her mind. He'd been there in her dreams. He'd been with her, running. Always running away from the demon, the bracelet safely hidden but carried with them.

Darn it, stupid tears. Nathan wouldn't work on so many levels. He was from Hollywood. There was no way he'd stay here. And he didn't believe in the bracelet, which in some ways was just as well, because if he left, it meant that nothing could happen to him.

That was right. That was what she had to hold to. She'd know Nathan was okay if he left Kelowna. Then she could do what she'd always done—remember their time together in Hollywood with the little extra pain of what had happened between them here. She could live with that. She could, and she didn't have to worry about packing it up for evacuation.

She took a long sip of her coffee. Her laptop. Her personal jewelry collection. Her clothes. She grimaced. She could fill her car with them alone, so some of them would have to be left behind. Some of her antiques—a mirror, a vase or two. Grandma's silver brush and comb set. The Alice in Wonderland tea set that had been far too expensive, but that she hadn't been able to pass up because of its exquisite warped shape. She'd love to save the dining and living room furniture that had been her grandparent's. And there were the copper pots on the front porch that her grandmother had spent a fortune on.

There was no way that all of this was going to fit in her car.

A soft tread in the hall said that Chloe was up. She pushed into the kitchen wrapped in Lila's plush winter robe, because neither she nor Jas had gone home last night for clothes. Her long hair was unbraided and fell in a thick, rippled waterfall down to her hips.

"Hey. You're up awful early," Chloe said. "I thought I heard someone stirring."

Lila rubbed the telltale tear tracks from her cheeks. "I could say the same right back to you. What are you doing up when you've got a perfectly lovely man in your bed to cuddle up with?"

Chloe sighed. "Would you believe I'm getting psychic messages from Clyde that he'd dying from hunger?" Clyde being the huge, blue-point Siamese cat who shared her apartment down the lake. "I figure I better get a move on. That cat loves me to pieces and I love him right back, but if his needs aren't met, he can be a total brat. On days when he doesn't get enough attention, I've found him on his side using all four feet to push some of my big crystals off their shelves. Aside from the damage it can do to the crystals, do you know what the crystal points can do to hardwood floors?" She looked around the kitchen. "I smelled espresso. Please tell me there's more."

Lila shoved out of her chair. "There might be dregs in the pot, but let me make you some fresh." She got busy filling the base of the little pot with water and tamped fresh grounds into the portafilter and then screwed the top on before putting the whole contraption on the gas burner. Behind her Chloe shuffled to the table and slid into the nook. She studied Lila's list.

"Hard choice to make, isn't it? I packed up boxes right after I saw the smoke arrived. Better safe than sorry." Chloe sighed. "You look like you've had a tough night."

Lila stood over the coffee pot as it burbled. "I hardly slept. Bad dreams and worrying about the fire."

"Not surprising, I suppose."

The coffee pot finished its work and Lila poured the rich dark brew into an espresso cup and brought it to Chloe. "There you go."

Chloe sipped and a blissful smile filled her face. From upstairs came the sound of movement and then the faint sound of water running.

"Jas's in the shower." Looking up at the ceiling, she smiled. "You know, it's surprising, but I like having a man around far more than I ever imagined. I'd always thought I was going to be on my own because no one was going to get past my history. No one would ever forgive me, because I couldn't forgive myself. I didn't think I deserved someone. I've come to realize that we all do."

Chloe's gaze slipped down to Lila's wrist, where Lila's fingers worried at the small door with the ornate-scrolled hinges.

Lila stopped herself. "Chloe, if you've got something to say, why don't you just come out and say it. We've been friends too long."

"All right. What are you going to do about Nathan? You went after him last night because you realized that you'd made a mistake. What are you going to do about it in the light of day?" She nodded at the murky yellow light coming through the smoke.

There it was: the question. Trust Chloe to ask it. Of course, if it hadn't been Chloe, Kylee or Reggie would have. Her friends were like that and even Victoria had a keen fashion-designer's eye for spotting things that weren't quite right and the bluntness to face things head on.

Lila sighed and fingered the ceramic handle of her espresso cup. "Well, that's the thing, isn't it? I'm not sure. A night of no sleep leaves a lot of time for thinking. There's no question that we feel something for each other, but I can't get over the sense that 'feelings' aren't enough to make anything work between us. It's all about the logistics." It came out as almost a cry and the stupid, idiot emotions tangled in her chest somehow infected her eyes. Tears pooled and then fell.

"Damn it!" She palmed them away until Chloe caught her hands and pulled her into a hug.

"For a woman as wise as you, you sure want to focus on the wrong stuff."

It was true. She had no time for all this emotional stuff. She had a business to run and a second partnership beginning, not to mention some creature—some djinn—trying to kill her. Her life was a mess, and the last thing she needed was to become an emotional wreck like some of her friends had been when they wore the bracelet.

"You're right, of course." She pulled loose from Chloe and stood up from the table. "Victoria's store opens at the end of the week. We've got permits from the town to hold a garden party on the sidewalk. In this murk that's impossible. I've got to come up with an alternate plan—that's if the entire town doesn't go up in flames and I don't get killed by a djinn."

Chloe looked her in the eye. "That's not what I meant and you know it."

Lila had to look away. "Well, that's where I'm going to focus my attention. There's too much going on. I have to pick something and focus there."

She pushed past Chloe to place her cup in the sink and then headed for the hall and the stairs.

"You know, sometimes, for a very smart woman, you can be a bigger fool than all of us," Chloe said softly.

Lila set her jaw and kept marching.

§

Nathan woke face-planted on the glossy amber-colored bedspread of his hotel room bed, strange yellow light streaming through the broad uncovered window. He winced his eyes open and groaned at the intrusion. Rolled over on his back and wondered what truck had run over him. His mouth tasted like the garbage from three film set catering trucks. His head felt like it had been scoured out as well as any studio set after the end of a shoot.

What the hell was wrong with him?

His arm across his eyes, he fought for the memory of just what had happened, for something had. Of that he was certain. He'd made a point of greeting each day of his life like an adventure, so why did he have the overwhelming sense of impending doom?

Because he had failed with Lila? Well, not so much failed as walked away as he would from a bad script or a bad investment.

Though he might have cut his film-making teeth on fantasies like Lila's, he'd never been drawn to fantastical beliefs or the occult. Clearly Lila and her friends were. Even the police officers, which on the face of it seemed strange, but then there were police who believed they'd seen UFOs, so why not believe in possession by a demon. *Pardon me, a djinn.* A damned genie, of all things.

He rolled to the side of the bed and sat up. He still wore the clothes he'd worn to dinner last night. The thought of how he'd stormed out left his stomach twisting. The drive through the soupy air hadn't helped any. He remembered going into the bar for a drink. Remembered the waitress saying that someone had taken care of his bill, but he'd be damned if he could remember drinking with someone.

It was like a shadow passed over the window and he shivered. There was something—a thought that hid from him like a child quivering in a corner. Now what was up with that?

He remembered a documentary he'd done on human trafficking and the defiled, untrusting looks on some of the kids' faces. That was how his brain felt: muzzy and used up and like it would never be clean again. As if something unclean had been slithering through his brain, checking out all his most sacred places.

Yes. That was how he felt. It made no sense, but it captured what he was feeling.

"Last time you get into the scotch when you're feeling sorry for yourself. Next thing you know, you'll be believing Lila and her friends."

Stripping off his clothes, he staggered into the shower and spent five minutes in steam and pounding hot water. It helped. When he rubbed the steam off the mirror, he almost recognized himself. A quick shave, a comb through his hair, and he padded out to the bedroom to dig through his clothes. A pair of tan chinos, a golf shirt the color of tropical waters, and a cream sweater because he still felt chilled to the bone. Then he went out in search of breakfast more out of habit than because he was hungry.

The hotel restaurant was a typical hotel place, though the décor was more upscale, with white tablecloths, wicker and cloth furniture, and what could have been a gorgeous view of the marina and lake. Unfortunately, through the yellow murk he could barely see the sailboat masts and the lake was invisible. He settled at a table, glanced at the menu they gave him, and his stomach did a slow, heaving roll.

He ordered a coffee—black—and dry whole wheat toast and sat there considering his plans. Being trapped in the interior of British Columbia wasn't exactly what he wanted to be doing with his time. Backwater, that's what it was. The City of Kelowna and environs not much more than a string of strip malls and parking lots that stretched from the airport to the lake, across the bridge, and right down the lake. Peachland might still have its charm, but it was clearly next on the hit list for development from what he'd seen.

It was a shame, really. The little town had its own special charm and the fact that Lila and her friends lived there didn't hurt either.

"Damn it, Lila, why'd you have to go and get yourself mixed up with a bunch of craziness?" He rubbed at the throb in his temples.

His toast arrived and he spread it with jam, took a bite and chewed. The toast was almost tasteless, the strawberry jam tooth-achingly sweet. He shoved the plate away and nursed his coffee, watching a family of husband and wife and small blond boy in the corner. The little guy was fussing, but mom and dad made funny faces and the little guy squealed in delight.

Once upon a time, he'd envisioned himself with a son. Teaching him baseball or hockey or to swim. Going on adventures together and watching him grow. There's always been a beautiful auburn-haired woman in those dreams, too.

Damn it, it was too early in the day to be maudlin and that wasn't his way. Make a decision and move on—that was how he did things. Hell, if he dwelt on regrets in his business, he'd never move forward. You made a decision and it worked out or not. Life in the movie business was too fast and too cutthroat to second-guess yourself all the time.

But this was Lila he was talking about. Walking away from her. She'd been part of him for almost all his adult life, and most of that had been a sense of regret. Wasn't that why he'd come here? Because he *did* live his life moving forward and yet he was haunted by a woman from his past?

Shit. He was hopeless.

Around him the tables had filled up with other hotel denizens— the honeymooning couple, the businessmen, the family that had perhaps delayed their holiday until school started to catch lower hotel rates, the seniors drawn to the hotel casino.

A stirring of air at the restaurant entrance made him look in that direction as a man entered. It was as if the world parted around him, people and furniture pushed away as if by a force field around him. Wait staff seemed sucked back into the kitchen. The young couple with the toddler protectively scooped the youngster out of his high chair. The honeymoon couple seemed to wilt where they sat, the businessmen's animated conversation went flat, the family hurriedly finished their meals and left. It was the human equivalent of what fish did when there was a shark in their midst. The air, already tainted with the smoke from outside, suddenly took on the scent of scorched earth.

The man was tall and blond, with that Teutonic jutting brow and square jaw that could have got him a cover on a *GQ* magazine when he was younger. His hair was cut short over the ears, but had just enough forelock to be charming to women. Broad shoulders, slim hips, and a gray power suit completed the image. The damndest thing was, Nathan was sure he'd seen him before.

The man seated himself next to the window where the yellow light silhouetted him, making his features harder to read. The man accepted the menu from the hostess and she almost ran from his table. He opened the menu on the table and then appeared to scan the room. Nathan dropped his gaze, but it was like a searchlight cutting through fog so he could positively hear the ripple through the conversation as the man's consideration touched on each table group. It was as if all the air went out of the room when the man's gaze found him. When the sensation ended, Nathan found he was holding his breath.

Holy crap. What was that? And who the hell was blondie?

Blond. And big. Big enough Nathan wouldn't want to face him in fight.

A shiver ran up Nathan's back. Stranger still. He didn't think he'd ever had such a visceral reaction to someone before, and judging how people avoided the tables around the blond man even though they had some of the best views even with the smoke—well, that just piqued Nathan's curiosity even though the man's presence actually repelled him.

He motioned the waitress over on the pretext of having his coffee refilled. "Who is that man by the window? I think I might know him," he asked holding the cup up for her.

The girl's hand shook and a few drops of scalding coffee splattered Nathan's hand. Her friendly gaze flash froze. She shook her head. "Don't know, sir. A hotel patron, I think. Sorry about the coffee. Let me get a cloth."

She was gone in an instant and it was another waitress who brought him a fresh napkin, but no more willingness to talk.

Nathan sipped his coffee, the swell of headache momentarily forgotten. There was something about the man—something that should mean something. He just couldn't put his finger on it.

On a whim, he pulled out his cell phone and made a show of checking his messages. Then he switched to camera mode, zoomed in and took a shot of the blond man. Not a great one, but it was something and he had no idea why it was important. It was, though.

He signed the bill for his meal, added a generous tip, and left the dining room. Stepping beyond the room, it was like a weight was raised off his chest and he realized the entire time in the restaurant it had been as if he was running a race. He'd almost been panting. He'd felt like a prisoner.

Stupid and yet it wasn't. There was definitely something about the guy.

He checked with the concierge again—still no commercial flights getting in or out of Kelowna airport. Maybe he should take it as sign that he wasn't supposed to give up on Lila just yet.

The little flutter of excitement in his belly said maybe he was happy with that.

"Fuck me," he swore under his breath. He'd already made up his mind that she was not the woman for him. He was not going to surround himself with people who believed in demons and genies! That was all there was to it.

But the way his hand tightened on his phone, he knew he was going to call her and suddenly he needed to badly. He headed for the bank of elevators and stabbed the button. The elevator dinged and the door slid open, empty. Nathan stepped in and hit the top floor button.

"Hold the elevator," a deep voice called and Nathan turned in time to see the blond man step into the elevator with him. Their gazes met for an instant and suddenly Nathan remembered Jas Stone and Danny talking about blond hairs recovered from a black ski mask.

Then all Nathan Moon's thoughts went away.

Chapter 15

The call came just as Lila finished putting the last of her must-have keepsakes in boxes in the kitchen. It wouldn't take long to get them into her car if the evacuation order came and the jewelry could be scooped into cases fairly quickly. She just wished that contingency plans for Victoria's *The Next Thing* grand opening were as easy. So far the local seniors' hall was fully booked during that time and the community center had programs scheduled. She just couldn't see the mayor providing an opening speech when the air was so thick the local media couldn't even get a reasonable photograph. For that matter, neither could Victoria, and that was something they'd hoped to have for their website. They could postpone the event, but all their media packages had gone out and a rescheduled day was likely to get a lower media response. It was a choice she and Victoria were going to have to make.

The buzz of the house phone brought her upright from where she adjusted some photos in the box to protect the glass. The yellow-and-white kitchen didn't look so bright today with the overhead lights off. The light through the window was a weird yellow-gray. The smoke had been around long enough that the air inside the locked-up-tight house smelled stale and yet still carried a tang of smoke that caught at the back of her throat.

"Hello?" She caught the phone off the counter and adjusted the blue-grey boat-necked top that she wore over same-color loose trousers. A single, long, silver chain of large hammered links hung on her chest.

There was silence a minute and then, "Lila, hi."

Nathan's voice sounded gruff and brittle, as if he wasn't quite sure what to say.

"Nathan." Funny. She wasn't either. "I thought you'd be gone from Kelowna by now." She thought she heard people in the background. "Or is this just a last call before your flight?"

Darn it, why did her heart feel squeezed tight and her chest blocked for air?

"No. No flight. The airport is closed. The smoke."

Terse, terse, terse, as if he could barely stand to speak to her. Understandable after what had happened, she supposed. The story of the bracelet wasn't something she would have easily believed, either, if she hadn't lived it.

"Listen, I'm sorry things happened like they did last night. I—I actually tried going after you, because you left your jacket. I couldn't find you in the smoke."

"Then perhaps it is good that I phoned. Lila, I wish to speak with you about something."

She settled into the kitchen nook. "I've got time now."

"No. What I have to say must be said in person. I must show you something."

Puzzled, she looked at the phone. He was speaking so formally it put a barrier between them.

"You can come here. I'll be here all day unless the evacuation order comes."

There was a pause on the phone. "I think not. After last night, I do not want to be around your friends. I do not think they appreciate that I put you through pain."

"Oh, Nathan, is that what this is all about? You sound so—well, worried. They're all fine with you. They understand just how strange this all must sound. You're welcome here—by all of us." She had to smile. That was more like Nathan. He cared what others thought. But then maybe he didn't like the way all of her friends stood together. Maybe he felt bullied. "I could meet you at the bakery café? Would that do? I have to be down at Victoria's store anyway and you and I could go for coffee."

There was a pause as if he considered. "That will do."

"Say three thirty?" she asked. "I should be able to get what needs doing done by then."

"I will see you then." The phone went dead in her hand and a shiver ran down her back. His voice had sounded so leaden, as if all their emotional connections had been cut. She was going to have to work very hard if she was going to rebuild their friendship.

The vise around her heart squeezed a little tighter. It really was over, and though she'd found all manner of reasons to rationalize that a relationship with Nathan could never work, it still broke her heart a little.

She scrubbed at her eyes. Well, maybe more than a little.

But the best cure for feeling blue was putting your effort into something worth doing. That was her grandmother's lesson, one that her mother had espoused as well. She stood. It was still too early to head to Victoria's; they'd arranged to meet at noon and it was barely eleven. At the front of the house, the store was quiet. Kylee had stayed home to work on the website and on-line marketing, leaving Chloe in the store alone. She'd call if she needed Lila.

She shoved her curls behind her ears and the hammered loops of earrings she wore. She could tidy up her office after the explosion of her files that had been necessary to contact Reggie's customers when the lawsuit against Reggie had started. She'd never really had a chance to put things back together. She could use the morning to get started...

The thought left her so exhausted that thoughts of her bed filled her head. To curl up. To pull the covers up over her head. That would be good.

Yeah, and then where would you be? A mess of emotions over something you can't undo.

But maybe she could. Maybe—if it was meant to be—this afternoon with Nathan she could set things right again. Maybe there was still a spark of hope. After all, he'd called her, hadn't he?

She distracted herself scrubbing the kitchen and when she was done her watch said eleven-thirty. After pouring her bucket of wash water down the toilet, she went out to the shop.

With the limited light through the windows, the shop's lavender-gray paint and dark wainscoting had an even mistier feel. The glass cabinets gleamed from their interior lights and soft classical music played on a portable radio. A tendril of incense threaded up from the brazier before the small bronze Buddha above the antique cash register.

Chloe looked up from the tedious task of labeling their latest merchandise. Each piece had to be marked with the price, but also with the name of the artisan who made it.

"Hey," Chloe said. She wore a midnight-blue caftan and leggings with an amber and jet bead chain. "From all the clattering and bumping and banging, I thought you were remodeling the kitchen."

Lila grinned. "Nope. Just cleaning."

"Uh-huh. You realize you were singing?"

"Singing?" There was no way. She wasn't any great singer and certainly wasn't the kind of person who sang in the shower. Singing while she cleaned?

"Yup. To tell you the truth, I thought you had that old Disney *Snow White* movie turned on and the birds were going to join in. Or they would if you had a window open." There was a mischievous light in Chloe's deep blue gaze as she came around the counter. "I heard the phone ring. Anyone I know?"

"Boy, you are one nosey Parker," Lila said and went to the front window. The beach—from what she could see through the smoke—was woefully empty, the lake itself an empty bathtub. For all the wind from the coast was driving the massive fires closer, the lake itself seemed trapped in the shadow of the mountains, with no wind to strip the smoke away. There was barely a ripple on the water, and yet—was that a hint of the bulk of mountains across the lake?

She turned back to Chloe. "If you must know, it was Nathan." She couldn't help the smile that crept onto her lips. "He said he needs to talk—to show me something."

Chloe came around the counter to catch her in a hug. "That is good news. So you're obviously seeing him. He's coming here, of course."

"No. He's not." Lila pulled away. "We're meeting at the bakery. The bunch of you clearly scared him off."

"Really?" Chloe looked a little stunned. "That doesn't sound like the Nathan I met. We're all pretty easy going." She did a little fluttering pirouette as if to demonstrate her harmlessness.

"Well, the bunch of you must have made him uncomfortable because he doesn't want to meet here. Let's face it. Together, the bunch of you can be a pretty daunting."

Chloe frowned. "Maybe... We were going pretty hard into the bracelet thing. That might scare someone off, I guess. I would have thought a little time and the prospect of seeing you would have overcome it."

"I guess it didn't." She checked her watch. "I've got an appointment with Victoria to discuss the opening and also to do some contingency planning re the fire. Any news on that front?"

Chloe's cheerful expression faded. She shook her head. "None of it good. Overnight there was an increase of wind and the fire leapt the fireguard. The back of Mount Coldham is on fire and evacuation orders have gone out to the folks at the top of Princeton Avenue. If it keeps going like this, the whole town's going to be in danger."

Not good news. Lila looked back to the window. If anything, the shadowed bulk of mountains seemed a little clearer. "Maybe we don't have to worry. Doesn't it look like the smoke is clearing a little?"

Chloe glanced out the window. "It does. A little.' Course, that could just mean that the winds have changed."

Lila rolled her eyes. "I thought you were the optimist."

Turning back from the window, Chloe grinned. "I am. Like I'm optimistic your meeting with Nathan will go well—if you don't blow it. You have to admit that you like him, Lila. That is not the kind of man you let just walk away—especially not when he likes you." She held up her hand when Lila went to speak. "Yeah, yeah, yeah. I know. There's all these logistical difficulties and you want different things. What you want is to find someone you love and care about. Logistical difficulties are things to be overcome." She hooked her fingers around logistical.

"Thank you, Chloe Main. Now to change the subject to something more pertinent to the moment, if we do have to evacuate, I've got plans to just grab a box I've got ready in the kitchen and toss in the inventory. If there's anything you can think of to improve that plan, I'd appreciate you putting it into action. I'd like to get as much of this stuff out of here as possible."

"Already on it. I've taken some of the pieces out of the displays and I've rearranged things so the most valuable pieces are in the three counter displays. That way, if we can't take everything, we can at least get the most valuable stuff first. And I've got Reggie shifting her most expensive equipment and all the precious stones and metals over to her place in West Kelowna. God forbid the fire should get there, too."

"Good. Would you ask her to take the chemicals, too? The last thing we need is something that might fan a flame."

"Consider it done."

Lila looked at her friend, and a soft spot formed in her chest. She slung an arm around Chloe's shoulders in a half hug. "Have I ever told you how glad I am that we did this together—opened the store?"

"Not lately, but it's pretty cool, isn't it."

Lila nodded. "I really got lucky in this life. I've got the very best of friends." She pulled loose. "And now I've got to move or I'm going to keep another friend waiting."

She headed out the front door for the two-minute walk to Victoria's new store. Chloe dogged her heels.

On the porch Lila stopped. "Just what are you doing? I don't need an escort. I'm a big girl and it's light out." She motioned at the empty beach. "See. No one lurking."

"Fine. I'll just watch from the gate." By the set of Chloe's jaw and the steel in her gaze, there was no denying her.

Lila went down the porch stairs. "Fine. But I feel like a little kid on her first venture out of the yard."

Sure enough, Chloe stolidly followed her to the gate. Lila set out down the sidewalk.

"Make sure you call and let me know what your plans are with Nathan," Chloe called.

Lila turned, disgusted, but understanding Chloe's concern. "Yes, Mom."

Chloe grinned and waved her away.

§

Victoria Angelucci's store sat in Peachland's most modern complex, a terra cotta-colored concrete building that housed a couple of boutique furniture and knickknack stores, the bakery, and a string of *très* chi-chi condominiums on the second floor that each cost upward of a million dollars for the views across the lake.

The shop space that housed Victoria's fledgling store had previously been a day spa, but now the windows were swathed in opaque white plastic with tastefully framed posters in the display space that advertised what the shop would hold and the date of the grand opening. The posters showed the back of one of the beautiful hand-painted kimonos that a Milanese designer friend of Victoria's had sent on commission, and some of Victoria's own lovely, classic designs. The posters had been successful enough that there'd already been a number of messages left at *This and That* enquiring whether certain pieces in the poster might be put on hold for certain prospective buyers. Lila had had to turn them down because Victoria was insistent that her opening day would have many things for sale, not just display.

The smoke was rough in her eyes and nose as she knocked on the store door that was flanked by large, concrete Greco-Roman urns filled with spiral topiary. The metal tables of the bakery café were all empty this morning, instead of full like they usually were.

The front of the café was closed up tight, light and noise from inside telling of a full house, but no one wanted to sit out in the smoke. There were virtually no dog walkers this morning either, when usually there was a steady parade of the canine-inclined down the promenade.

The plastic twitched on the back of the door and the lock snicked open. Then the door swung back to reveal Victoria—or at least the toned-down Peachland version. Victoria Angelucci had arrived in Peachland in an Italian peplum power suit, platform heels, and full war makeup. Now, from the carefully sculpted creature she had been, this morning she wore jeans, a Michael Kors shirt of robin's egg blue silk shantung that set off her vivid eyes, and a set of simple silver earrings that had *"Regulus Designs"* all over them. She still wore the platform heels, which Lila thought was probably because Victoria was so much shorter than Danny Forester, her police detective sweetie.

"Lila! Welcome! I have the coffee ready." She let Lila in, closed and locked the door behind her, and handed Lila a cup of Taste Bakery/Café espresso . "I wish the smoke would go. It leaves everything smelling like fire. My hair. My clothes. And I have no view from my lovely apartment." She pouted prettily. Victoria had leased and was planning to purchase one of the condominiums above the store. She came from an old Milanese industrialist family and could afford the steep prices.

The shop was fully renovated, with the main space painted in modern tones of gray with bright circles of red that matched Victoria's favorite lipstick shade. The effect reminded Lila of all the bussing of cheeks you received in Italy. It was a perfect way to set off the racks of lovely clothing. On one wall above the clothing hung the kimono from the poster, the hand-painting of the Italian countryside displayed for all to admire.

"The place looks ready," Lila said as she settled onto one of two stools at the cash counter.

"It is. There are a few little things like a few new pieces that the seamstresses are completing and a couple of sketches that I am having framed for the walls, but otherwise we have only to open."

Victoria sipped her coffee and Lila joined her. It was strong and black. One of the first things Victoria had done was make an arrangement with the bakery-café owner that she could bring their china cups to the store as long as she returned them. So far, the arrangement had been working.

Lila nodded. "I've been looking into places in town to hold the reception and fashion show, but everything's booked with programs. I'm still waiting to hear back from the Blue Hills Restaurant, but I'm concerned because the best part of their space is the terrace outside. It's no different than what we'd be facing outside here."

"Do we delay the opening?" By the little lines between Victoria's arched brows, she did not like the idea.

Lila shook her head. "It wouldn't be my first choice. We've got enough money committed to this place that we need to have money start coming in. Do we open without the ceremony and then have the big ceremony after the smoke has cleared?"

Victoria thought a moment, then shook her head. "No. It will mean no one will want to come to the event. It is all about the suspense, is it not? In Milan during fashion week, the energy goes high as the sky with everyone waiting to see the new creations. I want that here, though it will be a smaller energy."

She smiled ruefully and Lila caught her hand, feeling sympathy for her Italian friend. "You gave up a lot to help Reggie. I hope you know how much that means to all of us."

"It was nothing. Besides, it is better that I am out from under Erminio's control, and even if I had left him to open my own house, he would have made my life difficult. He is a very small man. Thank goodness Cesare's dealing with Reggie's lawsuit has brought to light Erminio's involvement. My contacts back home say the media are loving it and he is—how do you say it?—scrambling to save House Erminio."

"Hmm. If he was really serious about saving House Erminio, maybe he should pack up all Reggie's files and send them back,"Lila said.

"Eh. Perhaps he will. Cesare has included that in his list of damages and his countersuit. Imagine how strange it was when the German jewelry firm that laid the suit suddenly became no more than a puff of smoke. Poor Erminio is left holding the bag, I think."

"Don't you dare feel sorry for him. He made money off your ideas for too many years! Now come on, let's figure out how to get this store open so you can start making money on your own."

Lila took another sip of coffee. "I know we'd planned to have the reception out on the sidewalk, but in this smoke, that's impossible. We could go farther afield for the grand opening. Perhaps look for a golf club or something and have a hosted event. I thought of Elkhart Winery, but they don't have the space, either, and they also have the smoke. Either way, getting a different venue means whoever comes never gets to see your shop."

Victoria grimaced. "I would rather have the opening near to the shop so that people can see the clothing and the wonderful space. I wonder—do you think it would work to have the reception in my apartment? It is right upstairs and then people would not have to be in the smoke so long as we cut the ribbon and enter the store."

Lila thought a moment. "It would be very crowded if we tried to get them all into the shop at once. What about if we held the reception upstairs, but then had an additional reception area back in your sewing area? We could have the shop and the change area, but also a lovely place of flowers and couches where people could model the clothes for each other!"

"Or we could have the reception upstairs and then bring them down the back way and into the sewing area for a fashion show. Then they could go into the shop themselves!"

Lila set her coffee cup down with a clatter. "That's a fantastic idea! It would be like fashion week for House Victoria. And we're almost right in tune with Milan's fashion week. Kylee can have a field day marketing Milan's Fashion Week Comes to Peachland with your opening! Let's take a look at the space; and if the smoke clears, we can still have the fashion show, but perhaps on Peachland's very own sunny promenade."

§

For Lila the afternoon unfolded as the two women inspected what was currently a bare bones concrete-walled industrial sewing space and Victoria's clean-lined apartment to make lists of what was needed. From the cream leather couch in Lila's apartment front room, the two-story windows gave a smoke-obscured view of the lake and a hazy view of the mountains. The smoke had thinned enough to show light waves on the lake and the humped backs of the hills beyond the water, but the sky was still yellow, the sun a red ball so the world looked like it was ending.

"We should start phoning," said Lila. "I'll contact the florists. Can you give Kylee a call? She's made all the contacts. Tell her we need the long cloth banners to cover the sewing space walls, the carpet, too, to stand in for a runway. And padded chairs. The fashionistas of the Okanagan are going to eat this up. She'll want to get right on this." This was what her life was all about—her business. Her whole body felt buoyant, her stomach filled with butterflies.

Lila grinned at Victoria as they both picked up their phones. Then Lila stopped. "This can't be right, can it? Three thirty?"

Victoria frowned and checked her phone. She nodded. "My phone says three thirty-one."

"Damn." Lila stood. "I have to run, but I'll call the florist. I'm meeting Nathan at the café."

Grabbing her purse, she ran out the door and took the elevator down to the lobby that gave onto the quiet street at the rear of the building. She stepped out into the smoky afternoon and followed the sidewalk around the building.

Something was happening. The patrons of the café were just emptying out as she arrived at the door. All of them were scattering to their cars.

She tried to enter, but the narrow-faced youth who was the assistant manager stopped her. "Sorry, Ms. Weber. We're closed."

"Closed? But it's the middle of the afternoon!"

The harried young man shoved his fingers through a tangle of brown hair. "I guess you haven't heard. They've just issued an evacuation order for the entire town."

Chapter 16

Evacuation.

"I didn't hear anything—get any notice," Lila said.

"They're sending people door to door. You must have just missed them or something." He went to pull the door closed.

"I was upstairs. No one contacted us."

He shook his head. "Sorry. Don't know anything about that."

He pulled the door shut and Lila stepped back from the door. She'd better warn Victoria and get down the street to her store. Chloe would want to get home and get her own keepsakes.

"Lila!"

She turned around, recognizing Nathan's voice. Across the street through the scattering people, he stood beside his Mercedes, looking eminently Nathan-like. A small shiver of lust ran through her. She still hadn't gotten the darn man out of her system. In the middle of a fire evacuation, it was the last thing she needed.

Winding her way through the people, she came to his car. The tinted windows were yellow in the smeary light.

"Nathan, hi." She leaned up to give him a peck on the cheek, then shook her head. "I'm sorry. The timing for this really isn't going to work. They've just announced a fire evacuation for the town."

She turned back to look up at the mountain that backed Peachland. Wind ripped at the tops of the trees, and above the town, the swirls of yellow smoke cleared enough to show ragged blue sky and the tops of the mountain. Huge, lifting, gray plumes of smoke were ripped away by the wind.

"Holy God." She turned back to Nathan and pointed. "See? I need to get back to the store and retrieve my things."

Looking at him, she suddenly realized he hadn't said a thing other than her name. He stood more stiffly than he usually did, but that could simply be his discomfort at the situation between them. Still...

There was something about his eyes. Instead of the usual turquoise gleam, there was a yellow cast that dulled his gaze.

"Nathan? Are you all right? You—you look funny."

Someone down the street shouted and the voice sounded familiar. She glanced away in time to see Danny Forester climbing out of what was obviously an unmarked police car. What the heck was he doing here? But she knew, didn't she? The darn man had been here watching her, just like he'd kept an eye on Victoria. Was he possessed like he had been then?

Nathan's hand came around her wrist.

"Get in the car, Lila. There's something you need to see." His voice was terse and his grip said he wasn't going to let go.

"Nathan!" She tried to twist her hand away. "You're hurting me!"

He didn't seem to hear. Instead he pulled the Mercedes' rear door open. "Get in."

"I will not! Nathan!" She jerked back, but it did no good. His grip was unbreakable. The side of his car yawned open and there was something there and suddenly she was deathly afraid. This wasn't Nathan. This wasn't Nathan Moon at all. Had the thing taken him over like it once had Danny? Was he doomed to spend years in the psych ward like the others who had been possessed? Her knees went weak at the thought.

"Not you. Please, not you, Nathan."

He used her momentary pause against her and, twisting her arm behind her, forced her up on her tiptoes before he shoved her head down and headfirst into the rear of the car. She landed on her knees, her face up close to a blond-haired man she had never seen before.

§

Slouched in his car and bored out of his skull after a morning spent making investigative phone calls from his smart phone, Danny kept an eye on Lila's place; he'd watched her head up the block for Victoria's place. He'd gotten the call from Chloe that that was where Lila was going, because Jas had prevailed upon his girlfriend to help them keep Lila safe.

The Mercedes rolled down the block, shouldering the smoke aside like a shark through deep water and he sat up. There was something about the vehicle—something in the dead-eyed look of its reflective windows. All the little hairs on the back of his neck stood on end. When the vehicle had performed a U-turn and come back to park across the street from the café, he had a bad feeling, but he couldn't just go and arrest someone because their car gave him the willies.

His portable radio crackled in the background and caught his attention. The evacuation order for the entire town had come. Down at the corner, a sudden flood of people out of the café said that the word was spreading. Cars started to fill the street, probably the product of the local emergency call-out tree. All good, but the flood of people made it hard to see what was happening. The crowd parted in time for him to see the Mercedes driver door swing open. Someone climbed out. Nathan.

That meant everything all right. Nathan was cool. He'd been told what was happening and he was clearly crazy about Lila, even if he stomped off like a fool last night. He'd come to his senses. A man in love did.

But still... The way he stood beside his car, even when Danny spotted Lila talking to someone at the café entrance. If it was him, he'd have been heading across the street to surprise her, not standing there like some teenager expecting his date to meet him at the car.

All his Spidey senses went on alert. It could be nothing, but on the other hand... He climbed out of the car into the smoke and started up the street to talk to them.

The Peachland waterfront promenade was a lot like some post-apocalyptic movie scene—people running, smoke in the air, the stench of fire making his eyes water. Ahead, Lila had crossed the street to Nathan and Danny's Spidey sense kicked into high gear.

"Lila!" he called.

She glanced in his direction.

In the apocalypse that was Peachland, all that was missing was the sound of screaming—that was until Lila Weber was suddenly flung in a car by none other than Nathan. Her scream cut through the sound of too many car engines, but only until the Mercedes door slammed shut. The luxury car baffling effectively cutting off the sound.

"Shit." It was happening. Something was going down and here he was, halfway up the beach from his car, while Nathan slid in behind the Mercedes wheel.

Idiot.

Danny turned tail and ran, weaving through the people hurrying back to their homes and the vehicles already loaded and leaving. Ash sifted through the air and made it hard to see.

By the time he turned his key in the ignition, the Mercedes was gone.

§

Nathan woke in darkness—at least he thought he awoke. Or perhaps this was a nightmare because the darkness was complete. Utter. Devoid of light. He couldn't see. He couldn't move. Then he realized that he couldn't even feel his body.

That was when the panic started. And then he screamed.

At least he thought he did, but that could be in his own mind, because he couldn't say whether he heard any sound. He tried to fight against the darkness, tried to wake, but nothing happened. What the hell was going on? It was like he was trapped in some B-grade screamer movie.

The man trapped in the buried coffin.

The man trapped in the rubble of a collapsed building.

The man trapped in a coma.

Scree-scree-scree—the horror of his situation built to almost bursting.

But if he was buried in a coffin, he should be able to feel the sides; and he couldn't even feel his hands.

If he was trapped in a collapsed building, he should be able to feel pain. There was none.

A coma, then. That would explain the rapid thump-thump-thump of a heartbeat that he suddenly realized he heard. A heartbeat. A frightened heartbeat. He'd take a deep breath to slow it, but he had no body to breathe? What the hell had happened to him?

What. The fuck. WAS HAPPENING TO HIM????

No. No. No. Panic wouldn't help anything, least of all him. He had to think. Hell, thinking was all he had at the moment. Something had happened. What was it?

He'd been having breakfast in the restaurant at the hotel and had made a decision to get over himself and see Lila to work things out. He'd gone to the elevator to go up to his room and that was the last he remembered.

Wait a minute. There's been someone in the elevator with him—someone he recognized.

A fragrance of incense-strong aftershave, an impression of size.

You can do better than that, Moon. In Hollywood you learn quickly to recognize people and remember their names.

Blond—he'd seen a blond!

The man's image flooded back. Big, blond, and broad-shouldered as if he lifted weights and took pride in his body. Broad, pale forehead with aggressive brow ridge and pale eyebrows that shadowed even paler eyes. But he'd seen the man before. The man smiled at Nathan as if he knew him. And while Nathan wracked his brain for the man's name, he met his pale gaze.

And then he was here, locked away in black nothingness with nothing but his heartbeat.

Wait a minute. Maybe there was something else. A sound of muffled voices that was reminiscent of the wah-wah-wah of the adults in the old Charlie Brown TV specials. He strained to hear, comforted by the thought that if he could hear, he must still have ears.

"Nathan!" As if wax seals had been pulled from his ears, Lila's voice thundered in his head. He'd recognize it anywhere.

"You're hurting me!"

What the hell? What was happening? He got a sense that he

spoke, but not what he said. Then there was movement. Yes. He moved, and that was a relief, but if he moved, why couldn't he feel it? How could he move if he wasn't doing it?

Equal flushes of hot and cold ran through him, fear and more fear.

It had to be impossible. It was idiocy, a fairytale, a contrivance of special effects in the movies. That was all.

And yet. And yet, hadn't Lila's friends told him? Hadn't that Danny Forester told him how something had possessed Danny until he nearly killed the blonde Italian, Victoria? Could...could it actually be true?

Horror bloomed through him. Now was the time for the *Twilight Zone* theme song.

Was he killing Lila right now?

He wouldn't let that happen! Couldn't let that happen.

"You listen to me, you bastard! I'll destroy you if you hurt her!"

The darkness rippled like a sheet around him as if it laughed at his words. He was cold, so cold, but he also caught a whiff of roses—Lila's scent. He'd dreamed of the scent of her soft skin and in the elevator had wanted to go to her—wanted to whisk her away from everything so they could be alone. So they could work things out.

And now she was here. Near enough he could touch her. Near enough he could hurt her.

The flush of cold fear sent him curling back into himself. If this was the creature Danny and the others had spoken of, he'd allowed it to take him over. Hell, it had probably taken almost nothing because he already wanted what the creature wanted. To get Lila alone.

And once he did, the creature could do what it wanted because, locked in the darkness, Nathan wasn't much good to himself, let alone anyone else.

"Nathan, you're hurting me," Lila had said.

Chapter 17

The rear seat of the Mercedes reeked of smoke and fire. The blond man's pale face was barely three inches from Lila's. He grinned, showing a row of perfect white teeth that seemed perfectly capable of leaning in and biting off a nose or an ear. She yanked back and found her back pressed against the car door. Frantically fumbled for the lock, but the damn door wouldn't open.

"Electric locks, my dear. So sorry." Almost perfect British English with a hint of German accent.

She pounded on the window. As the driver's door opened, she lunged for the front seat, but strong, too-hot hands yanked her back; they thrust her into her seat as Nathan Moon slid behind the wheel.

"Nathan! What are you doing?"

She tasted blood from where she'd bit her tongue at the blow, but it wasn't Nathan driving, of that she was sure. It might be him in body, but it wasn't him in soul.

She was suddenly too aware of the man seated beside her. In the enclosed space of the Mercedes' rear seat, she felt his heat like a too-hot radiator on a summer night. She yanked away to the far side of the car, then turned to study him. Tall, blond, with a physique like he worked out. Almost colorless blue eyes that showed an inhuman intelligence. Cold, so she shivered, unable to get warm in his heat. She'd do anything to get away from this man, but instead she was trapped with him.

Shielding the bracelet behind her, she squared her shoulders. "Johan Fehr, I presume, though I believe we've met before—like on a dark street?"

His lips curved in what might be a smile, but so predatory she felt like a seal before a shark. "So you figured it out—you and your little friends. I have to admit that I am a trifle surprised." He peered forward out the front of the car and made a small motion with his hand. Nathan turned south onto the highway instead of north, where most of the evacuation traffic appeared to be going. Northward, the single lane highway out of town was bumper-to-bumper and crawling through thickening billows of ashy smoke.

Southward there was much less traffic, probably because most of the evacuation stations were in West Kelowna and Kelowna, not southward. The Mercedes sped up.

"Where are you taking us? Why not just kill me now?"

At that he looked at her again, and she really needed to rethink anything that made him look her way because just his gaze made her skin crawl.

"Now where would be the fun in that? Human emotion is quite delicious, don't you think? Like now. You fight the fear, but it grows slowly, deliciously, and finally will come the terror." Slowly, his bright pink tongue flicked across his lips.

She couldn't press into the door any harder, so she forced herself to face him regardless of the threat of his gaze. "What—what are you? What have you done to Nathan?"

"My, you are a surprise. Others have whimpered and prayed for mercy before me. But then your kind have forgotten that you share this earth with others, far older than you."

"A djinn, then. You really are such a creature." Keep him talking, gather as much information as she could. As long as he was talking, he wasn't killing her and maybe she'd learn something that could help her.

He went still, his pale glare suddenly wary. "How do you know this?"

It was her turn to show a small, secretive smile. She held his gaze and just hoped that she could pull it off when everything inside her just said RUN. Run fast and far. "We're not as stupid or as forgetful as you seem to think. We've bested you every step of the way."

He ignored her, but maybe—just maybe—there was a slight line formed between his brows. Worry? Was he scared? Could she use that to her advantage?

"You know someone saw us and they're after us now." At least there had been Danny. He'd seen. But had he come after? Had he realized he was witnessing an abduction and not her simply leaving with Nathan? Surely to goodness he'd seen how she was thrown into the back of the car. He'd come after if he had. He would. Whether he'd be any help against this creature was another matter altogether.

"Up the hill," said Fehr and Nathan guided the car onto Princeton Avenue that led up toward the old Brenda Mine Road— and the fire.

"What the hell are you doing, Fehr? Didn't you hear that we're supposed to be evacuating?"

The traffic in the other direction was vehicle after vehicle filled to the gunnels with families with children and pets and precious personal treasures. Trucks loaded with horses were among them. A cattle trailer with someone's herd. Virtually no one was heading in their direction.

"You need to rethink this, Fehr. You've got us headed to the fire."

Ahead and to their right, the mountain backing Peachland was aflame. Through the billows of thick smoke, beyond the small enclaves of houses spread amongst the drought-stricken ponderosa pines, the green flanks of Mount Coldham and Pincushion Mountain were pock-marked with bright gouts of crimson that seemed to leap across the tops of the tinder-dry trees. It was like an advancing army.

A fire truck came clanging up the hill behind them and Nathan pulled the Mercedes over, then pulled in behind the truck as they followed the road. Princeton Avenue curved around the base of the mountain, the number of neighborhoods diminishing as they rose higher, but there were still roads leading up to new developments being cut into the mountain's rocky flanks.

Ahead was a police roadblock that let the fire truck through. If they were stopped, she could get attention—escape. She readied herself, but Johan Fehr just motioned at Nathan. Just before the roadblock, the Mercedes turned onto a side road that led up the mountain.

Fear clamped down on her chest. He was going to do this. She was going to die and Nathan would, too. "Where are you taking us?"

"Me?" he said mildly and then turned his inhuman gaze on her. "Why, everyone will say that it was Nathan. I am not even here."

"Then why *are* you here?" Darn it, she was not going to let him see her afraid. She was strong. "Maybe it's because you're weak. You've used up your power trying to get the bracelet back. Otherwise you would never have come yourself."

The backhand was so fast and hard it threw her head back against the window and for a moment she was stunned. The car lurched a little as he growled at her—truly growled.

"You will not speak. Do you hear me?" His presence grew, filling the car like a fog.

She tasted blood and realized he'd split her lip, but the pain just made her angry and anger was good. It held power. Let him think she was cowed, but she was reserving her strength. She'd fight him somehow. Tooth and nail if she couldn't find a weapon.

The car wound up through tall ponderosa pine, spruce, and poplar and then ended in a cul-de-sac of new suburban houses on what must be half-acre lots. Lots filled with trees gave the subdivision a casual country feel, something that had been picked up in the wagon wheels and old tractors that a few yards displayed as lawn ornaments.

Fehr flicked his hand at Nathan again and the car stopped in the middle of the pavement. Lila swallowed. There was no sign of any people. Smoke rolled down the mountain to billow between the houses. There were no cars in the driveways, no dogs in the yards.

Evacuated all, which meant they were alone.

§

Danny urged his car forward in the snarl that was the northbound traffic and came to a stop *again*. He craned his neck out the window. It had been a guess that the vehicle had turned north away from the fire just like everyone else in Peachland. Surely that was the dark grey Mercedes about ten cars up. But he wasn't going to sit here any longer. It didn't look like the log jam of cars was going to break up any time soon.

Abandoning his car, he climbed out onto the road. The air stank of heat and fire and the ending of so many dreams up in smoke. Yup, that had to be the Mercedes. Same dark shape. Same tinted windows. He hauled out his cell and stabbed in the number.

"Stone," came the solid voice of his partner, a counterpoint to the pounding of Danny's heart.

He was going to face Johan Fehr, finally. If the circumstances were right, he'd kill him.

"Jas. It's me. It's going down as we speak. I saw the Moon guy haul Lila into a car and it didn't look like she was willing. I'm pretty sure I heard her scream, even if no one else did, but I couldn't get to the car in time to help her. So I followed. Now I'm stuck in the flipping traffic on the highway, a few cars back. I'm going to make an approach."

"No way. Danny, you listen to me. If you approach, he might make the leap to you again. I do not fancy having to take out my partner." There came the screech of chair rollers and then the sound changed to hollow. Jas was moving from their detachment office out into the open hallways. "Stay on the line. I'm coming to you."

"No time, Jas. This traffic snarl could clear anytime and they could be gone."

He hung up and pocketed the phone, ignoring how it hummed in his pocket. Jas calling back, no doubt. Nope. He was going to rescue Lila and in the process prove to himself that the thing couldn't do it to him again. Otherwise how could he ever fully trust himself?

Hand at his shoulder holster, he started up alongside the line of cars, reached the rear bumper of the Mercedes, and drew his gun. The damned tinted windows made it impossible to see how many occupants or what they were doing. Damn things should be illegal.

Gun down at his side, he eased forward and leapt even with the driver door, weapon up—

And found himself staring down his gun barrel into the face of a woman in her mid-fifties with perfectly coiffed steel-grey hair and a realtor suit. Her painted-on face was drawn up in horror.

"Please, no! Don't hurt me!" she shrieked.

He lowered the gun. "RCMP, ma'am. Sorry. I'm looking for a suspect in an abduction. He's driving a car exactly like yours." He quickly checked over her shoulder—no one else inside. Heard car doors opening behind him.

"What's going on?" demanded a man who'd climbed out of a Cadillac behind the Mercedes. He was joined by another man from a pickup, this one younger and brawny and clearly planning to flex his muscles.

"Stay calm everyone. This is a police matter and as I was just explaining to the driver, I'm looking for a similar vehicle that's been involved in an abduction. Sorry for frightening you, ma'am."

Just get out of here and where the hell was Lila? He holstered his gun and began speed walking back to his car.

Mr. Pickup truck grabbed his shoulder. "You pigs—you can't just do that to people."

Danny yanked away and ran back to the unmarked police car. Leapt inside and cranked the engine over, then pulled out of the line. If Lila wasn't in the Mercedes in front of him, then the car had to have gone in the other direction and by now they could be almost anywhere.

Disobeying all the rules, he fished out his phone and stabbed Jas's number. "They're gone. They fucking went south instead of north."

"Nice talking to you, too, partner. So how'd you figure that out?" The sound of a siren was behind Jas's voice. He was headed Danny's way.

"Caused a scene. Pulled a gun on a realtor."

He heard the groan through the phone.

"Couldn't be helped. It was the exact same model of car."

"You can bet your ass the Inspector's going to be hearing about this."

"Don't I know it. Plenty of witnesses, too. I apologized."

"You sure something's wrong with Lila?"

Danny came to the junction on the highway where the highway headed south and Princeton Avenue headed up the slopes of Peachland. A seemingly endless line of vehicles on Princeton waited at the stoplight for the traffic headed north to allow them to turn onto the highway. On impulse he turned up Princeton.

"I'm sure. I know what I saw. That was not a woman who went willingly into that car." And he was even more certain as he said it. "Something was clearly wrong. Now I'm headed up Princeton. You take the highway southbound. They're in a dark grey Mercedes S-Class sedan. I didn't catch the license, but if we contacted the rental agencies we could probably get it."

There was silence at the other end of the line. "You sure I shouldn't come after you?"

"Hey, partner, I resent that remark. I'm fine. You come after me and there's a fifty percent chance that Lila Weber's going to die. No, let me take Princeton and you take the highway."

Silence again and then, "Keep me posted."

The line went dead. Danny hit lights and siren and put the pedal to the metal up the hill.

Chapter 18

The stink of smoke and flames was so heavy in the rear of the Mercedes that Lila thought she might be sick. Fehr's pale gaze seemed to freeze her in place against the door and Nathan sat like an immobilized robot in the driver's seat.

She found the strength to glare at her captor. From everything Danny had said, she had to cling to the hope that the reason Johan Fehr was here in person was because he was desperate. Somehow she and her friends had weakened him and she needed to hold on to that. He might be able to do something to Nathan, but whatever it was, it wasn't what he'd done to Danny. Then it had been like something other had looked out of Danny's eyes—at least that was the way Chloe had described it. This was more like Nathan just wasn't there. As if Fehr controlled him like a robot. That had to take energy. If he was weak, that had to be energy he couldn't afford to lose.

So weaken him further. Make him use more energy.

"So are you going to kill me here?" she asked, but her voice didn't come out quite as calmly as she'd hoped. Not surprising given everything inside her was as taut as a cord.

Fehr's shark-smile returned. "In some ways I am almost glad that you waited so long to put the bracelet on. Your attempt to hide your fear makes this most delicious, indeed. Did you know that fear feeds me? My kind inhabit the gray spaces between the light and the dark. In the ancient days of my people, it was fear that sustained us in the barren reaches of the world. Fear that we evoked from unwary travelers was an elixir to our being. Fear of us in the cities was like a bath in fragrant oils. Our flames burned brightly in the night—far brighter than the puny torch and fire light.

"So many of us were banished by Solomon's ring, but I, one of the strongest, remained. I refused the call of the ring and kept to my palace, taking what I wanted—until that puny fool Acacius came. He robbed me of something precious and so he had to pay the price."

"You killed him and you killed his wife—the precious woman he had stolen," Lila said. Let him know that he was no longer so unknown. Most of all, keep him talking. Danny had seen them get into the car. He had to be coming.

Fehr's smile broadened. "So there are still tales about me, then. Tales to chill a young child's blood."

"Tales to put a child to sleep, more like. No one's afraid of fairytales anymore." Boastful creature needed putting in its place.

"No, today it is the terrorist, the child molester, the mass murderer. But I will have you know this—I have been and am all of those and more, and today, with the bracelet, I will once more transcend my need for this body."

Once more he grew to fill the car, shadow oozing out of him to surround him and, please God, not now. If what Fehr said was true, he'd have no need of his body once he had his power back— or hers or Nathan's. They were all going to die and the fire would destroy the evidence. She didn't want to die. She wanted a chance to live and sort things out with Nathan. She wanted to have the chance to figure out how to make the logistics work.

Nathan. If Fehr was focused on her, then maybe he was less focused on Nathan. Maybe—just maybe he could break free like Danny had.

The darkness pressed in around her, the stench of smoke and fire so intense she gagged. All light disappeared through the tinted windows and there was only terror and darkness. Her heart hammered in her chest as Fehr seemed to lift from his seat to hover over her as if they were in some gigantic cave.

No! Blood pounded in her ears, but he'd already he said that fear fed him strength. She would not be afraid.

She swallowed it back like a too-large pill and shoved herself from the false safety of the door. She pushed her face into his instead. "You've come to the wrong place, Johan. I might be afraid, but I'm not going to cower from you. Just like the women in the story wouldn't cower. So you can take your smoke and your pyrotechnics someplace else."

The swelling darkness stilled. Fehr's ice-blue eyes blazed with a ruddy light as if he was lit from inside. All of his attention focused on her and the utter malice in his eyes sent her heart hammering again. His hands reached for her neck; she fought them away. Nathan had to come-to now or it would be too late.

"Nathan!" she screamed as she clawed Fehr's face. "Nathan!" As Fehr's fingers finally found her throat and she was choking on his miasma of smoke, begging for air.

"You think he can help you, but you're wrong, little one. A pity, really. You are almost as beautiful as Laelia was. You would be a good plaything, but never a bride. A bride must be trusted and Laelia taught me that women can never be trusted."

His eyes flared red as she scratched Fehr's fists. They blocked the air from her and squeezed out her life. She kicked at him, but the space was too small. Kicked the back of the driver's seat in faint hope that Nathan would wake.

No air, but the creeping darkness seeped inside her. Seeped into her hearing, her sight. Sounds became distant. Her vision a tunnel that narrowed further. Her hands so distant she could not feel them. Darkness flooding in and only Fehr's infernal eyes for light.

They would be her last sight.

§

Something happened in the darkness. Nathan knew it as surely as he knew it was something horrible. Worse than being locked in a prison in his head. Something he should care dearly about, but it was so easy to simply drift on the clouds of dark that held him prisoner.

To drift and sleep and remember old joys.

Yes, that was the way of it. Simply sleep. Far better than the panic.

But something jarred through the darkness.

"Nathan!" A voice he should care about. A voice to dream about.

A voice in need and he should recognize it.

What was going on? He felt as if he floated in a kind of cannabis stupor. What the hell was that? He might have experimented as a kid, but he wasn't a drug user. Hadn't touched the stuff since he was a university student. Drugs might be rampant in Hollywood, but the successful with staying power abstained.

The realization brought him more awake and he shed the stupor like an unwanted cloak.

Around him the darkness had thinned. He could actually feel his limbs. It was as if the darkness had mostly fled, perhaps focused on other things. And he was left seated *in his car.* The realization jarred him further aware.

*"Nathan, you're hurting me!"*Lila had said.

He bolted upright, the darkness shredding in his limbs. He *had* hurt Lila. He'd forced her into the back of his car. He knew he had, though the actions were like a scene viewed through a hazy filter. Lila and that crazy story of her friends was true and he had to help her.

Move. Move your ass out of this car and help her.

Easier said than done.

From the back seat came the sound of a struggle. Someone kicked the back of his seat. It had to be Lila.

Shifting his hands off the steering wheel took as much effort as moving a pallet of bricks. His hands fell to his lap. His right hand crept slowly up his leg to the seatbelt closure, fumbled there a minute, before he found the control of his fingers to press the release button. The belt clicked free.

A small cry came from behind him, but the sound grew fainter. He had to do something, and now, if he was going to save the woman he loved.

He focused on his left hand. Inched it toward the door latch. So slow. Too slow. Sweat stung his eyes, but he found the door lock. Pressed. The soft thunk of the doors unlocking was masked by the thud-thud-thud of feet against the rear of his seat.

Damn it, he needed to move. Needed to act. Hand crept up the side of the door and found the door handle. His breath came in short, sharp gasps as eerie chuckles of glee came from the back.

Lila!

He pulled the door latch and the car door swung open. He threw his weight sideways and fell after it, tumbling out onto pavement in the midst of a smoke-filled neighborhood of houses. How the hell he got here he didn't know.

The smoke sent him coughing as he struggled to his knees, grabbed the rear door of the car, and yanked it open.

Lila hung limp in the blond man's hands, his hands fisted around her neck. The blond man from—his mind was blank—but he knew him from somewhere. He grabbed Lila's shoulders and yanked. The big man's glare shifted to Nathan and darkness began to coalesce in his brain.

Nathan clocked the blond upside the head.

Lila tumbled into his arms and he stumbled backward, swung her into his arms, and ran for the nearest houses uphill. Through the billows of smoke, the mountain slope above them was aflame. Not that direction, then. He turned back, but the blond was already pushing out of the car. Nathan felt the darkness flooding in, the need to simply turn around and return to his master.

The master, yes.

He realized he'd stopped running. Stood frozen in the middle of a driveway as Lila lay like she was dead in his arms. Not that. Please, not that.

But she would die unless he got her away from this man, this *creature,* for what else but a creature could control another person like Nathan had been controlled?

"Bring her to me, Nathan Moon."

The command was irresistible. Nathan turned. In horror he watched as his body obeyed and crossed the pavement. Lila stirred in his arms. Her eyes flickered open and then her unfocussed gaze settled on him.

"Nathan?" Her hand came up to touch his face as a smile touched her lips.

"Kneel. Kneel before me and do me the honor of taking her life."

"Nathan, no!"

He knelt, struggling against the darkness. It didn't help. His hands were no longer his, a compulsion moved them. He let Lila spill from his arms at the feet of the blond man and saw the fear and pain flood into her face.

Then she kicked him. Her knee caught his face and then she was on her hands and knees scrambling away, the blond man after her.

The dark bonds shivered on Nathan's body.

She made it to her feet and sprinted through the smoke toward the houses on the uphill side of the road and disappeared into the trees. The blond man went after her. The dark bonds faded away.

The blond man was big and athletic. He'd catch Lila if she didn't have help. Nathan struck out after them, aware of the distant sound of a siren coming up the road behind them.

Far too little and far too late to help.

§

Red light flashing on the dash of the car, Danny steered the car up the long, two lane hill that was Princeton Avenue. The street took broad, sweeping arcs across the benchland that would normally provide panoramic views of the lake and the eastern mountains. Not today. Today the yellow-grey pall of smoke obscured everything but the houses and trees close to the road. The neat subdivisions of view homes fell behind as he drove higher, to be replaced by the long-needled ponderosa pine and small hobby farms half-masked by smoke. Here and there, owners were fighting uneasy livestock into trailers. People were loading cars. It was the worst of the great Kelowna fire come to Peachland because all he had to do was raise his gaze to the hillside to see the wall of flames eating its way down the mountain.

Damn it, where the hell was that Mercedes? The farther he drove, the more certain his cop Spidey sense was that whoever had guided that car had come this way. He knew it like he knew when a suspect was lying. The tells were there, he just couldn't describe them. Something in his gut just *knew*.

So where the hell were they? If they kept going, they'd most likely run into a road block set up to stop people from getting in the way of the fire crews. There were always the crazies drawn to flames, and the police set up perimeters for their safety. That meant the Mercedes had to turn off somewhere.

But where?

The neighborhoods weren't an option. There was still too good a possibility some straggler householder would still be loading his truck or car with valuables. Thus Danny had driven right past them.

So where? He slowed as he passed a wooded driveway, but through the trees he saw people loading a car. Not them. He kept going, following the winding road up around the mountain's flank and had to slow for the thickening smoke. Even with headlights, there was barely a few hundred feet visibility.

Another curve and the road was blocked by a marked RCMP car and wooden stanchions, the red and blue lights barely visible in the thick air. He slammed on the brakes and a young uniformed police officer in a face mask came through the smoke to Danny's car.

Danny turned off his siren and rolled down the window. The acrid smoke filled the car. The constable leaned down to him and lifted his chin at the light on Danny's dash. The constable was young, dark haired, and smooth skinned as if he hadn't seen much of the ways of the world—yet. He was right out of Depot training if Danny recalled.

"You on a call?" the kid asked.

Danny nodded. "You're Hermanson, right? Corporal Danny Forester, General Investigations Section." Set the kid straight on rank right away. "I'm looking for someone. Might be involved in an abduction. I thought they'd come this way." Damn it. They had to be up here somewhere. He was almost certain of it. "They were driving a dark grey Mercedes S-Class Sedan. Seen anything like that?"

The young constable frowned. Then he paled. "Sir. I think—I think I might have made an error. We just moved the road block down here from where Princeton becomes the Brenda Mine Road. The fire was getting too low and the fire crew had to pull back. We'd cleared the housing developments up there, but there might have been a car. One like you describe. I—I think it might have turned onto the last road just before the road block point. At the time, I was tearing down the roadblock and it slipped my mind." He cast a glance over his shoulder and he swallowed. "Sir, if they're up there, they're in trouble. They pulled the fire base camp back to below that point ten minutes ago."

"Shit." Ten minutes while he'd been sitting in a traffic lineup. While he'd been scaring the crap out of a realtor. "Let me through."

"Sir, I'm not supposed to let anyone into the area."

"You take down that barrier or I'm going through it. Now." Danny ordered. The kid, thankfully, obeyed and Danny accelerated through, then grabbed his phone and stabbed Jas' number and the speakerphone on.

"Stone."

"Jas. I got them. A Mercedes matching the description was seen turning onto a side road off Princeton about ten minutes ago. Only problem is, it's now on the wrong side of the road blocks for the fire. I'm through, but it's like hell up here. I can barely see."

"On my way." Jas' voice cut off.

Danny drove as fast as he dared, siren on, keeping an eye on the road and on the mountain slope above. The flames were a sullen glare through the smoke. It was getting hellishly close. Way too close for comfort, and that thing had to have Lila up here in the fire, because no sane person would come up here of their own free will.

The point where Princeton Avenue became the Brenda Mine Road wasn't a specific place, it was more a general locale where the houses ran out and the forest and animals took over for the approximately fifteen miles it took to reach the now closed copper and molybdenum mine. The road flattened out, following Deep Creek that eventually flowed down through Hardy Falls to Okanagan Lake. Somewhere in here had to be where the roadblock had been.

The smoke was so bad he could barely see the trees to either side of the road. He slowed the car, but left the siren going. Hopefully the sound would reach Lila and, if she'd had a chance to escape, give her a direction to head for.

Ahead, on the uphill side of the road, came a break in the trees. Road. A discrete sign beside it said Hillcrest Acres in white paint on brown wood. The kind of place that might offer nice homes for people without a lot of money, though Danny couldn't figure why anyone would live in the Okanagan without a view.

Keep going or turn here. He stopped the car and closed his eyes. Was this the place? If Jas saw him, he'd laugh. Danny Forester gone just as woo-woo as all the weird events they'd dealt with over the summer—and this wasn't something taking him over.

His Spidey senses were on high alert; the little hairs on the back of his neck stood on end. Opening his eyes, he turned the car up the road and suddenly was more certain of this than of anything he'd been sure of in his life, except maybe his love for Victoria. He gunned the motor and the car cut through the smoke and roared past the trees into an open cul-de-sac surrounded by houses on large, treed lots. The Mercedes rose out of the smoke in the center of the pavement, both driver-side doors hanging open. He slammed on the brakes to keep from rear-ending it.

He grabbed his phone and called Jas back. "Found the car. No one seems to be around." He described where he was.

"I'm at the bottom of Princeton," Jas said. "You sit tight 'til I get there."

Still holding the phone, Danny climbed out of the car. From somewhere above, a scream cut through the smoke and fire roar.

"Something's happening, Jas. I'm going."

Chapter 19

Eyes tearing from the smoke, Lila ran between two of the vinyl-sided homes and out into a backyard. Johan Fehr was right behind her. In the yard, the usual brush that lay under the ponderosa pine had been largely cleared, leaving space for lawn and a cleared area that sported a swing set, two swings idly swinging in the smoky air. Beyond that lay only trees and burning mountain.

She plunged through the smoke for the trees. Glanced over her shoulder. Fehr was partway through the yard.

Almost no lead at all, and he was bigger and stronger. If he caught her, there was no chance she'd live.

She plunged into the forest. Branches grabbed at her hair, her clothes. Her stupid shoes, tan and black, open-toed spectators with a two inch heel that were lovely for town, almost sent her sprawling as the heels sank too deep into the soil. Twigs gouged at her toes. She leapt over fallen trees, crossed a gravel patch that might channel run-off water in spring. Up the hill. Keep going. The smoke was thicker uphill and there was a chance she could lose him.

In the thick air, she gasped for breath. Her blood roared in her ears. As long as she was running, she wasn't at the mercy of the creature that she'd met in the car. Her neck and throat were worlds of hurt, but that didn't matter. She was alive and she was going to stay that way.

She could feel him behind her like a force in the wind, pushing her farther and farther up the mountain toward the fire. She stumbled on rocks that poked through the forest floor, tore her biceps open on a branch, and felt the warmth of the blood pouring out of the wound.

A pillow of smoke almost doubled her over, coughing. The heat was intense. The fire couldn't be far. Going uphill like this, she was running right into it and she'd be trapped between Fehr and the flames. She needed to cut across the hillside in order to circle back to the houses—get back down to the road and the cop at the road block. That would save her if she could get there.

She glanced over her shoulder and saw only smoke. At least it gave cover for her movements. Her eyes and throat burned. The sound of her strained breathing filled her ears. She turned across the hill, her foolish shoes slippery on the pine needles covering the uneven slope.

Still no sign of Fehr. Had she escaped him?

Something burned her arm. Fire ember. She brushed it off. More sifted through the smoke like burning confetti to land on the parched needles at her feet. Tiny flickers of flame shriveled brown grass. The needles caught.

Fire. Spreading. She looked to the trees and saw a branch catch, and suddenly became aware of a horrible roaring. Not blood in her ears. Not her tearing breath. The fire.

An explosion ripped the air just uphill from her and a gout of flame cut through the smoke into the air. Sparks showered down on her, and the tinder dry needles ignited around her. Fire in her hair. She turned downhill and ran, madly swatted it out.

Where were the firefighters? Where were the water bombers? But she knew the answer. Their flights had been restricted due to the poor visibility, leaving the ground crews to go it alone. In this wind, this aggressive a fire would be too dangerous. She wouldn't be surprised if they'd pulled back and decided to give up on these houses to try to build a fire break that might save the town.

If that was the case, they'd have pulled the roadblock back, too. If they had, that meant that she was up here alone with the creature that wore Johan Fehr like a piece of clothing, and Nathan, who the creature controlled.

She was alone. She was alone being chased by the creature and the fire.

Fear tightened her chest, but there was nothing she could do. She would just have to go farther. She'd still aim for the road. She could take off her shoes and run on the pavement. She used to run with Chloe all the time before she took up yoga and the store took up too much time.

Keeping her panic in check, she set out as fast as she dared. She could do this. She could. But the smoke, if anything, was getting thicker and it was harder to breathe. She had to stop again and again to catch her breath, bent over to heave in great gasps of clearer air from down by her knees.

Another explosion just uphill rained more of sparks and flames.

Damn it, she had to go faster. The fire was leaping ahead through the treetops. The steady rain of burning sparks kept catching in her hair, at her clothes. She kicked off her shoes and started to run.

Was that something darker up ahead? Had she reached the cul-de-sac of houses? She lengthened her stride and angled sideways, diving blindly into a thick layer of smoke that streamed down from the fire.

Something in the haze.

A figure. Male.

Too late.

She slammed into him and arms closed around her.

Caught. She screamed.

§

Danny moved cautiously away from his car through the smoke, his service revolver in his hand. If Fehr was out here, and everything said he was, then he was a very dangerous man. This gun might be the only thing that could save Lila and Nathan.

The fire's roar was like the rumble of a train in a battle zone. Too many trees exploded on the slopes above him as the heat got their sap boiling. The air tasted of heat and flame, and the wind carried a steady stream of ash and cinders down over the pavement so that it had already hidden the windshield of the Mercedes. Danny checked the car. Scuff marks on the back of the driver seat suggested a struggle, confirming what he suspected: there was someone beyond Nathan Moon involved in Lila's abduction. He could pretty well guess who. Hell, even in the fire smoke, he could smell the hint of incense. The creature was here.

Yes, that was it. The creature's scent reminded him of the incense smoke in *This and That*. That meant that he might be able to track it.

He abandoned the Mercedes and headed for the houses in the direction of the scream he'd heard when he first arrived on scene. He following the faint trace of myrrh on the air, far more heady than any pine resin. In the backyard that overflowed with smoke, he almost walked into a children's swing set and stopped to consider. The trail said up the hill, but there was something as well that said he should go eastward, angling along the edge of the house yard.

Gun in hand, he threaded his way through the trees, the houses' almost invisible black bulks down slope from him. The brush was thick and tinder dry from the long hot summer. Branches snapped off when he brushed against them. Perfect for a firestorm, and the fire was coming. A spark caught in the hairs on his arm. He brushed it out with his hand. Others fell into his hair, burned his face. A tree exploded just behind him, and overhead, with every gust of wind, the fire was spreading far more quickly than it had. Damn it, this was getting too close. If they didn't get out of here soon, there'd be no way out at all. The fire's heat had already set sweat running down his face, his chest.

Call Lila? But that would alert Fehr to his presence and he didn't relish the opportunity to face him. Not that he could get out of it. The thing had to be destroyed and if its host was Fehr, that meant Fehr had to be destroyed. Everything he'd sensed when the creature had taken him over this last time suggested that it was getting weaker. He had to hold onto that hope.

Six doors must open so that the seventh can be free and the evil slain.

That was what Lila had read from the diary.

There was only Lila and Nathan left and then whatever needed to happen with the seventh door could happen.

He needed to find Lila. He needed to find Nathan and bring them together. How the hell he was going to do so in this smoke was another thing entirely.

A burning ember in his hair brought him back to himself. The thick smoke doubled him over coughing. The fire was too close. He had to get moving, downhill preferably. He struck out, back toward the houses, because surely the fire would have driven Lila and Nathan that way, too.

A second scream cut through the fire's roar and Danny stopped dead. Behind him and above him. Directly in the path of the flames.

Chapter 20

Caught in the smothering smoke amidst the trees, Nathan fought the struggling woman in his arms. Fists caught his cheek. A heel came down on his instep and sent fire up his leg.

"Lila. Lila, it's me." He choked out the words as loud as he dared, for the creature that was Johan Fehr couldn't be far away and he would not be trapped by the thing again.

The fighting stopped. "Nathan?" barely a whisper.

"That's right. Come on." He kissed her lips quickly, then caught her hand and started them around the subdivision of houses. "If we can reach the road, we might find help."

Lila shook her head. "We're behind the fire line. Otherwise there'd be firemen trying to save these houses."

"The car, then. We get to the Mercedes and leave Fehr here. Maybe he won't get out." It was a hope anyway.

The heat was almost unbearable, the ash thickening so it was hard to breath. Lila's face and clothing were streaked with soot and seared through in places. Burned patches showed where her hair had caught fire.

The bulk of the houses were barely visible through the smoke and it was hard to breathe. The trees here were spaced farther apart and they were walking on grass, marred with black patches where sparks had caught, then burned themselves out. In this heat with the constant rain of sparks, it wouldn't be long before this lawn, these structures went up.

They reached a house with a broad wooden patio and lawn furniture lying in wait like some macabre, sunny day in hell. Skirting round the side of the house, he headed for the street and the Mercedes. Another car sat behind it and maybe that meant help. Lila suddenly grabbed his arm and yanked him back.

"The other car?" he asked.

She shook her head. "It might be Danny here to help. But look." She pointed to their left.

He followed her gesture and the smoke parted to show Johan Fehr standing in the shadows of the front door of the house across the street. As they watched, from somewhere he produced a match, lit it, and tossed it out into the front yard. The brown grass caught and flames flickered at the base of the structure.

"What the hell's he doing?" Nathan whispered and looked down at Lila. When he looked back, Fehr was gone and Lila grabbed Nathan's arm and pulled him back between the houses.

"Cutting off our escape. He saw us. He's coming. Run!"

Lila led across the backyard like a frightened deer, leaping around the trees and plunging into the smoke-filled forest.

He caught up to her. "This way."

He caught her hand and led farther up the hill. Dangerous because of the fire, but if they could outrun Fehr to the other end of the housing development, they still might be able to get down to the road.

A tree, exploded only a few yards away, sent him backpedaling down the hill. He turned them across the slope, Lila running beside him, but the fire seemed to be always just beyond them and where was Fehr?

A coughing fit hit Lila and they had to stop. She doubled over and tried to catch her breath, inhaling the clearer air lower down. The fire was coming at them from three sides.

"Love, we have to get going. The fire's too close. We wait much longer, it'll jump in front of us."

He grabbed her arm and dragged her after him even though she was still coughing. They had to get out of here. The world was an inferno exploding around them as boiling pitch exploded in the tree trunks and spread more deadly sparks through the tinder-dry forest.

Thick smoke blinded them. They walked into tree trunks, tripped over stones, over fallen logs. Burning grassfires forced them to change their path so many times he wasn't sure where they were, but he had Lila and he was leading her downhill. That was all that mattered.

He led her downhill past a copse of new poplar.

Lila started coughing again. She stopped, but he dragged her after him. Kept going, even though she protested.

He tried to stop. Tried to open the fingers he had clamped on Lila's hand—for naught. Tried to warn her, but his mouth was not his own; the world had gone black all around them.

Then Johan Fehr stepped out of the smoke toward them.

"Nathan! Run!"

The blond man flicked his fingers and Nathan couldn't move.

Johan Fehr turned to Lila and his lips curved in a caricature of a smile. "As I said, Lila, your end was ordained as soon as you put the bracelet on. I may call you, Lila?"

No! This couldn't be happening. Nathan tore at his invisible bonds, but it did no good. He was captive as surely as if he was in an iron cage.

Fehr grabbed Lila's arm. "I'll take it from here, my boy."

Fehr flicked his fingers and Nathan released Lila. His body turned uphill toward the flames. He started walking.

"What are you doing?" he heard Lila ask and the sound of struggle.

"He is not needed anymore. Neither are you, I'm afraid."

"Nathan! No! Nathan!"

Lila's screams were lost in the roar of the fire as Nathan began the climb uphill. The smoke thickened and his chest begged for air. The heat seared his skin and the fire was all around him, the trees to either side in flame. If any of them exploded, he was a dead man.

Embers fell on his clothes and caught fire, but his body marched on to meet the inferno.

§

At the sound of the third scream, Danny turned and almost fell. Shit. He'd been going entirely in the wrong direction and he was too high up the hill, too close to the fire. Maybe he'd just been living in hope that Lila had made it into the clearer air this side of the subdivision. The scream rose higher on the air. There were words there, pleading. Unlike the first time when he arrived and the second when he'd headed up the hill. Those earlier screams had quickly been cut off.

The first time he'd thought she'd been killed immediately. This was worse, as the sound died away.

He knew Fehr. Knew the merciless gaze that had looked back at him from the reports of international business dealings. The man would take his time to torture Lila, just like he had played cat and mouse games each time he'd come for the women. He liked their terror. Perhaps he fed on it. That could be why he brought them here, because the fire could only compound her fear. Of course, Johan Fehr himself might be trapped in the fire. That suggested the creature wasn't too concerned about getting his host out of the situation. The damn djinn could just leap heads again.

Shaken at the realization, and knowing that it could even be him who had been targeted for possession, he started running, keeping low through the smoke and the burning trees. Maybe— maybe if he could come in up the hill from them, he could catch Fehr unaware. The roar of the fire distorted everything, but the scream hadn't been far, otherwise he wouldn't have heard it at all. The flames were leaping through the tops of the trees. They caught in the branches around him, leaping like small animals from branch to branch as if trying to get between him and his destination. He slapped away burning embers, his clothing so hot he thought it might weld to his skin.

The billowing smoke was thick and almost impenetrable, and yet gusts of fiery wind let him catch glimpses ahead. Something moved there, lumbering like an animal. A deer escaping?

A man!

A man strode directly up the hill not looking left or right, the back of his shirt already in flames.

Blond haired, but surely Fehr wouldn't be walking into the inferno.

Nathan. Had to be.

His usually easy stride was stiff and unnatural. His arms simply hung at his sides and the fact he headed directly for the wall of flames above them said something was seriously wrong.

Danny looked down the hill. The scream had come from that direction. Looking at Nathan, he'd bet good money that the man before him was being controlled by someone other than Nathan. The man might have walked out on Lila. He might even have grabbed Lila and thrown her in the Mercedes, but Danny'd bet good money that it was Johan Fehr behind the abduction and now the apparent suicidal actions of the Hollywood producer.

"Shit." Danny plunged through the burning forest after him. He caught up as a billow of smoke closed around him. It caught, burning in his throat as he grabbed Nathan's shoulder and hauled him around. The man's face was immobile. No sign of recognition.

"Shit." Danny clocked him in the temple with his pistol butt.

Nathan sagged against him and Danny holstered his weapon, slapped out the flames in the back of Nathan's shirt, then dragged him up into a fireman's carry and staggered downhill. The fire was everywhere and so was the smoke. Too thick to see and barely able to breathe. He coughed, hacked, and the heat burned his lungs. The heated earth burned through his rubber-soled shoes. A primal part of him wanted to dump Nathan and run, just run. Forget Lila. Just get free of the flames.

But he owed Lila. She had been the first person to trust him again after the creature had released him after that horrible first time. It was her trust and Jas' that had given him faith that he could be his own man again. That had given him the confidence to do the best thing he had ever done in his life—fall in love with Victoria.

Damn it. He was going to get through this for Victoria and he was going to save Lila and Nathan while doing it.

But he had to find Lila and Fehr to save her and it had been at least five minutes since he heard her scream. Five minutes was a lot of time. She could be dead by now.

Nathan groaned across his shoulders. "What the hell? Put me down."

Definitely sounded like Nathan. Danny let him slip to the ground and drew his gun.

Nathan staggered up and held up his hands. "It's me, Danny. It's Nathan."

"You were walking up into the fire."

Nathan shook his head. "No. Whatever that thing is walked me up there. I was the passenger. But it's gone now and it's got Lila."

It was hard to judge whether Nathan was truly free of the creature, but Danny made a decision. Lila and the bracelet were too important. He wasn't going to allow some "great evil" to be loosed into the world.

"Where is she?" he asked.

"Come on." Nathan led downhill through the woods. There was less fire here, the flames busy eating their way down to them. He rubbed his head. "You really plowed me."

"Had to," Danny said. "The only way I could make sure I wouldn't have to kill you."

Nathan shook his head and winced. "Well, he's gone, now. And that means he's just focused on Lila. That can't be good."

"Our only ally is the fact that he likes to take his time. It's like a game to him—or seems to be," Danny said. "He likes their terror."

"I got that, too. He was happiest when she was most afraid, and angry when she stood up to him." He stopped. "I—I think we were here."

Smoke oozed around them like oil through reeds.

"How can you know?" The place looked like any other piece of forest to Nathan.

"Those trees." Nathan motioned at a copse of six-foot-tall new growth poplar, beyond which a few trees burned. "This is where he caught us. I'm almost sure."

Danny bent to check the ground and there were scuff marks that could be signs of a struggle. He inhaled and caught the faint scent of incense and glanced up at Nathan. The man was grimacing with pain, but there was no time. "Come on."

The two of them headed down the hill together. Soon the bulk of the houses rose through the smoke. The roar of the fire was less here, but there was another sound—a deep throated rumble overhead. Danny looked up and caught a glimpse of blue through the smoke and a fleeting shadow across the sky. What sounded like a huge explosion came from up the hill.

A burst of black steam filled the sky and scalding heat came through the trees.

"Run. This way. They're bombing the fire. They got the planes flying somehow."

Nathan led through the backyard of the houses and through the space between them to the cul-de-sac in front. Through the smoke by the Mercedes, Johan Fehr stood over a kneeling Lila, his hands around her throat.

"Stay back, Nathan. He can take you over again." Gun in hand, Danny stepped out from between the houses. Fehr glanced toward him.

Overhead more rumbling spoke of another water bomber run.

"It is almost done. Her life spark fades," Fehr said dreamily and turned his flat gaze on Danny. "But if you prefer, I can break her neck before you can stop me."

Danny squeezed the trigger, but so fast, Danny barely saw it, Fehr hauled Lila in front of him, her head in both hands.

Lila drew a huge shuddering breath. So she lived, but all it would take to kill her was a simple twist of Fehr's powerful wrists.

§

Air. There was only air. Smoky, rancid air, but it was air! Lila choked and gasped in another huge breath and ignored the pain in her neck. She'd been sure it was over. Nathan gone and surely dead in the flames.

Thick, acrid smoke set her coughing. Fehr's furnace-hot hands held her neck and the reek of burning tore up her nostrils. A hopeful rumble filled the air overhead and even less believable was the way the smoke parted to reveal a figure before her.

Danny, soot-covered and singed, a gun raised.

The grip on her neck tightened and she knew what it meant. Knew she was to die imminently, but perhaps she'd meet Nathan in a next life. Chloe would say that was possible.

Another figure materialized beside Danny. Hair singed and scalp burned. Shirt nearly burned from his shoulders. Nathan.

He lived. He lived and she was going to die!

Her heart broke with the horror. Her eyes filled. *Sorry for the pain I've caused you. Sorry that I said "no."* She opened her mouth. "I love you."

Despite all the difficulties they might face, she meant it. But her words were so soft she barely heard them herself. Still, Nathan seemed to. His mouth curved in a small, private smile—the kind his face had held when they first made love.

The world slowed.

Heat seared through her body like an electric shock and the silver bracelet flared on her wrist.

Then it was gone. She felt the clasp let go, the silver links slide from her flesh, just as the hands on her neck began to flex.

A flash exploded from Danny's gun and suddenly she was falling, released from Fehr's grip. She collapsed on hands and knees. Fehr reeled back, clutching his left shoulder, his left arm limp at his side.

"On the ground, Fehr!" Danny ordered through the acrid smoke.

On the ground beside them gleamed seven links of silver.

Lila threw herself at the bracelet just as Fehr shoved her aside. Another shot rang out, but Fehr barely staggered. Smoke closed in around them as she fumbled for the bracelet. Silver links on rough pavement. Silver links in her hand as Fehr tossed her aside. Danny shouted at Fehr. Nathan plunged to her aid. Fehr roared as he realized she had the bracelet and came for her, hauled her into his chest, his grip on her hand crushing her fingers, but she wasn't going to let go. No way was she letting him get the bracelet. Pain screamed through her hand. Small bones broke and dislocated.

Nathan grabbed Fehr's neck, but the man was like a bull. Nathan's efforts barely had an effect and the bracelet was slip-slipping as Fehr pried her broken fingers open. She frantically grabbed for the bracelet with her other hand as he ripped it free of her grip. Her fingers caught on a bracelet chain. She held on as Fehr dragged her with him. One step. Another. Then the chain gave and it was gone.

Lila fell to her knees, her broken hand almost more than she could bear.

"The power is mine again!" Fehr roared his triumph and held the bracelet to the sky. More planes rumbled overhead, shadows through the heavens. The smoke billowed around them. Lila started a lopsided crawl. If she could get to Fehr, maybe she could stop whatever he planned to do.

Another roar as Danny fired and Fehr staggered back a step and then straightened. Another shot and the man was laughing

Nathan's warm hands caught Lila's shoulders and pulled her up into his arms. She turned to his shoulder, her broken hand between them, and Nathan edged her away back to Danny's protective weapon.

"Fool!" Fehr roared. "I have the bracelet!"

Danny shook his head. "It's over, Fehr. The bracelet came off. Lila and Nathan have found each other and the sixth door has opened. Wasn't that the old curse? Six doors open so that ancient evil can be killed?"

Fehr stopped his celebration and looked from the bracelet to Danny. Fehr's pupils had eaten even the whites of his eyes.

"Curse." He spat. "Made by a little man who I destroyed. You think you can destroy me—you and your gun? Never. Not now that I have the bracelet." As he spoke, dark flames oozed from his body, thicker and more oily that the smoke from the fire.

"The bracelet doesn't mean anything now that the sixth door is open, Fehr. You know that." Was she right? Was that what the curse meant? "Six doors have opened, Fehr. Most of your power's gone," Lila said. She hoped.

Fehr threw back his head and laughed. Through the smoke he grew bigger, the dark flames from his body enlarging his limbs.

His oily fire ate the afternoon's dim light, but the bracelet still gleamed in his hand. His body swelled larger until it loomed over them, consuming all light. In the burning landscape, she, Nathan, and Danny were like children in a nightmare under a night-darkened sky.

"You have to kill him, Danny. Before he escapes," Nathan said.

"He's taken four bullets already and it's like he felt nothing."

"You kill the body and he can take over someone else," Lila said.

"Do you know how long I've waited for this? What the rush of power feels like?" Fehr said, like the voice of God in the wilderness. "Six doors may have opened, but there is still power in the silver. With this power, the world is mine. The human race is no longer the master. The ancient doors between the worlds will open and the most ancient lords of dark will rule again as it was before the sunlight came."

Fehr's darkness had spread, eating up the two cars behind them, devouring the subdivision, the smoke on the hillside, and heat of the fire and of the sun. There was only darkness and all hope was gone. Darkness weighted her shoulders.

"On your knees before me!" Fehr's voice roared.

It was over. They had lost. In despair, Lila clung to Nathan.

Danny fired again, but the darkness swallowed the explosion of sound.

The bullet hit Fehr mid-chest and his body staggered, but more darkness flooded out of him, completing the darkness around them. Smothering darkness and she could barely breathe. No hope. No life. There was only the sound of their labored gasps, the roar of the fire behind them, and the gleaming silver still clutched in Fehr's hand.

The bracelet glowed as if it held its own beam of starlight. It flickered and burned and then its light increased.

Fehr roared and tried to throw the bracelet from him, but the silver appeared welded to his hand. Its light seared like lightning through Fehr's flesh. His body crumbled to ash that was consumed by Fehr's darkness. The bracelet fell from his hands. On the pavement, the silver glow increased. Fehr's dark flames swirled, congealed, and, like a smothering pillow, settled over the light.

All darkness. Everything lost. Lila sobbed into Nathan's shoulder as he eased her back.

A spear of light thrust through the darkness, intensifying until Lila had to look away. Nathan shielded his eyes. Danny lowered his gun and backed them away. "Could be an explosion."

"No. No, I don't think so," Lila said and refused to go further. "This is the other part of the Egyptian psychic's prophecy.

Remember what Colonel Bristol wrote in his diary? Six doors must open so that the seventh can be free and the evil slain?"

A brilliant flash of light blasted through the darkness like a door suddenly opened. The air shook with a scream so dark and malevolent Lila's knees buckled.She pulled Nathan down beside her. The brilliance passed. She blinked once, twice, three times, before her vision returned.

The darkness was gone, leaving ordinary smoke billowing across the ground. Before them, in front of the ash-covered Mercedes, stood a man so beautiful he could break her heart. Tall as Jas, as dark-haired as Cesare, with Nathan's breadth of shoulders and Danny's grin. She saw hints of Brett in the blue of his eyes and promises of Séamus' humor in their light. All of them represented in this man as he swung toward them clad in simple drawstring trousers and a coarse tunic that carried the same light that he did.

§

The blinding light cleared from Nathan's eyes leaving him kneeling with his arms around his precious Lila and a stranger before them in the smoke-and-flame-filled afternoon. He needed to undo what he'd done and get Lila out of here away from the fire, but the stranger in the unnaturally white clothing stood between them and the car.

"Danny, tell him to get away from the cars. Lila needs medical help. She's in pain."

Danny just stood there, shock on his face as the stranger stepped toward them.

"*Grazie,*" the stranger said, his voice low-timbered and strong. "You have done well to free me."

"Free you?" Danny said.

"Who are you?" Nathan asked as he held on protectively to Lila's shoulders.

"You opened the doors. You broke the chain that bound me." He stooped to the ash that had been Fehr's body and picked up the still-gleaming silver bracelet. "You see?"

The bracelet looked the same—still silver, still seven doors. Then he spotted the change. One end of a small silver chain hung loose from the door at one end of the links.

"The chain on the seventh door," Lila said. "It truly held the door shut."

The stranger nodded. "As securely as a prison. My only hope was that my curse might someday be realized, so that the one that held me might be lifted. When I stole the creature's power, I could not absorb it all. What I could not take, I placed in each of the doors. The creature hated human emotion and hated love most of all. How fitting that I cursed the bracelet so that the power was released each time the bracelet's wearer fell in love. Love is so natural that I thought it would happen quickly and that I could reunite with my beloved Laelia." The man sighed. "It was not to be. The bracelet was hidden too well. My love is long lost to the world."

"Your servant stole the bracelet and ran. She hid the bracelet where it might never have been found—wasn't found for over a thousand years," Lila said as if in a trance in Nathan's arms.

The stranger's gaze found them and he smiled. "You—you two hold the spirits of the lovers who fled before the creature's wrath. Sarah was our serving girl and a beauty she was. She was to be married but the creature came. She and her betrothed ran together until you were trapped in a cave, and even then you stood together to face the thing that finally killed you. You did well."

Which made no more sense than anything else about this craziness. The smoke from the hillside rolled in a thick bank around them, obscuring the houses and the vehicles again.

Nathan's eyes teared and Lila started choking. "We need to get moving. The fire's too close and you're hurt, Lila."

He helped Lila up as he stood and urged her toward the Mercedes, but she stopped him. "Look!"

From an eddy of smoke and embers, a slim figure coalesced. A long flow of ash-black hair, flesh fine and glowing as a haze over the sun. Dark-eyed, with a dress of smoke that moved as one with her flesh, a woman floated out of the smoke and destruction of the forest on the mountainside. She had Lila's hair and Chloe's wide gaze and the voluptuousness of Victoria as well as the hint of sprite he'd seen in the little one, Kylee. Around her biceps were coiled silver bands reminiscent of Reggie's Celtic tattoos.

The stranger's eyes widened. "Laelia?"

The roar of the fire dimmed around them and a whisper ran through the air. "I have wandered the world waiting. I knew you would come."

The woman's figure rode the coiling smoke and reached out her hand. The stranger reached for her and their hands met—light and smoke joined. The writhing smoke glowed. The figures grew in size but their details became indistinct, like a fade-out from one movie scene to the next.

The figures filled the pavement, they towered into the sky, and then the brisk wind from the coast caught them, and with a sound like the tinkling of small bells, they blew away, leaving a scent of—was that jasmine?—and a momentary fragment of blue sky.

Nathan shook his head. Had that really happened?

Then a rumbling plane flew in low above them to dump water or fire retardant on the mountain above them, and a tree exploded in the front yard of one of the houses.

Nathan dragged Lila across the empty pavement as flaming embers swirled around them. "We have to get out of here. Now."

He urged Lila to the Mercedes. She was shaking in his hands. Pain and shock. Her poor, poor hand, her badly bruised neck. She stumbled, barefoot, as she walked.

He helped her into the Mercedes.

"The bracelet. We can't leave it behind," she cried.

Nathan left her and scrambled to the last place he had seen it. Already the falling ash and embers muddied the heap of ash that had once been Johan Fehr. The wind had picked up and sent the embers and smoke swirling. It was too dangerous to be here. Leave the bracelet and head for safety was the wiser move, but Lila was concerned for the bracelet.

He sifted his fingers through the ash and came up with tarnished silver links. The bracelet looked old and worn as if he could crumple it between his fingers. Stuffing it in his pocket, he dashed for the car and climbed in behind the wheel. Danny was in his police car. The key was still in the Mercedes' ignition so Nathan hit the start button. The engine turned over, coughed once, and went silent. He tried again, but though the starter whined, nothing happened. The engine wasn't getting enough air. The ash.

He sat, flummoxed for a moment, his hands on the wheel, but the windshield wipers shoved the ash away and he could see the fire laying claim to one of the houses' roofs. They had to keep moving.

He leapt out of the car to see Danny doing the same. "Damn thing won't start," Danny said.

Nathan helped Lila out, but the shaking in her hands and the glassy look of her eyes said she was almost spent. Dragging her with him, he joined Danny.

"Where to?"

Danny led off in a trot down the road. The fire had spread toward the lake. They'd be lucky if Princeton Avenue wasn't blocked, but they had to try. He had Lila's safety in his hands and he'd be damned if he was going to lose the woman he loved just when they'd found each other.

The planes continued overhead, fighting the flames that came after them as if Fehr inhabited them. The road dove through the trees. To either side, spot fires had burst into being. The wind still drove the fire right down on the town. Nathan kept going, dragging Lila with him.

"I can manage on my own, Nathan," Lila said quietly.

He glanced down at her. The glazed gaze had passed, but the lines around her eyes spoke of her pain.

"You're hurt and I'm not losing you again." He kept a firm grip on her hand.

"So are you, but trust me. I can walk on my own."

And that was the thing, wasn't it? If they were going to be together, they had to trust that even though they were fiercely independent people, they both cared enough about the other to make it work. For an instant he had a vision of a never-ending dusty road and a woman much like Lila, though in archaic clothes, hurrying beside him, back bent with fatigue but never bowed.

He released her and she swayed a moment, her injured hand cradled against her chest. "Come on. We can do this."

Arm around her shoulder, he ushered her down the hill, the roar of the fire behind them.

Together the three of them stumbled out onto Princeton Avenue just as an unmarked police SUV came roaring around the curve of the road below them. Its lights were on, its siren wailing. Danny waved down the vehicle and it screeched to a halt before them.

Jas Stone leapt out. "Thank God. I would have been here sooner but the damned Fire Commander wouldn't let me through. He wouldn't believe there was anyone stupid enough to be up here until a spotter plane spotted your two cars and thought they saw movement."

He clapped Danny on the shoulder and must have seen him wince.

"Into the car. There's doctors waiting just past the road block."

"Lila needs more than triage," Nathan said and pulled her into his side.

"And Nathan's badly burned. Leastways his shirt was in flames when I found him," Danny said.

Jas just nodded. "The hospital it is, then."

Chapter 21

The day of the opening of *The Next Thing* dawned clear and cooler as only the onset of fall could bring. Lila stood in her apricot silk kimono, sipping a maple-flavored mug of tea on the front porch of *This and That,* enjoying the quiet and the smooth, cool waters of the lake. Behind her, on the ottoman, waited a second cup and the teapot that she had miraculously balanced out to the porch on her own. Along the lakeshore, the first hints of yellow and red edged the maple leaves, poplar, and willow. The few joggers running past wore long-sleeved shirts instead of just singlets and sports bras. The air still carried the taint of burning wood from the fire on the mountain, but the winds had miraculously shifted to the east and blown the fire back on itself, allowing the firefighters to contain it. Jubilant Peachland residents had been allowed to come home.

Of course, the easterly winds had brought the cooler weather, too, but it was a natural course of events that came with the seasons. The summer was almost over and soon it would be Thanksgiving and the holidays would come around. They would be different this year with not only her friends, but also Nathan in her life.

So much change had happened over this summer. So many lovers' matches. Even herself.

It had been such a near thing with Nathan. She'd come so close to letting him go again and as a result she'd almost lost him. She wondered what would have happened if Johan Fehr had not become involved. Would things have worked out as well as they had?

She looked down at her injured right hand, engulfed in a cast to keep her from using it. She grinned ruefully. The darn doctors had known her too well, apparently. But thankfully the prognosis was good after a brief surgery and she'd been sent home from the hospital. Chloe had lived in for a few days until Lila could manage on her own.

Nathan had been another matter, kept—or held prisoner, as he put it—in the burn ward so they could care for his back. Thankfully, the prognosis was also positive; and over the two weeks he'd been there, the second degree burns had mostly healed, leaving only one spot on his left shoulder where the fire had gone deeper into his flesh. How he'd managed to walk out of there when he was so damaged still amazed her, even though the nurses had said with the nerve damage he likely didn't feel a thing.

And today he was coming home. Yes, home. Because in Lila's daily visits to the hospital, they had agreed that Peachland was a good home base for Nathan to work from. It could be more than that, too, if Nathan would only give the place and the people a chance. So far she wasn't too sure whether that was working out.

A jaunty figure in a knee-length, grey caftan and leggings came striding down the sidewalk. Chloe, early as usual, so she had time to check on Lila. Lila grinned at her as she turned into the picket gate and took the stairs onto the porch. Lila pointed out the second cup of tea. "Right on time, as usual."

Chloe raised a brow. "Don't tell me I'm getting predictable."

"Let's face it; you're a mother hen where the rest of us are concerned."

"Pot calling the kettle much?" Chloe poured and tested the tea. "Mmm, good. But you don't need to be insulting. I'm no mother hen. I'm—I'm just concerned. Spoken to Nathan this morning?"

"Of course. Cesare is picking him up and they'll meet us at the opening. Nathan's chomping at the bit to get out of that hospital. I tell you, the cell towers have been burning up with all his calls about some secret project or other he's got going." She shook her head.

"And you're going to invite that into your home?" Chloe's deep blue eyes twinkled as she asked the question.

"And are you going to invite a fact-finding, no nonsense policeman into yours?" Lila crossed her arms over her chest.

Chloe sipped her tea, thoughtful. Then she grinned. "Guess you could say done and done. Who knew we'd learn to accommodate men."

"Heck, who knew they'd accommodate us!"

Laughing, Chloe carried their cups and the teapot into the house and together the two of them loaded the last few displays that were going to be taken down to *The Next Thing's* grand opening that was scheduled for eleven in the morning—exactly the time that Nathan was due to be released.

At ten o'clock they arrived at the clothing shop, Lila wearing high, cream-colored heels, with narrow trousers of the same shade that ended just above the ankles and a long-sleeved tunic that came down below her hips. The lower half of the tunic was a diaphanous fabric that shifted in the breeze and showed off her slim legs.

This morning the paper had been removed from the shop windows so they showed the lovely drape and sweep of Victoria's clothing displays. A tasteful green awning had been built so that the sun couldn't fade what was in the windows, and the two concrete, Grecian-looking urns framed the doorway, holding huge displays of lilies, twisty wood, lupine, gerbera, and baby's breath, all in shades of white and purple reminiscent of the *This and That's* misty interior.

The party supply company had arrived and placed a tasteful velvet rope to block off the area that would house the reception—Victoria's apartment was to be spared in the glorious fall weather—and an actual red carpet led to the front door. Tables had been set with white linen and awaited the bountiful finger food that had been arranged from Taste Café.

Chloe let them in through the black velvet rope and stopped. "Look at this. Look at what you've created." She grabbed Lila's good hand and motioned at the storefront. It looked lovely and posh and welcoming, all at the same time.

Lila took a moment to soak it all in. The fresh air that carried the scent of good coffee overlaid in a hint of autumn, the soft breeze that barely rippled the immense lake's water, and the green and brown of the mountain that slumbered across the lake. She turned back to the satisfying scene of the fledgling shop and allowed herself the immense satisfaction of a job well done. "It is good, isn't it? The shop."

"The shop, sure." Chloe slid her arm around Lila's waist. "But there's so much more. You've built a lovely enclave here—an enclave of women and men who all care for each other. This shop is just a—a symptom of the good you've done."

As if to prove a point, a racing green Miata pulled up at the curb and Kylee climbed out wearing a pair of high-waisted cream trousers that showed off her long legs and a sleeveless turquoise silk blouse that set off her bright blonde hair.

"Hey!" She waved and hurried over and the Miata moved off down the street to a parking spot. "Brett's come, too. He thought we might be able to use a male hand for any last minute heavy lifting." She grinned up at them.

"Nice trousers. I like," Chloe said.

Kylee swept her hand self-consciously over the fabric. "I thought that if I'm going to be part of the grand opening of a fashion store, I should probably dress a little more upscale."

Lila eyed the trousers that looked suspiciously like something of Victoria's. "Are those...?"

"Victoria's," Kylee said shamefaced. "I was bemoaning that I could never find trousers that fit or anything that allowed me to look grown-up. The stuff you find in the stores is usually either super casual or all business. Victoria heard me and pulled me aside. I love them, though Brett says he'd rather see my legs."

"I'd rather see what?" Brett Main, Chloe's brother, came up and swung an arm around Kylee's shoulders. He pecked a kiss on the top of her head. "Looks pretty fabulous, doesn't she?"

The front door to the store opened and Victoria stood there in a simple, dark grey sheath that was similar to the items she had for the store. Of course, this piece molded to her as if it was part of her.

"Come in. Come in. There are last minute plans to make and I am so nervous I think I might be sick."

"You'll be fine." Reggie stepped from the shadows of the shop clad in dark grey trousers and a tunic shirt, also of Victoria's design. Around her neck as a splash of color she wore a bright red scarf that was tamed by a silver rope chain woven into its length. A pair of dangling silver earrings with dark red stones peeked through her Cleopatra-style black hair. "Now come on, guys. We need to hold her together until Cesare gets back from picking up Nathan and get this whole party started."

There were last minute things to do like making sure the cash register had a float, confirming that the credit card machine was working and that the workshop area was spotless. Part of the grand opening would allow patrons to see where their clothing would be made and to meet the fantastic artisans who did the work. Victoria's two seamstresses fluttered around the room but came up to Lila to admire their handiwork.

"It looks so wonderful on you," Birdy, the gray-haired head seamstress said and ran her fingers down the sleeve of Lila's top.

"It's a wonderful piece of clothing and made magnificently. Thank you for your work." Lila squeezed Birdy's hand. "Thank you both. I think it's high time you two were celebrated for the artists you are. Who knows, maybe people will ask you for more custom clothing."

Birdy shook her head. "I couldn't do that. I'm going to be too busy with *The Next Thing.*"

"And that's the kind of confidence we all need to have."

"If people see you all in the clothes, they're going to want to wear them, too. You wait and see," Emma Scott, the other seamstress, prophesized.

At ten forty-five, guests began to arrive, milling outside the velvet line as Taste Café staff set out the food. At exactly eleven o'clock, they opened the velvet rope and a fluttering group of elegantly clad women with their men entered the reception area. Clusters of potential customers crowded around the windows. Lila found herself instantly cornered by women admiring her outfit and for a moment regretted their decision to bypass the fashion show by wearing the clothing themselves. Still, she took their questions as they drank champagne and orange juice and ate the tiny croissant and egg sandwiches, prosciutto, and melon wraps and the tiny lemon curd tarts that the bakery had prepared.

It was eleven thirty when Lila was called to perform the master of ceremonies duties. She accepted the microphone that Reggie handed her.

"Ladies and gentlemen, if I can have your attention please. At the start of the summer, I had no idea that it would bring so many wonderful changes to my life and to Peachland. I've been reunited with high school friends." She met Kylee's bright blue gaze. "I've been through trials with dear friends." She smiled at Chloe and Reggie. "And I've made new friends." She caught Victoria's hand.

"Victoria Angelucci came to Peachland to work with Reggie Lewis—of our own *Regulus Designs*—because Reggie's work was supposed to grace the walkways of Milan. Unfortunately, due to circumstances that were no fault of Reggie's, that opportunity fell through; but those same circumstances brought Victoria back here. She liked it enough she considered staying and, well, with some convincing, we've opened this shop together and we're happy to report that her business visa has just been approved." She gave Victoria a hug. "Now, opening a store was not Victoria's first thought. It took some work to get her to consider the opportunity. Wearing her beautiful clothes today, I am so glad we prevailed over her common sense. I'm sure you will be, too, when you see the treasures that she has brought us. Victoria, a few words, please."

She handed the microphone to Victoria, just as a maroon Camry pulled up to the curb. Looking Latin and dashing, Cesare Angelucci climbed out from behind the wheel and the passenger door opened. Nathan.

He wore pressed grey trousers and a light blue dress shirt with the collar open. His blond hair was cut extra short because so much had been burned in the fire. It caught the sunlight, as did the strong lines of his handsome face, as he turned to look up at her. His blue eyes seemed to still when he caught sight of her and everything went quiet.

She knew Victoria was speaking. Knew she was supposed to accept the mike back from Victoria and ask the mayor to cut the ribbon that was strung over the doorway. So many things she was supposed to do, and all her life she'd tried to do them. A hand on her back urged her away from the door and she took that as permission. Shoved through the crowd as Nathan walked toward her.

She met him at the velvet rope and his arms came around her and he buried his face in her hair. "Oh God, I've missed you. Visits at the hospital just aren't the same. "

"You're right there. Meeting with the sun on your back and the wind in your face is better." She smiled. "How's your back?"

"Same as it was, but this morning the doc said even the spot with the third-degree burn is healing nicely and doesn't look like it'll leave a major scar."

She nodded up at him. Leaned up to kiss him and rested her cheek against his. "I'm so glad we found each other—that you came looking."

"You and I were meant to be together and it didn't require the bracelet to tell us. The stranger in the fire said it all. We've been together through lifetimes, determined to be together." He swung her around to the gathering, where Victoria had smoothly assumed control of the MC duties and had the mayor cutting the ribbon. "So how's it going? The opening, I mean."

"Well, I think. Everyone is very keen to see her designs, especially after a few of us tempted them by wearing some of

Victoria's clothes." Leaning her head against his shoulder, she watched as the bevy of well-dressed women and their men pressed into the shop behind Victoria. She had Chloe, Reggie, and Kylee to help her, but she really should be there, too, to support the business.

She straightened, not really wanting to go. "I guess I should go in and lend my support. Duty calls and all that."

"Before you go, I've got some news for you. I just got the call this morning. I sold a concept to one of the big production studios and they want me to work on the script."

A script would be good. It would mean he wouldn't be traveling a lot and it was something Nathan enjoyed. "Fantastic, Nathan. You know, I do have an extra room in the house..."

"Hold on." He held up his hand. "There's something else you should know. The concept I sold is a romance—sort of a *Practical Magic* meets *Romancing the Stone,* with a whole lot more evil thrown in. I—I based it on what the bracelet put you through this summer."

Nathan released her with a rub on the shoulders as if almost afraid of her reaction.

"So you're going to fictionalize our story?" Her mind raced over what this could mean. "If it goes into production, where would you shoot it?"

In answer, Nathan spread his arms and looked around.

"Peachland maybe?" he grinned. "Can you think of a better place?"

There was so much to think about. If such a movie was made, it wouldn't have to identify them, but it might. It would bring production crews to the town, and possibly more people to the town after the movie was made. It was free advertising, but most important, if Nathan directed the movie, he could be here, too. "Not at the moment, but I need to get inside."

But her mind was racing as she pecked him on the cheek and turned for the store, then stopped. "You're sure you're okay?"

He rolled his eyes. "Go on. Cesare and I will just hang out and graze a little of the leftovers."

He nodded at the picked over hors d'oeuvres table. "A healing man needs his strength and all that. For a variety of important functions." He winked at her. Actually winked.

She knew exactly what he meant and felt a flush of heat up through her body. "Hold that thought."

She left the two men talking and ventured into the shop. With so many people crowded inside, it was a heated mayhem of clashing perfumes that the air conditioning couldn't quite keep up with. People were queued up for the dressing rooms and Kylee was tied up at the cash counter making appointments for fittings. Victoria was torn between her sketching table, where she'd planned to display a variety of pieces that could made by special order, and answering the questions of a reporter from the largest Kelowna newspaper. Reggie was busy helping women match pieces of clothing with jewelry, and Chloe, with Birdy and Emma's help, was giving the brief tour of the shop and construction area. It was all working like clockwork. Everyone seemed happy—both customers and staff.

She stood there, feeling the swell of satisfaction, even though her mind still buzzed with Nathan's news. It looked like the store was going to be a success and all her friends were doing well. All had met their match and the lovely silver bracelet that had plagued them for the summer was back in the store, but this time framed in a shadow box display as a very valuable ancient artifact. She'd even had a call from the Museum of Anthropology that had heard about the bracelet due to the metallurgical testing completed at the University of British Columbia. They were interested in possibly purchasing the bracelet for their collection. So far there hadn't been consensus amongst the wearers of the bracelet about what to do. It was hard to think of the silver links as harmless—so much so that none of them had even tried putting the bracelet on since the events in the burning forest. It could be that the bracelet was just harmless jewelry now, but none of them wanted to take the chance.

"What are you doing here?" Reggie whispered, having come up beside her.

"I helped plan all this, remember. Isn't it sort of my duty?"

"Not when that sweetie of yours is waiting outside."

Lila glanced through the door. Nathan looked eminently handsome, deep in conversation with Cesare and munching on one of the tiny croissants.

"He's got Cesare to keep him company."

"No. He doesn't." Reggie said with a twinkle in her dark eyes. "Cesare, could you give me a hand in here?" she called and gently shoved Lila toward the door. "Go have a life, would you. We don't need you to take care of everything anymore."

Lila was pretty sure she should protest, but Nathan stood there waiting. It was a lovely end-of-summer day and when she thought of it, she hadn't taken a single day for herself all summer. There'd been too much to do and too many worries.

She gave Reggie a quick hug. "All right. I will, you brat. If the world ends, don't bother calling. We'll be busy."

She stepped outside to greet the sunshine, the lake, and Nathan. Her future.

If you enjoyed the Unlocking Series,
turn the page to read a sneak preview of Second Spring.

About the Author

Karen L. Abrahamson is a well-traveled writer who has explored cultures and countries around the world, but south central British Columbia, Canada is one of her favorite places to come back to. She is the author of literary, romantic and fantasy fiction including the highly regarded Cartographer fantasy series. She lives on the west coast of Canada with two Bengal cats that aren't quite as well traveled as she is.

When she isn't writing she can be found with a camera and backpack in fabulous locations around the world.

If you would like to get an automatic e-mail when Karen's next book is released, sign up at her website:
www.karenlabrahamson.com.
Your email address will never be shared and you can unsubscribe at any time.

A Special Request from the Author

Word-of-mouth is crucial for any author to succeed. If you enjoyed this book, please consider leaving a review at Amazon, Barnes and Noble, or any other e-tailer, or on Goodreads; even if it's only a line or two, it would make all the difference and would be very much appreciated.

To find more of her writing, visit

www.twistedrootpublishing.com.

Also by Karen L. Abrahamson

and available through _www.twistedrootpublishing.com_

Romance

Ashes and Light
Shades of Moonlight
Judas Kiss
Second Spring
A Different Nightmusic
Shadow Play
Coming Down Christmas
Surviving Safe Harbour

The Unlocking (Peachland) Series:
Unlocking Her Heart
Unlocking Her History
Unlocking Her Grace
Unlocking Her Dreams
Unlocking Her Chances
Unlocking Her Doubts

Mystery

Through Dark Water
After Yekaterina
Mareson's Arrow

Sneak Preview – Second Spring

Chosen as consort of Spring at age twelve, Letha Rivers yearns for freedom from Spring Lake, but each year the duty to bring the season of new life and growth holds her captive.

When Ty Hunter, prodigal son, returns to the valley, it ignites old attractions, but Ty brings with him the specter of a past that pursues him. Letha must choose between her valley and the man she loves, but freedom and love come at a price that Letha may not be capable of paying.

Karen L. McKee once again introduces a unique cast of characters in a vivid setting. A richly evocative romance with a tinge of magic, Second Spring, introduces readers to the ranching community of Shelter Valley. With its wonderful characters and unique story-telling, Second Spring will be a book readers will love to return to.

Prologue

Shelter Lake, British Columbia

Before the sun rose, the pickup trucks rumbled through last year's hay stubble to stop by the unlit bonfire. Shadow figures climbed out of the trucks and the people came together quietly in the dim light amid the frosted Queen Anne's lace of the lake shore.

Once each generation they came to witness the choice of a gift bound to Spring — a sacrifice to bring new life and new sap in the leaves, through the breaking of ice.

In the cold of the lake, Letha resented the fact she was here, shivering, with Kristienne, Sylvia, and five other girls.

"How long will it take, do you think?" Kristienne, one of Letha's best friends, shifted in the knee-deep water so that the lake's surface shattered the reflection of her eleven-year-old face, glazed by dawn's first glow.

"As long as it takes, Mom says." Letha crossed her arms over her body, hating the fact that her mother and Valley tradition had forced her here. It wasn't a choice she would have made, but when had anyone ever listened to her preferences? No one ever listened to what you wanted when you were eleven. So she gave in like always. What she wanted didn't matter. Besides, doing what she was told made life easier for everyone.

But since her granny died, an unspeakable dread had kept her awake at nights with bad dreams of the lake that left her queasy. Standing like this made it worse. She looked at the other girls around her.

Let it be one of them. Don't let her be chosen.

All of her granny's old stories shivered in her, sending nervous energy coursing through her blood and making her stomach churn. The uncertainty of her future chilled her more. Brushing red hair back, she looked defiantly at those on shore, but her teeth were chattering too hard, and they were too far off for her defiance to show.

"It's freezing out here. Your lips are blue as Mom's Saskatoon-berry jam." Kristienne whispered, as she rubbed her palm briskly down Letha's thin, goose-pimpled arm. The blue cotton shifts they all wore were no guard against the chill wind.

They both looked at Sylvia, their third. Grandma Meyers said they were like a three-legged stool, always propping each other up, but Letha wasn't so sure. Her mom was always upset that they got in trouble a lot in school. Mom said she thought Sylvia might be a bad influence. Her granny had just laughed and told her mother they'd get their growth and common sense soon enough. Letha missed Granny.

Sylvia, on the other hand, waited reverent and calm. Her eyes held a firm acceptance, knowledge this was her place and time, even though her skin had gooseflesh, too. All their short lives, Sylvia had waited for the time of the choosing.

"We all knew it would be cold this morning. It's all part of the test. Spring wants to know we're strong enough to be married to him." She smiled a look of knowing.

"*I'm* not marrying anyone." Kristienne's emphatic words sent the water shivering again, and that was just like her. Kristienne got away with saying things like that because her family was 'from away'. Letha sighed, wishing she had the same right. But if she'd said that, her mother would have washed her mouth out with soap — if she'd heard.

"Good. *I* want to be chosen."

"Aren't you special enough? I mean, come on Sylvia, I'd love to be able to talk to my filly or that old barn cat, like you. I'll bet they'd have stories," Kristienne said.

"It's not like that." Sylvia snapped. Then she stopped herself, biting her lip. Sylvia was always the quickest of them to anger and the quickest to smooth it away. Of course, that didn't mean it didn't simmer below the surface. "Sorry. It's just — I've — I've always known that something was out there for me. You know that. Shelter Lake is important, and since Letha's Granny died it's like I feel something waiting out here in the lake — for me."

"It's like — darkness." Letha spoke dreamily and caught her friends' hands, suddenly afraid they'd let her fall into a nightmare. Or they'd vanish. The dread had been like that — as if she'd be left all alone. Or like one of those horrible dreams where you're standing naked in a crowd and everyone sees. "Grandma always talked about sacrifice and being in prison. I don't want to live my life like that."

The thought of it made her heart pound faster. She thought she might be sick. Kristienne's fingers tightened comfortingly on hers.

"It's not darkness. Or prison," Sylvia lectured. "The lake is good. Can't you feel it? Besides, the animals all depend on this choosing. Just like the people."

Sylvia scanned the shore, the groups of waiting Valley people. "Uncle Joseph says they need our sacrifice for harvest. Without the chosen one, the land can't renew."

Her words sounded like she'd memorized them, but then Sylvia was always studying and always at the top of their class at Shelter Valley's one-room school.

"Then I hope the lake chooses you." Letha felt the lake's darkness stir slowly. "Not me." Not me. Please, not me.

"How can you fear something so beautiful?" Sylvia demanded, motioning around them. The water glistened darkly along the shore, but just beyond where they stood, a thick white layer of ice waited for Spring to come. Overhead the night sky faded toward dawn's pale blue. The morning star glittered at the horizon's edge.

Letha shivered at a sense of pending doom.

"Uncle Joseph says it can't be wrong for the chosen one to bring Spring. Someone has to maintain the Valley's balance. Is *that* wrong?"

Letha rolled her eyes and Sylvia reacted. Her gaze flashed with resentment, quickly hidden. As if Letha had everything — well, at least she had a mom and dad.

"You take belonging for granted. You don't understand how important this is."Sylvia's grimace smoothed away. "Now stop saying things against the ceremony. I don't want to be angry. Letha's Granny said you can't feel anything bad."

She dragged in deep breaths and lifted her chin at the shore.

"The boys are all waiting. There's Tyler. They act cool, and like they don't care what happens to their younger sisters."

"Ty cares about us," Letha said, peering into the predawn to where Ty hunkered next to the unlit bonfire with his friends. She could always pick him out because he was so much taller than the rest. And because, even though he was five years older, he looked at her instead of ignoring her like the other boys always did. Like now. She caught his glance out to the group of girls huddled in the water, and it warmed her a little. Ty was — well — special. A special friend.

"Ty cares about *you*, Letha." Kristienne tightened her hold on Letha's fingers.

"And you. Us."

Kristienne snorted. "He has to care about me. I'm his sister."

"So." Sylvia looked at Letha, pale in the predawn, and fervently hoped to be chosen. It would mean so much to really be part of something great and wonderful like Spring. "They just want to know who's chosen. The boys always like the Consort of Spring. She's the most popular girl. Marry her, and you're almost as important as she is."

"Ty doesn't care about that."

"Maybe." Trying to rid herself of jealousy, Sylvia squeezed Letha's cold hand in hers. "Don't be afraid of the lake, Leth. It's part of us. Part of a plan, and if we're chosen we keep this place whole."

"It might be your plan, but I want out of Shelter Valley. I want to see all those places in the magazine pictures."

Sylvia rolled her eyes. Letha and her darn plans and pictures. She was never happy, even with everything she had. Everyone liked Letha, even the boys, and Ty Hunt especially. Why would she ever want to leave? Sylvia wouldn't.

"It's not my plan. It's something bigger. Can't you feel it? Something wonderful?" Sylvia could. A tremor of energy, like excitement, that ran up her legs from the soft lake mud.

As the sun lifted a burnt edge over the horizon, Letha felt the lake stir — the girls faced each other and joined hands. Wind rippled across the ice-burdened water, and on shore the bonfire flames leapt skyward in ancient greeting.

The eight girls formed a huddled circle, eyes closed.

Dread rising, Letha heard the wind hum.

"I just want to be myself, not the Valley's chosen. I want to be able to choose where I live," she muttered.

"You won't be chosen saying things like that, Letha. Me, Kristienne, the others — the lake will chose one of us. It wants reverence, not distrust and fear."

"Hey! I'm only here because Mom made me come," Kristienne said. "She said we're part of the Valley now." She shrugged. "'sides, you guys were here — and there's hot chocolate after."

Her disbelief in the power of the lake showed in her face. Then water sparked around Kristienne's knees and she jerked and frowned.

"What the heck? The water's glittering. It's circling Sylvia. Look, Letha, see? Around your feet."

Letha opened her tightly clenched eyes. The water glowed, the wind warmed. A tingling power rose through hers legs. It held questions, found answers. She clenched her eyes closed again.

"I want to leave Shelter Lake. Not this, not this, not me." Letha pleaded. "Take Sylvia. She already hears animal thoughts, she's the one who's ready to serve you. I could never serve you properly or bravely like Granny did. It's not me, can never be me."

The power rose like a river flooding her, a wind in her head, a green-gold lightening in her flesh. There was the ache of her father's diabetes. There was awareness of the new-born kit foxes on the shore. She heard Sylvia scream betrayal as the Valley folk sang the sun up into the sky, as the power lifted Letha's hair, became her life blood.

All the Valley's life swelled in her.

And Letha's thin legs gave at the burden she bore.

Chapter 1

**Shelter Lake, British Columbia
Fifteen Years later**

The Valley, Tyler Hunt mused, was a lot like the Tennessee backwoods. At least, that was what you saw when you first drove in. Small, ramshackle homesteads suggested people minded their own business. And didn't talk. 'Course that hadn't been true when he'd tried hiding in a Tennessee valley.

But this would be different. Here in this place where light glowed distinctively golden, he knew the people kept secrets across generations. Or had.

And it was home, or had been. Question was whether they'd remember Tyler Hunt, the young man who'd left for school and never returned. Ten years away left changes and deep wounds. And anger. He wondered if it were possible to return.

Once he had been part of this landscape as he rode his Quarter Horse through lodgepole pine, along streams, and across beaver dams, up into the folded hills chasing his father's roan cattle. He'd spent hot, dusty days training Hunt Ranch's prized reining and cutting horses.

He rubbed the numb patch on his right leg and the throb in his back, resenting the wound the bullet had left near his spine. At least he was walking and riding again — regardless of the doctor's concerns.

And seeing the Valley before him, with its poplar-edged ice-bound lake, reminded him he was damned lucky he'd survived the hit, and that the FBI had hidden that fact.

Coming here allowed for new beginnings, even a healing. He touched his truck brakes, checking his horse trailer in the side mirrors. He'd stayed in William's Lake last night, even though it was only a two-hour drive and his friend Matt Kelly had readied everything in the Valley. Avoiding the inevitable, Tyler supposed. A coward's avoidance, and he was never a coward. His father, dead now, would have homed in on anything like that as a sign of weakness.

That was one reunion he wasn't sad he'd miss. But then, he'd proved he wasn't weak anymore. All those Bureau years, all those undercover investigations and living on the edge had earned him respect. He'd been looking for the daily rush. 'The game' he had called it, until the last one. Disaster, total disaster, when a stupid phone call had betrayed him to the Russian mob. He'd gone to ground in Tennessee, until they'd somehow tracked him. The hit had almost succeeded and he'd lain hospitalized and dreaming of a golden lit lake. Dreaming of peace...

Abort that thought. Time at the lake was time to heal, and that was all; agents had no peaceful times. His Bureau buddies would clean up the situation and then he'd have his life as an agent back.

The truck neared the lake, which filled the landscape to his left, and he turned onto gravel that fronted the last cabin. The truck rocked, with impatient movements transferred from the oversize horse trailer. Hauberk — demanding to be noticed. Ty grinned. Stallions were up-front about their feelings. He supposed that was why he still rode. Horses were honest. Horses were something to be part of; when you rode, you could be something greater.

He backed the trailer up next to the cabin and stepped out into chill morning wind. Inhaling the sweet scent of ice-melt, Ty realized he'd missed this place.

§

Kristienne brushed her dark hair back from her eyes. The motion, Sylvia knew, was Kristienne's way of hiding her emotion. Given how she clenched her callused hands, how her shoulders stiffened her plaid cowgirl shirt, and how her full lips held a disgusted downturn, she wasn't exactly successful in her attempts.

"I can't believe you'd do that."

"I provided an opportunity. It'll help her, and in the long run she'll only thank me," Sylvia said.

"You trapped her. Letha finally works up the courage, takes a huge chance, tries to finally leave, and you use it to entangle her more. That's some friendship, Sylvia, buying a store and then having her sign papers as co-owner. Knowing you, you guilted her into it, too. You know how responsible she is. She makes a commitment and she always follows through. But then you were counting on that, weren't you? Some friend. How're you goin' t'deal, when she realizes what you've really done?"

Sylvia thought of the visit into town. Letha *had* been excited — and trusting. In fact, Kristienne had been pretty accurate in her assessment of what Sylvia had done, but darn it all, after all these years Letha was getting too close to working up the courage to leave. Someone had to do *something* to hold on to her. The Valley couldn't chance the alternative. And so she'd done what she had: bought a cabin to transform into a store, and made Letha cosign — responsible for Sylvia's money. Letha wouldn't let her down. Not Letha. It was like overcompensation for her refusal to embrace her Consort duties.

"You've always taken her side in this."

Kristienne scowled, the frown placing hardness around her eyes that made even cowboys wince. "Someone bloody-well has to in this crazy Valley."

Sylvia smoothed her hand down the colt's leg and lifted the dainty hoof. "Letha has to accept her larger responsibility for her place. She might be responsible in other things, but not that. She wants to leave — for good, this time. Surely to goodness you know what that'd bring. The Valley almost died before."

"So the stories say. I don't choose to believe it. Besides, it's still her decision."

"One that's always terrified her. I just took away the terror." Releasing the colt's leg, Sylvia collected her vet gear and turned toward her white "Shelter Valley Veterinary Services" truck. It took all her control not to tell Kristienne what she really thought. Her brown-haired friend could so easily undo Sylvia's resolve to stop swearing. "Your colt's got a bold spirit to nurture. He'll make a good cutting horse. He already hates cattle."

"Don't change the subject, you know this's wrong."

"Letha's not trapped here, it's her place. She needs it. It's different for her," Sylvia said as she hefted the tools into the truck. "You'll see it's all for the best."

"Let her be herself."

Sylvia turned around as a chestnut horse and rider came through the trees.

"Looks like she is. Herself. Don't make this harder, Kristienne." Sylvia pleaded as she glanced at her stubborn friend. "Just let her try it. It'll make her happy, having something of her own to do." Then, raising her voice as Letha approached, "Hey, fine morning, stranger. We were just talking about you and the store."

"Fine morning." Her face flushed by wind, Letha reined in. "I couldn't resist a morning ride. I'll open the store later, okay Sylvia?"

"Whatever you think. You're co-owner. How's it coming?"

"Well, fine, I think. I moved my things in last night."

"Whoa, you're parents are okay? They take the change well?"

"As well as expected, Syl. I came over to borrow your cell phone."

"Help yourself." Sylvia waited until Letha had climbed in the vet truck and turned triumphant to Kristienne. "Real unhappy, I'd say."

Kristienne's glare could peel paint. "She's used to pretending."

After about fifteen minutes, Letha returned. Her eyes shone as she waved a paper at them. A hint of mischief showed in her half-swallowed grin. "That was easier than I thought it'd be. The co-op had some of the supplies, but I'm going to have to get catalogues."

"But the order list, I showed it to you. Right?"

"Yeah... but woman cannot live by bread alone, so I've expanded. Maybe you can come over to the store later. Come see..." She swung up on her mare, smile flashing as she gathered her reins. "Come. Okay?"

"She seems happy," Sylvia drawled as she and Kristienne watched Letha leave. "Happy to plan. Yup, she's definitely been trapped. Written all over her."

"She's expanded." Kristienne tried to hide her satisfaction. With Letha, there was no telling what expanded might mean.

Late that morning, excited and feeling proprietary pleasure and fear, Letha greeted their trucks. The cabin-cum-store stood by itself at one end of the lake. Grey-weathered logs had settled comfortably onto an earthen foundation. It had a pleasant porch that faced the lake and a red-painted door beckoned welcome. Behind the cabin stood a falling-down corral and small barn. A pair of chairs and small table stood on the porch.

"So what do you think?" Letha asked. "I happened to see Johnny Warner when I was home collecting my stuff. Um, what's your opinion, Kristienne? I know you have different taste than Sylvia, so you'd know if it'll suit the summer people's tastes."

"Sure." Slowly Kristienne did a 360 scan of the yard. "Not what you'd expect." She returned Letha's gaze, then stepped onto the newly-swept porch.

The cabin's yard was populated with strange metal sculptures and statues, rattling whirligigs, and delicate carvings of wind-weathered wood. A four-foot wide, spider-fine spirit catcher that Letha'd had in her room for years hung at one side of the front porch, and held twists of sweet grass and eagle feather tassels. Chunky blue pottery and blue glass bottles lined the porch and window ledges in casual display.

By the door, etched into a slab of wood, were 'Letha's Store and Artwork'. A huge black raven Letha had always called Roscoe sat on the eaves, tugging at the leather cord that held the spirit catcher.

"Darn it, Roscoe, would you quit that!" Letha waved at the bird that just croaked and hopped back. She turned back to Sylvia. "You know, I still don't feel comfortable calling it my store. It should be "Sylvia's Store and Artwork.""

Sylvia pursed her lips. Her gaze was tight as it swung around the yard, but she smiled as she looked back at Letha. "We agreed the store was yours to run. You run it; your name goes on the sign."

The interior wood floors gleamed under a small braided rug, strong coffee scent wafted outside, and a comfortable chair had been positioned near a small display of paperback books. Behind a small counter waited the single bedroom and bathroom of the place.

Sylvia slowly turned, taking in the room as if she couldn't believe her eyes, as Letha stood hands clasped and swallowing a smile.

"I started thinking about who I wanted to serve here. I know the Valley people buy supplies weekly in town, but the newcomers never think of the distance to stores. So they'll need milk and butter, but there's more. The newcomers and tourists have money, right? And they're looking for something unique, like a trophy to remember this place by. Then I ran into Johnny and remembered his carving. Then I asked if he wanted to help, 'cause some of his art styles go back generations, but he has never had the chance to show it. It might even bring more people to the Valley—"

Letha's excitement faded when Sylvia's face stiffened. "You're trying to bring more people here."

"Sure. Business. A business succeeds on planning how to grow." She looked at her partner, then at Kristienne's face, and all the blood seemed to depart Letha's head.

Lips taut, Sylvia scanned the room, picked up a book. As she scanned the title, her frown deepened. "*Backpacking in Central Asia*, Letha?" she questioned, then put the book down. "If this was what I'd envisioned, I'd have arranged for an artist to manage the store. The locals won't like it, and they're the economic base here. I'm really not sure, Letha."

"What d'you think?" Letha, straining not to appear stubborn, turned to Kristienne. "I really thought I'd done this right. I worked all night," she said as she clenched her fists at her sides. "If I can't leave, I want the world to come here."

"*I* like it, but my opinion doesn't count. Think; if Sylvia's got her knickers in a roper's twist about your store, think how the Valley folk'll react."

§

Letha didn't rightly care what the Valley folk thought, but silence ticked around her when she was alone again. When the delivery hadn't arrived by two o'clock, she was going stir-crazy waiting. Every time a truck slowed outside, she ran to the door. When she went outside barefoot for a walk, figuring that even time by the lake was better than her anxiousness, she let the land and water's soothing convince her Kristienne erred.

Power whispered in the soil, revealing it was almost time for this year's ceremony, for breaking ice, for spring. Her fingertips tingled slightly, her body ached deeply as she scanned the poplar and the willow shoots along the lake for hints of the coming that would satisfy what she felt. Hints of change ran through the air. Something was coming, bringing ill-ease, like crows in storm. It had troubled her dreams.

Nothing was there, as usual. Power existed only in the lake. No matter that Sylvia had said Letha's freedom could only be bought if she found an alternative way to consecrate the Spring. The lake knew she'd tried.

She stopped in a cool patch of snow under the eaves of a poplar grove, leaves still furled tightly closed, and listened to the wind. Not Spring, not yet. She wasn't going to allow it to come, any more than she was going to do Sylvia's bidding about the store.

"Right. I'm right." Rebelliously, she turned back to the cabin and stopped dead.

'Wild' was Ty's first thought of her. Wild red curls around a porcelain, heart-shaped face, and a shirt-jacket that kept slipping off her shoulder. Her dark eyes made him think of taming fearful horses, and his hand half-rose in gentling response.

"Sorry about startling you, but I was just exploring the lake shore."

"Exploring's allowed. And I don't startle."

"A nice talent. Good. All the whirring oddities drew me here. I'm Ty. Tyler Hunt."

"I know. Letha." She looked past him, fighting to calm herself. She knew Ty Hunt's regular features from her dreams. He'd been the one teenaged boy she'd been drawn to back then. And the one who'd refused the sexual advances of a confused thirteen-year-old who'd been trying to gain her freedom.

Older, a slight hint of old pain edged his firm lips. Lines, collected during ten years away, radiated from calm brown eyes. The nose, not quite straight, from a boyhood brawl that, Letha recalled, ruined a long-time friendship. Brown hair, a little curly, that hung a little too long for Valley folk's taste. Something to like about him. And a steady gaze with a calm, deeply-intent focus and a smile that seemed to urge quiet and trust.

She remembered Kristienne's brother as forthright. Patient, kind. But the tremble that surged through her, said this man was the source of the darkness she'd been dreading.

His broad shoulders carried a rider's strength. He wore low-riding, well-worn jeans that hung loose and a plaid flannel shirt-jacket. But the strength of his arms and his callused hands made her take a step away from where he stood. The fear she'd felt—was it for her or the Valley?

"Just visiting?" she asked as she avoided his shadow.

"Guess you could say that. I'm setting up in the cabin down the way."

"Thought you'd go home." She started toward the store, aware she was being rude but afraid to stay.

"Not the best place, and besides, here I can visit your art collection." He raised his chin at the cabin. "The inside as interesting?"

"No."

Ty frowned at her. "That's not very neighborly. Poor for business, too," he added when she glanced back at him.

"No." She climbed the steps to the porch, white-knuckling the rail and shook her head. "I'm sorry. I guess you did surprise me — I was thinking. A new business requires it, though." Her voice was stiff and her gaze wouldn't quite meet his straight on. "I suppose that's why I'm not showing that Valley hospitality right this moment."

"Must be."

"Howdy, stranger."

Ty turned as a rider arrived, and grinned at his old friend and ranch hand, Matt Kelly. "Howdy, yourself Matt."

"You gone around home to see your mom and that sister of yours?"

"Held off so far."

"Your mother's really been havin' a time of it lately. The winter's been lastin' a little long this year, ya know. Your mom's been a little down that spring ain't come. Pardon me for sayin' what's true, Ma'am." Matt, ever the tradition-bound buckaroo, tipped his broad-brimmed cowboy hat in Letha's direction, his smile buried in his handlebar moustache, then turned back to Ty.

"Trouble?" Ty asked.

"Yer sister's gotta keep an eye sharp all the time."

Not what Ty wanted to hear. "Then I'll try to make it over sometime today. Seems your Letha here's attempting to beautify the lake, Matt."

"Looks like ya got all th' kid's art." Matt scanned the yard's whirling display, shifting his batwing-chaps-covered legs in the saddle. "That's Johnny Warner's work, ain't it? Heard Sylvia bought you a store."

"Yes." Letha's resentment rose in her chest. The Valley folk were all just humoring her. "The art. You think the tourists'll like it?"

"A simple man like me don't pay much attention to what city folk like or dislike. Got a feeling, though, that yer parents might not approve. Not too sure o' the old folk, either. They're the one's as matter. You get yerself over to visit your ma and your sister, Ty," he tipped his hat. "Before your ma does something else."

"Sure, Matt." Ty fought down the disquiet Matt's words brought, but then he'd known things weren't good with his mom for a while. He watched Matt turn his horse, then purposely looked back at Letha, somehow wanting to comfort the brief vulnerability he'd seen bloom in her eyes at Matt's comments. "The artwork's good, Letha."

She tossed her head prettily. Fussed with the blue-bottle display, the pottery, waiting for him to leave.

Letha Rivers, he thought, he'd have never predicted the carrot-topped kid would've grown into this ethereal woman. Of course, he remembered as he limped home, she'd always been like a pretty filly, all legs and timid curiosity.

His age-grayed log cabin sat back from the lake shore at the far side of the copse of white-barked poplar and willow that separated his place from Letha's. His horse trailer and truck were parked around back near the four-stall, hip-roof barn and broken down corral. At the cabin's front porch a white truck sat parked, a familiar petite blonde leaning against the driver's door. Wouldn't hurt, Ty thought, to know a little more about his lovely neighbor. He walked up to the driver.

"Long time, Sylvia."

"Long time."

"What brings you here?"

"Letha." Sylvia straightened and stretched her arms behind her back.

Still proving herself strong. Still plagued by those childhood insecurities he'd noticed so long ago.

"Matt told me 'bout your conversation. She's breaking tradition, and this valley is about as hide-bound in tradition as any," Sylvia said.

"She's selling Valley art. And that means she's breaking covenant?"

"God's truth."

"You honestly think that's true, Sylvia?"

"Might be, Ty." Sylvia wouldn't meet his gaze, instead studying his horse trailer. Her brow furrowed prettily and he remembered Sylvia's odd so-called talent, as she got a far-away look in her eyes. "I hoped the store would settle her. She's been hell-bent on leaving, so I was always afraid she would run. But with all this art rigmarole, she hasn't even brought in the Spring. You saw the ice on the lake."

"Yeah, I'm just suggesting maybe the Valley's being pretty hard on her for doing something creative."

Sylvia snorted, then lifted her chin back toward the cabin down at the lake. "Creation sits in the lake, Ty. Selling art, now... Spring's never operated a store." She shook her head. "I must have been nuts."

"There's nothing in the covenant that forbids selling art."

"Ty, maybe you've been away long enough to forget."

"I would never forget," he denied.

"So maybe you remember. Maybe it's Letha, maybe she's caught your sympathy."

"My sympathy? Maybe you should question why you're bothering me when you got business to attend." He held back his smile, knowing she'd wonder if she had him upset — and that not knowing would bother her. Miss Sylvia always was just a little too sure of herself.

She stayed silent a moment, then, "Ty Hunt, always a taskmaster." She motioned to the barn. "You still picking up strays, or have you actually bought yourself a horse? Stallion, huh?"

"Jokes, now. I'd ask if you're still making like Dr. Doolittle, but the truck and your question, it kinda answers me."

"You got a problem with that?" Sylvia's fists closed white-knuckled at her sides, and with that Ty knew he'd gotten under her skin — not that hard to do. Hell, he'd always been good at it even when not intending to, but right now her not-too-subtle warnings just plain pissed him off.

"Subtlety, Ty, a quality you're missing."

"I'm just guessing, but maybe your heart wasn't in exactly the right place when you bought Letha a store."

Sylvia's derisive laughter rang loud, but as she climbed into her truck Ty looked down the lake shore, recalled Letha's eyes, and felt compelled to see her again.

After Sylvia left, he checked Hauberk where he'd left him in the barn, fed the stallion, and unpacked his gear. Then he headed toward the store. The afternoon wind rattled the whirligigs and sighed in the willow, counterpoint to soft singing from inside. Tire tracks, Ty noted, fresh in the soil, and the clatter and humming from inside spoke of new merchandise and a life newly begun.

"You busy in here?" he asked, ducking his head to peer in the door.

"Yup. Town truck finally came with my order." Letha looked up from unloading condensed milk onto shelves. "Supplies for Valley folk. Old 'uns like sweetened milk, but it's the art that'll make the money."

"You're preaching to the converted," Ty said, smiling. "And I'll take on anyone who disputes it, unless it happens to be some big time New York art critic."

Across from her, Ty hefted himself onto the counter, considered the view. "You should come by my place after. I've got some beer cooling."

"Right. And I've got nothing better to do."

"We can fix that, too. Give us a chance to get reacquainted and all that?"

"I already remember you." But she did straighten, and look him right in the eye. "My place is here."

"You're saying you're happy in the Valley?"

"Never said that. But this store is supposed to earn me money, money I'll save. It's something that's mine, something I can do my way — no matter what Sylvia says. When I save enough,

I can leave. I make the rules here. You think I give a damn about complaints? No way."

"The folk's feelings don't matter, then. But I was just being neighborly. Thought you could update me on the Valley's news." He grabbed a box on the counter and saw Letha start when he began passing her boxes of matches. "So Sylvia Hill bought the store."

"So what?" Letha intently finished stacking a shelf, then surveyed the results. "Yeah. She did. An investment, she said. Her, and the bank, secretly, but there're no secrets in-Valley."

"And Sylvia's not exactly a confidence-keeper, is she? But her heart's always been in the right place. Caring," Ty murmured casually. "Weird gal — at least you could say that about her hearing animal emotions."

Letha looked up at his calm regard, somehow needing to come to her friend's defense.

"You've got her..." Saying he'd got Sylvia "all wrong" seemed inappropriate when he seemed pretty astute otherwise. "You don't know her anymore."

"No? I don't," Ty agreed, "But I'm generally a good judge of people. It's sort of a hobby I've developed and honed over my years outside the Valley. Sylvia now, she hasn't changed that much. Her needs still drive her."

"Sylvia's always been my friend."

"Good, then. So that's why you're working here? As friends?"

Letha avoided him, so Ty decided to bow out. "Letha, I remember as a kid you planned to leave. Given I've been around in the world a couple of times, I'd be happy to talk."

"You don't remember much if you think that'd help. Now I need to tidy this store." Like that, she shut him down. He placed the emptied box on the counter.

"I'll leave." Whirligigs whined outside, the wind having picked up across the lake. "But, my cabin's there," Ty looked back at her and saw how fear filled her eyes. "The Valley doesn't hold me the same. I don't hold the same views, either, Letha Rivers. If you want to talk about it, I'm there."

Trembling inside, Letha watched his shadowed form. Late afternoon sunlight on the cabin's porch placed his silhouette across her gingham curtained windows. The whirligigs' howled in a wind that chilled her. She swayed, and felt the cabin walls press in, press lungs, check her breath. She couldn't breathe. Caught and imprisoned. Trapped and dying.

How had she let Sylvia do this to her, when everything inside her throbbed and demanded something more? But it was so typical of her life, wasn't it? Always doing what made others happy. She'd been like that as a kid and as a young woman. It was just that now she wanted more — even if she wasn't sure how to get it. Tyler Hunt had suggested as much in his not so veiled words. She remembered him as a horse-crazy teenager, with intense green eyes. That detail came easily, why did she remember? Tyler Hunt was nothing. He meant nothing.

And she was only biding her time in the Valley. She would leave. He was wrong about Sylvia trapping her.

Leaving the half-emptied boxes, she stepped onto the porch as Ty studied the lake. The cold wind across the frozen water picked up more force, tearing branches and rocking the whirligigs.

It blasted into her and sent her stumbling, so that she fell against Ty's left side. A bright flash across her vision, a sense of heat and long unanswered desire. Hers or his — the feelings were all mixed up and as dangerously confused as a rattler nest newly awakened in spring. She yanked away, inhaling old-ice and man-scent.

She couldn't slow her heart, couldn't quiet its pounding in her ears, as loud as horse herd hooves. She pushed her hair from her eyes and found herself caught in Ty's serious green gaze.

"What'd you do? Shock me?" But she knew that wasn't it, saw an answering awareness form deep in Ty Hunt's eyes. Warm gaze, surprised, knowing, denying.

"I can't... I won't..."

"Yeah, bloody strange." Ty's voice had a strangled edge, as if he choked back emotions he'd never wanted to find. "Shit, I don't need this."

"Don't need what?" Hesitating, Letha brushed Ty's shoulder. Another spike of need and darkness sent her reeling back.

"Nothing you need to know. Nothing. It's just the Spring wind." But it wasn't Spring, he thought. Letha, the Spring, she hadn't brought it yet. "Tourist season soon. Better ready the store, Letha," he said softly, and left her.

§

Holy-shit-mother-of-god-damn-it, he didn't like this feeling. The sensation that had rammed through him when the wind had thrown her against him, its intensity, had almost overwhelmed. Being overwhelmed was bad. It could get you killed. For all the Valley's remoteness and distance, he knew he had to guard against people wanting him dead. Letha Rivers was a danger to him.

He strode down the path along the lake shore that linked his log cabin to Letha's store. Shit, there was no such thing as the human embodiment of the marriage of Spring. That was an old wife's tale. He was an FBI agent, his buddies would laugh.

What the hell drug had he been on when he decided to hide in *this* tradition-bound community, in the very place he'd spent his early years, fighting his father's iron-bound rules and the hide-bound beliefs of a community he'd always planned to escape?

He passed his cabin for the barn, entered. Horses had always taught him calm. When everything else was going to hell, the animal's need for calm consistency salved him. Most of the time — but there were exceptions, like today.

A snort, coming from the stall with the open window, told him he was right. A stallion was a good judge of character, better than any FBI agent. Better than Sylvia Hill, regardless of his memories of her talents.

He entered the dim-lit stall, and feeling the stallion's unease, stopped and exhaled his pique.

"Sorry to leave you like this, friend. But the corral here needs mending, and I don't need you breaking loose. I promise you'll have more space soon. But for now, I need your help."

The dim lighting gradually receded. Stallion movements. Hay scent, snuffed breath on his hand, a brown eye, uncertain, awaiting calm. Hauberk formed like darkness birthed from the darkness, his deep brown coat glowing. His bloodlines were of the famous Hanoverian breed, bred for greatness if his spirit agreed, but just as likely to be uncontrolled when aroused.

Just like Ty was aroused by certain events by the lake. They raised a devastating wave of desire.

He wouldn't respond. He'd no need to interact, no need to see her. Hauberk snorted his displeasure, a kick slammed the stall wall. The Valley wasn't Ty's place anymore; he belonged outside, but when he closed his eyes all he could see was the Valley fading to nothing, a blackened road forever before him, if he failed to answer the call.

He stroked Hauberk, the stallion's coat smooth under his hands. "You think you can control me?" he said to the air. "I'm not yours anymore. You'll see, I can leave again." He rested his forehead on Hauberk's neck. "Or stay if I want."

§

Letha, tired from the emotional roller-coaster of the day, was on the porch in her heavy jacket checking lists and watching the sunset, when Sylvia's truck wheeled into the gravel lot. "Still at it," Sylvia said as she climbed out of the truck. "Always knew you had work ethic. Thought I'd come see how you managed today." She grabbed the other chair and slumped down, pulling her fleece collar close around her neck. "You got your stock. How's the shelving and pricing going?"

"Good enough," Letha sighed. It was good to see the shop really come together. Cleaned, shelves all stocked, prices in place. She'd accomplished it all with only minor interruptions. And not quite so minor. "Ty Hunt dropped by. He's different than I remember."

"Yummy." Sylvia glanced at her amber-haired friend, caught in the failing sunlight, a worried look niggled the edges of Letha's eyes. "He hassle you? Probably just worried about his mom's drinking."

"Not again?"

"Yeah, poor Kristienne. Sad... but ya can't heal those as don't want ta be." She gazed across the lake ice to the distant Hunt house. "So, was this good, Letha?"

"As good as honest work, Pa would say. But I need to re-rail the corral."

"You should take some time to relax and do what comes natural, maybe go down among the mint sinks. The weather's fine and the wind even has hints Spring might come." She said it hopefully, and Letha stiffened.

"And I'll just bet the Valley elders put you up to that comment."

Sylvia's lips bowed. "You seem kind of tense right now. It couldn't be the change of season now, 'cause that would mean you have duties to attend. What happened today that's got you so on edge?"

"Nothing."

"Well nothing doesn't leave you sitting on the porch in a cold wind. You should be inside, snug and warm and satisfied at your work."

"All right, something did happen today. With Ty."

"What'd he do? He's always been good people."

"I stumbled and fell against him, that's what. There was a flash, and then darkness. Like an... explosion inside me."

She was being stupid and she knew it, but she kept going. "He felt it, too. His eyes showed he did. But he wouldn't admit it and he left."

"Probably got angry at you; never much for imagination, our Ty."

"If that was imagination, then it's verging too close to real." Shivering, Letha stood and pushed past. "Either way it startled me — and likely chased away my closest neighbor."

Sylvia studied her and chewed her lip. "Might have. But I'll bet he comes back."

"Comes back."

"Spring draws people," Sylvia frowned. "My assessment? Probably not anything more than two people attracting each other. He's not hard on the eyes and you could do worse than to follow your attraction."

The wind tugged Letha's hair and she held it back. Held her emotions back, too. "That's not what I felt."

"Might be true. Might even be fun to find out. He likes you, you like him. What more's required?"

Letha shivered and felt the darkness swell over her again, but this time it was an old darkness. "I couldn't possibly be like that."

"You tried it once, didn't you?" Sylvia reminded her of things best forgotten. "Didn't hurt. You had a bit of fun then, sowed some oats with some young men. It doesn't matter what you do, Letha. As long as you don't leave."

Letha couldn't find breath. The pain, it choked, and Sylvia didn't understand how trapped she was, how she died inside. The only time she'd felt something different was in the sensation from Ty. And that frightening desire wasn't to be repeated. Frantically she sought for something to say.

"I'm going over to Johnny Warner's tomorrow to see some different stuff, paintings, and talk prices. All that and I'll be too busy to leave."

"One way to do it, I guess, but I really think you should focus on the store — not this crazy arts and crafts notion." Sylvia paused as she stepped down the stairs. "Letha? You could still have some fun, you know."

"When has my life been fun?" Letha snapped. She turned and closed the red door, shutting the world behind her.

Chapter 2

Up with the sunrise, Letha had gone on horseback to visit Johnny Warner — a slim-fingered seventeen-year-old who made art between schoolwork and ranch chores. Letha had spent time in his tarpaper shed, looking at delicate watercolor paintings of leaves and flowers, and helping him set prices.

She left feeling happy. Even if she wasn't leaving the Valley, she was doing something for herself and helping others while doing it. She was helping Johnny step out in the world when everyone else in the Valley thought his artwork was silly.

It was a matter of purpose. Johnny'd been born to a ranch family, so he was expected to ranch. Just like when she'd been chosen by Spring, everyone just assumed that was her only purpose in life. Well, people had choice, too. They weren't like a tree, held in place by roots that would never let go.

Once she'd been chosen, her mother hadn't even wanted Letha to go to school, but the law had been on Letha's side. She'd gone to school, had even brought home one of Kristienne's cast-off computers, and had begun her own explorations of the world outside. Yes, the Valley was her home, her birthright, and her responsibility — and she'd been glad of that — but there was *so much more.*

That knowledge had grown into a longing that ached like a missing part of her.

The problem was, Spring must have chosen wrongly when it selected her, and no one understood how that could be. It should have chosen Sylvia.

If she left it could have Sylvia — or someone else.

And she *would* leave. All she needed was money, a ride, and to deal with the darned sickness that took her every time she passed Jed Hartley's cabin, and Sylvia could have her rightful place. Next time Letha left she wouldn't be coming back. There were pills for motion sickness. With money, she could buy them. It was as simple as that. They had to work.

Had to.

Still, Sylvia hadn't set up the store to help Letha's escape. And even though Sylvia's empathy worked mainly with animals, she could sense human emotion a little. That meant Letha had to be careful. She had to hold her plans close. If need be, she'd just take the money and run.

Staying wasn't an option.

She reined in her chestnut mare by the Spring Lake Ranch house and studied the old building. Frost still lay in the shadow of the old peaked structure. Last year's Queen Anne's Lace stood brittle and laced with crystals. But just a light nudge would bring Spring. It hovered in the air, waiting. She urged her mare forward, knowing she was being bitchy with her denial of the Spring rite, but it was her right to choose when Spring came. The only important choice she'd been allowed to keep.

One day soon, she thought, as her mare forded Brewster Stream toward the store, she would have so many choices. It would be fascinating to see what she did with them.

Would she become a woman like Sylvia, who had left the Valley for a time to go to school, but who had chosen to return? To be so confident this was your place. To be so sure about who you were, what you wanted, and how to get it. That must be what the outside world did, build certainty about who you were, because you could do and be anyone at all.

The thought made her hands tremble.

Yes, and while Sylvia had her own unique talents, anyone could learn to make choices, to become their own person. Sylvia was teaching her that, though she might not realize it, nor agree with Letha's choices. The store had taught her that she could stand her ground — at least on little things. And that was a surprise.

Ahead lay Ty Hunt's cabin and she urged the mare into a trot. She didn't want to deal with him on such a fine morning. Instead, she'd fix the mare's corral, so her horse could enjoy more freedom just as Letha was doing. Maybe she'd even plan a website for the store's artwork to bring in outside customers.

And that was her choice.

§

She finished hand-painting a sign and put it up next to the turnoff from the main Valley road to the two lake cabins. It was a fine bit of artwork, if she did say so herself. A spirit catcher drawn as an outside frame, 'Letha's Store and Artwork' woven into the web. She'd even found a few of Roscoe's feathers to hang from the sign so they dangled and fluttered in the wind. It should attract attention — even from the Valley folk.

Maybe even gain her respect for herself — beyond that which came with her position as Spring Consort. Let them see her as something other than that. Let them learn about Letha the entrepreneur and shopkeeper. Letha the person.

Setting her toolbox down beside the two-stall shed that served as home to her mare, Inca, she inhaled the sweet scent of new hay from the stall and studied the corral. Putting up rail fences wasn't her favorite thing, but she'd be darned if the mare was going to have less fun than Letha was out of all this change. From the stall window, Inca turned a dark eye on Letha and snorted.

"No, I haven't forgotten you, you and your need to kick up your heels."

Work gloves on, she grabbed one of the cut poles Sylvia had arranged to be delivered and dragged it to a spot where one of the old fence rails had rotted, then leaned down to grab her hammer.

Dangerous curves ahead, Ty thought as he paused in his traipse along the lake. He really had just been headed out for a walk. The store just happened to be along the way, along with its attractive proprietor. Somehow Letha Rivers brought a whole new perspective to a man's work shirt and old jeans — one that deserved to be appreciated.

The wind shushed cool through the willows, but Letha didn't seem to notice as she used the hammer to haul down the broken rail and wrestled the new one into place.

"Looking good."

Startled, she almost dropped the end of the rail, and swore soft cowgirl epithets against the son-o-gun piece of wood. It made him smile, the gentle remonstrations of the Valley, as did her quick glance at him and the way she turned and finished the rail. He sauntered across the yard, straightening a metal statue that had settled askew in yesterday's wind.

"Easier with two sets of hands." He strolled over to grab another rail, but she caught it from him, careful not to touch him, he noted.

"I'm fine, thanks. I can manage."

"You've got a heap of rails here. Something of a job." He reached down and grabbed a few more rails, hefting them between himself and Letha. "So where do you want them?"

She looked him in the eye and he shrugged.

"I figure the top rail needs replacing all round. There're a few others. But I really don't need —"

He was already dragging the poles into position, checking the strength of the others in each panel. The horse in the stall caught his eye. "Nice horse. Mare?"

He climbed through the fence at a break and went over to the stall to hold out his hand. The horse snuffled his fingers, snorted, and he rubbed the spot behind its ears. With a sense borne of years of undercover work, he felt Letha come up behind him.

"Her name's Inca, 'cause every time she gets scared she sacrifices her rider. Couldn't tell you how many times I've been dumped." Why the heck was she telling him this? The best way to get rid of him was to focus on the fence. She turned back to the rail she'd been nailing and hefted the other end into place. "I've gotta get a place for her to exercise or she'll eat me alive. She's not getting enough riding."

"A bored horse is nothing but trouble, my trainer used to say."

"Trainer?"

"Outside I used to ride horses competitively. Here, I'll hold this end in place while you nail yours."

A quick bang-bang, and the long spike was in place. She was good with a hammer. They continued on to the next rail and the next until she paused and wiped sweat from her eyes. "Thank you, neighbor."

"Nothing to it. Works up a thirst though, even in this weather. You got drinks in that store?"

"Yeah."

"You figure out which other rails need replacing and I'll get the drinks." He grinned casually and she knew he'd spotted her hesitation.

"Fine. Thanks." Damn him, he'd done that on purpose. Too neighborly for his own good. Or hers. Or the Valley's.

He covered the ground to the cabin in a sure, easy stroll that carried a slight limp. She didn't want him here, taking her choices away, pushing her to hurry.

She fumed as she used the hammer to haul other rotten rails loose. At least the hammering used up some of her anger.

He returned juggling two bottles of Coke and two of uncarbonated spring water, making soft oaths at how cold the bottles were. She smiled.

"Guess I should turn the fridge down." She took a bottle of water from him, careful not meet his fingers, watched as he kept the other and set the Cokes down beside her tool box. Very precise. Nice he preferred the water. But that could just be because she chose it. She turned back to the fence. "I was just worried things would go off if I didn't keep 'em cold."

"Well, cold they are. Here." He held out a five dollar bill. "Let me pay for these. I'll take the Cokes, too."

"Ty," she said and shifted to look at him. She wanted to ask him why he was here, why he was helping. Instead she said,

"You're helping. The least I can do is offer cold drinks. Keep your money."

"Well now, that's mighty neighborly."

He stuffed the bill back in his pocket and took a long pull on the bottle of water as she rolled her eyes at his affected drawl. He hadn't lived in the Valley for friggin' ten years. But there was something about the way he leaned back against the new rail, the way he studied the landscape — masculine, appraising — part of the landscape itself and yet... not. It lit a small tingle in her body.

She remembered the feeling she'd had when she was thirteen. Her pre-teen crush turned aside by the much older and wiser Ty. He was eighteen then, and this was like that crush only more so. A woman's feelings for a man she was attracted to.

Not to this man. No way in heck.

"I gotta thank you for your help. Would have taken me all afternoon."

"No problemo." He looked back at the mare, then at her with a slow casual glance that sent another jolt through her, reminiscent of the flash she'd felt the night before. She had to fight the small moan in her throat.

He took another swig of water, then, "This a red-headed league or something?" He lifted his chin, his brown hair gleaming in the sunlight. "You. The mare. You got something against blondes or brunettes, 'cause I might feel unwelcome."

She rolled her eyes again. "Jeeze, Ty. Chestnut mares're a dime a dozen and every one as ornery as the last."

"Yeah, but chestnut women, now..."

She froze, wanting him to stop, wanting him to leave, Ty saw, but not knowing how to tell him. Well, he could respect some of that, but — he hefted another rail and pulled it into position, took the hammer from her, and with a single blow, nailed the end in place. Repeated the action at the other end. "Hmm, still haven't lost the touch." He handed the hammer back to her.

She'd wanted to finish this herself, she thought. She wanted to keep busy until customers came. She wanted the time to plan.

Otherwise this could be just more waiting — just like all her twenty three years. But it just wasn't to be.

Helplessly, she watched as Ty brought another load of rails. They started nailing them up.

"So, you been to see your mom and Kristienne yet?"

"My mom," he said, but it came out with a sigh. "I stopped in yesterday evening. Got forced into staying for dinner, and Kristienne can't cook to save her life." He blew his hair up over his forehead. "Yeah, I saw my mom."

There was grief in his tone, in the way he picked up his water bottle, saw it was empty, and carefully set it down. He looked up at her and smiled, and the sad curve of his lips made her heart go out to this man. It was never easy seeing a parent fail, and Elizabeth Hunt had fallen far from the graceful opera singer who had come from New York with her husband. No wonder Ty'd left and never come back.

"You must have seen a lot out in the big world. A lot to keep you busy."

"There's a lot, all right." She had such steady eyes, he thought as he looked back at her. Steady and not really grey, just a blue as deep as denim that seemed to catch everything around her and just... be. When she looked away it was like suddenly being alone and empty. She didn't look away for long. Curiosity, he thought. Like a hunger. "A lot of people. A lot of crime. A lot of shit going down, pardon my language."

"You were a cop?"

"Could say that. Law enforcement. My dad was a cop before he decided to come to Canada and take up ranching. His dad was a cop, too. Hard to believe we're still considered newcomers to the Valley. I feel like I've lived here my whole life. You know, this is going to make a pretty solid loafing corral for that mare of yours."

"You think so?" She pulled back on a new-hung rail, testing its strength. Even a horse leaning into it was going to have to work to get it loose. Another choice: of a job, and the job well done. She nodded her pleasure. "Good work."

"I'd say you've got one hell of an arm on you. Good with a hammer, can set up a home pretty well, too, from what I saw in your shop. Going to make some Valley beau one happy fella."

"I'm not." Her body went stiff as the rail she stood beside. "Not ever."

"Never's a pretty long, lonely time," he said softly.

"It's not going to happen. And it's none of your business." She turned toward him, eyes flashing.

"Hold on there. I was just making a joke, okay. I just — know what it's like alone."

"I'm sorry," she said archly.

"So am I."

"So how long are you planning on staying in our fair Valley?"

"Long enough." He climbed through the fence and looked back, daring her. Letha's flares of temper were something to be watched, something that spoke of too much pressure inside. How does Letha Rivers let off pressure, he wondered. "Fence's fixed. How 'bout we set that mare of yours loose and see how big a fool she can make of herself?"

"Big as her owner," Letha grumbled, joining him inside the fence. "Pretty big."

"Let me be the judge of that. I've met some pretty big fools in my day." And you're making one of yourself right now.

"All right. Just you wait." For some reason she didn't want to annoy him — perhaps it was fear of the darkness she felt associated with him, or perhaps it was that tingling sensation that still jangled in her belly. She went to the stall and undid the slide, the mare lipping her fingers. "Stand back. She can explode outta here. It's a bad habit I've been trying to break her of since I got her."

She stepped back and swung the stall door wide, the mare slamming out the door in a single wild leap. She squealed, tucked her head, and bucked her way around the corral, before collapsing into the dirt for a good solid roll, legs raking the sky as she ground her back into the earth. Letha's delighted laughter rang across the corral.

"Damn foolish," he said, grinning. "Right up there, I'd say. And after that display, I better head home put some time into my own corral. Pleasure seeing you, Letha." He nodded.

"Thanks for the help, Ty."

He headed back to his cabin following the path on the lake shore, thinking about Letha Rivers. Something about her... Strong, capable to be sure, good with animals, fiercely independent, and just a tad scared of something. The way she avoided his touch, it could almost be him.

He paused as he stepped over a loose patch of ice between the willows and pulled the collar of his fleece jacket up. The ice edge of the lake had gone clear, rotten, but it wasn't receding. It should be Spring, so the melts would come. Around William's Lake, loggers were off work due to the thaws. And that lake was half ice-free. But not here. The Valley might be higher in elevation than William's Lake, but it should still be seeing new green grass. Something wasn't right.

He glanced back at the store and knew the thing that wasn't right was Letha. Something in her was worryingly wrong.

§

Letha rang up the cash register and made small talk with old Mrs. Zigheld. Mrs. Zigheld had had her son Harry, the local Postman, drive her to the store just to see what all the fuss was about, and probably to report to the other Valley elders. After fussing about the store and sniffing at the 'new-fangled ideas of young people' however, she'd bought a pound of butter because, she'd said, she had a hankering for shortbread cookies, and a tiny wooden rabbit ornament carved by Tessa Rogers, another of the Valley kids. A little triumph.

Letha watched Harry help the old woman in her sturdy black boots and heavy coat to his truck that doubled as mail delivery vehicle, but before she climbed in the old woman stopped. She stuck her wizened face up at Letha. "'bout time fer ya to be thinkin' about Spring, girl. Been a long winter." She climbed in, shaking her head as the truck crunched out of the yard.

At least she'd shopped. She'd been impressed enough with Letha's goods, she'd probably be back. She might even give a good report to the others.

The lake lay like a white disc, the ice cold blue under the sun. She shivered at the cold, and the lonely sound of the wind through the willows, and the distant caws of crows. A thump and nearby croak brought her to the spirit catcher at the end of porch. Roscoe sat on the rail, tugging at the fluttering feathers.

"Git! Git away!" She shushed the darn bird with a sweep of her hand, but the raven only fluttered up to the peak of the roof. "You do that again, I'll get a gun," she warned, even though it was an empty threat.

The raven croaked a retort and she grinned, turned, and smacked right into a solid chest. A bright flash, and her knees wobbled. Ty. He tried to steady her, caught her arm, but she yanked away.

Shock and something else — panic? — filled her. "Ty! Sorry. I didn't see you. God, I really should watch where I'm going."

She tried to duck past him.

"Whoa there. I'm fine. I realized I didn't buy any jam or peanut butter in town for my lunch, thought maybe the store..." He let her pass and followed her into the store, taking care to keep his distance. "Nice and warm in here. Unseasonably cool morning, though."

"The fire." She nodded at the wood heater radiating warmth in the corner, and hurried to a set of shelves near the window where the jars of jam waited. Being surprised wasn't something she was used to. Usually she felt people's presence before they arrived. But not Ty. Except for the darkness. His presence now — it brought a fluttering sense of panic to her stomach.

"Peanut butter and jam. What kind of jam, 'cause I've got strawberry and raspberry and marmalade, but then you didn't say marmalade, did you?"

"Calm down, Letha."

"Pardon me?"

"Calm down." He smiled kindly as he stepped up beside her to examine the jam labels. "I didn't come to assault you or anything."

"Sure. Fine." Frustration flared at herself and at this man who always seemed to insert himself into her space. "There's the jam."

She ducked behind the counter and he had a tough time holding back the smile. "So what'd you figure goes best with peanut butter? I've never fancied marmalade, but strawberry can be kind of boring after a while."

"Raspberry, then." Just get the selection over with and leave. She didn't need him here, with his capable hands and his touch that made her go weak in the knees. His gaze on her was like a too-hot towel right out of her mom's dryer.

"Thought maybe you could make use of this. I found it in my barn." He came up to the counter and placed the jam jar and a bundle beside her hand.

Letha just looked at the bundle, wrapped in what looked like an old t-shirt. "What is it?"

"Something for the store."

She rang up the jam and peanut butter and accepted the money he put on the counter. Put his change there, as well, beside the bundle.

"Go on. Open it."

She didn't want his gifts, but curiosity got the better of her. She unfolded the three folds of cloth that protected the gift. A brass bell on a chain, newly shone to amber brilliance. She picked it up, and a single clear note seemed to fill the store and a hollow place inside her.

"It's beautiful."

"Great sound. It was buried in some old manure. I figured it needed a better home than that. Thought you could hang it by your door, so customers can call you if you're outside."

She was shaking her head. "No. This is an antique. It's worth something."

"And so it's worth giving as a gift." He looked around the store and grinned sheepishly. "Got any bread? I forgot that, too."

She packed the loaf of bread, the jam, and the peanut butter into a bag and watched him out the door. He waved back at her as she shut the door and stepped back to the counter. The bell lay, glistening. She picked it up and it rang again. The sound made her smile.

§

Kristienne Hunt looked up from the ugly truth of the account books at the sound of a horse in the yard. It was too late for Matt and the other ranch hands to be leaving — she'd heard them hours ago — and it was too early for them to be back. A small chill of concern ran up her neck.

God, what was it now? After the way her mother had taken a turn for the worse six months ago, Kristienne was always on edge. The coffee she seemed to consume in ever-increasing amounts wasn't helping, either. She pushed her mug away.

Of course she could manage it. She always managed everything, had learned how at her father's knee and had taken over when he passed so suddenly. Good thing she liked the ranch and the way the work and the finances ebbed and flowed like the seasons and harvest. Or the way the seasons were supposed to flow.

She glanced toward the front window of the log house. It sat on sheltered bottom-land overlooking the frozen lake. Her mother's crocuses should be pushing up through the last snows at this time of year, but this April the snow was still heaped around the house. Well, everyone deserved to have a tantrum once in a while, and Letha was no exception.

She, Kristienne, had had her tantrum the other night when Ty had dropped in outta the blue. Ten years with only the occasional phone call, and then he arrives and his whole presence said he expected to be the man of the house. After she'd held things together, there was no way she was going to put up with that.

Ty's voice reached her from outside — talking to his horse, she supposed. He'd said he'd brought one with him. Always was horse crazy. As if he preferred the animals to the people who owned them, even though people always seemed attracted to the old Ty.

As if living things — animals and people — were drawn to him. Unlike her. That was how he'd been as a kid before he went away to school. Always popular. Even when he came back for his brief visits he'd fit right in, been an open book for people to read.

But the Ty that had come back this time was different, Kristienne thought. He was still caring and concerned, but this time there was a wall blocking some of those qualities away. This time there was an aura of secrets about him, as if he wouldn't let you in. Their mom had felt it, too, and she'd been more difficult the past two days.

He should never have come back.

Hearing his booted footfall on the rear porch, she stood to pour him a cup of slightly-burned coffee, and handed it to him as he came in wiping his hands. His appearance stopped her dead, but Ty still accepted the coffee. What the hell was he wearing? High black boots and thigh-tight britches. Nothing any self-respecting cattle-man would wear.

"Damn cold out there. Gotta get some stuff from the barn to fix the flue in my chimney. Damn near suffocated myself on smoke. Then I opened the windows and nearly froze my ass off."

Wearing his well-worn working boots and comfortable English breeches, he settled into their father's old blood-red leather wingback, and Kristienne frowned and sat back at the ranch's business desk in the corner. She was doing books, he saw. He really should be asking her how the business was doing, but he supposed if she'd run the place the past two years she didn't need him checking over her shoulder.

"So how's Mom?"

"Fine. Sleeping," Kristienne told him. "Your little surprise visit really threw her for a loop. She spent yesterday in your old room, making sure everything was as she remembered, then she wanted Matt and the boys to go get you and your stuff. She thinks you should be here, Ty. In your old room, and we'd be a family again." She held out a piece of paper. "And someone named

Samuels called and asked if you were here. I told him 'no', but that I'd see you got his message. I'm not your messenger service, hear?"

"Yeah..." he said slowly as he scanned the note. He looked up at her. "Not going to happen — moving in, I mean." He stood up and shifted around the room. Samuels, his partner, didn't know he was here. No one but the Assistant Director Buckley, did, and Buckley knew better than to contact him unless it was an emergency. What the hell was going on? "You shouldn't take messages for me. Anyone calls, I'm not here."

Kristienne noted the distraction in his voice. He'd got like that when he was a kid, too. Mostly when he was busy chasing some girl or other, and too busy to entertain his younger sister and her friends. When he wasn't distracted, he'd been a good companion and sometimes a champion. Hmm. "So how's it going at your end of the lake? Met your neighbor?"

He glanced at her as she looked up at him. "Letha? She's grown up."

Kristienne sniffed. "A matter of years. We all do. So you saw her, spoke to her."

"Yeah. I'm kinda..." he stopped himself and cocked his head, his longish hair reminding her of when they were much younger together. "You're still her friend, right? Have you seen her lately? Checked up on her?"

Kristienne looked heavenward. The last thing Letha Rivers needed was another person checking on her. "Sure, we're still friends. But I'm a friend who believes everyone deserves space, and that's something not too common around these parts — the belief, I mean. Not the space. I saw the artwork, if that's what you're asking."

"It's not the artwork. It's just... hell, I don't know. I just get the sense that something's wrong — I mean, where the hell's Spring?"

His question sent a little shiver down her back. She'd put it down to Letha's orneriness, but maybe there was something more. "Tell you what. I'll go see how she's doing if you'll hang with Mom for a while. But first let's go look at this horseflesh that has you dressing like a pansy fool."

He looked down at himself, realized how strangely he was dressed for folk who preferred old jeans and shit-kicking boots, then grinned and shrugged. "Sounds like a deal."

The Hunt Ranch was her pride, the operations efficient. In Kristienne's world, a well-run ranch was one where the cattle were fat and happy, the horses were cattle-eating Quarter Horses, and the men were focused on keeping them that way. She didn't mind the long winters that came with Central British Columbia, nor the fact that the only men she met were cowboys and rich folk looking to buy a horse as a toy.

Hunt Ranch was well known for cutting and reining horses that carried the bloodlines of past world champions in both fields. A cattle-eating horse would get you to your cow and keep you there, and the prize money was big. Her horses were solid in body and mind — the product of good breeding practices and real-life work — not some trainer in Las Vegas or New York.

She hauled on her riding boots and her worn fleece jacket, and paused outside to inhale the healthy smells of fresh manure and spread hay from the paddocks by the main barn that stood beyond the house. Neat rail fences quartered the land satisfyingly into gardens, paddocks, and loafing sheds for cattle. A hay barn and the main horse barn lay beyond, for mares delivering in winter and horses that were in training. Activity near the covered riding ring told of two-year-olds being broke to saddle. All as it should be.

It wouldn't upset her if the rest of the world disappeared — except she needed outsiders as customers. The 150 acres of poplar and lodgepole pine forest, the meadow and hay fields their father had bought, and the range rights to a half section of Crown Land were a small, self-contained world, and all the world she needed right now.

She stepped off the back porch and stopped. Closer, in a small corral next to the house that she usually used for mares with new foals, waited Ty's horse. "Holy shit, is that a moose?"

The horse stood in the corral like a mountain — must have weighed close to 1400 pounds — not like the tidy 900-pound reining or cutting horses she rode — not even like the big old plodding ranch horses a lot of the Valley people owned. Black mane and tail, body a brown so dark it was like shadows in deep water. Muscled and well-made, but snorting and way too hellishly high off the ground to make a decent cattle horse.

And every horse worth owning had to be a decent cattle horse to earn its keep.

Not that she didn't enjoy leggier horses. There was something to be said for a horse that could run. Every morning before the ranch's demands took over her day, she'd take her gelding, Strata, out for a good ride and they always enjoyed a run together. She'd even toyed with the notion of jockeying before she got her growth, but this horse — he was too heavy for racing, too.

"Must be over sixteen hands tall." She stood at the corral gate and looked up — way up — and at 5-feet-seven she wasn't short. She tossed her long brown hair back and rested her cowboy boot on the bottom rail.

"What the hell do you do with a horse like that? You couldn't even ride in the hills because you'd get caught in all the branches."

"Hey, he's my horse — Hauberk's his name — European Warmblood, Hanoverian, and great bloodlines — that's why he's a stud. He's a dressage horse, Kris, takes the reining horse athleticism and raises it to art — like in the Olympics — or those Lipizzaner stallions. I'll show you some time."

She heard the pride in his voice and knew her face showed her doubts. She scanned the horse, noting the silly-looking English saddle that went with her brother's embarrassing get-up, and searched for something to compliment. She knew her face showed just how hard she was working at it. She never had been able to smooth away her emotions like Ty — even though their features were similar in their wide-set eyes and full mouths. "Got a good hip on him, I guess. Good legs. Good bone."

"And hooves like steel, and movement like a dancer. Just you wait, you'll see."

She nodded, wondering what had happened to her brother to make him go all prissy like this.

"Guess I'll head over to Letha's." She shook her head and lifted her chin at the horse. "Matt sees him and he's never going to forgive you."

"Maybe."

She ducked away to the truck and started the engine, sitting back in the seat while she fought to compose herself. Giggles demanded release and she slammed the truck in gear, laughing and hoping Ty wouldn't see. Her big brother — a damned, pansy, flat-saddle rider.

She was still laughing when she pulled into the packed snow and gravel lot in front of the store. Sylvia's white truck sat out front, and that choked out her mirth. What was the woman doing to Letha this time?

Sylvia was seated in the lone inside chair, but even at rest she didn't look relaxed. She held a sheaf of invoices in her hand, her eyes scanning their contents in quick, bird-like glances, her forefingers tapping a light dance on the paper. Letha hovered nearby, trying to look casual while her whole body radiated nerves.

Sylvia could do that to most people, which didn't make a lot of sense given how good she was with animals. She needed to stop doing it to Letha.

Kristienne pushed through the door and nodded at Letha. "Thought I'd see how you were making out, but I guess I know, given Sylvia's here."

"Kristienne." Sylvia rattled her papers as if to reprimand Kristienne for interrupting. "I thought the ranch brought in its own supplies from down south so it wouldn't have to deal locally?"

She ignored the jab and turned to Letha. "She been bitchy like this with you? 'Cause I can take her."

"Like hell. You might be taller, but I've wrestled a damn-sight more horses and cattle than you. I've got muscles. You — you've got spindly little rider arms."

"I'd tell you where to take your muscles, but you might need them the next time I've got a breach-birth foal. Letha, I really did come just to see how you were doing. How's business?"

"Fine. A few customers. Mrs. Zigheld and Harry came by."

Kristienne wrinkled her nose. "Harry say anything about Ty being back? I swear that guy still harbors a grudge."

Letha shook her head. "I got some of Johnny Warner's paintings that I think are going to sell real well. I'll show you." She ducked into the back bedroom.

"You putting more pressure on her, Syl?"

"Just minding the store, so to speak." She looked back at the papers. "Don't go putting ideas in her head."

"You should talk."

"What the hell's that supposed to mean?"

"She's got her own ideas, Syl. You notice anything about the seasons?"

"No."

"I never thought you were a liar before," Kristienne said as Letha returned with an armful of stretched canvases.

"You've got to see these. He had them stuffed in a corner in his shed at home and no one except his teacher has seen them."

She laid the wood-framed canvases on the counter, and leaving Sylvia to her papers and her disapproval, displayed the first one.

"You studied some art when you were away at school, and didn't your mom take you to galleries in New York? What d'you think?"

It was a watercolor of poplar leaves in water. They were caught at the edge of rounded stream stones, and the work was so fine Kristienne could see the veining of the gold-green colored leaves and could almost hear the burble of water. "Wow. This is great. Johnny Warner did this?"

"And all these others. I want to help him; get people to know about his work."

"That'll take some effort."

"Hey, it's what this is all about, isn't it? And when his stuff starts to sell, I'll start taking a bit of commission and earn money that way."

"What? Sylvia not paying you enough to run this operation?"

"It's Sylvia's store. She financed the whole thing. I get a cut of everything when we start making money, but right now we're not even break-even."

Kristienne heard wistfulness in Letha's voice, but also the enduring faith of a long-time friend. The friendship was something she admired Letha for, but the wistfulness was as if there was something pining inside.

Kristienne studied her friend as she lifted another canvas, this one of a heron in early morning mist. The kid had talent, that was for sure. But Letha, there were shadows in and under her eyes. Well, starting a new business could do that, Kristienne decided.

Letha seemed to have a good mind for it too, judging by the neatly stacked shelves and the tidy displays of charming, wood-carved ornaments hung on a tree branch she'd positioned by the window.

Kristienne looked through the other canvases, then went back to the first canvas Letha had shown her. She glanced over her shoulder at Sylvia, knowing what she was about to do would piss Syl off.

"I shouldn't be doing this."

Letha paused. She frowned. "You can come in here whenever you like. It's a store, for goodness sake."

"I mean I'm going to have to buy this painting, because if I don't, someone else will. These paintings — and the ornaments and the carvings out front — they're all unique and wonderful. They'll put this store on the map. You just wait — you'll have customers coming from all over."

A radiant smile bloomed on Letha's face.

"We don't need to bring in more people. We just need a general store," Sylvia said from her chair. "It'll disrupt things."

"You open a store and you need business. The Valley'll deal, just you wait and see. And all the local artists are going to be thanking you for the extra income. You'll be a hero, Syl. Just like you always wanted. So what do I owe you, Letha?"

Apologizing, she named a price that was on the low side for a piece of quality art — even if it was by an unknown artist.

"Okay. I'll have to come back with my wallet, but hold the painting for me, all right? I'd love to get something different for the house."

Pleased at Kristienne's reaction to her efforts, Letha wrote up the bill, a little song humming in her head.

Kristienne looked at the numbers and shook her head. "Cheap at twice the price. But Ty is going to laugh his butt off when he sees this."

Letha froze. "Ty?"

"Yeah, my long lost bro came for a visit this morning. Said I should look in on you."

Letha's eyes turned darker grey, like a gathering storm. She gathered up the canvases and hurried out of the room as a gust of cold wind suddenly rattled the store windows and seemed to rush through the room.

Kristienne looked after her, glanced at Sylvia, who still had her nose buried in invoices, and turned thoughtfully to go. Something *was* happening here. Something more than a delay of Spring.

§

Darkness and cold, the night sky hidden with clouds, and the air laden with ice and snow. A harsh wind blew through the benighted Valley, drifting the snow, smothering everything and everyone there — including Letha.

The lake lay glistening, the water hissing as the snow hit the water, and ice crackled at its edges. Along the shoreline, the pale green willow catkins shriveled and blackened. Birds huddled amid naked branches. A chickadee shivered and fell, its taupe and grey feathers lost in the drifts. Through the blizzard a figure rode through the snow, then toppled off the horse to lay still.

Creatures — people — were dying of the darkness, and it waited for her.

Letha shifted in sleep, contesting the vision. No. Spring would come, just as it always came. The valley could not be like this. There was too much she held dear.

She walked naked through the snow. Her skin was pale as lake ice, her eyes dark as the snowy sky. Wind caught in her hair, dragged it wild around her face and head.

The lake, if she could only reach the lake she could save things — the man, the bird, so many others. But something hunted in the snow. Something human and dark.

He was a figure just glimpsed. A sound of hooves at the edge of hearing. Wanting her. Wanting to help her.

No! Wanting to end life. Hers and all others.

Darkness, it followed him and it masked his face when he came to her on a dark steed. Her own heat filled her with need and sent her to him. Snow melted on her skin, trickled through her curls. She looked up for his face but saw only darkness, felt only his wanting and the ravenous darkness that followed behind him.

Darkness that tore her up, tore her, crying, out of the Valley, and spoke to her in a wind-swept voice. She felt hands on her waist. "The Valley's gone. You're free of it."

She stood in a place she had never been — a city of glass, broad concrete streets, the sound of engines and steam. The smell of diesel and urine. Cold. So cold. Still naked, she walked through the crowds and the people did nothing. Said nothing. Walked through her.

"I'm Letha," she said. No one responded.

Was she wrong? Who-what was Letha? She was, wasn't she? And the cold crept inside and froze her heat. She was coming apart, falling apart, forgetting herself except for the darkness's hold on her. She needed to get away. Needed the Valley.

She yanked away, fell away.

Fell, and landed in snow. The man, he would help her.

The wind and voice laughed cold as ice, colder than her heat, froze the man before her, his steed. Ice formed on his brow, on the horse's eyes. Tree limbs cracked and fell to the earth. The forest crumbled into darkness.

The lake. She had to get to the lake. To Spring. She ran through the snow, darkness at her heels. A wolf howled and died. A deer screamed. Another. Fire in the darkness. The old Lake Stage Coach house aflame. Human voices, afraid. Afraid like she was. Darkness pulsed as she ran, as her fear sent her on.

Black surface before her. She stumbled and fell, tumbling down a slope through frozen thistle and ice, coming up against a willow that had cracks through its trunk.

She scrambled to her feet, dry grass and snow caught at her ankles, held her back from the lake, the water, the Spring, and darkness had almost caught her, was almost upon her.

Crying, she looked over her shoulder; it came on black wings, slamming her back against the tree. Get free. Get to the lake and save them all.

She stumbled around the tree, hobbled the last few feet to the water on frozen feet — *"Oh, Precious Spring,"* she began the rite — stepped out...

...onto ice, and slipped to her knees.

The whole lake was frozen. She pounded at the ice with her fists, pleading with Spring to come, ramming her knuckles into the hard surface until bones broke, until her spirit broke, and all she could hear was darkness laughing. All she could feel were her tears and the unending pain as she kept on pounding.

Look for *Second Spring* at your favorite book store
or order it on line.

Romance, Mystery and Fantasy
from Twisted Root Publishing

If you enjoyed this book, you might enjoy other titles available from Karen L. Abrahamson in your local bookstore or wherever e-books are sold.

www.karenlabrahamson.com

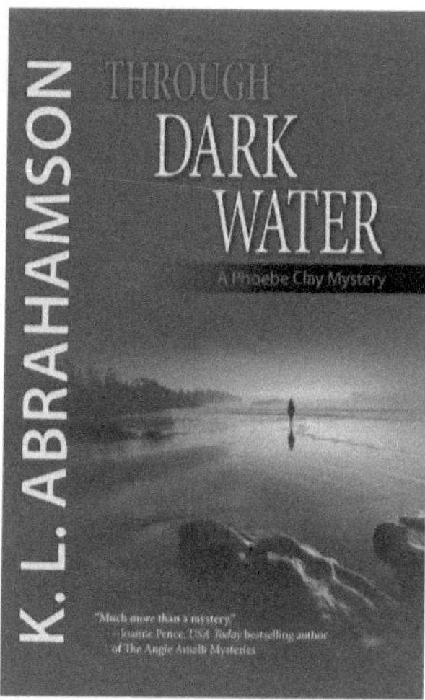

www.ingramcontent.com/pod-product-compliance
Lightning Source LLC
Chambersburg PA
CBHW051630180726
48284CB00006B/1673